The Unknown

The Unknown

Jack Smith

Copyright © 2014 by Jack Smith.

Library of Congress Control Number:		2014909984
ISBN:	Hardcover	978-1-4990-3097-6
	Softcover	978-1-4990-3098-3
	eBook	978-1-4990-3096-9

All rights reserved. No part of this book may be reproduced or transmitted in any form or by any means, electronic or mechanical, including photocopying, recording, or by any information storage and retrieval system, without permission in writing from the copyright owner.

This is a work of fiction. Names, characters, places and incidents either are the product of the author's imagination or are used fictitiously, and any resemblance to any actual persons, living or dead, events, or locales is entirely coincidental.

Any people depicted in stock imagery provided by Thinkstock are models, and such images are being used for illustrative purposes only.
Certain stock imagery © Thinkstock.

This book was printed in the United States of America.

Rev. date: 11/04/2014

To order additional copies of this book, contact:
Xlibris
1-888-795-4274
www.Xlibris.com
Orders@Xlibris.com
553362

CONTENTS

Prologue: The Uninvited 13

PART I

THE BEGINNING

Chapter 1	Twenty-Five Years Earlier................................	21
Chapter 2	Wednesday Morning, July 17..........................	27
Chapter 3	Wednesday Night—The Reunion	30
Chapter 4	Thursday, July 18—The Search Begins...........	34
Chapter 5	The Witness	37
Chapter 6	July 20–Run and Hide.......................................	42
Chapter 7	Monday, July 22–The Bloodhounds	49
Chapter 8	Unwelcome Guests..	55
Chapter 9	Questions	61
Chapter 10	Thursday, July 25–Bermuda	65
Chapter 11	Thursday, July 25–Stateside.............................	70
Chapter 12	The Protectors	74
Chapter 13	A Revealing Secret..	79
Chapter 14	The Uninvited..	83
Chapter 15	An Understanding...	87
Chapter 16	Interest Grows...	92
Chapter 17	Getting Prepared...	99
Chapter 18	Off and Running...	105
Chapter 19	Identities: Some Established, Some New, and Others Discovered	110
Chapter 20	Omens..	115
Chapter 21	The Intruders	117
Chapter 22	Good Luck, Bad Luck	120
Chapter 23	Plans of Action	125
Chapter 24	Quit When Ahead	128
Chapter 25	The Numbers Continue Changing	133
Chapter 26	Too Much Curiosity...	136
Chapter 27	Time to Leave	140
Chapter 28	Hide and Seek	143
Chapter 29	The Meeting—The Decision	149
Chapter 30	The Second Attempt	153

Chapter 31 The Identification 157
Chapter 32 I Do 159
Chapter 33 We Do and How We Do It 162
Chapter 34 The Escape 165

PART II

INFANT TO ADULT

Chapter 35 Exposure 169
Chapter 36 The Road Ahead 175
Chapter 37 The Growing Years 179
Chapter 38 What Lies Ahead? 182
Chapter 39 Death Reigns 186
Chapter 40 Introducing the High Priestess of Tarot 192
Chapter 41 A Promising Future 197
Chapter 42 His Name's Francis McDonald 200
Chapter 43 A Custodian with Influence 206
Chapter 44 Choices 209

PART III

THE ARCANA
THE SECRETS OF TOMORROW

Chapter 45 Times, Dates, Happenings 215
Chapter 46 The Funeral of the Welcomed and Not Welcomed ... 219
Chapter 47 Present, Absent, Present 223
Chapter 48 The Quad and More Lies 228
Chapter 49 "The Wife" 233
Chapter 50 Finding Stacey 237
Chapter 51 Surprise—You Have Visitors 242
Chapter 52 The Finale 246
Chapter 53 Advice 255
Chapter 54 A Decision! 258
Chapter 55 Relentless 260
Chapter 56 Stacey's Unacceptable Decision 263
Chapter 57 The Cat and the Mouse 266
Chapter 58 The Cat Scans 269
Chapter 59 The Cat Moves 272
Chapter 60 An Unexpected Surprise 275

Chapter 61 Positioning Themselves 280
Chapter 62 The Fourth Coincidence 282
Chapter 63 No One's Safe 287
Chapter 64 Once Again 290

PART IV

ANOTHER BEGINNING: A FINAL ENDING

Chapter 65 Discovery 299
Chapter 66 On the Offensive 306
Chapter 67 The Ruse 309
Chapter 68 Surprise! Surprise! 314
Chapter 69 The Making of a Believer 317
Chapter 70 Letters and a Phone Call 320
Chapter 71 Taking Eyes off the Ball 325
Chapter 72 Mismatched 329
Chapter 73 Another Time, Another Place 331

BIOGRAPHY

John G. (Jack) Smith

Career Path:

    2002—Retired

    1988-2002—President, PPRB: Developed sales and marketing programs for pharmaceutical/H&BA manufacturers, drug wholesalers, retailers, and consumers

    1986-1988—Founder/President, JGS and Associates; Sales/Marketing consultant to pharmaceutical/H&BA manufacturers, drug wholesalers, and retail drug chains

    1984-1986—President Ketchum Wholesale Drug Company, with distribution centers serving retail pharmacies in Connecticut, Michigan, Ohio, New York, and New Jersey

    1956-1984—Northeast Zone General Manager, McKesson & Robbins Wholesale Drug Company, servicing retail/hospital pharmacies throughout New England, Manhattan, parts of New York State, New Jersey, and Eastern Pennsylvania.

    1954-1956—Assigned to U.S. Army Intelligence.

Education:

1953-1954—MBA, The Ohio State University
1948-1952—BSBA, The Ohio State University

*Final position held, others not listed.

To Vera, my wife,

my inspiration, my love, my soul mate

of fifty-seven years

PROLOGUE

THE UNINVITED

Gong! Gong! Gong!

The *Bells of the Golden Age,* in the town center, tolled eleven times. Shops closed; roads were empty. A blanket of silence was everywhere. As far as one could see, the heavens were black and starless, a bright full moon the only exception.

Homes hidden from neighbors turned dark. Villagers, nestled in the arms of Morpheus, had dreams envisioning private worlds known only to themselves. All but two remained unaware of what was to happen, and those two as yet did not know.

A woman descended Rocky Mountain Pass, maneuvering the winding downhill curves with abandon. Observers would wonder why such a raven-haired beauty, with facial features of flawless perfection and eyes glimmering like amethysts, would drive so recklessly. Yet Stacey McDonald was troubled.

She was returning from dinner with a friend, a last-minute date set to ease anxieties coming from a stay in Bermuda and a frightening late-in-the-day disclosure arising out of a Tarot card reading. The island visit was to have been a relaxing vacation, one involving a singular love—tennis. Instead of pleasure, however, it became life threatening. Then to learn the reasons why, a reading of the Tarot cards proved vexatious. Three of the eleven cards appearing on the *Celtic Cross* were *The Tower, The Devil,* and the *Seven of Swords* each a forewarning of unexpected events from someone intending great violence.

Why me . . . why me, she wondered. *What violence, and by whom? The secrets of the Arcana are never wrong. What will reverse these life-threatening problems? Can the early forewarnings even be overturned? I not only need answers; I need guidance. Where can I turn? What can I do?*

Soon I'll be home. I'll kick off my shoes, pour a glass of Sancerre, and think, think, think. Oh, to find the answers.

At the outskirts of her hillside community, the driver eased off the accelerator as she passed the dark homes of her neighbors. Moments later, she turned into a driveway. From the mailbox she removed a pink envelope addressed with an unrecognized feminine flair. Placing the envelope in her purse next to a Tarot deck, she opened the car door.

Across the road, a cul-de-sac—Destiny Lane—circled away from Rocky Mountain Pass. Hidden under a willow's overhanging limbs was a black Chevrolet. The driver, a man in his late forties with clean-cut facial features, was committed to remaining unseen. He sipped coffee no longer hot, slouching against the backseat of his pitch-dark car. He had been waiting over an hour, patient and pleased that he had arrived at the house before her. He had known she was away and wanted to surprise her with an unexpected entrance.

The man knew her well. Previous undetected visits taught him a great deal—her interests, habits, customs, and peculiarities. All was committed to memory, all including the surrounding property features, the interior layout of her home, and the neighbors' activities as well.

Tonight's arrival was perfect. The man wanted her patience overwrought from the fears of the past week and the tiring flight from Bermuda. These would stimulate resistance, excite aggressiveness to his uninvited advances, and achieve the sensual fulfillment desired.

Out of the open car door, her long, gracefully curved legs appeared. Standing, she leaned back into the vehicle. The full moon cast light upon her calves and the white tennis skirt hugging her hips and bottom.

Enjoying the sight, the stranger reached for his car phone and keyed in a series of numbers. With the second ring, an authoritative voice commanded, "Go ahead! Speak!"

"The package arrived."

"Are you holding it?"

"Not yet, but soon!"

"Well then, get on with what we've discussed."

"First, I want to examine it . . . fondle it. The thrill has been long in coming."

"Do whatever pleases you, but be damn certain that once you've had your thrills, nothing remains. Nothing is ever found."

"Don't give it a second thought!"

But his reply remained unheard. The respondent had disconnected.

Retrieving her purse, Stacey stepped away from the car. Swinging her hip, she closed the door and ascended three sets of multiple slate steps angling to the front door.

Meanwhile, the unseen visitor retrieved from the floor both a black bag with shoulder straps and a small leather satchel. In the satchel was what he called his *passion playmates*—a choker clamp and four chains complete with wrist and ankle restraints, as well as bedpost and bed rail manacles. Each was placed in the backpack.

"Now for the final touch," he murmured.

Out of the bottom of the satchel, he removed a mahogany box. Within it was a latex, milky albino, over-the-head mask complete with glass eyes having blue-tinted irises and deep red sclera. Down the forehead, over an eyelid, and continuing to the upper lip was a pus-like yellow-white wound having the authentic appearance of tissue debris. Across the forehead, prominently printed, was *Remember Me*.

"Worth every dollar paid," he whispered. "Tonight, my ultra ego will inflame the fear, the combative rage, and the defensive actions that lead to sexual fulfillment. After all these years eluding me, you'll finally be mine. And I intend on receiving my just rewards before disappearing like a shadow in the night."

Leaving the car, he stretched his arms through the shoulder straps. In the anticipated excitement, he slammed the car door. Its sound carried through the distant, quiet night.

Damn, that was dumb. Studying the three-story house, all the windows remained dark and empty. *I've got to be quiet, or I'll be warning her and destroying the pleasure of seeing her startled, god-fearing look when I unexpectedly appear.*

Turning, he loped across Rocky Mountain Pass to partially spaced oak and maple trees bordering the western side of her house.

Inside, Stacey headed to a wall intending to turn on the downstairs lights before entering her library for incoming telephone messages. She stopped.

What was that?

On each side of the front door was a vertical window. Looking through one, she scanned the front yard. No movement. Nothing. Usually confident of her instincts, she became fearful.

Am I imagining things? Was there a noise? Are the readings coming true? Instead of going to the library, she, like a blind person familiar with the surroundings, stepped unhesitatingly down the unlighted hallway, beyond entrances to adjacent rooms, to a circular center staircase. Ascending carpet-covered steps, she came to a landing with three large glass-tempered windows, each one overlooking portions of the western, northern, and eastern sides of her property. At the left and right ends of the landing were hallways leading back to the front of the house, each hallway passing doors to bedrooms on its respective side.

Out of the west window, she caught a glimpse of something. It moved and disappeared quickly. Frightened, she darted to the second window. A figure, clothed in black and carrying a shoulder pack, ran across the yard and turned the corner.

Unable to see the figure from the third window, she moved down the hall, entered her bedroom, and tossed her purse on the bed. Through an unobstructed bedroom window, she watched the person maneuver a backpack in order to climb an oak tree no more than five feet from her room. Alarmed, she looked for a weapon. She had no gun, no knife, no club, not even a tennis racket. Yet if she had, she would not have known how to defend herself.

Stacey considered running but hesitated. On an adjacent table was a crystal bowl holding several dozen multi-colored glass balls. Removing the bowl and a polyester table cloth, she carefully laid the balls on the floor, hiding them beneath the cloth. Standing, she stared out the window at the scarred demonic face of a big man climbing toward her window.

Stepping back, she stifled a scream. She watched the monster grab an oak limb and begin swinging back and forth, gaining momentum to fly the short distance through her window. Turning, Stacey ran to the door. Glass disintegrated. Over her shoulder, she saw the trespasser's feet hit the floor-covered cloth. Momentum from the leap moved the glass balls, causing the backpack to swivel. The intruder lost his balance; his shoulder and side of his head hit the table, smashing it into a pile of wood.

For a moment, the invader remained motionless. Stacey, without waiting, headed to the door, stopped, returned to her bed, and retrieved her purse. Dashing from the room, she ran down the hall and through another door.

The aggressor rose tentatively to his feet, rubbed his head, and wiped, with his sleeve, blood seeping through the torn mask. He charged after the woman only to have his feet, once again, fly out from beneath him as they rolled over more loose balls on the bare wood flooring.

"Damn you, bitch!"

He rose to his feet and moved cautiously through the bedroom door. In the outer dark hall, he searched the wall for a light switch. Locating the switch plate, he flooded the upstairs and downstairs with light. He ran to the top of the stairs, looked down, but heard and saw nothing. At the other end of the hall, he noticed the open door through which his intended victim escaped. Sprinting past rooms, he exited the door and saw, from the upper landing, Stacey's descent on uncarpeted steps two flights below. He moved swiftly, taking the steps two and three at a time.

She heard him and glanced upward. He was gaining, less than two flights away. At the basement landing, Stacey could hear his breathing, smell his sweat. She stole another glance! Now he was only one flight behind. Quickly, she retraced her steps down the cellar hall to another door, running as fast as her legs would move.

The assailant leaped from the fifth step to the landing, stumbled, regained his footing, and sprinted after her, reaching the swinging door just as it was closing.

PART I

THE BEGINNING

CHAPTER 1

TWENTY-FIVE YEARS EARLIER

TUESDAY, JULY 16, 1985

Another night—starless, hot, and humid! A black limousine moved down Commerce Avenue, veering slowly from one lane across the yellow line to another. Cautiously, the driver avoided the ruts and holes of the neglected street.

Behind the vehicle and from an unlighted doorway, a prolonged but subdued whistle was heard. Stepping out to the sidewalk, a small woman in a tattered sweater and skirt, frayed hat, and long-since clean white gloves, stood immobile, staring at the back of the passing vehicle while unconsciously shuffling Tarot cards in her hands.

Putting the always accessible deck protectively in a timeworn purse, she mumbled, "If I hadn't seen it and somebody had told me about it, I'da said he was nuts."

To the community, the west end had become a forsaken area. Commerce Avenue was more commonly referred to as Pothole Parkway with both names complete misnomers. Commerce had departed the area years before, apparent from the deteriorating, abandoned buildings on each side of the road. And a *parkway* it certainly was not.

As the car eased to a stop, the curious woman stepped up her pace, pressing close to the empty structures. Out of the driver's door stepped a groomed chauffeur who walked behind the vehicle and opened a rear passenger door. From within, extended arms handed him a package, which the driver accepted before closing the door. Turning, he proceeded down an alley. The woman, now even more curious, walked rapidly toward the car. Within feet of its trunk, she hid in another doorway, listening for the sound of the driver's returning steps.

Moments passed, and at the alley entrance, the chauffeur reappeared no longer carrying the package. Before climbing into the car, she heard him say to the passenger, "I've done as you told me." Unable to hear the reply, the woman watched the chauffeur climb into the car and drive away. Now, even more interested, she entered a garbage-strewn alley, one inhabited by rats, stray dogs, homeless people, and other occupants ignored by the community's governing council.

Proceeding down the passageway, the woman walked slowly looking to her right and left for something unknown. Forty yards from the entrance, she quickly stopped, tilted her head, and listened. To her left was a dumpster. Moving to it, she placed her ear against the cold metal and listened. Lifting the lid, she grasped the upper edge of the receptacle, hoisted her five-foot body, and looked down into its half-filled contents. Then she let out a cry, dropped to the ground, and ran further into the alley to the opposite wall. There, she began kicking a pile of old newspapers and raggedy wool blankets.

"Stop it! Stop your damn kickin'! I'm sleepin'," groaned a voice from beneath the pile.

"Get your ass up, Roscoe! You gotta see this."

Pushing away papers from his face, he said, "Dora, what's got into you? It ain't even morning. Let me sleep."

"Roscoe, 'less you get up, I'll give you such a boot in the head you'll be dizzy for days. Now, get up, and I mean this instant."

Moaning unhappily, he stood in toeless stocking feet, yawned, and stretched, mumbling, "Dora, this better be damn important, or I'm gonna—"

"You're gonna what?" she fired back.

"Oh, nuttin'! Forget it! Just tell me what's crawlin' up your backside!"

"Just follow me and find out!"

At the trash bin, she raised the lid and pulled Roscoe to her side.

"Look down in there!" Over six feet tall, he could easily see into the bin.

"You mean that sound? Comin' from that box? Sounds like something's crying? Move, so I can climb in and fetch it!"

Up to his ankles in wet, loose garbage, Roscoe lifted up the box, wiped its dampness against his trouser legs, handed the package to Dora, and climbed out. As they walked back to his "estate," the crying continued. Dora removed the lid and held the box against her breasts, sliding it side to side, humming a tune softly in a baby's ear.

"What're you gonna do, Dora?"

"Me! Why me? What about you? You're now part of this too!"

"I know, but you're the woman!"

"Yeah, but I ain't never been a mother. And just what to do, I'm not certain. Keep quiet. Let me think!"

After a few moments, she said, "Bingo! That's what we'll do!"

"That's what we'll do? And just what in the hell is 'that'?"

"We'll find Doc! He'll know!"

"Doc? That old drunk! He's been away from medicine so long he won't even remember what a baby is."

"Don't kid yourself! He's got moxie. Under that gray head of hair is a wealth of knowledge. You'll see!" And off she scurried, juggling the infant up and down to ease its distress.

Watching this from further up the alley was Freddie, another homeless person. He recognized the couple and had watched Roscoe retrieve the box from the dumpster. But their movement down the darkened alley had taken them too far away to be seen or heard.

Now that's interesting, thought Freddie. *Wonder what's in that box. Had to be something worth a lot for Roscoe to climb in and fetch it. By damn, you two! If it's valuable, then I want some of it. You're sure as hell not going to keep it for yourselves.*

Dora, Roscoe, and the baby left the alley and moved to a large abandoned warehouse. Entering, they walked through rooms fraught with damaged goods and debris. At a rear door, they left the building, crossed Prosperity Road, entered a small vacant retail store, and exited through a back delivery door. Ahead of them was an overgrown hill with buried rocks and protruding roots, causing them to trip and stumble on their way to the bottom. Finally on level ground, they arrived at Settlers' Park.

In addition to the bushes and trees scattered across the lawn, there were blankets—brown, black, off-white, and tones of every hue.

"Take the kid, Roscoe! Hold him gently but keep rocking him. I think he's crying himself to sleep, so let's keep it that way!"

"He! Him! How do you know it's a boy, Dora?"

"I don't, but we'll know soon enough."

Passing by sleeping bodies, the woman peered into faces. Of those covered by blankets, she carefully lifted the fabrics seeking someone she knew.

"Hey, Rose! Rose! Have you seen Doc?"

"Not lookin' for him and don't care to. Let me sleep!"

Dora continued to search until she finally found someone who had seen Doc by the bridge. Together, the three moved in a new direction. After fifteen minutes of checking several dozen bodies, they found a source.

"Yeah! Saw him a while back down by the river. Had a jug of elderberry, nice and sweet! Sharin' it with everybody! If you hurry, maybe there'll be some left."

Rosco finally spotted Doc leaning against a stump.

"There he is, over yonder."

The medical man's legs were extended, his ankles past the edge of the embankment, inches above the water. Slightly built and only a hand's length taller than Dora, he rested a jug on his shoulder and with two fingers and thumb, clutched the spout near his lips. His feet were bobbing up and down, out of sync with an off-pitch Irish lullaby rasping from his mouth.

"Doc! Hey, Doc! Over here!" shouted Dora.

Stifling the tune, he squinted and then grinned, waving his jug.

"Whasha know? Fi-fi-finealee my buddies ha' come to party. Have some of life's precious juice and join in the singin'."

Still swinging his arms, he fell to the side and smashed the bottle against a rock.

"Oh, hell! Looka whatta I done! The prom . . . prom . . . promise of life's pleasure's lost and gone forever! Wha, whatta shame!"

"Forget the juice, Doc!" Pointing at Roscoe, Dora said, "Give us a hand with this baby!"

Focusing through squinting eyes, Doc muttered, "A baby? You Dora? Roscoe? When? Didn't even know you were intamunt?"

"It's not ours, you old coot. We found it, and we don't know what to do. He won't stop crying. Maybe he's sick. Help the kid, Doc! You're all he's got!"

Pulling himself up, the medical man once again leaned back against the rock. Looking bleary-eyed at the baby, he belched, his head falling to his chest.

"He's no help! He's out of it!" complained Roscoe. "Let's go!"

"We ain't leavin'!"

Dropping her purse, she stepped into the water and grabbed Doc's ankles giving them a tug.

As the lower part of his legs submerged into the river, Doc howled out in laughter. "If you wanna go swimmin', Dora, just ask?"

With a second tug, his butt fell from the embankment, splashing into the water.

"Damn, tha's cold!"

Buoyed by the water, Dora's third and final tug caused the man's head to sink beneath the surface. Twisting her captive on his front, she pressed one hand against his back, grabbed his hair with the other, and angled his face in and out of the water.

After thrusting him up and down several times, she commanded, "Sober up, you old goat! This kid needs help, and by diggedy, you're going to give it to him."

Again, she pushed Doc down and pulled his head out of the river. Gasping, he regurgitated a mouthful of water, bent his knees into the sand, extended his arms, and straightened up.

"Damn you, Dora! Stop it! You're gonna drown me."

Resting a moment, he pulled his wet shirt up and wiped his face.

"Are you mad, woman? I haven't practiced since I lost my license, and I'm not gonna batter my heart and soul by putting some infant at risk. Find a doctor who knows what to do."

"How? Where? And how'll he be paid? You know what to do! You've more sense and experience than hundreds of those shingle-practicing nincompoops bleeding patients in hospital beds. At least look at the kid. If he's seriously ill, we'll go from there. But at least look at him."

Reluctantly, the doctor took the baby from Roscoe's arms. Touching his forehead, he noticed no temperature. He checked the pulse, and the rate was normal.

"Wish I had a stethoscope."

Placing his hand on the infant's bottom, he said, "Well, a changing will help. I don't suppose you know when he ate last?"

"Not since we've had him," volunteered Roscoe.

With the child in his arms, he hitch-stepped to the dry ground and his resting rock. Near the stone was an old canvas bag packed with three clean T-shirts and other personal items.

A very surprised Dora said, "I'll be! Where'd you get them clean clothes?"

"It's the one thing, maybe the only thing I carry over from my profession. In my other life, cleanliness was ingrained in me. Good health and good hygiene are interdependent. Some habits just don't disappear."

Removing the dirty diaper, Doc said, "Well parents, your first lesson in caring for your baby is to know he's a she. Roscoe, wet this shirt in the river while I tear up another one."

He wiped the baby's bottom with the wet cloth and dried it with the second one. Then he took the torn shirt and fashioned it into a diaper. As he lifted her, he stared deeply into her eyes.

"Would you look at that?" said Dora. "She's smiling at you, Doc!"

"And a cute smile you have, my little ballerina," said her caregiver. "Bet it gets bigger with a full tummy. So let's go shopping!"

Kissing her on the cheek, Doc asked, "Roscoe, how much money have you got?"

Roscoe cast his eyes downward, lowered his head, and shook it barely.

Dora reached into her purse and removed one dollar and thirteen cents.

"Come on!" said Doc. "Let's go to that all-night grocery on the hill and get some formula. Similac, Mull Soy, Lactum, or whatever they've got. I'll do the shopping. At least I didn't spend everything on wine. After she's fed, we'll turn her over to the authorities."

"Turn my baby over to the authorities! The hell we will," shouted Dora. "No way is she going to some godforsaken foster home recommended by uncaring social workers or indifferent juvenile authorities. She's my baby, and she's staying with me. Don't give me any lip, either of you. And so we understand each other, make damn certain you don't spread the word about her. No one's to know she's with me. If you tell, you'll become high-pitched eunuchs."

CHAPTER 2

WEDNESDAY MORNING, JULY 17

"Mr. Jensen, you have a phone call."
"Anna, I thought I made it clear that I was not to be disturbed."
"You did, but it's Peter Grouse, and he says it's an emergency."
"All right. Put him through!"
"Peter, this better be important?"
"It is, Mr. Jensen. Earlier, on my way to Central City Bank, two squad cars with sirens howling passed me on the interstate and took the exit onto Commerce Avenue. I got curious and followed. Coming to where we were last night, I see a cop and a group of homeless people. Slowly, I pass the alley and see two black and whites along with one of those 'We Don't Refuse Any Refuse' trucks close to the dumpster."
"What were they doing?"
"I don't know, and not wanting to be questioned, I continued down Commerce. I was in my own car, not the limo, so it's unlikely that my presence was even noticed. But I thought I'd pass the information on."
"Thanks, Peter! You did the right thing."

Hanging up the receiver, Jensen turned to three men sitting at his conference table and said, "Gentlemen, if you'll excuse me for a few minutes, I have an important call to make. Go down the hall, get some coffee and Danish. We'll resume shortly."

Pressing four numbers, he waited. On the third ring, he heard, "Security Office! This is O'Malley."

"Tom, Walter Jensen!"

"Hi, Chief! What can I do for you?"

"Have a job! Hush, hush! Only you and me! Understood?"

"Fire away!"

"There's an alley at the west end of town off Commerce Avenue, between Oak and Maple."

"Know it well!"

"This morning, a couple of cruisers and one of those 'We Don't Refuse Any Refuse' trucks were snooping around a dumpster. Find out why and anything they learned. The quicker you have something, the happier I'll be. And the tip will be generous."

"With some luck, I should have an answer by morning. I still have some friends from my days as a cop who'll share what's going on."

"Good! Be circumspect and be certain to keep my interest out of it."

"Commerce Avenue Precinct. Sergeant Circerchi here!"

"Hi, Wop! How's my old partner?"

"My god! It can't be. I'm hearing things. Is it really the Mad Irishman, O'Malley?"

"The one and the same! How've you been?"

"Not bad for a gimpy paper pusher! Guess you heard? My being shot and pulled off the streets!"

"No? What happened?"

"End of a shift! Just got home and was stepping out of my car when a truck drove by with two or three gun happy perps opening fire. Lucky to be alive, but they sure played hell with my knees. Could have had full disability but talked the command into letting me be a desk jockey. It's boring as hell but better than sitting at home watching the soaps."

"They ever find out who shot you or why?"

"The case is still open, but the leads are thin. I'd been on surveillance, looking for scum. There had been talk about an organized gang dealing in white slavery of twelve- and thirteen-year-olds. Thought to be a major crime family! But we haven't been able to connect the dots. Now a chunks been taken outta my hide, and the shooters have disappeared. At least for now!"

"Dom, that's a damn shame. Wish I'd been around! I owe you a couple!"

"You owe me nothing! Oh, a beer or two might come in handy!"

"Count on it! How about tonight at the Lucky 13? Around ten or so?"

"Sounds good! See you then, partner."

CHAPTER 3

WEDNESDAY NIGHT—THE REUNION

As the minute hand struck twelve, the door to the Lucky 13 swung open precisely at ten o'clock. The place was crowded, and noisy cops were everywhere. O'Malley walked in waving to some, shouting hello to others, and slapping a few on their shoulders. It was as though he had finally come home. Passing slowly among the tables, he headed back to what was formerly known as "Red and Dom's Private Sanctuary."

Rising from a chair, Circerchi stepped forward, arms outstretched. The two embraced, renewing a friendship that would never be broken.

"Dominic! You don't know how good it is to see you. It's been too damn long."

Before the Italian could respond, a waitress leaned into the Irishman's back and wrapped her arms around his neck.

"Hi, handsome! Welcome back."

O'Malley turned, hesitated momentarily, then pulled the girl against him and stared into her eyes. Making no attempt to prevent her body from pressing against his, she accentuated the embrace with a prolonged kiss.

"Tom, it's been too long."

Slowly her fingers danced down his chest to his stomach.

"Under that shirt is one hunk of man. And while I can fantasize, you'd better release me and place your order. Otherwise, I might do something that'll close this place forever."

Laughing, O'Malley said, "I swear, Amy, you're more Irish than me! What a bunch of blarney! But you have a point. Dominic and I are thirsty. Get us a pitcher of ale, a couple of glasses, and some munchies. He and I have a lot of reminiscing."

Walking away, the security officer shouted, "One more thing, girl! Make certain the glasses are clean!"

"You gotta be kidding! Here, in this joint! If you think things have changed since you left, you're an optimist!"

His deep, hearty laugh carried across the room.

"Like old times, Dom! Good to be back!"

Looking at his partner's girth, O'Malley said, "How's Rosetta? Looks like she still making that delicious *rigatoni Bolognese*!"

Now it was Dominic's turn to laugh.

"Does she ever! And so much more! Red, I'm the luckiest guy in the world. How I ever convinced her to marry me, I'll never know. But she stays by my side and puts up with my crap. We're truly in love. Just the other day . . ."

Circerchi's voice trailed off as the muscular six-foot-two O'Malley fell deep in thought.

What ever happened, partner? When we were a team, you were always the one in shape, the one making the challenge—handball, foot racing, basketball, even arm wrestling. The first in the gym, the last to leave! Now look at you— fat, jowly, and even breathing hard. When was the last time you did anything physical? Months I'll bet. I wonder how long you could last with me now. Ten minutes? Twenty minutes? Half an hour? If you saw me at the gym, you'd know what it's like to work out. And I mean work out. Strenuously! Pressing weights, using the machines, and running—not jogging—around the track! No less than an hour a day, five days a week. I'm built like a bull, with a bull's stamina. I refuse to be a slob!

O'Malley's thoughts were interrupted by Amy with a tray full of munchies and ale. Leaning forward, she placed the order on their table, pressing her breast against O'Malley's cheek.

"Consider that a welcome-back gift," she whispered. Looking into his face, she said, "Well, whatta you know? Now I understand why they call you Red."

Chuckling, she left the table, only to stop when she heard her name. Looking back at the two partners, Tom was holding a sparkling drinking glass up to the light.

"Amy, me dear! Your tip has leaped to ten cents."

"Ha." She laughed. "That'll be the day!"

O'Malley filled his glass, raised it, and recited an Irish toast shared with only his closest friends. "May you live as long as you want and never want as long as you live." Together, they drank to a continuing friendship.

"Okay, Red, fess up. What's the reason for this get-together, even though it's long overdue?"

"Dominic, how can you question my motives? Can't this just be a friendly visit?"

"Nope! Not from you! I know you too well. You're after something, so spell it out! What do you want?"

"I should have guessed my intentions would be obvious. You're as perceptive as ever. And you're right. I do want something."

"Well, quit beating around the bush and give. What is it?"

Leaning forward, O'Malley lowered his voice and began to talk.

Hours passed! It was nearly two in the morning. Dora, lying on her side, looked at the baby next to her and then at Roscoe on the other side of the infant. Rolling off a mattress lying on a hard wood floor, she struggled to her feet. Once standing, she stretched, twisted the upper part of her body left to right, and then bent up and down several times trying to remove the stiffness from her joints.

"What's up?" whispered Roscoe.

"Can't sleep! Been thinkin'! Goin' out! Be back in an hour or so."

"Where?"

"You'll find out. Take care of the little one!"

Disappearing, Dora spaced a few lighted candles along her exit route to a lower floor. Outside the building, she left Commerce Street and hiked several blocks to a strip mall. All the businesses were closed, and the parking lot was nearly empty, except for two abandoned cars. The woman walked unhesitatingly to Home Depot.

Scanning the front lot, she saw only empty cart stands with the pushcarts likely inside for safekeeping. Annoyed but not discouraged, she headed along one side of the building, turning the corner at the rear. There she spied a single cart. As she pushed it, the right front wheel shimmied.

No wonder you're outside.

She nursed the cart to her abandoned department store dwelling, entered the side door, and headed to an unmoving escalator. As she pulled the wagon up the stationary steps, it bounced on two rear wheels. At the second landing, she turned and ascended to the third floor.

The banging echoed through the empty floors. Curious as to what was happening, Roscoe left the mattress and followed the candles to the escalator where he saw Dora.

"Woman! What in the hell are you doing? We already have three of those damn buggies filled with more stuff than we need, and you fetch another one. We only have four hands for pushin', along with carrying a kid. You gone mad?"

"Don't treat me like a dummy! I can count. This one's going to be the baby's crib. It's not healthy for the little one to sleep between us. She's bound to smell your tobacco-stinking breath, and who knows what she'll get from that. And then, during one of your nightmares, she's likely to be clubbed by your flipping arms. Until she grows more, this'll be her bed. Won't have to worry 'bout her falling on the floor. Now get me some towels and sweaters. We need to make a mattress."

When finished, they placed the infant in her new resting place. Dora then moved one of her "collected treasures"—a bowl-shaped grill—near the adults' bed. Putting charcoal from the previous night's purchase in it, she went to the ladies' room for water. Although there was no electricity, an oversight of not turning off the water became a major reason for choosing this "five-star hotel" as home. Washing a new unused baby bottle, she then filled two pots with water and placed the three items on the grill.

"In the morning when she wakes up, we'll light up the 'stove,' sterilize the bottle, and with some hot water, fix the formula the way Doc showed us. The little tyke's likely to be hungry, so we can satisfy her craving quickly. Now, let's get some sleep. Daybreak's gonna be here soon, and I'll need all the rest I can get."

CHAPTER 4

THURSDAY, JULY 18—THE SEARCH BEGINS

"Mr. Jensen, Tom O'Malley! Got some information!"

"So soon, Tom? That's great. What have you learned?"

"It'll take a few minutes, and it's better not to discuss it over the phone! Where can we meet?"

"Make it the Oasis? Luncheon crowd will be gone, and it'll be too early for dinner. Besides, it's close. I have a four-fifteen meeting, so be prepared to tell me everything quickly."

You're always in a rush. But maybe you'll start giving me more time once you learn what I know. "Sounds great, Mr. Jensen! Be there in less than ten."

Walking into the diner, Tom saw the president in a booth at the rear.

"Good choice! No one's close enough to overhear!"

After placing orders for coffee, O'Malley began relating what he had learned.

"My contact is a former partner now assigned to the desk. He's privy to most of what's going on. Seems some homeless person, seated on a fire escape at one of the deserted buildings, saw a driver—someone groomed as a chauffeur—leave a parked car and carry a box that was tossed into the dumpster. The driver returned to the car and left."

"What kind of car?"

"Snitch wasn't certain. It was a big car, make and color unknown. But what caught his attention was what followed. Another person appeared almost immediately and went directly to the dumpster."

"Did he recognize the person?"

"Before I answer that, let me tell you what happened. Apparently, this person was too short to climb in, but something in the bin made him or her curious. Immediately, the person began searching the alley for someone else. After finding who she or he was looking for, the second body went to the trash bin, climbed in, removed a box, and handed it to the short one. Each examined the contents. Seems whatever they found caused a frenzied discussion."

"Did the snitch learn what was in the box? What was found?"

"Can't answer that. He said nothing was removed from the box and claimed he was too far away to hear what was said. His opinions are based entirely on the two people's actions. He was some distance from the dumpster. Whether he couldn't hear because he's hard of hearing or deadened by the sauce he drank, the cops don't know."

"What about the two people? Who are they? Did he know them?"

"He claims he couldn't tell. Again, they were too far away to be clearly seen. The cops aren't totally buying his story, however. They think he may be holding back, possibly looking to gain something in exchange for information offered at a later time."

"Now what happens?"

"Hard to say! Apparently, there's some interest. The drivers of two squad cars confirmed part of the snitch's story. After seeing footprints in the garbage and hearing some talk, they climbed in the dumpster to see what could be found but came up with nothing.

"Now, the investigation appears to be—and I emphasize the words 'appears to be'—low priority."

"What's that mean?"

"Since there's no crime in a couple of homeless climbing in a dumpster, I imagine they'll do a quick check to see what can be learned."

"Will they continue?"

"My guess? It's an open investigation on the books. There've been a number of problems caused in this town by the homeless. Robberies! Assaults! Public harassment! But more significant than that is why an apparently wealthy person, someone with a chauffeur, would drive to this part of town—known for its high crime rate—and discard a box in an out-of-the-way dumpster. That's enough to make the higher ups' curious."

"So if they continue to investigate, what are they likely to do?"

"Again, only guess! They'll question the snitch a second time and see if he can either identify the two who took the box or offer names of others who might know. Because homeless people drift, an investigation of this type is likely to be time-consuming and costly. If nothing shows up quickly, the incident is likely to be shoved off to the side. Cops have too many crimes requiring an already restricted, overworked force to be used judiciously on investigations of lesser importance."

"You're probably right! But all the same, I want you to remain focused on the investigation. So keep me posted!"

Handing an envelope to O'Malley, Jensen continued, "You've done a fine job, Tom. Here's a small reward. The more you learn, the greater my appreciation."

After O'Malley left the diner, he opened the envelope and thumbed through a number of one-hundred dollar bills. He then put the envelope in his inner coat pocket, raised a cold cup of coffee to his lips, sipped, and stared ahead.

Fifteen hundred dollars! Very, very generous! But why so much? What's your interest, Jensen? Or better yet, what's your involvement? What's this box to you? And Dominic, why won't you tell me who the informant is? Yah, I know. It's an ongoing investigation, and the word coming from the top is to keep things close to the vest. But it's me, Dominic. Your former partner, Red! We never held out on each other before. Why now? Besides, you don't seem too excited about this dumpster caper. And neither do the department heads from what you've said. So why the hush-hush? Yet Jensen's overly interested. Oh, I'll give it my attention, all right. You can bet on that, Walter baby. Maybe a lot more attention than you would like. Who knows what'll turn up! Possibly, there's something more rewarding than a bunch of C-notes.

CHAPTER 5

THE WITNESS

Tom O'Malley, from years as a police detective, enjoyed working in the dark since he was accustomed to all-night stakeouts and limited hours of sleep.

When he left the police force, he was required to turn in his assigned weapon, badge, and other department material. But possessions unknown to the "brass" were never surrendered. A clean uniform, worn when he was a patrolman, along with a badge, revolver, and disguise kit, were concealed behind a false wall in his basement.

During one undercover assignment, he "found" an unregistered .38 caliber Colt Detective Special and "forgot" to report it. The badge, "picked up" years earlier, belonged to a dead police officer who had been part of a covert surveillance operation that had failed. In an attempt to cover the killers' tracks, the dead cops were tossed in a pile, soaked with gasoline, and set on fire. One officer's body, beneath the other victims and pressed against the earth, "protected" his badge from being marred. As part of the cleanup detail, O'Malley—a newly graduated police officer—discovered the shield and kept it as a souvenir.

Dressed in the old uniform, armed, and wearing the badge, the former policeman left his home around midnight and drove to Oak

Street. There, he parked behind a tenement house. Walking into a moonlighted alley, he disregarded those sleeping against the walls, paying particular attention to the fire escapes at various buildings. One held his attention!

He entered a side door to the third building away from the alley entrance and proceeded to the fourth floor. Working quietly, he eased open a window, stepped out onto a fire escape of choice, descended silently one flight of stairs, and leaped onto the landing next to a pile of blankets.

A body bolted upright, startled and wide-eyed, staring through bloodshot orbs at two hands; one holding a revolver, the other a badge. "Sh-sh-shit, oshifer! You scar . . . scared the piss outta me."

"You're lucky if that's all you lose."

"But I . . . I . . . I ain't done nothin'. I'm just sleepin' here with my bottle, minding my own business. And none of that's against the law. I know my rights, oshifer."

"I'll be the judge of that. You tell me what I need to know, and I'll leave you alone. But string me along, down to the precinct you go. What sleep you've already had will be the last because the cell reserved for you won't be as private as it is here. You'll have roommates. All kinds of guys! Those who like new bunkmates and can't keep their hands to themselves! Touching, feeling, exploring to find out what you have that's of interest to them! So if you want to stay here, alone, by yourself, then you'll tell me what I need to know. So let's start. What's your name?"

"Gra . . . Grape Juice!"

"No, your given name?"

"Been usin' Grape Juice so many years. There ain't no other name! Mention Grape Juice, and everyone knows who you're talking about. Use any other name, and nobody knows who in the hell you mean."

"Okay, for the time being, Grape Juice is good enough. But if I come looking for more, I'm going to make certain I know who I'm talking to."

"Go ahead and ask! I'll tell you all I know. Ain't got nuttin' to hide! And besides, I know all about that jail. And I damn well don't want to go down there."

"Good! Begin with Tuesday night, the sixteenth. Were you here?"

"The sixteenth! What's today?"

"The eighteenth!"

"Two nights ago? Ah, yeah! Thas the night of the 'citement. The big car! The little box! My two friends nosing round the trash bin! Yeah, yeah! I was here. Already told the cops about that night. Told 'em everything! Everything I saw, everything I know. Answered all their questions. Ask them? They'll tell you."

"I have, but there are some loose ends. Things that need to be tied together. Like the vehicle and the driver. And the box. And anything else you saw."

"Like I told them, I don't know the make or color of the machine." Pointing, he said, "Look for yourself! Pothole Parkway's a far piece! It was dark, too dark to see!"

"Well, describe the vehicle! Was it large? Small? Was it a car or a truck? Did it have two doors or four? You had to see something?"

"Nah, it wasn't a truck. It was a car, all right. A big one! A long mother! Guess I didn't tell the cops that."

"By big, what do you mean? Like a stretch? A limousine?"

"Yeah! That's it! Don't see many of them on Pothole Parkway."

"The color, was it—"

"Like I told you, I don't know what the color was. Nor do I know the make."

"Look, we can get through this a lot quicker if you let me finish with the questions before you answer. In other words, shut up and don't interrupt."

"Sorry! Sorry! Won't do it again!"

"Now, the color? Was it dark or light?"

"Oh, it was dark. Don't know if it whash blue, green, black, brown, or what. But it whash dark, definitely dark."

"That helps! Now, the driver! Was he tall, short, fat, thin, white, black, Hispanic? What do you remember about him? Anything, everything!

"Couldn't see his face. Don't know if he was a whitey, darkie, Spic, or what. Had on a hat and walked with his head bent, so I cudn't see his face. He just kept looking at the box! And . . . and . . ."

"And what?"

"Something funny! Something I'd forgotten till jest now. When he was passing below, his hands were shakin'. So bad that he had to pull the box close to his chest! Like he was 'fraid he was gonna drop it. Maybe he's got palsy or that—that Parkinson's stuff. I know all 'bout that 'cause one o' my buddies, Shaky Smith, had—"

"Forget Shaky Smith! Tell me about the box: big, small! What color? What happened to it? Everything you remember!"

"Sure! Sure! It was just a . . . not a big cardboard box, more like a flimsy carton. Maybe a foot or two long! And the color? Dirty white. Nuttin' unusual, 'cept the shakin'. But you know, oshifer, the thing that makes no sense at all is why'd he toss it in the trash. If he was scared, he was gonna drop it? Nope. Makes no sense. No sense 't all. And why whash Dora so interested? Sure some strange goin's on!"

"Dora! Who's Dora?"

"Oh shit," he mumbled. From the alarm on Grape Juice's face, O'Malley could see the wino had not meant to reveal the woman's name. But now that he had, he could only continue. "She's a friend. Her and . . . oh, what the hell . . . Roscoe! Two o' my best pals! Always sharin'.

"Seems like right after the car pulls away, Dora comes down the alley. Walkin' slowly. Looking all around. Real careful like. Then when she gets to the trash bin, she stops. Looks at it and scurries over to it. Lifts the lid and pulls herself up to look inside.

"But Dora, she's small! Not much . . . not much bigger than a bug's bite on my butt! But she can't see what she's looking for, so she goes searching 'round the alley for Roscoe. Well, he's sleeping and not too happy at being rousted. But with him, she's like a mother bear in control. Total control. She rants and screams, not taking any of his guff. And off he shuffles to the trash can, like a kid whose pride's been crushed.

"Now, Roscoe. He's big. Taller 'n me. She tells him to climb in, and though he always does what she says, he ain't happy. I hear him rummaging 'round and screamin' about the slop he's wading through. Then he finally finds the carton and hands it to her. Both of them look inside and begin whispering. I can't hear a word said, but whatever they found interested them 'cause they held the carton protectively when they left the alley. And then that's when Freddie appears!"

"Freddie! Who's Freddie?"

"Oh, he's another one of the gang who sleeps in the alley. Known as 'Frisky Fingers.' Let me tell you about him and that name. It's real funny."

After revealing all he knew about Freddie, Grape Juice concluded by saying, "Officer, that's all I know. Hope you're satisfied because there ain't no more!"

Whether it was the conversation or the threats, it appeared the homeless man was sobering up. It was officer instead of *oshifer* and phrasings more common to an educated man than a witless bum.

"Yes, Grape Juice, you filled in some of the holes. Guess you can stay here tonight."

"Well, if you're really happy, maybe you can give me a buck or two for a pint. My throat's awfully dry from all this talking. And I sure need to wet my whistle!"

So much for sobriety! Some chosen habits can't be discarded, thought Tom.

Reaching a gloved hand into his pocket, O'Malley removed a bottle of grape wine. "Here! Take this! I heard you like it, and I planned to give it to you if you tied together the dots. You have. You've earned it. Enjoy the privacy of your evening."

CHAPTER 6

JULY 20–RUN AND HIDE

It was a nice Saturday morning. Sunny, cool, and busy!

Doc was walking down Main Street, whistling and enjoying the sights. As he crossed the intersection at Oak Street, a bus approached, and a woman on a bench rose and boarded it, leaving behind yesterday's newspaper.

Walking to where she had been sitting, Doc lowered himself onto the bench and picked up a weekly tabloid, *Our Little World*. The newspaper, circulated on Fridays, summarized world and local area events over the previous seven days.

As he scanned the front page, he hardly noticed the news releases on Saudi Arabia's willingness to fund the replacement of an Iraq nuclear reactor destroyed by Israeli planes; or the riots in England; the scheduled meeting between the Senate Leaders and Sandra Day O'Connor, a Supreme Court nominee; or the lobbying efforts of President Ronald Reagan on his tax cut plan. Instead, Doc's attention was focused on the following article:

Former Councilman Suspected of Being Murdered
By "Tips" Wright

The body of Charles Evans Hughes, 54, was discovered early today in an alley off Commerce Avenue. The former attorney and once popular councilman had what many thought to be a political future destined for greatness. But his need for wealth and personal status led to the embezzlement of city funds, conviction, disbarment, and imprisonment. Following release, he returned to the city's streets as one of its unwelcome castoffs. Recently, he was questioned by the police on an open but under-seal investigation regarding an incident occurring in an alley off Commerce Avenue. On a follow-up visit by police, Hughes was found holding a pint of grape wine believed to be poisoned. Savoring the taste of fruity wines, the former councilman had acquired the familiar nickname, Grape Juice. The deceased has no known relatives and will be buried in the cemetery for indigent people.

Doc, deep in thought, sat tapping his knee. Rising, he proceeded down Main Street, stopping occasionally to ask acquaintances if they had seen Dora or Roscoe. A few of the conversations were brief, others lengthy and informative. The negative responses were discouraging but not relinquishing. He continued walking over to Oak, along Walnut, onto Forest, and then to High. Near the end, he approached Elm Street where a dozen standing people were intent upon something.

Crossing the road, Doc moved to the back of the group and observed a young man being encouraged by a female companion to sit down at a table and have a pressing question answered through the reading of Tarot cards. After some persuasive selling by the lady, the man finally agreed; and when he stepped forward, Doc saw the reader to be Dora. Curious, the doctor moved to the far end of the group, remaining hidden from Dora's view and possible distraction.

The person seeking the Tarot reading positioned himself at a ninety-degree angle from Dora. After a few get-acquainted remarks, she asked the man what he wished to learn, and he explained that he had been given the opportunity to change careers, and he wondered if it was in his best interest.

Handing him the deck of seventy-eight cards, she asked him to shuffle them, relax, and phrase the question he wanted answered. Through minimal instructions, Dora offered the querent a suggestion on clarifying his question by removing negative connotations with empowering ones. Once again, he was asked to reshuffle the cards, relax, and ask his first question precisely and correctly.

With his left hand, he cut the deck into three stacks, placing them in a leftward direction. Continuing to use his left hand, he picked up the rightmost pile, put it on top of the center pile, and then placed that combined group on the third pile.

Among the seventy-eight cards in a Tarot deck, twenty-two are illustrated and identified by names appropriate to each illustration: the Chariot, Death, World, Empress, Emperor, Fool, Hanged Man, Hermit, Hierophant, Judgment, Justice, Lovers, Magician, Moon, Star, Strength, Sun, Temperance, Tower, Wheel of Fortune, the Devil, and the High Priestess. These, the Major Arcana, are known to be one's inner great secrets, hidden privacies leading to the achievement of wisdom.

The remaining fifty-six cards are the lessons of everyday life known as the Minor Arcana. These fifty-six cards comprise four suits with each suit consisting of fourteen cards ranging numerically from ace through ten followed by a Page, Knight, Queen, and King. Each of the four suits is illustrated: *Cups,* the suit of love and feeling; *Pentacles,* considerations practical and of material comfort; *Swords,* conflicting forces of knowledge and reasonableness; and *Wands,* aspects dealing with business and careers.

Dora had him select ten cards and place them face down in a clockwise circular fashion, with the first card at twelve, the second at one, and continuing with the tenth and final card at nine. This created the *Magic Mandala Spread,* one of twelve formations Dora customarily used, with this one being selected because it effectively provided answers to one seeking personal insight and guidance on an issue.

Beginning with the first card, the querent turned it over from left to right, and Dora read the card in reference to how it applied to his self-image. When he went to turn the second card, he was told that he must flip it from left to right, as he had done the first card. While Dora had no requirement about turning the cards from left to right or top to bottom, she did require consistency of the chosen process.

Once turned, every Major and Minor Arcana fell into either an upright or reversed position. The latter does not necessarily imply a negative or unpleasant situation but merely an opposite meaning to the upright's present qualities, one signifying a fading or undeveloped power.

As the first card was turned, Dora's reading reflected how the man viewed himself. The following six cards disclosed information about his desires and intentions, inviolate needs, achievements, determinations, abilities, and vulnerabilities. A secret appeared with the eighth card, and the ninth recommended an initiative to be taken. The tenth and final card showed how the man should proceed. With the reading completed, the customer ecstatically rose, thanked Dora, and kissed the woman who had persuasively talked him into the sitting.

When they left, another man stepped forward, holding a roll of cash. Seeing the money, the seated Dora welcomed him, and he explained what he desired to learn. Before she could answer, Doc moved into her vision and tilted his head backward, motioning with his thumb for her to leave. Hesitating momentarily, she picked up the Tarot cards, completed a rapid shuffling, and laid five cards face up in front of her. Then she turned to the man and said, "Sir, I am troubled and deeply sorry, but the cards tell me that now is not the time for another reading. Possibly later this afternoon at four or five o'clock! But for your benefit, now will not be suitable."

"Oh no! From what I just saw, I know you can help me. You say possibly in a couple of hours! If I return at four, am I likely to be refused again?"

"No, that I promise! Manifestations like this have happened before, but the delays are never permanent. Please come back. I'll be waiting for you."

Disappointed, the man departed along with the crowd. Dora stood directly in front of Doc and said, "Did you see the money he was holding? You needing to see me had better be important because I can't afford to lose opportunities like that."

"It is. But tell me. Did the cards really say it's not a good time for a reading?"

"No! But I had to have some excuse since you seemed so rambunctious."

"Clever! Fact is I'm surprised to find you back with the cards. When did that begin?"

"Two days ago! With the baby, I need cash. Can't risk being broke. Have to take care of my little girl. Roscoe's a big help. He's right handy but sure as hell ain't a walking bank. So it's up to me to do the providin'. And frankly, being away from the cards as long as I have, I'm pretty rusty. But it's comin' back, and the response is good. People are anxious to hear what will empower them. So they're lining up for self-discovery. But 'nough about Tarot! What's up? Why this rush-rush?"

"It's all about Grape Juice. I guess you heard what happened to him?"

"No! Ain't heard nothing? What about him?"

Handing Dora the paper, he said, "Read this."

"My gawd! The poor old guy! Why? He never hurt anyone. Why? Why?"

"Obviously, it has to do with the baby you fetched out of the dumpster. Grape Juice was always on that fire escape, and he probably saw you and Roscoe. So it's not safe for you and the infant. Too many folks know about you living in that abandoned department store. If you really love that baby, and I know you do, best you move and stay out of sight. This Tarot reading's got to stop. Otherwise, the same thing that happened to Grape Juice is going to happen to you."

"Doc, there's no way I can just drop out of sight. Besides, me and Roscoe have already moved. We're no longer at the 'hotel.' No one knows where we're living. And I just can't hide! I need money to care for my little girl. That's all there is to it."

"Where are you living?"

She remained silent for the moment, merely staring at her old friend. "Only Roscoe knows, and we're not too happy about sharing it with others."

"Theodora Rochelle! This is me, Doc! I've been with you since the beginning of this new family. And if you can't trust me now, then I'm washing my hands of all three of you."

"Oh, quit gettin' a burr up your behind. 'Course I trust you. Go fetch Totem, while we close shop. I'll do more than tell you. I'll show you!"

Going to where she pointed, Doc retrieved Dora's most prized found treasure, a small mobile steel cart on four inflatable rubber tires. Longer than it was wide, three vertical plates extended up from the platform base—two along the sides and one in the back. Extending from the rear plate were two movable handles used for pushing and turning the cart with ease. Above the handles and attached to the back plate was a steel utility box with a hinged cover.

About thirty-six inches high, the cart was easy to move and made it possible for Dora to transport her card table, two chairs, decks of cards, and other essentials. The conveyance was the envy of every homeless person, and Dora guarded it with her life.

As they moved away, Doc asked, "Where are we headed?"

"Down by the old tracks! The ones no longer used! You know, those left to rust once the new depot was built. There's a work shack there. Abandoned a couple of years back! Me, Roscoe, and the baby have moved in."

"You mean that old dump? The one with the weeds growing all around it and the walls and roof falling in? How can you take a newborn infant into such a hovel?"

"Like I said, Roscoe's real handy. Used to be a carpenter! A gem of a workman! Jack of all trades! You'll see how he's spruced up the old shack. I'm right proud of it."

"Well, it's not safe. You want to protect the child? Leave the area! Get away! Far away!"

"You gotta be kidding, Doc! I don't know any other place! And why? Why do you think it's so necessary to get away? No one cares about us or where we are."

While saying this, the couple passed an unnoticed homeless man sitting in a doorway.

"Well, I can think of three reasons why you need to leave. First, there's too much interest in that recovered carton with its unknown contents along with the two people who took it. Second, with the killing of Grape Juice, the police investigation is bound to intensify. And then there's Frisky Fingers Freddie! He's getting a great deal of attention with his mouthing off."

"Frisky Fingers! What's he got to do with all of this?"

"Rumors going around, he knows who poisoned Grape Juice and that he's got an idea who the unnamed couple is that took the carton."

"That bastard! If he knows about Roscoe and me, then all hell will break loose. He'll stop at nothing to seek revenge!"

"Revenge! What are you talking about, Dora?"

"Oh, it goes back a couple of years. Was a warm summer night, and I had gone to the river for a bath. Had stripped down, scrubbed myself, and was back on the bank getting dressed. All of a sudden, two hands reach around from behind, one grabbing one of my titties, the other against my stomach sliding to a no-hands-allowed area. So I grabbed a finger on that roaming hand and jerked it back. Two sounds! One, the breaking of a bone and then a scream! With the release of his hand on my boob, I pivoted around while tugging on the broken finger. Then I knee this creep in his jewels, and he falls forward, clutchin' his privates, screamin'. Near my feet was a big hunk of wood that I lifted up and smashed over the back of his head. Down he went, unaware of everything other than the stars in his head.

"Good old Irma had gone to the river with me for a bath. She saw this and broke out, howling in laughter. From that time on, he's been known by the moniker she gave him, 'Frisky Fingers Freddie.' Boy, did it catch on. Like wildfire! Now, when anyone stops to say, 'Hi, Frisky Fingers,' he goes bonkers knowing that the person heard that he was accosted and beaten up by a woman nearly half his size. So if he finds out I took the box, it'll be payback time."

"All the more reason for you to get away!"

"I hear you, Doc, but that's easier said than done."

"Maybe, maybe not! Let me mull on it."

Together, they moved away, with Dora calling over her shoulder for Doc to quicken his slow-moving hitch step.

Unseen to the couple was a homeless one who exited a darkened doorway and followed in the distance. *Just what are you up to? Time to find out.* Nosey Ned thought.

CHAPTER 7

MONDAY, JULY 22–THE BLOODHOUNDS

The phone rang. "Security Office, O'Malley speaking."
"Tom. Walter Jensen."
"Hello, Chief! What can I do for you?"
"Just wondering how you're progressing on that little assignment I gave you.'
"Slowly, sir. Very slowly! There have been some developments. The death of that street person, Grape Juice, and some scuttlebutt about a Frisky Fingers Freddie!
"Grape Juice! Frisky Fingers Freddie! Who the hell are they?"
After revealing what O'Malley knew, Walter remained quiet.
"Mr. Jensen. Are you still there?"
"Yes, Tom. I'm here. Just thinking. I want you to spend whatever time you need on this new assignment. I'd like some quick answers."
"I understand, sir. But the security of the company's important, and it requires quite a bit of my time. It's not a small organization, as you well know."
"True. But you report to me, and your priority is this job. Delegate the rest."
"Whatever you say."

Hanging up, Jensen telephoned his son, the vice president of sales.

"Hi, Dad! What's up?"

"I've been thinking and made some plans. Now that Sara's back, I want you to take your mother and wife on a vacation. Your mom's not a complainer—as you know—but during breakfast, she was in a great deal of pain. That Lou Gehrig's disease is advancing, and Bermuda this time of the year is a favorite. Maggie and Gerard should be at Elbow Beach by now. Had them fly down to freshen up the place. A week on the island will give you and Sara time to work out your difficulties and give your mother the companionship she needs. We're lucky the two gals are so close."

"Dad, I'll be glad to do it, but it sounds like you want this to happen tomorrow."

"Wednesday, actually."

"But that's not possible. I have to meet with Mathew McQuillen on Friday and finalize the agreement for comarketing his British-made products."

"I know that, and I also know he loves to take his wife to exotic places. So I've booked a one-week stay for the two of them at the *Fairmont Southampton.* Its pink, sandy beaches, *Willow Stream Spa,* and historic *Waterlot Inn* should provide the ideal setting for you to clinch the deal."

"But, Dad, you're talking about next week. It's quite possible he can't pick up and leave on such short notice."

"He can. I've checked it out, and he and his wife are available. All you need to do is make the offer. Fly them on our jet. Wine and dine them for a week, and everyone around here will be saying that young Walter is a chip off his old man's block. And on your way out today, stop by Anna's desk. She's got the itinerary and listing of reservations I've made."

After disconnecting the call, he dialed home and asked for his driver and guardian.

"Peter, bring the Ford Ranger to the office. And hurry."

"Do you need anything else?"

"Good question! Bring your night-vision glasses, binoculars, and a camera."

"Appears we're going to be busy."

"I hope so. We'll be looking for a couple of people."

He hung up the phone and remained seated, tapping fingers on the desk.

The dependable and the questionable: an ex-policeman motivated by money; an employee never questioning but always willing; and the third man, a mystery. Much like a shadow. Here one moment, gone the next. Am I more dependent on him or him on me?

Reaching for the phone, Jensen depressed eleven buttons, numbers known only to him and the private-line subscriber.

After three rings and a recorded message, he briefly said, "Everything's in motion. Go with the plan. I'll touch base later."

Disconnecting the call, he walked to his office closet and replaced his suit jacket and tie with a sweater, sunglasses, and a Yankee's cap. Then he swung back a hinged picture frame concealing a wall safe. Rotating the dial, he opened the door to five shelves. Two had confidential papers; two had bundles of cash; and one supported a Glock 22 .40 caliber pistol, a Smith & Wesson Bodyguard .38 Revolver, and a Baretta 9mm pistol with two magazines holding seventeen rounds each. Beneath the handguns were licenses to carry concealed weapons.

After a few seconds of thinking, he palmed the Glock, but instead reached for a roll of cash. Swinging shut both the door to the safe and the picture frame, Jensen left his office while notifying Anna to cancel all appointments. Although surprised by his casual appearance, the dutiful secretary made no comment other than merely saying, "Goodbye, Mr. Jensen. See you tomorrow."

* * * * *

O'Malley entered the precinct. Walking to the front desk, he hesitated while waiting for Circerchi to finish a phone call.

"What a day!" the desk sergeant groaned. "In ten minutes, I clock out, and I'll be damn glad to get out of here. So what do I owe the pleasure of this visit? Considering what's already happened, it can't be good."

"Come on, Dom. Smell the roses. Tell you what. I'll buy you a pitcher of suds, and we'll spend an hour unwinding. How about it! Say twenty minutes?"

"You're on. But make it a bathtub rather than a pitcher!"

At their private sanctuary, Dominic extended his hand to accept the offered beer. Immediately, he quaffed the pint and motioned with his free hand for a second.

"Slow down, wop, or you'll end up on your ear."

"On this stuff? Doesn't have enough juice to give my dog a buzz. Not today anyway."

"Something's really wound your clock. Well, spit it out and confess to Father O'Malley all your problems."

"After you fill this glass."

Taking a swig of the third pint, Dominic let out a sigh.

"Remember our conversation the other night? The one about the dumpster in the alley? Off Commerce."

"That low-priority case?"

"Yep! Only it's no longer low priority. It's at the top of Parker's unsolved 'Get me some answers quick' list. All because IA is involved."

"Internal affairs? Why them?"

"You heard about the Hughes killing?"

"Who hasn't? It was front page in *Our Little World*. But what's that got to do with IA?

"Rumor has it a cop did the old guy in."

"A cop! You got to be kidding!"

"Wish I were, but Hughes, before he went off the cliff, was a pretty prominent defense attorney. Appears an eyewitness saw a cop talking to him the night he died."

"Any identification?"

"That's why the IA. Description received, though not solid, fit a few assigned to the precinct. So IA's taking over the investigation and questioning damn near everyone. So far, the most likely ones have airtight alibis. But everyone's on edge. You remember Steigerwald?"

"Fritz? Sure do."

"Well, he was one fitting the ID and, when fingered, went ballistic. I thought World War III was taking place. He began bitching about all the crap falling on him—a guy with nineteen years of service, a closet full of commendations, favorable reviews, and an unhesitating willingness to do whatever shitty detail someone wanted done. When finally cleared of suspicion, because he was working undercover with three others, he was not pacified. I bet he'll never be. And because Steigerwald is looked up to by nearly everyone in the outfit, morale is really low. That's why Parker's a bear. Hell, I hate going in tomorrow."

"Tell me about the suspect. Describe him."

"That's part of the problem. Other than the uniform, the description's vague. It could be nearly anyone. Even you, if you were still a cop! With it being night, poor lighting, and up high on a fire escape, we're not even certain what color the guy is."

"Are they sure it's a cop?"

"Good question. Just the uniform. There are tons of clues—fingerprints, hairs, fabric samples, DNA, and other bullshit from who knows how long. All different, all unknown. With so many clues, a cop's DNA is like a grain of sand on the beach. So IA wants to be sure and is taking command. It's a crock."

"Any matches to the data bank?"

"Not yet. Because of the location of the killing, it's likely the perp's not even worried. Hell, he probably wore gloves."

"What about the witness? Anyone question him?"

"Name's Frisky Fingers Freddie. But we haven't been able to find him. And everyone, and I mean everyone, has his description and is looking for him. We all want this case put to bed."

"Dominic, it's times like this when I miss the old job. But, friend, what pleases me obviously doesn't please you. So let's have one more. Then I've got to shove off."

* * * * *

It was nearly seven o'clock in the evening, and Nosey Ned was walking along the riverbank. Up ahead, he saw Freddie sitting on the ground with a burger, fries, fruit, and a large container of coffee.

"Freddie, my friend, look at what you've got. And here it's dinnertime. You will share with your old buddy Ned, won't you?"

"That honker of yours could pick up freebies miles away. But your willingness to go out and beg like the rest of us takes too much effort. No, Ned! I'm not sharing with you because you never have anything for me. Go out and scrounge like the rest of us. Today, I hit it rich, and there's no reason why you can't do the same."

Touching his crooked nose—one broken in a bar fight and not properly reset—Ned replied, "What if I have something to offer? My friends call me Nosey not only because I smell a good meal but because I have a nose for news. And I've got something you want!"

With a skeptical look at his visitor, Freddie asked, "And what might that be?"

"Well, I hear you've been looking for Dora and Roscoe. What if I tell you I know where they live? Is that worth some food?"

"If you're going to tell me about the abandoned department store on Commerce, forget it. I know all about that place. Besides, they're no longer there."

"You're right! They left for a new place. Pretty nice from what I hear!"

"And just how do you know that? They certainly wouldn't tell you, and I don't see you following them. Even with a hound dog, you couldn't track a stumblebum."

"Don't underestimate me, Freddie. Like I said, I've got a nose for knowledge. But if you're not interested, keep your damn food. There are others who'll share!"

Turning to leave, Freddie said, "Hold on! I'll risk some food. If you're right, it'll be worth it. If you're wrong, that nose of yours will never smell food or anything again. So whatta you know? Here, take some fries, the apple, and banana. And have a cup of coffee! Now give!"

"Not unless you share some of the burger."

"Oh hell! Okay! Tell me where they are and how you found out."

And he did.

Sending Ned on his way, Freddie finished the few remains of his food and coffee. *With darkness settling in, it was a good time for a surprise visit.*

CHAPTER 8

UNWELCOME GUESTS

The Ford Ranger drove down Commerce Avenue before going over to Main, Oak, and Walnut Streets. Along the way, it occasionally stopped at a curb, allowing Walter to speak to people wandering the streets.

"Aren't you worried some bum will tell the cops they talked to you?" asked Peter.

"It's not my neighborhood, so it's unlikely anyone knows me. Plus it's night, and I'm wearing this Yankee cap and sunglasses, so who'll identify me? Besides, with all the wine these lost souls consume, its unlikely conversations will be remembered an hour after spoken."

"Yeah, but ten- and twenty-dollar bills make impressions."

"True! But only one guy, the old geezer, got any. Others, who didn't know who Freddie is or where he is, ended up with nothing. So far, we're safe."

"And just what are you going to do if you catch him?"

"Talk to him! Bribe him with money. Learn what he knows."

"And if he refuses? What then?"

"That's why you're along. To persuade him."

Continuing down Walnut Street, Walter interrupted their conversation, saying, "Look over there, under the street light! Pull over! See what that woman can tell us."

Several blocks earlier, a Monte Carlo, passing the Ranger, made a U-turn and followed at a distance.

Glad I know you, Peter, thought O'Malley. *Otherwise, I would have missed the two of you. Now, just why are you in this godforsaken area?"*

The Ranger F-150 came to a stop, and the tracking Irishman eased beside a curb, reaching for his binoculars. He noticed a street woman hesitate and then move closer to the Ranger. A few minutes lapsed while the woman and the occupants in the Ranger conversed. Then a hand reached through the window, offering several bills which the woman quickly grabbed. Smiling toothlessly, she shoved the money into her bra and watched the car pull away.

O'Malley left the curb, drove to where the woman was standing, and turned off the engine.

"Lady, care to make a few bucks?"

"Depends on what you have in mind, mister?"

O'Malley showed her a ten-dollar bill. "You can have this by telling me what the guy in that other car wanted to know and what you told him."

Squinting, she said, "Worth more than ten. He gave me twenty!"

Removing from his wallet another ten, O'Malley said, "Okay, but no more!"

She made a grab for the money, but the Irishman pulled it back.

"Information first," he told her.

"Sure, sure, sure! He was looking for Freddie, Frisky Fingers Freddie. Know him?"

"I know of him but not what he looks like. Describe him! Tell me where he is!"

"You want a lot for twenty bucks."

"You may be right. But now that I know who I'm looking for, I can probably get it for less."

Thinking but not answering, the former policeman started the engine.

"Guess you don't want the twenty?"

"Hold on, Sonny. I ain't said no. You sure are an eager one. Slow down and live longer."

"Tell me what I'm asking, and you'll be paid. I need to get going, and I don't have time for your words of wisdom."

Leaning in the window, the woman described Freddie and where she had told Jensen to look. O'Malley gave her the money and drove toward the park.

Upon arriving, he cruised around looking for the pickup and questioning people about where he could find Freddie. No one seemed to know until he ran into Nosey Ned.

"You're interested too? Seems everyone's lookin' for Freddie. First, the two guys in the Ford. And now you! Sure is popular! Like I told them, I ain't seen him."

"Thanks anyway."

As he shifted into gear, Ned says, "Though I haven't seen him, I have a pretty good idea about where he might be."

"Oh! Where's that?"

"What's in it for me?"

Rather than hand out more money, O'Malley flashed the recovered police badge and said, "How about a trip to the precinct? I'm sure I can give you something down there that'll make you tell me what I want to know."

"Now hold on, officer! I don't want no trouble. Just want to cooperate. Freddie's looking for Dora and Roscoe. Told the other guys they moved down to the old train yard to the empty workmen's shack. That's where he probably is."

Now that's something, thought O'Malley. *A lot of people interested in this caper. First Walter Jensen, then Grape Juice, next Dora and Roscoe, and now Freddie! Why him? Where's this going?*

* * * * *

Lighted candles illuminated the interior of Dora and Roscoe's new home, extending a welcoming invitation to unannounced guests. Alone and surrounded by only a few abandoned train cars, railroad tracks no longer in use, and a distant fence, the converted workmen's shop stood accessible to visitors from every direction.

"Doc, mind feeding Stacey?"

"My pleasure!"

Taking the baby, he tilted the bottle into her welcoming lips.

"Anastasia Victoria Adronicus. Twenty-five years from now, that pretty face, jet black hair, and amethystine eyes will bewitch dozens of young men. I foresee you breaking many hearts. And that comes from not reading seventy-eight Tarot cards either. It's from me! So I caution you to use your beauty wisely."

"She will," Dora said. "I'll see to it. With her Greek intelligence, she'll know what to do."

"Greek intelligence? You don't even know her national origin. She might even be one of the fortunate Scots, like me."

"Not in this house! Not my baby! I'm a descendant of Andronicus of Rhodes, the eleventh successor to Aristotle, founder of Peripatos. And she's destined to have his wisdom. It's in the cards."

"Dora! What's this crap about you being a descendant of some noted philosopher? I don't recall seeing that in the cards?" responded Doc who was now being taught by Dora on how to read Tarot."

"No, Doc, you didn't see it in the cards because it wasn't in the cards. I haven't always lived on the streets. How I came beholden to the cards is a secret that will follow me to my grave. But there was a time when I was well educated, and that knowledge and wisdom will be passed on to Stacey. That I promise.

"But that's enough about me. Let's get back to the reading. To that question you asked, flip a card, and I'll reveal the answer. Then we'll discuss it, and you can tell me if you understand why I say what I say."

But instead of answering, she gasped, "Oh my god!" and jumped out of her chair.

"Now what," asked Doc. "What's the matter?"

"Quick! Give me Stacey! Grab her blanket! We've got to get out of here!"

"Why? Where're we going?" asked Doc.

"Quit asking questions and just do what I say."

On the table, there were seven cards laid in the form of a *Lucky Horseshoe Spread*. The first card was an upright *Ace of Cups*. Representing the past, it signified a new beginning.

Love was arriving, and she associated it with Stacey.

The second card, *the Fool*, reversed rather than upright, described the present: *look forward to a changing life filled with exciting dreams*. This was not the time to be impetuous and thoughtless but instead a time to exercise caution, especially with new people entering Doc's life.

The third card, representing the future, was *the Chariot*, reversed. It was a warning of possible failure and defeat: *be on the lookout for impediments and obstacles; rethink and revise plans. This was not a time for emotions to take charge.*

The fourth card was the *Seven of Swords*. It forewarned of people gathering to oppose and cause failure.

Without turning cards five through seven, Dora raced from the house, holding Stacey protectively to her breast. The three of them headed to an abandoned freight car. Handing Stacey to Doc, Dora climbed aboard and then took her little girl in order for Doc to enter.

Sliding the door to within inches of closing, the two adults remained behind the crack, giving vigil to the house.

After a restless, quiet wait, she turned to Doc and said, "Let's get some sleep."

"Dora, what in the world's gotten into you? We dash out of your house to sleep in this dirty old freight car. Why? What the hell's going on?"

"I'll tell you when I wake up. Now, either get some sleep or at least shut up."

* * * * *

Twenty minutes later, a lone figure walked brazenly into the house. Entering, the man spoke softly. "Dora? Roscoe? Anyone home?"

The one-room building revealed Roscoe's handy work. Cracks in the floor, walls, and ceiling were repaired with odd-shaped pieces of wood and siding. A broken glass window had been partially boarded. Cabinets, three folding chairs, two tables, and a desk—all rejected by the railroaders—were carefully positioned and, like the walls, freshly finished with varying colors from whatever paint Roscoe could find.

The worn mattress, from the "residential" department store, was pushed against the wall, and the Home Depot orange pushcart-converted-crib and charcoal grill were still available.

As rudimentary as the possessions were, Dora had exercised her decorative touch by carefully positioning each item and using candles to create a homey appearance.

The door opened. Roscoe returned.

"Who the hell are you, and what are you doing in my house?"

"Not a very friendly welcome for a visitor. Especially one who's been looking high and low for you and Dora! Seems you have something I'd like to see."

"Oh! And what might that be?"

"You know! That item you removed from the dumpster in the alley. Now with that crooked lawyer's departure from this world and the interest the cops have in his death, my help can be a blessing to the two of you."

"Is that so? Well, we don't need your help. So scram!"

"That's not very polite."

As the visitor pulled back a chair to sit, Roscoe moved forward, aggressively but awkwardly. The "guest" pushed his chair aside, fainted, and with ease, parried the taller opponent's outstretched arms. Roscoe, experienced in the skills of street fighting—biting, kicking, choking, and headbutting—proved to be an unworthy combatant.

As the visitor slipped between Roscoe's two widespread arms, he grabbed the wrist of his taller opponent with one hand and front of his shirt with the other. Pivoting to his right, the visitor launched Roscoe over his extended, outstretched leg to the floor. Twisting the immobile Roscoe's arm behind his back, the judo expert dropped his knees to the base of the fallen victim's spine, causing a whoosh of air to escape the injured man's lips.

Clutching Roscoe's chin with one hand and grabbing a fist full of hair with the other, the visitor pulled Roscoe's head upward and then slammed his face to the floor three times, causing blood to flow from a broken nose.

* * * * *

Earlier, Freddie, hiding near the fence, saw the unknown stranger enter Dora's home and witnessed Roscoe's entrance and verbal outburst—"Who the hell are you and what are you doing in my house?"

Curious, Frisky Fingers dashed to the window and witnessed, through an unobstructed slit in the partially covered glass, the stranger defeat Roscoe. When the victor exited the house, Freddie entered and, with satisfaction, eyed his enemy's unconscious condition. Smiling, he looked around the room and reached for a candle. He placed the lighted wick against the mattress. The pad burst into flames. Leaving, he raced across the open yard to the fence and scaled it with ease.

Outside, two vehicles arrived—one from the west, the second from the south. Knowing where Jensen was heading, O'Malley approached the workman's shack from the southernly direction in time to see a person climbing the fence but too distant to be identified.

Fire inside the house spread with every combustible item blazing. Quickly, the two vehicles left the area.

CHAPTER 9

QUESTIONS

Dora and Doc became weary from waiting for Roscoe to return and quickly fell asleep. With the passing of time, the sky turned from starless black to predawn gray.

In the distance, sirens grew loud. Doc, a light sleeper from his medical days, rolled over and listened. Vehicles were nearing the railcar. Standing, he peered through the boxcar opening. Fire engines and police cars were sliding to a halt. The blazing fire had dwindled to burning wood planks, ashes, and embers as firefighters hosed what remained of the building.

Doc stepped cautiously down from the railcar and edged his way closer to the activity. Other street people were already arriving to see what was happening. Slipping among them, he was able to get as close to the burnt building as the police cordon off area would allow.

"Chief! Over here! We've found a body."

"Man or woman?"

"Can't be certain. Not much left—a piece of cloth, badly burned ankle, foot, and possible sneaker! Rest of the body's under a pile of rubble. But the cloth appears to be from a trouser cuff or a woman's slacks. It's wool fabric—blue, green, and gold check."

Oh damn! That's Roscoe. What a hell of a way to die, thought Doc.

Slipping away from the crowd, Doc disappeared into the night, sneaking back to the railcar. Then he climbed up and walked silently over to Dora who was still asleep.

Oh, how I hate this!

He shook her gently, and she jumped to a sitting position

"Wha-wha-what's the matter?"

Kneeling down beside her, he wrapped an arm around her shoulder and, with his other hand, gently touched her face.

"Dora, I've terrible news. Your home's gone. It went up in flames. Police and firemen are here, and they've found parts of a badly burned body. Among the visible remains is a piece of fabric, and it's the pattern and color of Roscoe's trousers. He must have entered the house, and whether he saw someone starting the fire or attempted to stop it himself, I can't say."

"No, no, not my Roscoe," sobbed Dora. "He's too good to die. Maybe cantankerous but big hearted and kind! He's everything to Stacey and me. What am I going to do, Doc? How can I care for my baby? I need him. Why, why do bad things happen to good people? Why, Doc? Why?"

"Folks have been asking that same question for years, Dora. If you ever find the answer, spread it around. You'll be the oracle of information others want to know.

"But now, don't worry! I'm here, and I'm not going to let anything happen to either of you. Try to get some sleep. We'll make plans later, plans for the three of us."

* * * * *

In the company's near-empty lunchroom, Tom O'Malley was having a breakfast roll and coffee. Walter Jensen came in behind the security officer and tapped him on the shoulder.

"Morning, Tom!"

Turning, he replied, "Hi, Chief! Early as usual! Can I buy you a wake-up cup?"

"No, I'll get it myself. Stay seated. I want to talk to you."

Returning with cup in hand, Walter Jensen pulled out a chair and sat opposite the Irishman.

"You own a two-door Monte Carlo, don't you?"

"Yes, I do! Why do you ask?"

"Thought I saw you on Walnut Street last night and then later near the old railroad yard!"

"Well, I was out, all right. Working on the assignment you've given me. I was on Walnut Street in the early evening, but I never got over to the yard. Had no reason to!"

"Monte Carlos are pretty common these days. You must have seen someone else. Were you by any chance near the railroad yard during the fire?"

"Fire? At the railroad yard! No! I'm not aware of one. What happened?"

"The story I was told, just before you came in, had to do with that old railroad engineer's office. Supposedly went up in flames! Heard it was no longer used after the new depot was finished, but apparently someone was inside. A dead body was found."

"Have they identified the man?"

"Last I heard no one knew whether it was a man or a woman. The medical examiner at the morgue is doing an autopsy to find out the cause of death, as well as the sex and other details."

"See what you can find out and keep me posted. I'll be in the office all day."

Returning to his company-leased Cadillac, Jensen entered the back door.

"You look down in the tooth, Mr. Jensen," Peter said. "Something wrong?"

"Just had coffee with O'Malley! Said he was on Walnut Street last night but not at the railroad yard."

"Proves he's a liar."

"That's one problem, but it's the other one that worries me more."

"What other one?"

"Why he was following us! Parker, over at the precinct, told me he was one hell of a cop. I can use him to keep me up-to-date on what the police are finding out, but I damn well don't want him knowing what we're doing. If he does, then there's likely to be others, besides the baby, who'll need to be eliminated. We have to be careful, Peter. Can't afford to be careless! Need to plan our moves and carry them out perfectly."

Slowly drinking the last of his coffee, O'Malley mulled over the conversation. *What am I? The fox or the hound? Must be getting sloppy for him to have seen me! He no more believes I wasn't at the yard than I believe he wasn't at the fire. Certainly was a dumb comment of mine. Just wasn't thinking! Now I've got to be doubly cautious. I just don't get what's going on? I'm paid to learn about some strange happenings in an alley, when unexpectedly the guy who wants me to do that begins sniffing on his own! Then there's the box with the unknown contents. And a whole lot of people interested in it! Yet none of them knows where it is. Now* **suddenly***, a guy dies who's witness to it all, and the killer's a suspected cop. Since I was with Grape Juice that evening, I wonder how long it'll take for someone to finger me as the killer cop. And what about the missing three—Dora, Roscoe, and Freddie? Where are they? What do they know?*

And what are they hiding? One hell of a lot of unanswered questions! Won't be long before this Jensen-O'Malley parade has every cop in the area working to pull the loose ends together. So I need to be watching over my shoulder. Can't afford to become the hunted, have to be the hunter. Too much at stake and too much to lose for being sloppy! Time to get invisibly nosy and menacingly dangerous! Just the way I like it.

CHAPTER 10

THURSDAY, JULY 25–BERMUDA

"Oh, Mrs. Jensen, I'm so pleased. You've finished all of your soup," said the servant as she gently wiped the invalid's mouth with a napkin.

"Maggie, of all the foods you prepare for us, your gazpacho is among my favorites. Its cool, spicy flavor is especially enjoyable on these warm days. I hope there's more so that I may have another serving at dinner."

"Yes, ma'am, there is. Now, how about a little iced tea? I've sweetened it to your liking." Holding the glass near Mrs. Jensen's mouth, the maid inserted the straw between her lips. As she sipped the tea, the attendant held the napkin beneath her chin to catch the drippings escaping her mouth.

The attention Maggie gave Ginny Jensen evolved out of genuine love and respect, feelings arising over the years more from a familial kinship than a thoughtful employer-employee relationship. Many solitary moments were spent in tears as Maggie watched her mistress's health deteriorate to a condition now requiring wheelchair straps to prevent the woman from falling because of diminished muscle mass and nerve cell shrinkage caused by the amyotrophic lateral sclerosis.

Seeing Sara at the porch door, Ginny said, "Honey, come inside. It's delightful in here."

"Oh, Momma Ginger, this is heaven. So cool and comfortable! It must be more than one hundred degrees outside."

"Well, sit down and relax. Maggie will get you something cool to drink. What do you crave?"

"A large, ice-cold gin and tonic will be ideal, Maggie. Do you mind? I'll stay with Mrs. Jensen."

"I just can't believe Wally is playing golf on a day like today. It's unbearable."

"You know how he loves sports, Sara. Just like his father. Look around! This is more like a trophy gallery than a living room."

Pictures of the senior Jensen were everywhere—playing golf, shooting skeet, hunting wild animals in Africa, Canada, and the States. But one picture held Sara's attention. It was a photograph of him serving the winning ace at the club's annual tennis tournament the previous year. Her gaze was not on his form but on a birthmark, an image embedded in Sara's mind.

"Here is your gin and tonic, Ms. Sara. Also, I took the liberty of preparing a variety of finger sandwiches. You haven't eaten since breakfast, and we don't need you getting run down in this warm weather. I'll put the plate on the table.

"And how about you, Mrs. Jensen? What do you say we mosey over to your room and get you in bed? It's time for your nap, and a rest will do you good."

"You're right, Maggie. Rest is what I need. I am a little tired. However, before I go, give me a moment with Sara."

Maggie moved the invalid next to her daughter-in-law and left the room.

"Sara, you can never imagine how happy I was when I saw you at the front door yesterday. I was certain when you left New York eight months ago, you'd be gone forever. Oh, how I prayed. And then you showed up. I knew my prayers had been answered. Please, please resolve your differences! You are everything Wally needs, and a divorce will not only break his heart but be unbearable to all of us—his father, Maggie, Gerard, me, everyone!"

"Wally and I are working on it, Momma Ginger. But it may take some time. I promise we'll try."

"That's all I want to hear. Your promise. Maggie, come back now! It's time for my nap. Roll me to the room, doctor!"

"Have a good rest," said Sara. "Don't worry, and remember, darkness always turns to dawn."

Sara picked up the drink and sandwiches and headed to the outdoors. The lush green lawn led to rippling blue ocean waters glimmering beneath a golden glow of light from the sun resting at the horizon. Though lovely, Sara's mind was elsewhere, occupied with troubling thoughts.

Oh, Momma Ginger, if you only knew. Will our marriage last? I really can't say. Since my youth, I've prided myself on making things work, but that no longer seems to be true. Back in Canada, at an early age, I was crushed. My classmates ridiculed me. I was the shy, poor kid who wore second-hand, out-of-date clothes. The girl who was never accepted! And so I turned bitter, obsessed with showing them they were wrong. I made up my mind to make things work. And I did but only with great mistakes. Big, big mistakes!

They first began with Johnny Comstock, our high school star quarterback, the guy who had every girl's eye. But fortunately for me, he was my next-door neighbor. Oh, how well I remember how I captured him. I was blossoming and noticed he couldn't keep his eyes off my breasts. They were something, I'll admit. Equal, if not larger in size, to those of many of his classmates! So I decided to prove to the other girls I had something they didn't have. Appeal! The ability to attract the biggest catch in school! It began on my birthday. I picked the tightest, sexiest sweater and shortest skirt I owned and then waited for Johnny to come home. When he did, I waved to him and offered some ice cream and cake. He couldn't resist. And while we were eating our servings, I let the plate fall against my blouse. Oh, what a performance I put on. Screaming and laughing at my clumsiness, I had him grab a towel from the drawer. Of course, some of the ice cream had slipped inside my blouse. As I unbuttoned it and complained of its coldness, he pleasured himself by wiping away the dampness, allowing his fingers to explore beneath my bra. I knew then and there to whom I was going to lose my virginity. Not that day but within the week.

It was late on a Friday afternoon, and the team had a big game on Saturday. Johnny was walking home with a football in hand. When he headed toward his front door, I came out on the porch and waved hello. I was dressed for the occasion. Another tight sweater and short skirt! He eyed me and decided to come over. I gushed at how excited I'd be in seeing him play the next day. This led to my asking a bunch of dumb questions on how he gripped the football when he was going to pass and how he handed it off during the running plays. Then I cast my hook. How, I wanted to know, does the center know when and where to place the ball if he was in the T formation? In response, he explained his signal calling techniques—a changing tempo, his hard count, a rotation of numbers, and other silly things. Playing dumb, I said, I just didn't get it and begged for him to show me. I offered to be the center and him the quarterback. After several practices, I suggested reversing the roles. And my hand, like his hand earlier, explored areas of the body centers and quarterbacks avoid. Some fifteen or twenty minutes later, I allowed myself to be led behind the house where I helped him take my virginity. And that became the first day I started making plans for whatever I wanted.

After graduating from school, I was hired into the secretarial pool at your husband's company. And the first time I saw the vice president of sales, your son, I knew I had to reel him in. Finally, an opportunity arose; his secretary was out sick, and I was the replacement. On our first day together, other than noticing me, no sparks flew. But on the following day, in the hope that his secretary would still be away sick, I dressed appropriately. Not only couldn't he keep his eyes off me, he found flimsy reasons for coming to my office and having me go to his. Then shortly before five o'clock, he had me take some needless dictation. By the time we finished, it was nearly six thirty, and he offered amends by suggesting an after-hours drink. Of course, I accepted. From the next day on, he found reasons for me to help him, even though his secretary had returned. These get-togethers led to dinners, meeting engagements with clients, weekend trips, and finally a marriage proposal. For a while, all went well. But eventually, I became bored. I wanted Wally to be the decision maker. But he wouldn't. He couldn't. He was too weak, and I couldn't accept that. Then something happened, something I didn't initiate but something in which I became involved. Something so unacceptable it has changed my life forever. It occurred after returning to Canada where things became worse. Now I harbor secrets that someday will have to be known. And they will be. If not by me, by the one person I trust. However, Ginger, your ill-health demands that they remain hidden at this time. Once everything becomes known, the backyard whispers will turn ugly; people's lives will not be spared. For some, I am deeply saddened; for others, I care less. But now for the time being, I need to be careful. I must relax. Clear my thoughts. A good swim will help. It always does. Then I can go about doing what needs to be done.

Finishing her sandwiches, Sara walked to the beach. She dropped the towel, empty plate and glass on the sand, and waded into the ocean. The water's cooling touch and pebble-free and sandy seabed were inviting.

She dove into the surf and gracefully swam to the deeper waters. Nearly a mile from shore, she tired, rolled on her back, and floated, smiling as the still warm sun glowed on her face.

From under the water, an arm suddenly encircled her waist, and a hand grabbed the back of her one-piece bathing suit. The overpowering strength of her attacker flipped Sara on her front and forced the struggling, screaming woman beneath the surface. Down, down, down she went, swallowing seawater through her open mouth. Deep beneath the surface, the scuba diver released his grip on the back of her suit, pulled her body against his chest with the encircling arm, and guided his free hand across her front to her opposite forearm.

Her resistance forced him to wrestle for control, inhibiting his movements and accelerating the consumption of oxygen from his tank. Yet he refused to relax his hold, and when the remaining air escaped Sara's lungs, a yielding body became easy to guide.

Taller than the victim, the assassin reversed direction and flutter kicked his unrestricted swim fins further out to sea. Blanketed now by a darkened sky, he released Sara's dead body beneath the surface and swam to a location distant from the Jensen home.

When he got back to land, he walked to a moped and from the attached sidecar removed a towel, dried himself, and dressed casually for an evening in town. With a cell phone in hand, he depressed a series of numbers and listened to a recorded message: "Unavailable! At the beep, leave your message."

"Assignment complete! Problem solved!"

One day passed! Sara was nowhere to be found. Walter Jensen Sr. flew to Bermuda, contacted the police, and reported a missing person. During the ensuing investigation, Sara's towel, empty glass, and plate were found. Days later, her body washed to shore.

Ginger was unable to suppress her tears. Walter Jr. remained quiet, never expressing thoughts or feelings. Maggie, like Ginger, was overwrought, and Gerard was both consoling and attentive. A released medical examiner's report, issued for publication, stated, "Sara Jensen's death was caused by drowning."

CHAPTER 11

THURSDAY, JULY 25–STATESIDE

"Ever since the fire, Doc, you keep harpin' on the same thing. I don't want to hear it anymore. I ain't gonna do it."

"Theodora Rochelle, I will not take no for an answer. It's just not safe for you and Stacey to stay here. You have to get away. At least for the baby's sake!"

"And where are we going? I've been here too long to try new places. My roots are here. And now people are coming to learn about divination. The money's starting to come in, and I can provide for Stacey and me. And you want me to give all that up? Go someplace I don't know? Where no one knows me! You gotta have a screw loose, Doc. I won't do it."

"Dora, what if I take you someplace where you can make lots of money? Just temporarily! Like a vacation! To a place where there are people, crowds of people! A place where they go to have fun and enjoy themselves! A place where it's nice to stay! What can be better than that?"

"And where is this utopia? Other than in your head!"

"You think I'm lying? Making all this up?"

"No! I think you've been consuming too much of the sauce."

"Theodora Rochelle! How dare you? Apologize this minute!"

"Oh, loosen up, Doc. I mean no harm. It's just that I'm too old to believe in fairy tales. When you've lived the number of years I have—clawing for meals, sleeping in vacant buildings, having friends you can count on—these are realities to me. Why should I give away sure things for the possible? Sorry, Doc! I just can't get my hopes up on the uncertain."

"Dora, you and I have been friends a long time. More years than I can remember. I've never misled you and won't start now. I have a friend, not known to you, who owes me a favor. A big favor! He's got a place. One he seldom visits. If I call him and ask him to let you, Stacey, and me stay there for thirty days, he'll do it. That'll give us time to get away, time for things to cool down. Then we'll return, and you can live the life that makes you happy."

"Why would this guy do such a thing? Let a stranger stay in his home? For all he knows, I might be some cat burglar who'll walk off with everything."

Doc burst into laughter.

"That's something he'll neither think of nor worry about."

"If you say so! Where is this utopia?"

"Upstate New York!"

"Near the Appalachian mountains, I suppose. That'd be great! A mob of mountain people just waiting to learn about their futures from the cards I read!"

"No! Actually, it's near a famous racetrack. Saratoga Springs! During the month of August, people from all over the country go there. After a week or so, we might even head north to Lake George and Lake Placid. More people!"

"And just how do we get to all these places? On foot?"

"The last few days I've been doing pretty well panhandling. Along with some money I've saved from my old medical practice, I can get us north on a bus. Whether we go from Saratoga Springs to one of the lakes, we'll decide later. But don't worry! You'll have enough money to travel in style."

"Why's he in Saratoga? What's the big attraction?"

"He's got a thing for horses."

"I haven't even met the man, and already I'm getting to like him. Anyone interested in animals is an A-OK guy with me! Does he own any ponies?"

"I doubt it, but I don't really know. All I know is that his business interests involve, among other things, horses and dogs."

"Dogs too! What kind?"

"Greyhounds!"

"They're runners too, aren't they? Just what does this guy do?"

"I'll tell you on one condition. You have to keep the information to yourself. He's a little, shall I say, shady. His interests are rather vast—construction, trucking, and gambling. A variety of things."

"In other words, he's a mob boss! No way am I getting involved. Not with Stacey. You do what you want to do. We'll stay here."

"Dora, don't worry! He's not a mob boss. He's an entrepreneur. This man can be trusted. As I said, he owes me, and he owes me big. As long as you don't cross him and you keep close to me, he'll watch over you like a father."

"If you knew my father, you wouldn't say that. And just why are you so certain you can trust him?"

Staring at the woman, Doc remained silent. Finally, he said, "I'll tell you, but remember, this is strictly between you and me.

"When I was licensed, a friend of mine, a prostitute, who I—on a regular basis—took care of medically, came to me. She had a friend who had been shot really bad. Four bullets! She was with him at the time. Since he couldn't go to a hospital without having the gunplay reported, she urged him to see me. He did because he trusted her. Two of the wounds were superficial; a third was near his heart, and the fourth was lodged close to his spine. She and some people he relied on brought him to my home. I removed the bullets and kept him there, hidden, until he was able to move around. He never forgot, and he's willing to do damn near anything for me. I haven't spoken to him yet, but I know he'll do what I ask. He has two codes: honor your debts and keep your promises."

Before answering, Dora mulled over what she had heard. Finally, she asked, "Did the medical profession find out, and is that what caused you to lose your license?"

"No, they never found out about him and me. I lost my license over a dumb mistake." He again fell into a silence. "Dora, I'm sensitive about explaining why my license was revoked. But you're a dear friend, and if anyone deserves to know, it should be you.

"I had a patient. A notable, prominent, big money—a well-respected woman. She had colon cancer, and I was confident I could eliminate the growth surgically because the CT scan indicated the cancer had not spread. During the operation, I removed the tumor but failed to notice a second polyp developing. It was something I should have seen but didn't. It too had cancerous cells, and by the time it was discovered, months after the surgery, the malignancy had spread and become inoperable. The woman died, and the hospital and I were sued. After a thorough review, the hospital denied me the right to practice, and soon after, I lost my license. The reasons: negligence and incompetence."

"Sorry, Doc. I had no right to ask, no right to know. And be assured, I'll mention it to no one. But there's something about this friend of yours I don't understand. If he's into the things you say he is, then he has to be stepping on some toes. Big toes! Like skimming money out of the head man's territory! You know who I mean. The godfather who controls this area!"

"I don't have the answer to that, Dora. Only he does. And between you and me, I don't intend to ask him. And if I were you, I wouldn't either."

"I hear you. Don't let my curiosity do to me what it did to the cat. Besides, how important is it? Why should I do anything to alienate him? So how do we go about getting Mr. Good Guy's help?"

"Smart thinking! That's my girl. Let's go across town. He has a club that few people know about, and I think it's time for you to be introduced."

CHAPTER 12

THE PROTECTORS

As they proceeded down a near pedestrian-free road, Frisky Fingers Freddie came out of a store on the opposite side of the street, carrying a cup of coffee. Seeing Doc and Dora pushing a grocery cart, he smiled. *'Tis my day! Whatever the two of them have been hiding is probably in that cart. And soon I'm going to know what it is.*

Remaining on his side of the street and trailing well behind, Freddie walked and walked and walked. Just when he was about to give up, he saw them stop and knock on a door. When it opened, Dora's eyes bulged. A big man—about six feet seven inches tall and 275 pounds of bone and muscle—appeared.

"Hello, Giant!" Doc uttered. "It's been a long time."

Freddie, too far to overhear the conversation, saw the two men shake hands with the big one listening and nodding to Dora. After a moment, he retreated and closed the door behind him. The visitors waited. Once again, the door opened, and the three entered, leaving Giant to observe people on each side of the street. His eyes quickly passed over Freddie and scanned the street for others who might be known and unwanted.

Satisfied, the hulk closed the front door and walked to the back where Doc was already knocking on a second door. It opened, allowing the four to enter a large oak-paneled room sparsely decorated with brown leather chairs, a center table, floor lamps, and pictures of people, both respectable and somewhat questionable.

Behind a desk extending nearly wall to wall sat a man casually dressed in an open collar short sleeve chocolate brown custom-tailored shirt sprinkled with tiny gold images. Within arms' reach were two telephones, a humidor, lighter, ashtray, pad of paper, and two desk pens. No computer, no letters, no documents, no incidentals. To the unacquainted, he was obviously a well-organized, no-nonsense man. Not apparent was his intolerance to windy, overstated excuses. Five others seated and standing around the room all had one thing in common—unsmiling, "don't fuck with me" expressions.

With Doc's entry, the host rose from his desk and walked with arms spread to receive his friend and lifesaver. He embraced Doc, kissed him on each cheek, and welcomed him with glowing, near-embarrassing terms.

One of the groups, standing against a side wall, walked directly toward the grocery cart that Dora was controlling. Before he reached the baby's "crib," Dora stepped between it and the much taller man and extended her arms with hands only inches from his chest.

"That's close enough, fella," said Dora.

"That's okay, Louie. They're guests, and I'm certain I have nothing to fear."

Extending his hand to Dora, he said, "I'm Vincent Shomazzi. And who might you be?"

Turning from the intruder, Dora hesitated, then reached out, saying, "I . . . I . . . I'm Theodora Rochelle. Dora, for short, Mr. Sho . . . Shomazzi!"

"Call me, Shoe, Dora. All my friends, enemies, and media know me by that name. It's a pleasure. Any friend of the doctor is a friend of mine. So tell me, Doc, what brings you here?"

"It's a favor, Shoe. Unfortunately, it'll take some explaining, and I know you like everything concise in a neat little package. So I hope you'll excuse my rambling."

Receiving both a nod and hand motion to begin, Doc avoided the events involving how the woman found the baby, the burning shack, and the people killed. Instead, he created a story about how the two had enemies and were facing difficult times, needing to get away from the area. Hinting at a developing relationship between Dora and him, he made his request.

"I'm all she's got, and the two of them mean everything to me. For their sake, I'm hoping you'll let us spend August at your place in Saratoga."

Stepping forward, the boss turned to Dora and said, "May I see the baby?"

Surprised but without hesitation, she nodded.

The man's hardened mannerisms softened, gently picking up the sleeping girl, cradling her in his arms, and smiling down at her.

"She's adorable. I once had a daughter. Equally as pretty. Unfortunately, God made his calling, and she's no longer here. You can be very proud of this . . . of your daughter. What's her name?"

"Anastasia Victoria Adronicus. Stacey for short."

"Stacey! That's a nice name.

"Doc, I have no problem with you staying at the house. You, that is! But Dora, while you seem okay to me, I don't really know you. And based on my years and past experiences, I just don't automatically extend hospitalities to strangers. Nothing personal. Just habits, over the years, that have made me more comfortable."

"I understand . . . Mr. Shomazzi. In fact, I'm not surprised. If you were to ask Doc, he'd tell you I questioned such a generous gift. Thanks anyway for your time."

Rising to leave, Doc said, "Hold on, Dora! Shoe, I see you're still wearing the horseshoe."

Reaching beneath his open collar, the man unconsciously rubbed his thumb and forefinger on a small charm extending from a chain.

"It never leaves my neck, Doc. It's brought me a lifetime of good fortune and good health, as you well know. Thanks for noticing."

"Well, considering that you place so much faith in that horseshoe, what if I were to tell you that Dora can do more. In fact, she can see into your future."

"Don't push it, Doc! I don't like to be mocked about my beliefs."

"Shoe, I'm not mocking you. Never would I do that. I'm just explaining a fact about this woman that you don't know. It pertains to destiny and how a great many people have placed their faith in her ability to interface the present with the future."

Chuckling, Shoe asked, "And how does this mystic do that? Tea leaves, palm reading, or crystal ball gazing?"

"No, Shoe. Tarot cards."

"Ha, ha, ha! Just as I thought. Charlatanism!"

"Now—" Dora interrupted, "you're mocking me and all the oracles—Chinese, Europeans, and Egyptians—that over the centuries reached out and embraced the omniscient Divine. It's too bad you're such a nonbeliever. In hiding from your destiny, you only deprive yourself. Come on, Doc, let's go."

"Wait a minute, young lady! Maybe I'm being shortsighted. So read the cards. What have I to lose? If I don't believe what I hear, I'll ignore it. If, however, you have the powers that Doc claims, then I benefit."

"Yes, assuming one thing."

"And what's that?"

"That you're *willing* to be receptive to the guidance offered. If not, let me not waste your time . . . or mine."

The man stared at the woman, amazed at her gumption, her outspoken disregard for who he was.

"Fair enough! I'll be open-minded. Where and when do we do this?"

"Here and now, if you're willing? All I need is an empty table and two chairs."

"Use that table. Giant! Windy! Pull up two chairs. And the rest of you, leave the room. I don't want either my reader or me to be distracted."

Two hours later, when the reading was completed, Shomazzi sat quietly, his expression revealing nothing. Scratching something on a piece of paper, he pushed a button beneath the center desk drawer, and immediately the office door opened.

"Giant, take our guests to the front door. They're leaving!"

"Doc, here's a phone number. Keep it to yourself. You're one of six people to know it. Call me promptly at five o'clock. I'll give you my answer regarding the house.

"Dora, nice meeting you. Thanks for revealing the Tarot secrets." He folded his arms, and the visitors knew they were being dismissed.

As they left the front door, Giant eyed the people on the street. This time, his attention was drawn to Freddie who had remained on the opposite side, waiting for Dora and Doc to reappear. As they walked away, Freddie stood up and followed.

Giant closed the door and returned to Shoe's office. Upon entering, he walked to Shoe and whispered something in his ear.

"Windy, come here!"

A small man drifted to Shoe's desk. The sobriquet, not a criticism of being too talkative, was instead a compliment for one who was like a gentle breeze, present yet never seen.

Whispering into his ear, the inconspicuous man hastened from the room. Outside, he moved swiftly in the direction given, looking for a man described facially and physically down to the color and styling of his clothes. Within three blocks, Windy saw Freddie and began shadowing him. Still on the opposite side of the street and one block removed, Frisky Fingers concentrated on his acquaintances, unaware of Windy who remained behind. Freddie decided the time for a confrontation had arisen and dashed across the street.

The light turned green, and Dora, Doc, and the baby crossed the intersection. As Freddie approached, the light turned yellow, and a hand clutched his elbow.

Turning, Freddie faced Windy who quietly asked, "Sir, will you kindly direct me to 33 Winter Street?"

"Get lost, fellow! I'm in a hurry."

Struggling to pull away, Windy held firmly, saying, "Sir, you don't need to be rude.

I'm lost, and I'm running late for an appointment. Please point the way!"

"I haven't got time, buddy," replied Freddie. "I'm also running to meet someone. Let me go!"

"Look, it'll only take a second. Please, please help me."

Looking ahead, Freddie saw Doc and Dora standing at a bus stop, waiting for the next public vehicle.

"Okay, okay! Go down three blocks. Turn left at the traffic light, and go one more block, bear right at the V in the road, and in one block you will see Winter Street. Where 33 is, I don't know. Now, let me go!"

"Certainly! But let me repeat so I don't make a wrong turn. I go down here three blocks and turn left at the traffic light. Two blocks further, I'll come to a V in the road where I keep to my right. After another block, Winter Street will be in front of me."

"No, no, no! After you turn left at the traffic light, you go only one block further and then bear right at the V in the road."

Seeing the light turn red, Windy released his grip. Freddie, anxious to cross, was delayed by heavy traffic. When the light changed in his favor, he made a dash for Doc, Dora, and the pushcart as they prepared to board the bus. But Freddie was too slow, and the bus pulled away, heading to an unknown destination.

"Shit!" mumbled Freddie. "Maybe not this time, but you can't avoid me forever."

Seeing Freddie stomping his feet, Windy headed back to the clubhouse.

CHAPTER 13

A REVEALING SECRET

Knocking on Shoe's door, the inconspicuous one entered and succinctly related what transpired. Shoe nodded and waved Windy out of the office.

Who is that guy, and what's he after? wondered Shoe. *Is it Doc? Dora? Or both? I owe Doc my life, and I'll let nothing happen to him. But what about Dora? She's a stranger. A gal with spunk. I like that! And her readings, well . . . they are . . . I don't know—puzzling at the least. Some general statements, applicable to nearly anyone; others, specifically troublesome if accurate!*

Twisting his chair to face the back wall, Shoe rubbed the horseshoe charm. By no means impulsive, this cunning leader of diversified interests was a careful planner. Priding himself on his memory, he reconsidered what he learned.

Dora had formed a *Celtic Cross.* Of the eleven cards turned, five were particularly annoying: (1) *The Devil,* in a reversed position, was a forewarning that someone had plans of his own; plans unfavorable to Shoe; (2) a reversed *Two of Pentacles* cautioned that the individual could be a scheming opportunist; (3) a reversed *Six of Wands* predicted bad news regarding a delay or postponement of anticipated rewards; (4) the upright *Five of Swords* was an alert that something might be lost but should be accepted as a lesson for future success; and last, as unacceptable as the *Five of Swords* was, the reversed *Ace of Pentacles* was most disturbing—a financial gain possibly lost.

Picking up the telephone receiver, Shoe dialed the number for his crosstown office.

"Shomazzi Industries, to whom would you like to speak?"

"Doris, put me through to Campbell!"

"Certainly, Mr. Shomazzi."

"Accounting, Mr. Campbell's office."

"Peg! Let me speak to the bean counter."

"He's not here, Mr. Shomazzi."

"Where is he?"

"I thought he was with you, sir. When he left yesterday at two o'clock, he said he was going to deposit the day's receipts at the bank and run some personal errands. He told me not to expect him today since he'd be in a meeting with you at the club."

"And no one called to forward messages?"

"He gave specific instructions not to be disturbed. In fact, he emphasized that no one was to interrupt the meeting."

"Thanks, Peg."

Shoe sat thinking.

Finally, his thoughts were interrupted by a voice. "Please hang up your phone! If you need assistance, dial the operator. Please hang up now!"

Depressing the receiver button, he dialed another number.

"Central City Bank. With whom would you like to speak?"

"Your manager, please."

"This is Greg Whittier. May I be of help?"

"Hi, Greg! It's Vincent Shomazzi. How are you?"

"Good morning, Shoe! This is a pleasure. I haven't spoken to you in some time."

"You're right! My apologies. Business in construction, and trucking have been so good. I haven't needed any additional working capital. My gain, your loss, I suppose."

"You're right. But nonetheless, I'm glad to hear things are going well. So to what do I owe the pleasure of this call?"

"A reliable source came up with an intriguing idea," explained Shomazzi. "One that peaks my interest. But before I grab onto it, I want to know if a deposit was made yesterday afternoon. My CFO, George Campbell, could tell me, but he's out of town. Mind finding out for me?"

"Not at all. Hold on while I review your accounts."

Minutes later, he returned.

"There's no record of a deposit, Shoe! You certain it was made yesterday?"

"So I was told. But apparently, my source is misinformed. Thanks for your trouble, Greg. I'll be calling you in a week or so. Maybe we can have lunch."

The livid Shomazzi sat thinking. *Were the cards right? Was he swindled by someone he trusted? And if so, how much was stolen?*

Shoe dialed the phone and interrupted Doris before she could even finish her greeting. "Put me through to Bob Woodson!"

"Treasurer's Office. This is Carol."

"Carol, let me speak to Woody."

"He's on another line, Mr. Shomazzi."

"Tell him to finish the call. This is an emergency."

Seconds later . . . "Yes, Shoe, what is it?"

"We have a problem! I'll be over in thirty minutes. Where's Jeff Nader?"

"Conducting an audit at trucking."

"Get him too. Immediately!"

In the office, Shomazzi related the conversations he had with Peg, Campbell's secretary, and Greg Whittier. But no mention was made of Dora and the Tarot cards.

"Woody, find out what happened to the money and the amount. Jeff, start auditing the records immediately. Woody, you used to run this department, so I expect you and Jeff and whoever else is needed to tear the place apart. Look at every ledger, every accounting entry, and every cancelled check to satisfy me that other things haven't been happening that we don't know about. And if it means working twenty-four hours a day, do so. Now get out of here and get started! And keep me posted!"

Calling the club, Shomazzi ordered Giant, Windy, and six others to his office. When all arrived, he told them about Campbell, the missing money, and the instructions given to Nader and Woodson. He then separated the eight men into four teams, giving each of them instructions about where to begin looking for the accountant— his home, an upstate hideaway, the airport, bus depot, cruise lines, girlfriends' houses, and other known haunts. Through covert tracers, he had sources monitoring Campbell's credit cards and telephone records. There was no place to hide.

In the quietness of his office, Vincent Shomazzi reflected on the events of the day.

The initial plans on locating Campbell, the money, and reviewing the corporate records are satisfactory but only for a start. New initiatives will be required, hopefully from leads uncovered. But waiting can lead to irretrievable losses. I need to be proactive. What else can I do?

He sat thinking. Slowly, very slowly, his expression turned from a contentious scowl to a less belligerent frown to a quizzical look and finally a decisive smile. He looked at his wristwatch. It was 4:53 p.m. He left his desk and went to a refrigerator for a beer. Uncapping it, he returned to his desk and took a slow sip from the bottle.

Exactly, seven minutes from when he looked at his watch, the phone rang.

"You're still as precise as always, Doc."

"My god, you know who it is before I even speak. Is there anything you don't know?"

"You give me too much credit. As I told you, only five others know of this number, and not one of them is expected to call. Enough of the idle chatter. I've made my decision. Dora and Stacey can stay with you at the house in Saratoga. On one condition, however!"

"And what will that be?"

"Dora has to give me a reading anytime I want one. And at the precise time I request it."

"No problem, Shoe. Now, how do we find the place?"

"Windy will drive you there tomorrow. You'll be going in the Lincoln. Pack lightly. A couple of changes of clothes. Whatever the baby needs. And that's all! Deodorants, toothpaste, razors, and other paraphernalia are at the house. Be ready by nine in the morning. I need to get Windy back by dinner. I've got him doing something important."

"How do we get around Saratoga? Neither of us knows the place, and Dora's got to find a good place to set up shop."

"There's a car in the garage. Do you still have a driver's license?"

"Yeah, but it's expired."

"You're causing a hell of a lot of problems, Doc."

Hesitating briefly, Shoe finally said, "Tell you what. I wasn't planning on going with you, but I think I will. But that makes it necessary for the three of you to be ready to leave at five in the morning."

"Five! Why so early?"

"There's something that needs to be done. For Dora and Stacey especially. And it'll require some time."

CHAPTER 14

THE UNINVITED

It was early morning, 3:00 a.m., dark and quiet. Freddie couldn't sleep. He sat alone at the riverbank, skipping stones over the surface of the moonlit water.

Dora! Doc! Now where the hell are you? Every time you're together, you're pushing that damn cart. Whatever's in it has to be worth some dough. And once I catch up with you, I'll find out. Then I'll share in the goodies. Count on it! But first I've got to find you. You're not at the usual places. Somewhere new. But where is that, and where do I begin looking?

Ready to skip another stone, he stopped, smiled, dropped the stone, and headed away.

Thirty-five minutes later, Freddie arrived at a building across the street from the door that his friends had entered the preceding day. Sitting down in an entranceway, he placed an empty cup on the ground beyond his extended legs. At this hour, with no one else on the street, he hardly expected any charitable offerings, but the cup gave the allusion he had a reason to be sitting there.

Minutes ticked by. First one person arrived, followed later by a second, and finally a group of four latecomers. All had entered the door across from where Freddie sat. A Lincoln limousine pulled up to the curb. A person, the little guy who had held Freddie's elbow the preceding day, stepped out from behind the wheel. Freddie pulled his extended feet back, pressing his spine against the building's door, safe in the darkness of the alcove. The driver disappeared through the same entrance the others had entered.

Minutes later, three people returned to the street: the little man and the giant, each carrying suitcases, followed by an older man, never before seen by Freddie. As they were about to step into the Lincoln, the sound of moving metal wheels pierced the silence of the night. The attention of the three men followed the noise. The giant began to move toward it, but was halted by the older man who merely shook his head. The three stood, watched, entered the car, and drove away.

"Hello, Fingers. What are you doing in this part of town?"

The moving sound had stopped at Freddie's alcove. A man, with his legs prone on a low four-wheel cart and his back resting against an upright metal plate, had used his arms and hands to propel the conveyance along the sidewalk.

"Hello, Knees! Decided on a change of location and came here. Seems to be a mistake. Too quiet and no traffic."

"Not surprising. Those three who just left. Did you see them?"

Freddie nodded.

"You do know who they are, don't you?"

This time Freddie shook his head.

"Well, my friend, that door leads into Vincent Shomazzi's private club, and it's best for you not to be here."

"Shomazzi, the hood? You've got to be kidding?"

"I'm not. That was the old guy and his two goons. He doesn't like strangers outside his door."

"Then why are you here? Or are you a friend?"

"A friend? Hell no! I'm an annoyance who keeps popping up."

"That's not smart. What are you going to do? Outrun him!"

"You've never heard the story, have you?"

"The story! What story?"

"Why I'm on this damn cart. It's not because I want to be but because I can't move my legs, and I can't bend my knees. And I owe all that to the hood."

"No shit? Tell me about it."

"As you probably know, he's notorious for his construction business, trucking companies, and gambling interests. And it's also rumored he's in prostitution, drugs, and protection to mention a few. I have no proof of this, but I do know about the gambling.

"Years back, I was a success. Had money. A lot of money. But life grew dull, so I started gambling for the excitement. Got in over my head. Especially on the ponies. I went to Saratoga for a day, but the day extended into a second, then a third. I was dealing through a bookie who knew the 'sure things.' I bet all the races, but his winners turned out to be nags. The ones I backed seemed to be stumbling around the track when the following races began. As it turned out, I was in over my head. My bookie was under the control of Shomazzi who either wanted his money immediately or in scheduled payments at an unaffordable percentage. Since I couldn't meet his terms, payback came. My knees were busted. My spine cracked. Paralysis set in. Now I come here just to remind Shomazzi I'm still around."

"Aren't you afraid?"

"What's he going to do, break more bones? Kill me? Death might be a blessing, though I've too many friends, especially lawyers and cops who suspect, without certainty, that they know what really happened. Shomazzi's smart. The punishment delivered could never be proven. Now, if something happened, he'd be a prime suspect. Possibly the only one. So he tolerates me. And while I know I'm pissing him off, it's not enough for me. This is one hell of a way to live, and there are days when I really wish I were dead. That he would blow his cool! But he won't. My disappearance isn't enough reward for the risk involved."

"Maybe yes, maybe no. Did you see the suitcases his guys are carrying? Your presence may be getting under his collar, and he feels it's time to get lost."

"No way. About now, the ponies are arriving at Saratoga for the August races, and since he has a place there, I'll bet he's heading north to arrive for Opening Day. It gives him a couple of days to arrange some investments. Oh, to hell with Shomazzi. I need to forget about the bastard, and so I'm taking off. Stay out of trouble, Freddie. And be careful."

Heading back to the river, Frisky Fingers stopped people along the way, held out his cup, and sadly bewailed how he had become an out-of-work unfortunate, falling victim to the rising unemployment in the depressed present-day economy. After appealing to many, he finally called it a day and went to the riverbank where he began counting the coins.

His concentration was interrupted by "Looks like you've made a big haul, Freddie. Going to share it with an old friend?"

"Well, if it ain't Nosey Ned? Amazing how you always turn up when things are going good for me."

Touching his nose, Ned said, "Like I keep telling you, it never fails me."

"And as I keep telling you, friend or no friend, I'm no charity. Go beg on your own."

"Might be that I have something to trade. For a couple of bucks, that is."

"Yeah, and what might that be?"

"What if I told you Doc and Dora are leaving town. That of any interest?"

"How do you know that? And just where are they going?"

"Can't tell you where, but they're traveling in style. Just saw them getting into a big black Lincoln."

"Who else was with them?"

"Don't know them! One was a monster! The second an old fart. And I couldn't see the third guy. He stayed in the car, behind the wheel."

Jumping up, Freddie hugged Ned, saying, "You're all right! And that nose of yours has become a damn pretty thing. Take care of it."

Handing Ned a handful of coins, he turned and began to run away.

"What's with you? You don't even know where they're going?"

"Oh, but I've a good idea."

Going to where his possessions were stashed, Freddie filled an old torn suitcase that he had taken from someone's trash. On sizable cardboard, he wrote, *Saratoga*. Finished, he hiked to the interstate and began thumbing the morning traffic.

CHAPTER 15

AN UNDERSTANDING

A cross-country semi pulled off the interstate into a rest area at the outskirts of Saratoga. The driver turned to his passenger and repeated directions leading to the city. Thanking him, Freddie left the truck. The driver closed his eyes and rested his head against the seat. It had been a tiring eleven-hour drive.

Across town, the Lincoln circled through an enclosed middle income neighborhood, passing similar three-floor colonials with shutter windows and frame sidings of white, red, yellow, and cream-stained woods. Shoe's house sat no further back from the street than his neighbors' homes, lost in a residential area of commonality, an obscure presence he demanded.

Turning left into the driveway, Windy steered the vehicle to the back of the house and opened the garage door by remote control. Out of the car, Doc, Dora, and the baby followed Shoe through a basement, up a flight of stairs, into a home that evoked from Dora, "My lord, this is beautiful." Not only beautiful but strikingly different from the building's staid outer appearance!

On tastefully textured walls were selectively framed landscapes, portraits, and abstracts—all artists' originals. Sconces and designated tables featured figurines: ivory, Dresden, Wedgwood, and

Royal Copenhagen along with other recognizable ceramics. The furnishings were of eye-appealing styles and periods, comfortably relaxing to both men and women. Planning and forethought had gone into decorating this man's residence.

"You are to enjoy every room in the house with the exception of the one behind the closed, locked door on this floor, the one at the end of the hall on the second floor and the entire third floor. The first room is my office, where no one ventures. The second room, on the floor above, is my bedroom. Private only to me! And the third floor has a suite of three bedrooms and three baths. Those rooms are occupied by Giant, Windy, and Martha who you will meet soon."

And as though beckoned, the lady appeared.

"Excellent timing, Martha! These are our guests: Dora, Doc, and the baby, Stacey. Martha is the boss in charge of this house. She cooks. She cleans. She'll do all the necessary ordering, bill paying, and planning while we're here. She's been with me for nearly twenty years. Completely trustworthy, responsible, and dependable. There are not enough adjectives to describe her. She's a widow, a mother of two adult women, and Dora, a baby sitter for Stacey unlike any you could ever find. So when you're off reading your cards, and Doc is tired of sitting around the house, you can leave the baby in her care, certain that the child will receive the necessary attention required. Now, you probably don't accept that just because I said it's true. So I encourage you to get to know Martha. It will prove helpful to you.

"Martha, we've been traveling for hours, and I for one am hungry. Set the table with whatever's available. Later, we'll drive around town, familiarizing Dora and Doc with Saratoga. Tonight I'm going to treat my guests to the most delicious restaurant food they've ever eaten. So leave us and pull together something appetizing. Windy, Giant, go to the cellar and get two bottles of Cabernet sauvignon. Then go unpack.

"Now, Dora and Doc, it's time to get down to business! I want to know some things. First, the baby. Whose was it, and how did it come into your possession?"

Dora looked at Doc with alarm. This was not the plan. He had no need to know anything about Stacey as far as Dora was concerned. And she had no intention of telling him either. The room remained silent. No one said anything.

Dora sat back, arms crossed, mouth closed. Doc bowed his head, looking nervously at the Oriental rug beneath his feet. Finally, Shoe broke the silence.

"I don't know what the two of you are hiding or for that matter, what you are concerned about. But if you love that little girl, you'll give serious thought to what I am about to say. I know, Dora, the child's not your flesh and blood. Your parental actions disprove it. So think about this. Today, Stacey is less than a year old. Where she came from is of no importance to her at this time, but in thirty, twenty, even twelve years, having an identity will be necessary. She'll need papers—a birth certificate, social security number, verifiable documentation that she is a citizen of this country, a person with a traceable past. As of now, she doesn't have that, and she needs it. If you love this child as you say you do, you'll see to it that she has everything she needs."

"How? How does she get that? You tell me!"

"I will. But first, I need to know who she is and from where she came. No secrets! I need and want to know everything."

Dora looked at Doc, who was still staring at the carpet.

"You're absolutely right," Doc said. "I've been concerned about this for some time. I haven't mentioned it because I don't have the answers. But if Shoe can give Stacey an identity, then it's up to us to provide our friend with everything we know. It's for Stacey's own good. You agree, don't you, Dora?"

Nodding her head, she murmured, "Doc and I had a reading last night. The cards turned confirmed that. An upright *Wheel of Fortune* foretold of help from others, people who were close, people willing to be of assistance. I see that now as meaning you."

And so Dora began with Doc interjecting comments along the way the discarded box placed in the dumpster, the intrusiveness of Frisky Fingers Freddie, the deaths of Roscoe and Charles Evans Hughes, and even the fire at the railroad tracks.

"Well, Shoe, now you know the entire story. What can you do to give Stacey an identity?"

"I know a guy—a printer, a master in the creation of documents that go undetected."

"In other words, a forger?"

"Now, Doc, is that necessary? Anyway, he's available. He's been away from Saratoga this week, but he can be here tomorrow at his office. He's not inexpensive, though. In fact, for you it'll probably be pretty costly. A birth certificate, wedding certificate, a—"

"Wedding certificate?" interrupted Dora. "And just who in the hell is getting married?"

"Why, you and Doc, of course!"

"I have no say in this? What if I don't want to marry Doc?"

"Look at me, Dora! I don't care if you sleep with him, live with him, or ever see him once you leave here. But for Stacey's sake, legitimatize her birth. Let a certificate show that she has a father and a mother. The marriage license is simply a diversion, a padding so to speak, to rule out future questions regarding where the girl came from and to whom she belongs. If you can't go along with that, then the three of you can leave this house and be on your own. I'm not going to become involved in this whole charade and suddenly become investigated by the cops because they suspect a kidnapping. Especially if 'Mr. Big Bucks,' who discarded the child, has a change of heart! With a lot of money and the right attorneys, who knows what trouble he might start?"

"Okay, okay, okay! I'll marry the old geezer as a paper formality, but you just said all this will be expensive. I'm here to build a nest egg for our future. Stacey's and mine. I don't have money to pay this guy. So what other suggestions have you got?"

Without hesitation, Shoe responded, "I've anticipated this and have given it considerable thought. My decision goes against all my established business practices, but I've come to a conclusion about you, Dora. And for your own welfare, don't prove me wrong. I believe you're an honest, forthright woman, one who will do what she promises. I'll lend you the money and not at my normal repayment rates. The interest which will be modest, along with the extended repayment terms, must be tightly guarded secrets between only you, Dora, and me. Even you, Doc, will not know the conditions of repayment. As a businessman, I don't want people to think I'm a soft touch, a pushover. So this transaction will be under the table, strictly between us. No one in my company will even know we're doing business. And if word gets out, Dora, you will suffer and suffer painfully. In ways unimaginable! That also applies to you, Doc. And be certain of this. Stacey will be lost to both of you, permanently. So be damn certain there's neither a slip of the tongue nor an ignored repayment of the obligation.

"One final thing! In addition to this agreement, you, Dora, will, as previously promised, provide me with a reading anytime I request one. I hope I'm making myself clear."

"We understand the conditions," replied Dora.

"Be certain that you also understand that the readings are to reveal whatever the cards say. I don't want you cushioning or modifying messages to satisfy something you think I want to hear. I want only the truth, regardless of what it conveys."

"Now, Shoe, you're overstepping your limits. I'm blessed with the ability to provide guidance to those who seek the truth in their lives. I will never misrepresent or falsify the Divine revelations of the Arcana. And I never want to hear that accusation again. I hope I'm making myself clear?"

Without averting his eyes from her intense gaze, Shomazzi thought, *Woman, you have one hell of a lot of guts to stand up to me like that. Yet the more I get to know you, the more I admire you. Doc's done me a great service with your introduction.*

"Enough of this conversation! I think we understand each other. Let's adjourn to the dining room."

CHAPTER 16

INTEREST GROWS

Days elapsed, and all was quiet. O'Malley had been traveling to all the haunts favored by the homeless, but no one was talking or even showing interest in the dumpster, the package, their former friends—Grape Juice and Roscoe—or the burning railroad shack. Even the police investigation, once active, had fallen into low priority, kept open only because of the two killings. Circerchi was of no help.

Prodded daily by an unhappy, often demanding Walter Jensen, the Irishman juggled the daily activities between his responsibilities at the company's security office and his travels throughout the city. Particularly aggravating was the disappearance of the often-present Frisky Fingers Freddie whose whereabouts seemed to be unknown to everyone.

Repeatedly, O'Malley chased down Nosey Ned and even the woman who had given the policeman information the night he and Jensen drove to the burning shack. But neither was helpful.

Giving thought to what else might be done, he played a long shot. Waiting for the police shifts to change, he sat in his car near the front door of the precinct. Finally, the man for whom he had been waiting headed toward a parked car.

"Fritz, Fritz Steigerwald! Over here! It's me, Tom O'Malley."

"Well, I'll be damned. Hi, Irish! How the hell are you?"

"Couldn't be better! Just stopped by to jaw with some guys, and here I see you. Must be my day."

"And why's that?"

"I've been looking for someone who likes beer, and so far, no one has the time. Now I see you, and I know how you like the suds. Will you join me? My treat!"

"With an invitation like that, who am I to refuse? There's a neighborhood bar uptown. One where we can exchange war stories without other cops being around. Mind going there?"

"Sounds good! Lead the way."

Entering the Four Leaf Clover, Red said, "Already, I like this place. The owner can't be Irish, can he?"

"Well, if McNamara is Irish, I guess he is. There he is behind the bar. Hey, Sean! I've brought some new blood. Meet Tom O'Malley. Tom, this is Sean McNamara."

"Well, I'll be! A kinsman! You from the old country?"

"Afraid not! Never been more than a couple of hundred miles out of this state! But I'm determined to get there someday."

"Well, make it soon. You've got to enjoy life while you can. And since you're Irish and a new customer, the first round's on me. What'll you have?"

McNamara led them to an empty booth and brought them glasses and a pitcher of beer. Knocking their glasses together, Fritz smiled, winked, and downed half a pint.

"What can be finer than two old friends having a bit of ale?"

"This is like old times, Fritz. I miss these moments. Along with the excitement and pressure of the old place. I don't suppose it's changed."

"Oh, it has, Tom. It's not like it used to be and never will be. I'm counting the days. Two years, four months, and twenty-one days! Then I'm gone, never looking back. The days of being a cop, respected, and looked up to are over. Now you have to be careful about who you are, and you have to think twice about what you do. When I think of all I've gone through, I keep asking myself, 'Why? For what?' The day I turn in my gun and badge can't come too soon."

"I can't believe what I'm hearing. This doesn't sound like the Fritz Steigerwald I know. What's gotten into you?"

"I don't know how well you're keeping up with what's going on in this town, so if I start saying things you're already aware of, stop me.

Back around the middle of July, a package was supposedly taken out of a dumpster in an alley off Commerce Avenue."

"Yeah, I heard something about that."

"What the package was, no one knows. Then a day or two later, a homeless drunk, known as Grape Juice—real name Charles Evans Hughes—was found dead on a fire escape in the same alley. Rumor was a cop killed him. Internal Affairs got involved and began an investigation. I became a suspect!"

"You? You're kidding? You, of all people? Why'd they suspect you?"

"My appearance, according to some unidentified sources. Seems the 'cop' looked like me. Damned if IA didn't make my life a living hell. I got pissed. In fact, I still am."

"You mean you haven't been cleared?"

"Oh, I've been cleared. Had an airtight alibi! I was on an undercover stakeout the night Hughes died. The fact that IA didn't recognize that early on still has my goat. I never trusted that bunch. And the way they mishandled the investigation proves they don't know shit about detective work."

"Has the killer been caught?"

"Hell, no! No one has a clue, and that really galls my ass. Every minute I'm in the precinct, I feel a dozen eyes staring down on me, accusing me as if I'm the perp."

"Fritz, I know how you feel. But you're overreacting. You've been a cop too long, with commendations that are the envy of everyone in blue. And with the undercover assignment, you've now been cleared. Forget it. Put the whole thing behind you."

"Wish I could. But I can't."

"Hold on a minute. I'm a fresh set of eyes, with a few years of experience, as you well know. Maybe I can come up with an idea that will help. Commerce Street, the alley, and Hughes—all have one thing in common. The homeless population. When I was working the beat, there were a dozen or so street people who stood out from the rest. Guys and gals who always knew what was going on. There must be some like that today, people with information."

"Oh, there are, and because of my involvement, I keep close tabs on what's learned and who's seen what. With the exception of two or three, most of the good leads you're referring to have been run down with nothing more than a complete blank coming up. Whether the homeless are keeping quiet because they're frightened or because they don't want to get their buddies in trouble, or for some other reason, no one knows."

"You say all but two or three. Who are they, and why haven't they been questioned?"

"There's this one guy, Frisky Fingers Freddie. But those who know him haven't seen him recently. Then there's a woman named Dora something, but she's nowhere to be found. Seems this Freddie fellow has a real grudge against her. Then there's Doc! A one-time prominent physician who lost his license. Apparently, this Doc and Dora are real close. But now all three have disappeared! Poof! Where? How? Why? Do they know things we need to know? Beats the hell out of me. But I sure would like to question them."

"Is anyone looking for them?"

"Who knows? If someone is, it's really hush-hush. This whole thing smells. The three of them nowhere to be found is too much of a coincidence. And I don't believe in coincidences."

Interesting! Fingers, Doc, and Dora keep coming up, and suddenly they're gone. And for no particular reason! Time to find out where they are.

"Damn it, Fritz. I feel for you. I know what you're going through. It's not right for someone as dedicated as you. Wish I could be more helpful. In the meantime, have another beer. I've got to be leaving in half an hour. A dentist is going to have some fun drilling holes in my teeth. But while I'm in his chair, I'll mull over what you've told me. You're too much of a friend to let this remain unsolved. If I come up with something later, I'll contact you. Now let's forget our problems and have some laughs.

Hey, Sean, how about a refill?"

* * * * *

O'Malley's dental appointment was a deception, an excuse, but years of police experience raised a real concern.

I've got to get moving before the trails leading to these three grow too cold and totally disappear.

For more than two hours, he cruised around areas of the city—Commerce Avenue, the park and riverbank popular to the homeless, Oak, Main, Walnut, and many of the lesser connecting streets. Along the way, he stopped and spoke to meter maids, hot dog vendors, paperboys, and vagrants. But common to what Fritz said, no one knew anything.

Nearing dusk, O'Malley drove down Winter Street, ready to call it an evening. On the sidewalk illuminated by the street lights, he saw an old acquaintance, an informant he relied on during his detective days. So he pulled to the curb and stepped out of the car and walked toward the man.

"Hello, Knees! It's been a long, long time."

Heading toward the Irishman, the crippled one—pushing his four-wheel cart along the sidewalk with both hands—broke into a smile.

"Well, saints alive! If it isn't my old friend, Sergeant O'Malley! What, by the grace of God, are you doing in my part of town? I thought you were retired."

"Oh, that I am. But seeing you, I had to stop and find out how you're doing."

"As well as can be expected! But I certainly miss seeing you around. You were always the one cop I could confide in without fear of someone finding out I was a snitch. Now, I kinda stay in the shadows. You know what I mean, Sarge?"

"I do, Knees, and I'm sorry about that. I know the money I paid for the info you gave was of some help. You still able to pay for your meds and food all right?"

"Sure! Sure! I'm getting by. Not that a few extra bucks wouldn't help. But I'm making due."

"Maybe we can give each other a good turn."

Reaching into his billfold, O'Malley pulled out two five-dollar bills.

"I'm looking for a couple of people. People who live in this area. I need to ask them a few questions. Nothing heavy, mind you."

"What I know, I'll share. Who you looking for?"

"Three people, actually—a Frisky Fingers Freddie and two homeless people known as Dora and Doc. Do you know any of them?"

"All three! Haven't seen Doc and Dora in a couple of weeks. But two or three nights ago, early morning I should say, Freddie and I had a conversation."

"Where and about what?"

"You know the Shomazzi clubhouse uptown?"

"What cop doesn't?"

"Well, I'm rolling down the sidewalk across the street from the joint, and as I pass by this dark doorway, I see Freddie sitting and watching Shomazzi and two of his goons about ready to get into a Lincoln and pull away. I don't know if they saw Freddie, but they saw me. One—the big guy called Giant—started to move toward me but was stopped by Shomazzi. I'm still an annoyance to them, but they leave me alone."

"How many times have I told you to stay away from him?"

"I know, I know! But like I told Freddie, Shomazzi's more concerned about what would happen to him if something happened to me. That's all you—oh sorry—not you personally but the cops would need to reopen an investigation on how I got these knees.

"Enough of that! Back to the other morning! Freddie watches them climb into the car, and shortly thereafter, he leaves the area. Haven't seen him since."

"Do you know where he went?"

"Nope!"

Handing the cripple ten dollars, O'Malley says, "Well, thanks anyway! Take care of yourself, Knees. I'll be seeing you." And he headed back to his car.

As he was about to get in, Knees shouted, "Say, I do remember something else. Don't know how much good it will be, but at least it's something."

Leaving the car door open, the Irishman returned to his invalid friend.

"I nearly forgot. The three of them—Shomazzi and his two hoods—threw some suitcases into the Lincoln. Freddie asked me about that, and I told him that the crook was big in horse racing. With it being August and him having a home in Saratoga, maybe he was heading north. This time of the year, that track's a goldmine to him."

Returning to his car, O'Malley gave thought to what he had learned. Another long shot, but it was all he had. He started the car and returned to the company headquarters.

Taking the elevator to Walter Jensen's office, Anna cleared his visit with the CEO.

"I've been beating the bushes with minimal luck, but let me bring you up-to-date." He began with the visit he had with Steigerwald, explaining how the police, with no suspects, once again placed the investigation on low priority. He then focused on the disappearance of Doc, Dora, and Fingers, emphasizing his thoughts on the three being involved in the recovery of the box. Finally, he mentioned the interest they appeared to have on Shomazzi.

"If I'm right, and my gut tells me I am, I believe all four are now in Saratoga, at the racetrack. Horses and gambling are the hood's lifeline.

"This case continues to get bigger and bigger. First, there's the throwaway carton, contents unknown but apparently valuable enough to be retrieved. Then two murders and an arsenal job! Now, three very familiar, well-established street people disappear, and a well-known hood makes his entrance. Something big is breaking. I feel it in my gut. So if you want me to continue with this investigation, let me tell you what I need. An advance on expenses. Travel money! Also, up to a week's leave of absence. I want to go to Saratoga and see if these people are up there together and what in the hell they're doing. Chief, I'm going to find something. Something very important! I know it just as sure as I'm sitting here. I know I'm right."

Jensen sat motionless. He stared at O'Malley, saying nothing. Finally, he grabbed two pieces of paper and scribbled out notes. Handing them to O'Malley, the security officer scanned the contents. One was addressed to human resources telling the vice president that O'Malley was going to be on a seven-day assignment away from the office. The second letter authorized accounting to advance a generous sum of money to be accounted for by a forthcoming expense report. O'Malley thanked his boss and left the office to finalize what needed to be done before going home to pack.

Jensen reached for the phone. He pressed the seven buttons known only to him and the private line subscriber. Before the third ring, a voice answered, "Yes!"

"I have an out-of-town assignment. Are you available?"

"Where, when, and what do you want?"

"Now, immediately. You're to go to Saratoga, and here's what I want you to do . . ."

CHAPTER 17

GETTING PREPARED

The Lincoln arrived in the garage following a splendid dinner of lobster, oysters, shrimp, and crabs. Shomazzi was the last to leave the car, holding Stacey as he had throughout the evening.

"Shoe, it's been years since I've had a meal like that. I've forgotten how good food can taste. Very generous of you to have taken us there," said Doc.

"It certainly was," chimed in Dora. "But you never had a chance to enjoy your meal, holding Stacey the entire evening."

"I eat there all the time, but seldom do I have the pleasure of holding a cute baby. I have no regrets. Doc, why don't you take Stacey? I need to talk to Dora. After you put her down, join us in my office."

Unlocking the door, Shoe flipped on the light and noticed Dora's eyes taking in the surroundings. The room was as handsome as all the others but designed in a masculine office setting, befitting the man's needs.

"Care for a drink? I'm going to have an after-dinner brandy. Join me?"

"No, thanks. I've had more than enough."

Opening a desktop humidor, he withdrew a Havana, snipped off the end, and moved the cigar slowly beneath his nose, smelling the fragrance. Carefully wetting the entire outer wrapper, he lit it and exhaled smoke rings into the air.

"From your expression, Dora, I see you dislike cigars. But here in my office, you'll have to tolerate it while we discuss things that will be important to you."

Shrugging her shoulders, she dismissed his criticism, saying, "This is your house. You're certainly entitled to do whatever pleases you."

Shoe removed the cigar from his mouth, smiled, and nodded, so much as to say, "You're absolutely right."

Instead of commenting, however, he began discussing his plans for the following day. After breakfast, the four—Doc, Stacey, Dora, and Shoe—would visit a forger's office where photographs would be taken and information gathered for the documents to be made. When finished, they would take a sightseeing trip around the area.

"There were times this evening when your comments and expressions indicated places you thought you could gather large crowds," volunteered Shoe. "I agree with two but not the others. Although you need to be visible to the racing crowd, your presence on the grounds close to the track could cause a hassle. While I don't know your business, I'd like to point out places you haven't seen. Then you make the decision."

"Fine, I like that." Dora realized Shoe had a wealth of knowledge, and there was much she wanted to learn. Over the years, she had trained herself to observe people's reactions and steer them to her advantage. To do this with Shoe, she decided to play to his over-inflated ego and encourage him to flaunt his knowledge.

"Tell me about the racetrack. Why does it attract people from all over the country? What's so important about a bunch of horses running around in circles?"

"Interested, are you? Where do I begin? Let's start with a history lesson. This month, the race course will be in its one hundred twenty-second year, the oldest organized sporting location in the country. It's known as both *The Spa* for its near-at-hand mineral springs and the *Graveyard of Favorites* because of some unexpected defeats in major thoroughbred racing. Man o' War had his only defeat in twenty-one races at this track. Gallant Fox, the bettors' favorite in the 1930 Travers Stakes, was outrun by Jim Dandy, a hundred-to-one long shot. And then there's Secretariat, considered by many to be the greatest racehorse of all time and a thoroughbred that won the Triple Crown.

Yet here is where he suffered his lone defeat to Onion in the Whitney Handicap.

"The Saratoga Race Course has three tracks. The main dirt track is a mile and an eighth in circumference; the outer track, known as the Mellon Turf Course, is a mile and ninety-eight feet in circumference, and the inner turf track is twenty-six feet short of seven and one-half furlongs.

"Each mount is assigned a handicap, a prediction of the horse's chance to win the race in which it is running. These handicaps take into account different factors—the weight the horse is carrying, the past performances and distances run in every race the horse entered, its odds in each of the previous races run, the horse's lifetime record, the amount of money earned, and other information of value."

"You mention weight as one of the factors. Wouldn't a horse carrying a light jockey have an advantage over a horse carrying a heavier rider?" questioned Dora.

"The weight factored into the equation is stipulated by the racing secretary. It includes not only the weight of the jockey and saddle but required lead weights that are placed in saddle pockets to equalize the poundage required.

"Because of Saratoga's history, the prize purses available, and the quality of horses running, it attracts sizable crowds, crowds equal to and larger than what you, Dora, witnessed on Opening Day. That day was merely an appetizer. Ahead is the main course. It consists of three Handicap and eleven Stakes races. Eight of these fourteen races have purses ranging from two hundred fifty thousand to four hundred thousand dollars. Then the biggies: the Diana Handicap, the Sword Dancer Invitational Stakes, and the Woodward Stakes each with a five-hundred-thousand-dollar purse; the Alabama Stakes with six hundred thousand dollars; and the Whitney Handicap with seven hundred fifty thousand dollars. Obviously, your presence needs to be seen during all of these races. But it is particularly important that you are visible on the day the Travers is run. For that Stakes race really draws the crowd and the fastest thoroughbreds in the country. Its purse—one million dollars."

"You refer to some of races as stakes races and others as handicap races. Is there a difference?"

"Actually, the Diana Handicap and Whitney Handicap are both stakes races. In the United States and Canada, there is an association consisting of thoroughbred owners and breeders. This group describes races with names that originate from the stake or entry fee, owners pay. To these fees, additional moneys are added by the track to form a pool of prize money that is paid to the first, second, third, and fourth place finishers in the named race. This process is referred to as a graded stakes race.

"There are different levels of graded stakes races at Saratoga. The top ranking with the largest purse available is a Grade I Stakes Race. This is followed by a Grade II and Grade III. Then there are the ungraded stakes races and the Steeplechase.

"Back in 1863, when the track first opened, racing lasted only four days. Over time, it stretched out. Now, it lasts six weeks up through Labor Day. And when people aren't at the track, they're enjoying festivals, wine- and beer-tasting events, food vendors, bocce ball tournaments, and beginning tomorrow, Tarot card reading. So depending on your stamina, the hours you work can be long, from early morning before the races, throughout the day at the races, and well, into the night.

"For now, that's enough background information. We'll be on our way tomorrow morning around seven thirty. That'll allow you time to get familiar with the area before meeting with the document's specialist. Then we'll be off to the track where you'll go inside, watch the people, and get a feel for why they're here and what they're doing. See the happy winners and the weeping losers. That should help you promote Tarot to the curious, the hopeful ones."

Doc, having returned during the early discussions, nodded his head in agreement and said, "Tomorrow, Dora, is a day of familiarization, a day to get a feeling. You have the entire month to accumulate money. If the offtrack pedestrian crowd is light during the racing hours, you can relax and watch the horses run. You'll need a breather. Now I think we ought to get some sleep. You have to be alert tomorrow."

"Not so fast," interrupted Shoe. "She'll be fine tomorrow. Tonight, I want a reading."

Stealing a glance at Dora, Doc said, "Come on, Shoe, not tonight! Sometime tomorrow! Look at her. She's about to fall asleep in that chair."

"Uh-uh," responded the host. "We have an understanding. One you both agreed to. I get my readings when I want them."

"Shoe, be—"

"Shut up, Doc. He's right. I'll get the cards."

To help her host get a better understanding of himself, Dora decided on the *Tree of Life*, a spread revealing the major factors influencing one's present-day status. Ten cards were spread in three vertical columns with four center cards extending above, within, and below the two outer three-card columns. The first two cards revealed had future significance. They were the upright *Ace of Swords* and the upright *Wheel of Fortune*. The first predicted the beginning of a victory; the second announced a special gain forthcoming from an unexpected event that would end recent problems.

* * * * *

The following morning at breakfast, Shoe was waiting for his guests to arrive at the table. He had finished eating, had read the morning paper, and was now enjoying a third cup of coffee.

Dora and Doc, though sleeping in separate rooms, entered the dining room together with Doc carrying Stacey. Martha brought to the table eggs hollandaise, Canadian bacon, buttered toast, jam, pancakes, orange juice, and fresh coffee.

Looking at Doc, Dora shook her head and said, "Getting adjusted to living on the streets again is going to be verrrrry difficult." And then she proceeded to fill her plate with servings of everything.

Martha approached Doc and said, "I can take the baby. I'm warming a bottle, and when I give it to her, I want to smother the darling with love." Everyone stopped what they were doing and smiled as the woman headed to the kitchen.

"You can read the paper, Doc. I've finished it."

Setting the paper beside his plate, Doc thumbed through the pages, glancing at the headlines between bites of food. Then he stopped, set down his fork, and lifted the tabloid to carefully study an article in its entirety. When he finished reading it, he noticed Shoe watching him.

"You knew about this, didn't you?" inquired the doctor.

"I had an inkling."

"When?"

"Recently."

"But you never mentioned it. Why?"

"Because Dora confirmed it."

About to take a mouthful of food, Dora stopped.

"I confirmed what?"

Before he could answer, Doc interrupted and read a headline: *Chief Financial Officer of Shomazzi Industries in Fatal Car Accident.*

"It appears the brakes on George Campbell's automobile failed and his vehicle crashed, killing him," said Doc.

"But I've never mentioned anyone dying," said Dora. "Besides, I don't even know a George Campbell."

"Directly no, but indirectly yes!" said Shomazzi. "During your first reading, you said a scheming opportunist was working against me, and a large financial gain was likely to be lost. Campbell not only stole a large amount of money but had been falsifying my company's accounting records for quite a while. Unfortunately for the crook, he lost his life before he could enjoy his newly gained riches. Then last night, the *Ten of Swords* confirmed the worst was over, with the *Wheel of Fortune* revealing that an unexpected event would end the problem. That event turns out to be the car crash. Never again will I question you and your cards, my dear."

"So you're saying you didn't have anything to do with this death?" questioned the skeptical doctor.

"Why would I? I wanted him alive so I could recover the large sums of money he stole. Money that now may never be recovered. I'm just as saddened by this as I imagine others are his family and friends."

Doc and Dora stared at their host but said nothing.

"As soon as you finish breakfast, we'll be on our way. Dora, I want you to see some places where in the next couple of days you may want to conduct your readings. Not tomorrow, mind you. Tomorrow, you'll be attending the races."

CHAPTER 18

OFF AND RUNNING

Nearly 11:00 a.m. and people were either searching for seats or shoving their way to a better view of the first race. Thoroughbreds left the paddock and trotted to the starting gate. Excitement filled the air! Bettors, counting fortunes to be made, moved anxiously to the windows and placed bets on "sure things"—horses with symbolic names, noticeable sweat in the hind quarters, a prancing spirit, the odds of either a favorite or long shot, inside information whispered, the jockey's lucky colored silks, and other "certainties." Hours later, there would be those who bemoaned losses, questioning why they spent what they did at the *Graveyard of Favorites*. Many, but not all!

****

After leaving the semi, Frisky Fingers Freddie walked and thumbed and walked some more to the track. Drivers were reluctant to pick up the disheveled hiker, but never discouraged, he covered the miles, unashamedly flashing his collection cup to those on foot. Coins and bills were generously donated by bettors, confident they would win at the track. Freddie, however, had no intention on betting; he was only interested in locating the woman he despised.

Standing not too far from the main entrance, Freddie scanned faces for Dora and Doc. Then off to his side, he heard, "You prick!" Jerking around, Freddie faced a man teetering on unsteady legs with a bagged bottle in one hand. A familiar whiff of wine drifted to Freddie's nose. The inebriate, facing a parking lot behind Freddie, continued mumbling profanities at a group of five stepping out of a Lincoln.

"You know them?" Freddie questioned.

"The old asshole and his two goons! But not the other two!"

Reaching into his pocket, Freddie removed two one-dollar bills and flashed them for the drunk to see.

"That's Vincent Shomazzi, isn't it?"

"That's the bastard. The biggest crook around! If you've got more of those green things, hide 'em. If he sees 'em, they're as good as gone."

"You don't hold him in very high regard?"

Spitting and then taking a big swallow from his bottle, the drunk said, "If you went through what I've been through because of him, you wouldn't either."

Freddie watched the five disappear from the lot. "Do you know where he lives?" inquired Freddie.

"East side of town! On Crestview . . . Broad Crest . . . something like that."

"Know the address?"

"Fella, me and him ain't the closest of friends. He never asked me to come and dine, and I sure as hell wouldn't go if I was asked. But when you see his house, you'll know it. It'll be the biggest, most expensive one on the street!"

Thanking him, Freddie handed the man the two dollars. "Spend it on food, not booze! You'll feel better."

Freddie began to hike toward the east side of town. Arriving in a residential area where there were hundreds of homes, he looked for but did not see anything resembling either Crestview or Broad Crest. Considering the long shot a lost cause, he was about to return to the track when he saw a Sunoco Station two blocks away. Heading to it, he entered the station.

Behind the counter, a teenager eased back against the wall, fear written all over his face.

Disregarding the look, Freddie asked, "Does Vincent Shomazzi live around here?"

The attendant's eyes relaxed, and a slight curve appeared on his mouth.

"Yep! Everyone around here knows him. Lives on Hill Crest. Don't know the address, but I can look it up in the directory."

"Never mind. He's not listed. Thanks, just the same."

Leaving, Freddie passed a number of streets before finding Hill Crest. It was a long curving road with homes of similar size and style. At a loss, he snooped through mailboxes located at the curb, looking for the residents' names. Some of the boxes were empty; others with mail were not addressed to Shomazzi.

He continued on the sidewalk and saw a woman on the opposite side of the street, heading his way. Crossing the road, the woman stopped, turned, and walked hastily back in the direction from which she came. As he continued his search, his attention was drawn away from the mailboxes to the sound of an approaching car.

He walked to the middle of the street and raised his arms, waving them back and forth. About twenty feet in front of him, the car pulled to a stop, and the driver leaned his head out the open window.

"Mister, can you . . . ?" began Freddie.

Seeing the coin collection cup hanging from Freddie's belt, the driver said, "Buddy, a little advice. Get lost! The police travel these roads day and night looking for bums like you." With that, the man rolled up the window and floored his car past the vagrant.

Freddie remained deep in thought. He came to a conclusion, left the neighborhood, and returned to an older section of Saratoga Springs. Walking around, he found a small dimly lighted retail shop, entered, and began thumbing through the racks. He chose a white, somewhat large pullover shirt, a pair of blue jeans, socks, underwear, a towel, washcloth, and a "Gone Fishing" cap. All clean and inexpensive! Exactly what he wanted!

Further down the road, he entered a drugstore and bought a disposable razor, a small can of shaving cream, a cheap comb, a bar of soap, toothpaste, and a brush. His cash was running low, but he was not concerned. The racing crowd would soon replenish his needs.

He left the store and walked to a public restroom where he stripped and began scrubbing his body before shaving. Finished, he put on the clothes purchased and threw the old ones in a waste basket. Now, cleanly groomed, he became someone from the past he could barely remember. Returning to Shomazzi's neighborhood,

Freddie sat at a bus stop near the access street, unobserved by the passing public.

The afternoon dragged on. The final race of the day was over, and people began heading to where their evening plans beckoned. Six o'clock, seven o'clock, eight o'clock slipped by. Freddie sat calmly. Finally, what he was waiting for appeared. Shomazzi's Lincoln!

As it entered the neighborhood, he left the bench to follow. Quickly, the car disappeared from sight, yet Freddie followed. It was a long road with cars parked on both sides of the street—Buicks, Plymouths, Hondas, Toyotas, and others. But no Lincoln!

Up one side and down the other, Freddie walked. From behind, a car drove by. It was the Lincoln. *From what house had it come?* Annoyed but not discouraged, Freddie knew he was closing in on the woman responsible for making him a joke. The woman behind the "Frisky Fingers" moniker! The one who ruined his reputation! *Oh, you'll suffer! You'll not only find out what it's like to be a fool but a very poor fool, as well. Soon I'll have that valuable you took from that dumpster, and you'll have nothing but memories. Sad, sad memories!*

Retracing his steps, he approached two neighboring homes, houses with no cars parked at the lawns or in either driveway. Across the road, in front of a vacant lot, was a parked station wagon. Freddie moved to the front passenger door, leaned against it with only his eyes and forehead visible above the car's roof. There, he remained watching the two houses. Minutes ticked by.

Finally, the Lincoln returned, turning into one of the driveways. Freddie heard the garage door open, then close. Rooms on the first and second floor were already lighted. The third floor, dark, soon came to life. A big man walked to a window and drew the shade. It was Giant. *Now, Dora, I've found you.*

The following morning, people started moving. Cars began to drive away.

Freddie awakened on the ground of the overgrown vacant lot. Rising but kneeling, he watched the Shomazzi residence for activity. A woman, one not seen before, came out the front door, holding an infant. She hesitated, looking at something, before walking to a carrier box where she retrieved the morning paper. Back at the door, she disappeared.

Is that Shomazzi's wife? His baby? She seems pretty old to have a newborn. I wonder who else is inside that I haven't seen.

Once again, the woman came out the front door, this time with Doc and without the infant. She pointed to a tree and spoke briefly. Then they reentered the house and returned with Dora holding the baby. Doc pointed to the tree, and then Dora whispered something into the child's ear. They laughed. Not loud but pleasantly cheerful.

Freddie, puzzled by what he was seeing, failed to notice a mother robin flying from the tree and returning with something to feed her baby nesting in the limbs. Then his attention was drawn to the sound of the Lincoln moving down the driveway and stopping for Shomazzi, Doc, and Dora carrying the infant. They walked to the automobile with both Windy and Giant attending to the passenger doors. After everyone was in the vehicle, it drove away.

Something's going on. I can feel it, but I don't know what it is. Got to come up with something, something that'll let me know what's happening. Think, damn it, think!

CHAPTER 19

IDENTITIES: SOME ESTABLISHED, SOME NEW, AND OTHERS DISCOVERED

Across town, a Monte Carlo pulled into a parking place in front of the Saratoga Springs precinct. Stepping from the car, Tom O'Malley—attired in shirt, tie, and sport jacket—entered the front door.

He walked confidently to the desk, removed his billfold, flashed a badge, and said, "Sergeant, the name's Kristopherson. I'm from the thirty-fourth downstate. Are you familiar with the recent car crash and death of a George Campbell, CFO at Shomazzi Industries?"

"Can't say I am. We have more than enough investigations up here for me to remember without trying to recall others outside the Springs," he chuckled.

"I know what you mean. Well, my captain wants me to ask Vincent Shomazzi about some company records found in the car. We understand he's up here for the races, and I need to talk to him. Mind telling me where he lives? All routine, you understand."

Without looking for an address, he spits out from memory, "179 Hill Crest. And Kristopherson, you'll be doing us all a favor if the questions you ask lead to some rest time for him in an open cell downstate."

Waving over his shoulder while walking to the door, Tom replied, "I'll see what I can do, Sarge!"

* * * * *

Miles away, five adults and an infant entered a brick building sandwiched between two taller buildings. They ascended by elevator to the fifth floor. One lone door gave access to the entire floor. On the door was the name TODD BURSEN.

They knocked, and a voice responded, "Identify yourself, please!"

"Shomazzi."

A buzzer was heard, and the door opened to a small reception area.

"Shoe, it's been a long time. Great seeing you!"

"It always is, Todd, when I'm bringing new business. Meet Dora and Doc and the baby, Stacey. You remember Giant and Windy from the last time I was here?"

Acknowledging each, the forger asked, "Anyone for coffee, tea, or a soft drink?"

Before any replies were heard, Shoe interrupted saying, "Bursen, we have a busy day. We don't need anything to drink. Just start by showing Doc and Dora around your various rooms, the equipment, and the documents to be provided. Be thorough but concise."

"Same old Shoe! Come on, folks, follow me."

One door led to a second room, followed by a third room, and then the fourth before finally stopping at a door not to be entered—the dark room. Dora and Doc were impressed. The rooms were spacious, dedicated for specific jobs, with each housing the current, most expensive photographic and print equipment available. If others worked for Bursen, it remained unknown. He was the only individual on the premises.

In a supply room, quantities of stationery with various textures and hues required to produce authentic-looking documents, either recent or decades old, were neatly arranged in organized cribs. From one, Dora removed several sheets of ecru paper and later, from another crib, three pencils with different shades of lead. Shoe watched with curiosity.

Returning to the main office for some discussion, Todd started by asking Doc a number of questions. According to the responses, the forger jotted down background information appropriate to the photographs and documents required. Shoe's attention remained on Dora who was applying various pencils to one of the sheets of paper she had taken.

Unobtrusively, Shomazzi approached Dora from her blind side.

"Damn, that's good," he said, startling her.

Todd stopped what he was doing and, along with Doc, turned his attention to the pair.

Taking the paper from her hands, Shoe walked to the photographer and jokingly said, "Maybe we don't need you after all. Look at this picture. Just as good as any photos you'll be taking."

On the page was a sketch of Todd's face, highlighted with various shades of lead.

"I didn't know you had such talent," said Doc.

"Why aren't you an artist rather than card reader?" questioned Shomazzi.

"There was a time—long, long ago—when I did. But I realized my abilities were limited and became interested in Tarot instead. Now, the only art I do is designing my cards."

"You mean to tell me that all those illustrations on the cards you read were drawn and colored by you?"

"That's right! It's important that I'm comfortable with a deck. It has to be the right size for my hands, have the right feel, and be appropriate to the readings I give. That's why you'll see different decks at every sitting."

"But where are your materials—the card stock, the pens, the ink, and the brushes? I haven't seen them," commented Doc.

"When the shed caught fire, I lost everything except the decks, which were in my purse. That's another reason why this trip is important. I need the money for my baby, for the food we eat, and for some card stock and art supplies. So let's stop gabbing and get on with the pictures and information Mr. Bursen needs. We need to get Stacey home for her feeding and nap before heading to the track. I want some action."

* * * * *

At the grassy vacant lot across from Shomazzi's home, Freddie had a plan. Brushing off his clothes, somewhat wrinkled but surprisingly clean, he combed his hair and then crossed the street to a brick walkway leading to the gambler's house. He stood on the front porch listening and waiting. Finally, he lifted the knocker on the front door and listened to a sound heard years before but no longer identifiable.

Banging the clapper, all turned quiet. Footsteps were heard approaching the door. Appearing before him was Martha, wearing an apron and pulling a vacuum cleaner a few feet behind.

"Mrs. Ackerman?"

"Sorry, you have the wrong house."

"Isn't this 179 Hill Crest?"

"Yes, but no one by the name of Ackerman lives here."

"Gee, I'm sorry! I was told this was the address. Do you know the Ackermans? They have five children."

"No, I don't. The man who owns this house is here only a short period every year. He's a bachelor who travels a great deal, and I'm only here when he is."

"Well, thank you, ma'am! Again, my apologies for the interruption."

Walking away, Freddie felt the woman's eyes boring a hole in his back. As he reached the sidewalk, he heard the front door close.

What the hell's going on? Obviously, the kid isn't his. And if she's the maid and the baby's mother, why has Dora taken the kid in the car?

Deep in thought, he headed away from the house before abruptly stopping.

Can it possibly be? I sure as hell bet it is! Could the box she and Roscoe took from the dumpster have held that baby? It was large enough. Why someone would toss a baby in the trash, and who it was, I can't say. But sure as hell, I know who found it. That pushcart! The move from department store! The sudden attention and continued presence by Doc with Dora! All of it makes sense. By damn, Dora, you found a baby. Ohhhh boy, am I ever going to get even now.

As Freddie walked rapidly away, a Monte Carlo eased out from the curb. Moving slowly, O'Malley, alert to his surroundings, eyed other parked cars, looking for people near the Shomazzi residence. He approached a black Toyota Corolla and intently studied the driver who was watching Freddie. The moving Monte Carlo caused the Toyota's driver to turn his head, eyeing O'Malley as he passed. Each now had a mental image of the other.

After the car disappeared from sight, the Toyota driver dialed his car phone.

"Mr. Jensen's office," answered Anna.

"May I speak with him, please?"

"I'm sorry. He's away from the office. I'll be happy to take a message though."

"This is the Lost and Found. Tell him his misplaced article has been found, and that I'll be calling back for delivery instructions."

"May I say who—"

Removing the phone from her ear, she stared at the receiver. The caller had hung up before Anna could finish her question. *Boy was he impatient!*

Now what do I do, the caller wondered?

Three houses away from the Toyota and another two doors from Shomazzi's, a lady and a man were having a party. Some twenty-five or thirty people were mingling inside and outside the house with cars dropping off more guests.

I know Jensen wants me to dispose of the kid, and if it were here at home, this would be the ideal time. But everyone's gone other than the maid. Time to go to the deli and grab a sandwich while I decide what to do! Now's no time for a hasty half-ass decision.

Minutes after the unknown one left the neighborhood, the Lincoln returned to the Shomazzi house where a hungry Stacey was affectionately received by Martha. Dora kissed the baby good-bye and returned with the four men to the racetrack.

CHAPTER 20

OMENS

At the main road, Freddie boarded a bus displaying a windshield sign, *Saratoga Race Track*. O'Malley followed. When his subject left the bus, the Irishman parked his car at a vacant curb, threw quarters in the meter, and followed at a distance. In a notebook, he jotted what appeared to be points of interest, including an entrance gate that held Freddie's attention.

The homeless one drifted around the perimeter of the main racetrack, until he spotted Dora surrounded by a small circle of people attentive to her reading cards for a female querent. Freddie stood away from the group, waiting for the opportunity to approach Dora with no one other than Doc in her presence.

Minutes before the horses saddled up for the first race, people dispersed. Shoe walked through the entrance nearest the gambler's private box. Giant and Windy, following Shoe's instructions, remained with Dora and Doc. Freddie's plans were changing. He had no intention of contacting her with all three present. Their meeting would have to be later. Freddie waited patiently.

Witnessing all that he cared to see, O'Malley returned to his car and drove back to Hill Crest. He had a feeling about the vagrant's interests and knew of the bus stop where he had arrived. He could always find Freddie later.

Dora and Doc remained at the table. She began shuffling Tarot cards, intending to lay the *Chakra Spread*. Giant, obviously annoyed, stepped forward, pointing, talking, and motioning for the two to fold their cards and go to the track. Ignoring him, they sat, and Dora began reading the cards Doc turned. Suddenly, she screamed. Jumping up, she placed her hand over her mouth. Doc, Giant, and Windy all began shouting questions at once.

Freddie was too far away to hear what was being said, so he remained fixed, watching with interest.

Then there was movement. Giant and Doc started folding the chairs, and Windy comforted the near-hysteric Dora.

With tears running down her cheeks, she began listening to the small man. Grabbing her cards, she and Windy dashed through the gate that led to the track. Giant, with table and two chairs in hand, headed toward the parking lot, leaving Doc standing alone. Freddie was confused; he was unable to understand the commotion.

Near the private box, Windy convinced the weeping Dora to wait. Going to Shomazzi, he whispered something, and the two left the box just as the horses broke from the starting gate.

Shomazzi approached Dora and asked, "What's wrong?"

"After you left," she stammered, "Doc and I decided to have a reading. The recent developments had caused me some concern. I wanted answers. To questions asked, Doc flipped an upright *Five of Cups* and then the *Judgment* and *King of Swords* in reversed positions. These are omens, bad omens.

"The *Five of Cups* portrays grief, mourning the loss of a loved one. *Judgment* conveys a possible loss or death of someone near and dear. To prevent this, there is a need for change. The *King of Swords* forewarns the presence of a controlling, abusive person with evil intentions. Deep within me, I know these cards refer to Stacey's safety. We need to get to her immediately. Oh, Shoe," she sobbed, "please, please, let's leave now."

"Come on!" Shoe commanded. "We'll go this way. With this crowd, it'll be the quickest way to the parking lot."

CHAPTER 21

THE INTRUDERS

After returning from lunch, the driver in the black Toyota watched a woman exit a house located between the one with the party and the Shomazzi residence. Viewing her noisy neighbors, she jiggled the knob, ensuring the lock was secure, and then reached into her purse for a key that was inserted in what he assumed was a dead bolt. Confident the house was impenetrable, she walked to her car and drove away.

A vacant house! That helps my plan, thought the driver.

Out of his glove compartment, he removed a necktie and knotted it neatly under his shirt collar. Locking the compartment door, he stepped from the car, slipped on a sport coat, and walked toward the house now teeming with people.

A taxicab stopped at a brick walk leading to the front door. Two Japanese couples exited the vehicle.

With an engaging smile, the Toyota driver approached the couple, bowed to the senior Asian male, and began a conversation. The Asian returned the bow and introduced the three people in his group. Together, they headed up the brick walk. The American extended his farewell to the four and moved nonchalantly onto the lawn as the Japanese mounted the steps leading to the front door.

O'Malley, who had returned, observed this. He discreetly parked a block away from the Toyota and stood behind his Monte Carlo observing the Corolla driver through binoculars. The uninvited visitor drifted among clusters of people, avoiding everyone and occasionally nodding his head in recognition without engaging in conversation. Finally, he reached the back of the house and became no longer visible when he moved behind it.

In the backyard was an outdoor bar with a man and a woman serving the guests. Retrieving a beer from an unattended cooler, the Toyota driver pulled the tab and placed the can near his lips, faking a swallow. Not moving, he scanned the crowd to be certain no one was paying attention. Satisfied, he walked around two groups of people engaged in conversation and slipped unobserved through a hedge into the backyard of the now-vacant home separating the party-active house from Shomazzi's.

Continuing through the second backyard, the stranger arrived at the third house and studied it for activity. All was quiet. He dropped the beer and sprinted from tree to tree, stopping at times to see if his movements aroused attention from the woman known to be inside.

At the rear of the house, he peaked through windows. Nothing moved! All was quiet! Crouching beneath the window ledges, he duckwalked to the rear door. There, he put on a pair of surgeon's gloves and pulled over his head a hood with holes for his eyes and nostrils.

Slowly, he opened the screen. Turning the knob, he found the door to be unlocked. Then he removed his loafers and tiptoed into the kitchen. At a closed door leading into another room, he stood listening. Nothing! Soundlessly, he inched the door open. There was no one in the dining room. Quietly, he peeked into all the other rooms, with the exception of Shoe's office, which remained locked. The downstairs was vacant.

With decisive steps, he ascended the carpeted stairs. Each of the bedrooms, with the exception of Stacey's, was empty. The infant was asleep in her crib.

A door, leading to the third floor, was open. Quietly, the stranger climbed the steps and looked into two empty bedrooms before coming to the third, occupied by the maid. She sat at her desk reading a book, her back to the door. Entering silently, a premonition—possibly—caused Martha to turn. A strong hand grasped her throat. Her eyes bulged with fear.

* * * * *

O'Malley, in the meantime, retrieved a Slim Jim from his car. With an easygoing stride, he sauntered to the Toyota and, seeing no one, slipped the door-opening mechanism between the front passenger window and door frame, popping the lock. Inside the car was a telephone. He attempted to open the glove compartment door, but it was locked.

More people arrived at the party house. To avoid attention, O'Malley lay down across the passenger seat. Slowly, he moved his hand beneath the dashboard but found nothing. Inspections under the floor mats and behind the sun visors also produced nothing. Then, reaching beneath the driver's seat, he felt a narrow box. In it were license plates for Montana, New Mexico, and Michigan.

From his pocket, he retrieved a lock pick and proceeded to open the glove compartment door. Inside was an envelope holding three driver's licenses, four motor vehicle registration certificates, and four automobile insurance identification cards. One set of three specified Montana, the second set New Mexico, and the third set Michigan. The two remaining documents—a vehicle registration certificate and an insurance ID card—were issued by New York for the plated Toyota. The driver's license, O'Malley reasoned, was in the possession of the owner. The faces appearing on the three driver's licenses were that of the man O'Malley had seen earlier, but each of the identifying names and addresses was different.

One remaining piece of paper, the one O'Malley wanted to find, was also in the envelope. It had a telephone number. Dialing the car phone, the Irishman cupped his hand over the mouthpiece. After two rings, a voice responded.

"Tell me about the misplaced article."

O'Malley remained silent.

"Have you got it or not?'"

More silence!

"Hello! Hello! Are you there? Damn it, speak up!"

With no response, the call was disconnected.

What the hell's going on? There's no hiding your voice, Jensen. But who's this man of many names? Three driver's licenses with multiple car plates, DMV certificates, and insurance IDs! What's his connection with you, and why's he in this neighborhood? And what's this misplaced article? Need to give this a lot of thought. But first, I'll look for Freddie. Once he's out of the way, full time can be spent figuring out what the hell you're up to.

CHAPTER 22

GOOD LUCK, BAD LUCK

O'Malley drove back to the racetrack with hopes that his drifter would still be there.

This'll be a challenge. Can't be certain where the homeless creep might be, but he desperately wants to find Dora. That's a starting point. She'll be in an area surrounded by a bunch of gullible believers!

Yet the grounds around the track were immense. Locating Freddie required anticipatory foresight and Irish luck.

The final race ended. A throng of people exited the grounds, walking to distant parking lots, bus stops, and taxi stands. The Monte Carlo moved slowly stopping at times in spite of honking horns by angry drivers.

A stroke of luck occurred when O'Mallley saw a car pulling away from a parking spot. He swerved into it. He was now a couple hundred yards from the entrance that had held Freddie's earlier attention and somewhat more than two miles from where the bus had stopped when the beggar first arrived.

O'Malley slid to the passenger's side, pushed the seat back, rolled down the window, and began staring out the side and rear windows. He anticipated a long wait with the possibility of not seeing Freddie at all. But once again, after only a ten-minute delay, the Irishman's luck continued.

Twenty yards back, Freddie was seen weaving in and out of the crowd, heading in the direction of the Monte Carlo. Nearing the front window, O'Malley leaned out and shouted, "Hey, buddy, will you come here?"

Pointing to his shirt, Freddie said, "Who me?"

"Yes, you! You in the white shirt! I'm not from around here, and I was wondering if you'd give me some directions?"

"Not me! I don't live here either."

Waving five ones, he said, "Thanks anyways! Hopefully the next person I ask knows where Hill Crest is."

"You looking for Hill Crest Drive? Oh, I happen to know where that is. In fact, I'm going there."

"No kidding! Damn, this may turn out to be a lucky day, after all." Sliding back to the driver's side, O'Malley said, "Hop in! I'll take you there, and here's a few bucks for your help."

Freddie climbed in, grabbed the money without a thank-you, and stuffed it in his pocket.

As the Monte Carlo edged onto the road, the Irishman said, "Better show me the way."

"Continue down this street. At the second traffic light, turn left and drive ten, fifteen miles. When we get closer, I'll show you where to turn."

"Good! Like I said, you might make this my lucky day. So far, it's been a loser. First day at the races, and already I'm out a couple hundred bucks. The nags certainly weren't kind to me. Hope your day's been better."

Without admitting he hadn't been betting, Freddie said, "Oh, I did all right. Not a lot but a few bucks! Like my old man used to say, 'Any amount won, no matter how small, is better than money lost.'"

"Your old man had it right. You say you're not from here. Where's home?"

"Down south. The big city, New York."

"Big difference—Saratoga and New York."

"Yeah! I'll be glad to get back. But first, I've got business here to attend to."

Continuing with useless conversation to keep Freddie's attention from wavering, O'Malley unexpectedly turned right.

"Where we going?" asked Freddie.

"Down here a ways. I'm thirsty and want a Pepsi. Buy you one too!"

Now, a skeptical Freddie questioned, "Since you're not from around here, how do you know there's Pepsi down this road?"

Removing a Colt .38 from inside his jacket, he shoved it close to his passenger's face. "You'd be surprised at what I know, Freddie!"

"Freddie . . . Freddie? Who are you anyway? How do you know my name?"

"As I said, you'd be surprised at what I know about you. Who you are, where you live, who your friends are—Knees, Doc, Nosey Ned, Dora, and others!"

Now frightened, Freddie inched his hand slowly toward the door handle.

Jamming the barrel of the Colt in Freddie's forehead, the captive shouted, "Ouch! Quit that. It hurts!"

"Then just stay seated. Opening that door won't be safe. Just shut up until you're spoken to!"

Turning down a desolate dirt road, O'Malley suddenly pulled the Monte Carlo to a stop.

"Now, slide off the seat and put your knees on the floorboard."

"There's no room. I'll do what you want. Talk, be quiet, anything! Just let me sit here."

Swiping the back of his head with the side of the revolver, Freddie again cried out, "Stop it, please. Have a heart. You're hurting me!"

"Nothing like how you'll feel if you don't start paying attention. Now! On the floor and fast!"

Sliding off the seat, his knees hit the mat, and his head bounced off the dashboard.

"Oh, shit!" he cried.

"Lean forward, lay your head against that panel, and put your hands behind your back."

From his pocket, O'Malley removed handcuffs and clamped them on Freddie's wrists, pinching the skin. Again, Freddie screamed.

"Now, answer some questions? Why are you here in Saratoga?"

"To be at the races! Why else?"

The Irishman struck him again, and Freddie shook his head to remove colored spots floating in front of his eyes.

"Don't shit me, Fingers! I doubt that you've even placed a bet. Instead, I think you're biding your time looking for Doc and Dora. I'm right, aren't I?"

"No, sir. You're mistaken, man!"

Once again, O'Malley swung his hand back, and Freddie screamed, "No, no! Don't hit me again! I'll talk. So you know who Doc and Dora are. Do you also know who Roscoe is?"

"The guy who died in the fire? Down by the old train station?"

"Yeah! Him and Dora found a box in a dumpster off Commerce Street."

"So?"

"Well, she's a bitch! She's responsible for destroying my reputation."

"The 'Frisky Fingers' handle?"

"Yeah, that and other things! So to get even, I wanted to find out what was in the box." Refusing to admit he now knows it's a baby, he adds, "It has to be worth a bundle, and I intend to have a piece. So after Roscoe dies, Dora pairs up with Doc and heads here. So I follow them."

"And!"

"I'm still trying to find out!"

Raising the gun, he said, "I don't believe you. And until I'm convinced you're telling me the truth, I'm going to beat the living shit out of you. And you'll either fess up everything, or you'll be facing your judgment day. You know what I mean when I say judgment day?"

"Yeah! I've been to church a time or two. I know what judgment day is."

Cocking back the hammer on his Colt, he said, "Well, start talking or begin counting your last few minutes on this earth."

"Okay, okay, okay! Every place they went, they carried the damn box. And just this morning, I learned it had a baby in it. Now I'm going to grab that kid and get even. Yes, sir . . . You bet . . . I'm going to get even!"

O'Malley reached behind Freddie, opened the door, and shoved him out on the ground. Lying in a pile, Freddie looked into the barrel of the gun, two feet from his head.

"Now, I'll tell you how you're going to get even. You're going to get out of their lives."

Reaching once again into his pocket, he withdrew a billfold and key. He placed the wallet on the seat and waved the key inches before Freddie's eyes.

"See this? It unlocks those cuffs." Pointing, he said, "See that dirt pile over by the tree?"

Freddie nodded.

"Then watch this!"

With a sweeping hand motion, O'Malley tossed the key some ten feet toward the dirt pile. It dropped short, falling in high grass.

"Now, you go find that key and unlock those bracelets. That'll keep you busy for a while. And if you're really interested in your freedom, you'll do what it takes to get them off. Once that happens, start heading toward the knoll off to your left. About a mile, maybe two, beyond it is the interstate. Thumb your way out of town. Where you go, I could care less. But if you want to live, don't ever let me see you again."

Picking up the billfold, O'Malley flipped it open and waved the police badge in front of Freddie's eyes.

"I'll repeat! Don't ever let me see you again. If I do, I'll have my buddies in blue chase you down. And when we get you, and we will, it'll be a long time before you walk freely in the sunlight again. The courts don't pay kindly to unemployed winos who want to kidnap children."

He slammed the Monte Carlo door, made a U-turn, and headed to the Shomazzi neighborhood.

CHAPTER 23

PLANS OF ACTION

Before Martha was able to scream, the man of many names smashed her face with his fist. Two teeth cracked, and the bone in her nose snapped. Releasing his neck-grasping grip, he dropped the unconscious woman to the floor and smiled as he stood over her.

Then he descended the stairs to Stacey's second-floor bedroom. Reaching down, he gently lifted the infant from her crib. A teeny smile appeared on the sleeping baby's lips as the abductor cradled the child in his arms.

"Sleep for now, little one, and remain silent," he whispered. "Our journey together will come to an end shortly."

He went down the steps and saw through a window the Lincoln coming up the driveway. He heard the garage door open. Moving rapidly to the front door, the intruder swung it open and darted back to the dining room where he placed Stacey on a chair. He pinched her three times. She let out painful screams, crying loudly as he moved through the door into the kitchen.

There he grabbed his loafers, left the house, and ran barefoot through the backyard toward the neighbor's home. Leaping over the hedge, he raced into the shadows of the vacant building. He slipped on his loafers, removed his hood and gloves, straightened his tie, and combed his hair. Cautiously, he slipped through more hedges onto the grounds occupied by the gregarious party crowd. Moving to the cooler, he retrieved a second beer, taking this time a lengthy swallow as he continued nonchalantly into the front yard and back to the Toyota.

* * * * *

With the sound of the baby screaming, Giant and Windy ran up the steps, followed by Doc, Shoe, and Dora half a flight behind. Windy moved to the crying baby, picked her up, and began rotating his upper body to quiet her. Giant dashed to the open front door, looked up and down the street, but saw nothing out of the ordinary. Shoe and Doc continued through the house, looking for Martha. When they found her, she was still lying where she had fallen. Doc applied a damp, cool cloth to her damaged face and revived her to a painful consciousness.

Dora took Stacey from Windy's arms and began to speak softly to her, kissing away the tears from her weeping eyes.

"Enough of this," roared Shoe as he reached for the phone. "Giant, Doc, Windy, take Martha to the hospital."

Dialing a number, he demanded to speak to the chief of staff. Endowments he had generously given the institution throughout the years resulted in his call receiving immediate attention. He spoke to the doctor, briefly reviewed Martha's condition, and requested a private room.

"Dora, I'm not leaving here until Martha's released from the hospital. Later today, we'll discuss plans for Stacey, you, and Doc if you want him included. In the meantime, you and your baby will receive around-the-clock attention from Windy, Giant, and others."

* * * * *

As the intruder slid into his Toyota, the telephone rang.
"I'm here," he answered.
"It's about time I heard your voice."
"Our last call wasn't that long ago?"
"Do you mean that one an hour ago when you wouldn't talk to me?"
"An hour ago? What are you talking about?"

"You called! I asked about the misplaced package and whether or not you had it? But you never answered. What's going on? Are there problems I should know about?"

Scanning the passenger seat and dashboard, he noticed something.

"We may have a problem. I'll let you know once I figure it out. In the meantime, know that I had the package only moments ago, but unwelcome visitors prevented me from keeping it. However, you needn't worry. I'll soon be getting it back. Until then, I'm going to be out of touch."

"Out of touch? Why? For how long? This doesn't sound good."

"Don't worry. Everything's under control. Have patience. I'll bring you up to date. Talk to you soon." And he hung up.

Down on the floor mat was a tiny sliver of paper. One with a crease in it. Opening the glove compartment door, he scanned the envelope. The contents had been rearranged. *Lucky for me the snooper's marker wasn't seen by whoever opened the door. Now I need to find out who's sticking his nose where it shouldn't be. Guess it's time to make some changes.*

Starting the engine, he pulled away from the curb and settled back for a thirty-mile ride to the Albany airport. In the long-term lot, he parked the Toyota and went to an on-site car rental where he picked up a Buick. Back at the parking lot, he transferred to the Buick items from under the Toyota's front seat, its trunk, and glove compartment. He then removed the mobile telephone and installed it in the rental.

Finished, he drove back to the airport, parked, and carried a satchel to the men's restroom. In a stall, he exchanged his shirt, tie, and suit coat for a wool button-down shirt and winter jacket. Then he applied a walrus mustache, put on horn-rimmed spectacles with plain glass lens and a stocking cap. Glancing in the mirror, he smiled.

Even my mother wouldn't recognize me now.

After retrieving the Buick, he headed back to Saratoga Springs.

* * * * *

It was past the dinner hour, and O'Malley, having returned from his confrontation with Freddie, was hungry. He stopped at a diner for a late supper. Finishing the meal, he returned to Hill Crest Drive. All was quiet in the Shomazzi household with Doc, Windy, and Giant now back from the hospital. The Irishman knew nothing of the attempted abduction hours earlier.

CHAPTER 24

QUIT WHEN AHEAD

After falling twice, Freddie began crawling to the key. Two minutes, three minutes, five minutes ticked by and still no key to be found. The grass was high but not so thick as to prevent it from resting in full view.

It's got to be here, and unless I find it soon, it'll be dark, and I sure as hell don't want to spend a night handcuffed in this miserable spot.

Reexamining the grass, his eyes spotted a speck of silver.

"Gotcha!"

He twisted his body so his butt would be close to the key, leaned back at a slight angle, and felt blindly where it had fallen. Touching the key, he grasped it between his right thumb and forefinger, then lifted it out of the grass. He stretched his left arm as far to the right side of his back as the cuffed hands would allow and searched for the keyhole on the left cuff with his right pinkie.

"Damn it!"

He dropped the key.

Starting once again, he repeated the movements, squeezing the key tightly between thumb and forefinger as he searched by touch for the hole.

Minutes passed. Frustration grew. His shoulders and fingers ached. But he kept trying. Finally, the key went in the hole, and Freddie clicked open the left handcuff. Freeing his wrist, he moved his arms to the front of his body and began rotating his shoulders to ease the stiffness. He dropped both the cuffs and key to the ground, mumbling, "At least I'm free."

Slowly, he massaged his wrists, and the blood began to flow back into his deadened hands. Now content, he removed a switch blade from another pocket and honed the blade against a rock until it was razor sharp.

You may have won the first round, cop, but that will be the only one.

The sky was overcast as Freddie started his long walk back, looking for a bus stop and public transportation to Hill Crest Drive.

* * * * *

O'Malley drove past the Buick without noticing the driver. He parked the Monte Carlo a distance from the Shomazzi residence and began watching people wandering through lighted rooms. A little after nine o'clock, an Olds 88 pulled into the driveway. Four men exited the car and walked to the front door. Giant greeted each with a hug.

One of the men, young and limping, held the Irishman's attention.

Hello, Charlie Spade. Now why are you in these parts?

After the four entered the house, Giant stood in the doorway looking up and down the street for activity. Seeing nothing, he followed the guests and closed the door behind him.

O'Malley left the car, avoided the street lights, and slipped into the adjoining yard of a darkened house. From there, he headed clandestinely to the back of Shomazzi's home, curious about the growing number of questionable people.

The driver of the Buick intently watched the driver of the Chevrolet disappear from sight. Interested in learning what might be found in the Monte Carlo, the man was about to leave the Buick when he noticed another man approaching. The person walked cautiously, turning his head left and right as though expecting to see someone. He stopped. Something on the opposite side of the road held his attention. Whatever it was, remained unknown to the man of many names.

After a moment's hesitation, the stranger darted across the road to the rear of the Monte Carlo. There he kneeled behind the left tire.

Staring at it, he remained deep in thought. From his pocket, Freddie removed his switch blade and hid the knife in his clenched fist.

The Buick driver, keeping his eyes on the stranger, removed a pair of surgeon's gloves from a satchel and slipped them on. Opening the car door, the disconnected ceiling light allowed the interior to remain dark. Stealthily, the driver moved quietly around parked cars, silently approaching Freddie from behind.

The pondering Freddie never noticed the approaching man until his powerful hands pressed down on Freddie's shoulders.

"What are you up to?"

Startled, Freddie wrenched, but his knees never left the ground. He tilted his head backward and looked into a pair of violent, black eyes never before seen.

"Don't try to move. Just tell me why you're here and what you're up to."

No sound! No explanation! Nothing!

"Mister, you don't want to be asked a third time!"

But a defiant Freddie remained silent.

Pulling the slightly built Freddie to his feet, he spun the captive around and pressed him against the car.

Clinching his fist, the driver of the Buick said, "Don't be stupid! Talk to me!"

With arms stretched across the trunk, Freddie cried, "D-d-don't. . . don't hit me. Please! Just give me some air. I'll tell you."

The man released his hands and moved half a step backward. Freddie, without warning, snapped open the switchblade and swung the knife toward the aggressor's face. Alertly, the man of many names tilted his head back, and the blade missed his face by inches.

Parrying the passing hand with his right arm, the unknown one grasped the wrist of the knife-held fist, clinched his right fist, and pounded it rapidly into Freddie's soft stomach. As vomit flowed from his mouth, Freddie's last conscious thought was that of the attacker clutching his head and thrusting his face to the pavement.

The assailant picked up the discarded knife and dragged Freddie back to the Buick. From a satchel, he removed duct tape and two clotheslines. After sealing Freddie's mouth and binding his ankles and wrists, the attacker lifted the unconscious victim effortlessly and tossed him on the passenger's side of the front seat. He then got in the car and drove away.

Nine minutes elapsed before Freddie stirred. With his left hand on the steering wheel and his right hand waving the knife in front of the semiconscious Freddie, the attacker pressed the pointed blade to his victim's throat.

"Don't move! Warm blood flowing down your chest isn't pleasant."

Miles later, the Buick entered a wooded area. Down a dirt road and over seldom-traveled terrain. The car finally stopped in an open area surrounded by trees. In front of the headlights was a large oak with a big limb, twelve feet high off the ground. Five feet below it, jutting from the side of the trunk was a smaller sturdy limb.

Pulling the now-conscious Freddie out of the car, the assailant swung the victim over his shoulder, carried him to another tree, and seated him facing the oak.

From the satchel, the attacker removed a long, thickly twined rope. He tied a piece of wood to one end and tossed the weighted end toward the higher branch. The first toss fell short of the limb; the second hit the limb and fell to the ground. Two more underhanded pitches were equally ineffective.

"Never was a good pitcher," chuckled the captor.

Finally, after two more failing throws, the weighted end of the rope cleared the limb and fell into his outstretched hand. Carefully, he pulled the rope down a foot before picking up the other end and wrapping it several times around the lower branch. Retrieving the dangling, weighted end of the rope, he removed the wood and made a slipknot. From the lower branch, he untied the other end, slid it through the slipknot, and pulled the noose up until it was tightened snugly around the limb. Taking hold of the rope, he swung freely, smiled, and cheerfully whooped Tarzan's yell.

The hangman dropped to the ground, circled the area, picked up strips of wood, and piled them into a platform two feet off the ground. He carried Freddie to this stage, gauged the distance between the stand and the rope's end, and dropped the captive. With the loose end in hand, he fashioned a hangman's noose. Teardrops trickled down Freddie's cheeks.

Looking at his victim, the hangman said, "This is one hell of a way to die. The rope tightening around your neck, oxygen no longer reaching your lungs. Your head stretched painfully up from your neck and shoulders! So agonizing, so time consuming! Yep! It's one hell of a way to die. But it's your choice. Tell me why the interest in that Monte Carlo and live out your life. Or die painfully!"

With that, he ripped the duct tape from Freddie's mouth.

"I'll tell you. I'll tell you. Just don't kill me. Please! Please! I want to live."

"Well, start talking. And be truthful! I know when someone's lying. So you have one chance. Don't fuck it up!"

The words poured out in a torrent—Dora and Doc, the dumpster, the package, the baby, the deaths of Roscoe and Grape Juice, the undercover cop, and the shackling of Freddie. The only thing withheld was his intention on kidnapping the child.

Exhausted and gasping nervously, Freddie said, "You've heard it all. Now, let me go as promised. You'll never see me again. And I'll forget all about this. All of it! I promise. On the soul of my dead mother, I promise. Oh yes, in God's name, I promise."

Seated, while Freddie regurgitated all that he knew, the abductor remained thoughtful and quiet.

Interesting! A cop, the baby! Why's a cop prowling around? What's his interest in all of this? And just who is he? I've a lot to learn.

Standing, the assailant idly wandered around. Picking up the hangman's noose, he slapped it against the palm of his hand. Saying nothing, he continued walking. Freddie eyed him with anxious, hopeful eyes. Yet he remained silent, fearing that anything said might ignite the man's anger.

Continuing to circle Freddie, the killer finally dropped the noose around his victim's neck.

"No, no, no! You promised. Have a heart? Forgive me. Free me! Oh, please, please, please! Don't do this to me. Don't kill me. I'm too young to die."

Insensitive to the outbursts, the villain circled his arm around Freddie's chest and lifted him onto the pile of wood.

Though sobbing, Freddie tried to balance himself as the wood shifted. The killer pulled the rope tight, securing it around the lower branch. Facing him, the abductor laughed and then kicked away the top strip of wood.

"Sorry, but you know my face."

On tiptoes, the homeless one screamed. Another piece of wood was kicked away. Airspace appeared between Freddie's toes and the platform.

Tiring of the time he was wasting, the killer finally kicked away all the remaining wood, heard the last sound uttered—"A . . . a . . . ugh!"—and watched the homeless one slowly swing to his death. The killer gleefully commented as he walked back to the Buick, "You are really one dumb, gullible puissant."

On the way to Hill Crest Drive, he pulled the Buick into a Texaco Station. Briefly, he spoke to the attendant and made a purchase.

CHAPTER 25

THE NUMBERS CONTINUE CHANGING

O'Malley stood silently, peering in the back window of the living room. Shomazzi was lecturing the seven: Dora, Doc, Windy, and the four recent visitors.

All are here but Giant! Wonder where he is?

Unable to hear what was being said, the former policeman was captured by the emotions of the people. Everyone was taking part in the dialogue. Seeing what appeared to be an end to the meeting, O'Malley dashed back to his car. Upon entering it, he noticed the Buick was nowhere to be seen.

The porch light went off, and then the front door opened. Three unidentified bodies appeared in the dark entrance with two continuing on toward the Oldsmobile. An interior light exposed the two entering the vehicle. Charlie Spade slipped behind the steering wheel.

As the car backed out of the driveway, O'Malley turned on his engine and slowly pulled into the street half a block behind the 88. From the front door, Windy watched both cars leave the neighborhood. Returning to the living room, he whispered something briefly to Shoe. The host excused himself from Dora, Doc, and the two unidentified men, motioning the inconspicuous one to follow him to his office.

"So tell me!" Shomazzi commanded.

"Since our arrival, I've been watching the street. Not too many cars in this neighborhood, so it's easy to get familiar with the ones belonging to the neighbors and the ones stopping by for a visit. But there have been three cars that always park in different spots. They made me wonder which homes the drivers were visiting. A Toyota Corolla, a Chevrolet Monte Carlo, and a Buick LeSabre. Never was any one of them near the same house twice. The Corolla and Monte Carlo were here originally. Now the Toyota has left, and the LeSabre has appeared. It seemed unusual and got my attention."

"What about the drivers?"

"Occasionally, I'd see one or the other in a car, but often the cars were empty. And I never got close enough to get a description of the driver in either the Toyota or the LeSabre, but I have a good mental image of the one in the Monte Carlo."

"You say they were here before and after Martha's beating?"

"The Monte Carlo and Toyota were. But shortly after the beating, the Toyota left, and the Buick appeared. What the drivers of those cars are up to, I can't say. But my curiosity has me walking the neighborhood often. Thought you should know!"

"Good work, Windy! Always on your toes! Keep me informed, but don't say anything to Doc or Dora. I don't want them spooked more than they already are. When Giant comes back from the hospital, clue him in. You and he are to keep a close watch over Stacey."

* * * * *

The 88 pulled into the hospital parking lot. Charlie Spade and his riding companion entered the emergency room door. Minutes later, the riding companion and Giant drove the 88 away.

What's going on? wondered O'Malley.

Getting out of his car, the head of security entered the hospital and walked to the cafeteria. Looking around, he watched a man leave his chair and head to the dessert section. Carelessly, the diner left his suit jacket on the chair. Attached to its lapel was a visitor's badge.

Walking casually to the chair, O'Malley detached the ID and left the room. He pinned the tag on his coat and proceeded down the first floor halls. At the elevator, he went to the second floor and continued his tour. On the third floor, beyond the nurses' station, he came to another corridor entrance. Opening the door, he saw Charlie Spade sitting outside a room, reading a magazine. Not wanting to be seen, the Irishman entered a restroom where he patiently waited. Periodically, he opened the door to see if Spade was still sitting by the door.

Among your many bad habits, Charlie me boy, are your needs for coffee and smokes. I can wait. You'll be going outside soon to satisfy your craving for a Camel.

Five minutes! Ten minutes went by! Looking out the door, the seat was now vacant. Walking to the empty chair, O'Malley scanned the patient's name posted at the side of the door. *Martha Brown!*

Back in his car, the Irishman headed to Hill Crest Drive, pondering the woman's identity.

Who's Martha Brown, and why's she so important to Shomazzi, Dora, and Doc? And why is Charlie Spade sitting at her door? Was Giant there before him? If so, why all this attention? And does it have something to do with Mr. Toyota and Jensen? I may be knee-deep in shit without even knowing it. Time for some deductive reasoning! But where do I begin?

CHAPTER 26

TOO MUCH CURIOSITY

Near Shomazzi's residence, the driver of the returning Buick passed the already parked Monte Carlo. It continued down Hill Crest, turned left at an intersecting street, and pulled into a driveway. Then it backed out, returned, and parked facing but some distance from the Chevrolet.

Dialing the phone, he waited. After five minutes, he redialed. Still no answer.

Hungry, he drove to a Jewish Delicatessen and ordered a carry out of matzo ball soup, pastrami on rye, and large black coffee.

Back on Hill Crest, he redialed. Still no answer! He began eating, and when finished, punched in the numbers one more time while sipping his coffee.

"What have you to report?" was the response.

"Thought for a while I wouldn't locate you."

"Had a meeting!"

When don't you have a meeting, the assailant silently thought. "I've got some news! There's a homeless one from the city. Name's Freddie! He's been poking around."

"I've heard of him but never met him."

"Well, you won't be. He's no longer around. However, I now think I know who called you. The one who didn't speak when you answered!"

"Who is he?"

"A cop! Don't know his name. But I'll get it."

"Then what?"

"Like Freddie, he'll disappear."

"Is that necessary?"

"Unless you want more people finding out about the package?"

"You know I don't. Make certain his disappearance is permanent and untraceable. And that reminds me! I want everyone—now understand me, I mean everyone—involved with this package eliminated. Am I making myself clear?"

"There's no need to worry."

"Good," he said, and he disconnected the call.

The hangman smiled! Removing his disguise, he dropped the mustache, glasses, and hood in the satchel. He then started the Buick and drove slowly past the Monte Carlo, staring directly into O'Malley's eyes. Flooring the accelerator, he sped away. The Monte Carlo pulled out from the curb and made a U-turn.

Ah, the fish is hooked!

Continuing on the curvy Hill Crest Drive, the pursued came to a stop sign and waited for the Monte Carlo to appear. As the lights came around the bend, the Buick turned left and eased between two other vehicles. Purposely driving slowly, the unknown one watched O'Malley through the rearview mirror.

Tailing a car and remaining undetected requires skills. But wanting to be pursued without alerting the follower requires expertise also. Each driver allowed several cars to remain between them. As they reached the city limit, the Buick picked up speed but not so fast as to lose O'Malley.

On a dirt road, the lead car alternated between moving rapidly, braking, and reaccelerating, throwing a stream of dirt into the air. It was easy for the former policeman to follow. Extending the distance that separated the two, the killer intently kept the Monte Carlo in view.

Suddenly, the Irishman stopped. It was in a clearing, only a hand-shaking distance from Freddie. The corpse—not completely stiffened with rigor mortis—and its contorted white face swayed in the howling, gusty wind.

Suddenly, a rifle shot. Blood splattered across the windshield and roof of the Chevy. O'Malley's head fell to the steering wheel. Out of the woods came the man of many names, a rifle cradled in his arm. Staring for a moment, he turned and reentered the woods. Minutes later, the Buick appeared and stopped within fifty feet of the Monte Carlo.

With the engine left running and the front door open, the unknown one stripped off his jacket and shirt and threw them to the ground. He then removed a satchel from the trunk and carried it to the Chevy. Out of the bag, he withdrew a terry cloth towel, surgeon's gloves, and hatchet.

Opening the car door, he covered the victim's head with the towel and twisted his face toward him. Hammer and screwdriver in hand, the killer chipped away at the Irishman's teeth, plucking pieces from his mouth and dropping them into a Ziplock plastic bag. Then, with the hatchet, he chopped off the ends of O'Malley's fingers and thumbs and placed the tips alongside the teeth in the bag. Casually, he threw the bundle onto the passenger seat of the Buick.

From the victim's pockets, he removed a billfold and other items of identification. One handwritten note held his attention. Folding it carefully, he placed it in his pocket. With hammer and screwdriver, he destroyed the vehicle identification number. Methodically, he removed stickers from the doorjamb and retrieved the automobile registration card, insurance certificates, vehicle maintenance records, and other papers stored in the glove compartment. All were set ablaze; the ashes scattered on the floor mat beneath the victim's feet. From the vehicle bumpers, license plates were removed and placed beside the plastic bag. Out of his car trunk, a rag and five-gallon can of gasoline purchased at the Texaco Station were removed. Soaking the rag, a foot of cloth was fed into the Chevy's gas tank, and another two feet dangled over the fender. The remaining gasoline was poured over the Irishman's body and upholstery of the car.

Replacing the can, tools, and satchel in the Buick's trunk, he dropped a lighted match onto the victim's lap and quickly ignited the dangling rag before jumping into his car and speeding away. The Monte Carlo burst into flames and exploded.

On the main highway, fire engines passed in the opposite direction, heading toward a forest fire raging out of control. Miles down the road, the killer stopped near a bridge. There, he picked up a handful of stones and placed them in the bag, holding the body pieces. He then wrapped a rope around the parcel, bent the license plates in half, and threw all the items in the river. Smiling, he watched the evidence sink.

Two jobs well done! Now for the dismemberment of the baby. Then all will be complete. My skills in disposing of bodies, and identifiable evidence will be heralded by future clients as justification of precautionary practices that will protect their invisibility . . . a very important reason for their willingness to pay the fees I charge.

CHAPTER 27

TIME TO LEAVE

The following morning, Doc and Dora came down the steps, lured to the living room by a television newscast. Shoe, leaning forward with a cup of coffee in hand, was engrossed by the reporter's announcement. Standing behind him, equally absorbed, were Giant and Windy.

"Finally, after three local engine departments extinguished the raging fire, all that remained were the trunks of some of the finest trees, two unidentified bodies, and a possible Chevrolet Monte Carlo.

As the investigation continues, it appears the bodies may be the result of murders, with one man hung and the second killed in a car explosion. A partial hangman's noose has been found near the first body, and an accelerant is believed to have been applied to both the second man and the automobile in which he sat.

As more evidence is uncovered, Channel 11—The First and Best in News Coverage—will keep you informed."

"What do you think?" Shoe asked of no one in particular.

"The Monte Carlo isn't in the neighborhood," offered Windy.

"What's that mean?" asked Doc.

"The house has been under surveillance," replied Shoe. "First, a Toyota and a Monte Carlo then a Buick and the Monte Carlo! Now, both the Toyota and Chevy are gone. What about the Buick, Windy?"

"It's down the street. Returned late last night!"

"Obviously, we've got visitors. Unwelcome ones at that!" offered Shoe. "Dora! Doc! I think we need to give thought to leaving here. With six men on hand, everyone, including Stacey, is perfectly safe. But too many eyes are watching us. We need to lose these guests—permanently. For your sake and Stacey's! We don't know who or how many are involved, but obviously someone, possibly with powerful connections, has an interest in . . . and I'm guessing . . . It's Stacey."

"Stacey! Why her?" asked Dora.

"The break-in the other day was well planned. And we were lucky! While your cards foresaw it, our arrival couldn't have been timelier. Martha is due for release today. Windy, you know the clothes she likes. Toss them, along with some cosmetics and toiletries, in a suitcase or two. When we get to where we're going, I'll bankroll her needs. The rest of you, pull together what you want and take your bags to the garage.

"In a couple of hours, Giant, you, and Windy, load the luggage in the Lincoln. Drive to a rental and pick up another car, one to be dropped off at a sister location somewhere away from here. Transfer the luggage to the rental, and park it in a lot at the edge of town. The two of you come back in the Lincoln and get me. We'll go to the hospital and pick up Martha. Tonight, the seven of us will crowd into the Lincoln and slip out of town.

"At the parking lot, Windy and I will ride in the rental and lead the rest of you in the Lincoln to our next home."

"And where will that be?" asked Dora.

"Temporarily in the city, but later, another property will become permanent."

"I appreciate your concern for Stacey, Doc, and me," interrupted Dora, "but you're assuming control without even asking for our input? Our opinions."

Staring at her, Shoe responded quietly, "You're right! You should have your say, but understand I don't need any extra attention. While I have no concern about my safety or the safety of anyone in this room, I don't intend to remain here. This investigation will continue, and who knows what direction it will take. While we have airtight alibis, I attract attention. Attention I don't need. Attention I don't plan on having.

"Since meeting you, Dora, I've become a convert. I believe in your ability to see the hidden secrets of the Arcana. And because of that,

I'd like to have you near, knowing where you are so that I can reach out to you when I want a reading.

"And equally important is the affection I have for your Stacey. Not since my daughter—God rest her soul—have I been so drawn to a child. I'd like to self-appoint myself as her godfather and be in a position to help guide her into adulthood. Yet as much as the three of you mean to me, I have myself and others—two companies full of people—to consider. I will not fail either them or myself by going against my better judgment. It's your call! Follow me and remain protected. Or move out of this house tonight and be on your own. The three of you! Your choice! Your decision!"

Silently, Dora stared at her host.

"Choice? Not much of a choice as I see it. You've been good to us and never went back on your word or your promises. And because of that, I trust you, just as you trust my cards. I'm just not used to someone else controlling my future. I've always been in charge. But now with Stacey, it's more difficult to move blindly ahead. And I won't. I'd be a fool. Understand this, however! If at any time, I feel it's in Stacey's and my best interests to go off on our own, we will. You're watching out for others. So am I."

"Fine, we understand each other! Now, start packing! We'll leave tonight. Windy! Giant! Once you're finished packing for Martha and yourselves, get me. We'll go to the hospital and pick her up. I'll call the chief of staff and issue instructions for her to be ready and waiting."

Everyone began filing out of the room with the exception of one. "And why are you waiting?" Shoe asked.

Smiling, the person said, "Just thinking! Considering what Dora's readings have meant to you and how that little girl has buried herself in your heart, I'm wondering if you'd really leave them, if Dora decided not to accept your conditions."

Slowly, Shoe's frown turned to a smile. "I guess now you'll never know, will you, Windy?"

CHAPTER 28

HIDE AND SEEK

The one who was always present but never seen entered the front door. "Mr. Shoe, the Buick just left. We have twenty-five minutes."

Punctually, at five thirty every evening, the unknown one drove to a fast-food restaurant, picked up a meal, and ate it in his car on Hill Crest Drive.

"Let's go," ordered Shomazzi. "We need to hurry." The six adults and Stacey crowded into the Lincoln and left the house.

At 5:56 p.m., the Buick returned, and the vigilante enjoyed his hamburger, fries, and coffee while watching electronically lighted rooms in the empty house. By seven o'clock, he was becoming anxious. There was no visible movement.

Dialing Shoe's house from his car phone, it rang eight times before the man disconnected the call. Aided by the dark night, he slipped into the yard, sneaking around the house looking in windows. No movement!

At the backdoor, he picked the lock but was unable to enter because of a chain. This he skillfully unfastened and entered. Moving cautiously and quietly at first, he became bolder as he visited every room, even the office which he unlocked. The desk drawers and dresser were empty. Bedroom closets, though having some articles of clothing, had many empty hangers. The basement and garage were bare. The quarry had disappeared.

Livid, he returned to the Buick with no indication of where they may have gone. *Jensen will be pissed. Best I don't let him know until I come up with something, and it better be damn soon.*

* * * * *

The Lincoln and rental were parked at one of Shomazzi's favorite Italian restaurants. The host, holding Stacey, ignored his dinner while the others conversed between bites.

"With the Campbell theft and some labor union disagreements, I have to be in the office tomorrow and possibly the next day. You'll spend tonight and probably tomorrow night, as well, at my Long Island residence, but don't unpack your belongings. We may be leaving on short notice. While the guy driving the Buick has been given the slip, it may only be temporary. If either he or the people with whom he works prove resourceful, he might very quickly come back into the picture. So be prepared to leave on a moment's notice."

"You still haven't told us where we're going," said Dora.

"I have a couple of places in mind. One in Florida on the east coast. Or possibly a small town in Georgia just across the Tennessee line south of Chattanooga. There are pluses for both. Once I've made up my mind, I'll let you know. Do yourself a favor and don't worry. Enjoy the food and wine. I'm content holding Stacey."

At the Albany Airport, the unknown one drove to the parking lot and transferred his possessions back to the Corolla. After he returned the Buick to the rental location, he walked back to the lot and drove the Toyota into the city.

Arriving, the assailant passed a construction site with Shomazzi equipment on location. Smiling but tired, he drove to a hotel, registered, and placed a call from the room.

An operator answered the phone and transferred his call.

"Mr. Shomazzi's office," a woman answered.

"Connect me with your president, please," said the unknown one.

"May I ask who this is?"

"It's Gregory Richardson," he lied. "I'm an attorney with Baxter, Bracket, and Reems. We have a client intending to sue Shomazzi Construction for noise and unsafe construction work at your Ninth Avenue installation. I'd like to discuss it with him."

"Mr. Richardson, Mr. Shomazzi is unavailable to take your call. Allow me to transfer you to our in-house corporate counsel, Mr. ...."

At that moment, as Shoe entered the office, the caller hung up.

The secretary, staring at the dead phone in her hand, evoked from her boss, "You seem perplexed, Anna?"

"I am, Mr. Shomazzi. A Gregory Richardson at Baxter, Bracket, and Reems called to speak with you about a potential lawsuit on the Ninth Avenue work site, and when I told him I'd transfer the call to John Jordan, he hung up. Strange, wouldn't you say?"

"Call BB&R. I've known Charles Baxter for years. I'll see what he has to say."

Minutes later, Shomazzi picked up his phone.

"Shoe, this is a pleasant surprise. Usually Jordan bends my ear. For you to call, it must be important!"

"Hello, Charles! Hopefully, this conversation can be easily resolved. My secretary just received a message from one of your attorneys about a potential lawsuit on the Ninth Avenue construction site. Bring me up-to-date."

"Lawsuit against Shomazzi Construction? Not that I know of. But then again, I may not have been briefed. We're rather busy right now. Who was the attorney?"

"A Gregory Richardson!"

"Gregory Richardson? Not here at BB&R! We have no Richardson. Could your girl have misunderstood?"

Thinking for a moment, he responded, "If she did, it's the first time in twenty-four years. Forget that I called. Besides, I don't need any more of your 'long-term, low-rate, favored-client hourly charges.'" He laughed.

Hanging up, he rang his secretary and had her book the earliest available flights to Miami Florida for six adults. The gambler decided the infant, Stacey, could fly free, comfortably seated on her mother's lap. Then he phoned the others and told them to be ready for a departure either later that day or in the early morning.

* * * * *

At the hotel, the man with many names put in a wake-up call for seven o'clock that evening. It had been days since he'd slept in a bed, and an eight-hour nap was going to be a pleasure.

Awakening to the hotel operator's call, the unknown one telephoned room service and ordered supper. As he finished shaving, the bellman knocked and delivered his dinner.

Wolfing down the food while dressing, the assailant vacated the room twenty minutes later.

Retrieving his car, he drove to an all-night parking lot three blocks from a multistory structure where the Shomazzi offices were located. From there, he walked to the building, and proceeded down a ramp, through a lower-level garage, to a locked door.

With picks in hand, he mumbled, "Never a door I couldn't crack."

Seconds later, he entered and climbed one flight of stairs to another door leading to the main concourse. Opening it slightly, he saw two security guards playing gin rummy at their station opposite the locked main entrance. The next floor was divided into three sections: the first third filled with files and storage cabinets for the construction company, the middle third with desks for employees assigned to construction and trucking, and the remaining third with files and storage cabinets for trucking.

At the dark third-floor hallway, he found three large empty rooms: an employee cafeteria, a mail room, and what appeared to be a typing area.

The entire fourth floor held the computer center. Operating twenty-four hours a day, the night crew was updating reports and files along with other maintenance responsibilities. On the fifth floor was a vacated company reception desk with a curtain wall concealing individual cubicles where the day staff worked.

The sixth floor housed the executive offices for accounting, credit, purchasing, human resources, vice presidents in charge of construction and trucking, and specific staff personnel.

Occupying the seventh floor was the executive luncheon area, its kitchen and a large conference room. Finally, on the eighth floor, the uninvited one found what he wanted—Shomazzi's office, his secretary's office, and a second smaller executive conference room. Ignoring the latter, he picked the lock to Shoe's office and did a cursory check for information relating to Doc, Dora, and the baby. Finding nothing, he left the room. Anna's desk drawers also revealed nothing. The top of her desk was clean and neat. Only a telephone, computer, pen, Rolodex file, and desk calendar were present. Disappointed, he was about to leave when he noticed that the blank page appearing on her calendar was not for this day but the following one. Turning the page back a day, he discovered a handwritten reminder: *6TCAM*.

Pulling back Anna's chair, he sat and pondered the cryptic note. He copied it and pushed back his chair.

Better get going. Those guards are likely to have hourly rounds, especially with the computer center busy. Leaving by the back stairway, the uninvited one exited the door just as the elevator opened.

The killer returned to his hotel room and pondered the note. *Just what is this telling me? Being a secretary, it's obviously an abbreviated reminder. But what does it mean? What could be so important that . . . No! It can't be as simple as that!*

From his briefcase, a packet of papers was removed. A volume of information about Doc, Dora, and Shomazzi had been collected, beginning when Jensen first gave him the assignment. It was this type of thoroughness that contributed to his success as a hired killer, and for the large sum promised for an undiscovered kill, the man had to be methodical and precise.

One of the pages listed properties owned by the gambler: homes, cottages, and condos within the United States, Bermuda, and Europe. One condo in Miami popped off the page. From a telephone directory in his room, he dialed Capitol Airlines and learned that there were a total of four morning flights leaving LaGuardia the following day. Being coy, he assumed Vincent Shomazzi's identification and spoke to an agent feigning ignorance about the reservations his secretary made.

The agent responded, "We're holding six tickets in your name on LaGuardia flight 5552 leaving at eight fifty tomorrow morning. Is there anything else you wish to know?"

Thanking the agent, the assassin decided on an early morning wake-up call with the hotel operator. *Too risky to chance some inquisitive airline inspector discovering the weapons and supplies I'll be needing in Miami, so best I drive. I'll get in bed now and have a good-night's sleep before starting my drive south.*

After breakfast the following morning, he telephoned Walter Jensen.

"Have you the package?"

"No, and that's why I'm calling. There have been complications, and I'm on my way to Florida to resolve them."

"Complications? Florida? What in the hell's wrong? And when will you have the package?"

"It's best we don't discuss this over the phone. Better eyeball to eyeball! Can you be at the Miami Airport day after tomorrow? I'll meet you there."

"Miami Airport? You've got to be joking. I'm running a multibillion-dollar corporation and just can't go hopping around the country on a whim. My company needs me, and the board won't tolerate it!"

"There are other things your board won't tolerate. Things like the lost package. And more! This may be an inconvenience, but there are a lot of things you need to know. And it's worth your time and mine for the two of us to sit down and talk things over. Otherwise, start thinking about another messenger."

"Hold on now! Just hold on! No rash decisions! I'll be there. Give you a call tomorrow night with my arrival time. But this meeting sure as hell better be productive."

CHAPTER 29

THE MEETING—THE DECISION

Jensen entered the arrival lounge at 1:05 p.m. and handed his carry-on bag to the assassin.

"I have a car in the short-term lot," said the assassin. "Best we go directly to your condo and talk, unless you want to eat first?"

"I can eat anytime. I want to find out what's taking you so long, and how we can quickly find and eliminate the kid."

When they reached the lot, the unknown one opened the passenger door of a Pontiac Bonneville Brougham. "Thought you had a Toyota."

"You and a dozen others! I'm leasing this for a couple of days, and then I should be able to leave this miserable state and go where I can enjoy myself. Buckle up! I've wasted enough time and plan on moving fast."

At Jensen's condo, the host removed a couple of beers from the refrigerator.

"I always keep a supply on hand. Have no munchies. Threw out what was here three weeks ago."

"A beer's all I need. As I said, I'm not interested in wasting time. Let me bring you up to date! Earlier this week, I'm watching the Shomazzi house, trying to figure out how I'm going to get hold of the baby without being seen a second time. Happens there's another guy interested in the old man's house as well. In fact, he left his car—a Chevrolet—and was sneaking around the house looking for something. As I sat there, a second dude comes up the street and takes an interest in this guy's car. He even attempts to break into it. Well, I'm curious, so I go up to him and take him by surprise. The guy was stupid. He tried to stab me with a switchblade. Not only was he dumb, but he was a loser when it came to handling a knife. Probably the only thing he ever cut was a piece of meat. Anyway, to shorten this tale, I knock him out and take him to some woods. After a little pressure and some scaring tactics, he tells me one hell of a tale."

And the killer reveals all he learned: Freddie's story about the dumpster; the discovery of the package by Dora and Roscoe; the deaths of Roscoe and Grape Juice; and Freddie's capture by the Monte Carlo owner.

"Turns out the Chevy owner is a cop."

When mentioning this, the killer was lifting the beer to his mouth and never saw Jensen flinch.

Recovering, the contractor said, "Well, go on!"

Swallowing two more mouthfuls, he continued with the hanging. He then told how he conned O'Malley into following him to the woods, distracting him with Freddie's body before shooting him and destroying the evidence that could lead to the discovery of the vehicle's history and the identities of the dead people.

With the intentional overextended and barbaric explanation of the killings, the assassin closely watched the man's changing facial expression. Feeling the moment of uneasiness had been reached, he withdrew from his pocket the handwritten note he had discovered in O'Malley's glove compartment. Handing it to Jensen to read, he watched the man's eyes blaze.

"You killed the head of my security force? Why in the hell didn't you let me know who the guy was before you slaughtered him?"

"Why should I? You know how I play the game. You knew the rules before any agreement was reached—what I demanded. I made it clear that if you couldn't accept my conditions, then any arrangement, even one paying the sum you offered, was of no interest to me. Rule number one: I was to be in charge—free to move wherever I wanted and to do whatever I thought necessary. And to do it alone. But you couldn't have it that way. You had to have me shadowed, and I don't like that. I don't want others to know how I perfected what has made me the best in the business."

"Perfected? Best in the business? Well, how then did a baby, one held in your hands, get taken away? Yes, I agreed to pay you a hell of a lot of money. But instead, what am I receiving? Dead bodies of people who are unimportant."

"Oh! Your daughter-in-law, the swimmer! She was unimportant? O'Malley, your head of security! He was unimportant! Freddie and those witnesses who have been complicating this mission. They were unimportant too? Maybe, we should reassess the entire arrangement? It's not too late for me to walk away. I have several offers waiting for my skills. I'll accept payment of what is due and go my way—immediately."

"You wouldn't do that. If word gets around that some jobs are too difficult to be finished, that you can't be relied on to carry out your contracts, others might start wondering if you're as good as you claim. How many interested buyers would then be waiting in line for the delivery of your goods?"

"Don't you threaten me? If I walk and others find out about it, I'll know you're the source, and I'll come after you. And Jensen, that won't make for a long pleasant life. So open your mouth and plan on spending the rest of your days looking over your shoulder, fearing what will happen. Something less swift and more painful than what happened to Freddie, O'Malley, or your daughter-in-law. Something like broken bones, crushed testicles, and gouged-out eyeballs. And other pleasant things I won't bother to describe. Do I make myself clear?"

"Yes . . . Yes! I've got the message. Forget what I said. Living that kind of life is not what I want. You have my word. I won't say anything! Let's put this whole misunderstanding behind us. I was wrong using O'Malley. A big mistake! One more person learning something that shouldn't have been known. And compared to you, an amateur! Go about doing whatever is necessary! I'll step back, keep quiet, and stop pestering you. Instead, call me whenever you have something you want me to know. Okay? How's that? That'll satisfy you, won't it?"

The killer stared at Jensen. The menace in his cold black eyes sent a chill through the CEO's spine.

"I don't know. I'm not certain I can ever trust you again. How do I know you won't sometime—in a week, a month, or even a year—break my rules once more?"

"I won't! You have my word! I . . . I'd be too frightened. To prove what I say, I'll up the ante! I'll . . . sweeten the pot! Give you double! Just do what you have to do. Please? Just do it!"

The room remained silent. Finally, the killer spoke, "Okay! You have a deal. But know this. I'll be watching you. If I ever have reason to question your actions—on anything—we won't have a second discussion. I'll cause so much pain your death won't come quick enough."

* * * * *

"Thanks, Remy!"

"Certainly, Mr. Jensen, anything you want, just ask."

The flight attendant handed him a second Martini, but before she even reached the row behind him, he had wolfed down part of it. Staring at the half-empty glass, he set it down on the tray in front of him.

Oh, the mistakes I've made. I should have never hired him. He's a madman with no consideration, no regard for another human's life. And no sooner had we finalized the contract, I knew what kind of psychopathic killer he was. Even then, I could have bought out his contract. He knew so little. Only that I wanted an infant located. Not why? Not what I planned? But now it's too late . . . too late to have even accepted his offer today. He knows the secret. He knows why she needs to die.

I can't believe I, Walter Jensen, president of a Fortune 500 Corporation, could make such a mistake. And then I compound the mistake today with a foolish, fucking threat. No way can I let him go. I can't afford to have this secret known. I'd be a disgrace. To my friends, to the community, throughout the industry! The industry? What about the company? Would it even survive?

Oh, Jensen! What a fucking fool you are.

"Remy! Remy! Bring me another. Better yet, make it a double."

* * * * *

Back in Miami, close to a piano in a popular cocktail lounge, the overlooked man of many names tapped his fingers rhythmically to "What Kind of Fool Am I?" Sipping a Johnny Walker Gold Label, he wondered. *Can I trust you, Jensen? Have I been stupid in agreeing to this new arrangement? I hope for your sake I'm not. But be assured, I'll be watching. If you cross me, you'll become an example to others. No one fucks with me!*

CHAPTER 30

THE SECOND ATTEMPT

Within the residential condominium that housed Shomazzi's fiftieth-floor suite were a variety of shops along with a popular four-star restaurant that attracted people from all over the city.

"Welcome to *Le Trésor Coffre*. May I be of help?" asked the garment sales clerk.

The customer smiled, shook his head, and scanned the shop for merchandise. Displayed on several gondolas were apparel items. Selecting two articles, the assassin went to the cashier, paid, and placed the folded bagged items in his outer coat pocket. He then exited the store for the elevator.

Arriving on the fiftieth floor, he walked to an emergency door, entered, and waited. Twenty-seven minutes elapsed. Shoe and his party finally left the suite. The unknown one watched the group enter an elevator on way to the restaurant. Their arrival prompted the maitre d' to attentively usher Shomazzi and his party to a favorite table.

Seeing how other diners were groomed, Doc—wearing an open-collar shirt and sport coat—excused himself and returned to the bank of slow-moving elevators that were receiving and discharging people on the upper levels.

On the fiftieth floor, the assassin carried his satchel to the suite's front door where he quickly picked the lock. Inside, he studied every room before entering Stacey's bedroom.

Behind the crib was a locked window and screen facing a porch that extended past two adjacent bedrooms. Moving the crib, the intruder opened the locked window and carefully loosened two side clips that secured the screen to the window frame. Not removing the screen, he left it installed but unfastened. Closing the window and leaving it unlocked also, he pushed the crib to its original location. About to leave, he saw the front door open. The unnamed killer ducked into Stacey's bedroom closet, sliding a less than fully quiet, loose-fitting door to within an inch of closing. Through the crack, the intruder observed Doc.

In his bedroom, Doc was changing his shirt when he thought he heard a noise. Stopping, he listened but could not identify any more sounds. Retrieving a tie and walking out of the room, he scanned the living room and two other bedrooms before entering Stacey's room.

The assassin withdrew from his pocket Freddie's knife and snapped open the blade. Doc headed toward the closet, stopped, glanced around the room, but failed to see the slightly open closet door. Standing in front of a wall-hanging mirror, he fashioned a Windsor knot in the tie selected. The assassin, alert and ready to drive the knife into the homeless man's body, waited. Doc smiled at his appearance in the mirror, turned, and returned to the main room before leaving through the front door unaware that he had not been alone.

The nameless killer silently followed to the entrance and peeked down the hall as the elevator door closed. Leaving the suite, he exited through an emergency door where he wedged a chair under the knob. He ascended one flight and arrived at another door, one leading out to the roof. There he placed his bagged purchases in an obscure corner before going outside. The bar and garden area, normally overcrowded with chairs and people, were empty.

Around the perimeter was a steel-safety railing. The intruder moved to a spot directly above the Shomazzi porch. Other than the automobile traffic below, few people were outdoors in the late-afternoon heat.

From his satchel, the assassin removed a rope and tied it to the reinforced railing. Dropping the loose end, it fell to the porch fifteen feet below. He smiled, hoisted the rope, and walked to a lounge chair where he lit a cigarette and began to think.

Tonight, after everyone's asleep, I'll lower myself, remove the screen, reach in, and muffle the brat's mouth before lifting her up out of the crib. Then byebye problem child as she falls fifteen stories to the street. Even if someone from inside sees me, I can scamper, hand over hand, up the rope, a mere fifteen feet. I'll secure the loose end of the rope under my belt to prevent anyone from following. With that floor's emergency door wedged shut, I'll be down the steps and out of the building before others can enter a slow-moving elevator. Not foolproof but doable, even with an unlikely intruder.

* * * * *

Two hours slipped pleasantly by. Shomazzi and his party savored their five-course meals, enjoying each other's company.

At the end of dinner, Shoe, again cradling the sleeping Stacey in his arms, said, "I think the princess should be in her crib. Martha, carry her to the room while I settle the bill."

Inside the suite, people moved to their respective rooms.

"Doc, Dora! Join me on the porch. The stars and moonlit sky are a sight to behold."

From the roof, the killer observed the three delighting in the evening beauty, amid cigar smoke and a pleasant conversation. After twenty minutes, the group entered the suite, and the sliding glass door closed. Thirty-seven minutes ticked by. The rooms began to darken. Another thirteen minutes elapsed. The assassin removed a bandanna from his satchel, wrapped it over his nose and mouth, and tied it securely around his neck. Over his head, he put on a stocking cap and pulled it firmly down, preventing it from blowing off in what was now an offshore ocean breeze.

Dropping the rope over the railing, he, hand over hand, descended to the porch below, pressing athletic shoes against the wall to control the speed of descent. Quietly, his feet touched the porch. All the rooms were dark, except for the one adjacent to Stacey's bedroom. The killer avoided that window.

He removed the screen, placed it on a lounge chair, and slowly raised the window. In the crib lay the sleeping girl. Reaching down, he stretched to take hold of her. She squirmed and let out a whimper. Lifting her, he moved his hand over her mouth to prevent further sounds. Unexpectedly, the door opened, and he heard Martha whisper to someone behind her, "Don't turn off the light. Once I find my book, I don't want to stumble in the dark." Seeing the intruder, she screamed, "It's he! It's he!"

The kidnapper dropped the baby in the crib, turned, and grabbed the rope. Giant pushed Martha aside and, along with Windy, dashed to the window.

Seeing the athletic intruder climbing rapidly hand over hand up the rope, he shouted, "Giant, the guy's going to the roof."

Giant bolted out the door, but his progress was slowed by the presence of Shoe, Doc, and Dora. Getting them to retreat took a moment with the big man racing to the main entrance where he unchained the door before throwing it open.

At the emergency exit, he found the entrance inaccessible. He turned and dashed to the elevator. Punching the up button repeatedly, the carrier finally arrived, and he rode it to the roof.

The intruder had by then dashed across the roof stripping his body of the hood, bandana, and shirt which he had thrown in a trash barrel. He exited the door and picked up his purchases, a brightly colored sport shirt and gaudy beret. Casually, he walked down the steps, buttoning the shirt, combing his hair, and donning the flashy cap. On the thirty-seventh floor, he entered a down elevator.

With no one on the roof, Giant descended the steps two and three at a time. At the main floor, he found Windy. Together, they scanned the lobby and outdoors. But they were too late. Earlier, a group of six people had strolled out of the hotel. In the center was a man wearing a colorful shirt and gaudy beret, tilted in a rakish style. But he was now long gone having disappeared into the night.

CHAPTER 31

THE IDENTIFICATION

In the living room, Dora, rocking Stacey in her arms, listened to Martha repeatedly say, "It was he, it was he. I know it was the same man who attacked me in Saratoga. I know it! I know it was he."

Doc and Shoe looked on with disbelief. Windy, who had been closest to the intruder, asked in a quiet, sympathetic voice, "Martha, how can you be so certain? He had a neckerchief around his face and a cap covering his hair. How can you be sure it's the same man?"

"Those eyes! Those black, violent eyes! I'll never forget their menacing look when he hit me. Never will I forget those eyes nor his face."

All remained silent. Finally, Dora spoke.

"Doc, take Stacey! Put her down. I think she's calm enough for a good-night's sleep.

"Shoe, have you any paper? And several pencils?"

"Yes, a drawer full of them! Why do you ask?"

"I have an idea! Other than when we were in Saratoga, it's been a number of years—many, many years in fact—since I've done what I hope I can do now. But it's worth a shot. Leave Martha and me alone at the kitchen table, and let's see if we can recreate a pencil sketch of this bastard."

And they began. With patient prodding, Dora recreated the assailant's face. It took a number of drawings to finalize the forehead, cheeks, and chin to look as Martha remembered them on the day of the attack. Then the nose and mouth! After many sketches and much erasing, the results were acceptable. But when it came to the eyes, a part of the anatomy that often proves difficult to recreate precisely, Martha's description was so explicit that Dora sketched them to the woman's satisfaction, rapidly and faultlessly.

With a deft hand and a careful eye for detail, Dora shaded the assailant's hair, jaw, and chin with proper tones of black, highlighting his swarthy five o'clock shadow and full head of hair. Giving the picture to Shoe, he passed it through a photocopying machine producing duplicates. Nearly, seven hours had passed from the time Dora and Martha began the apparition of the unknown assailant. Now, Giant, Windy, and the others knew who they needed to find.

* * * * * * *

Back at his hotel room, the assailant reflected upon his interrupted visit. *Once again, I've been stopped. If this keeps up, Shomazzi, his minions and guests will recognize me. Did I disguise myself well enough? That same broad I encountered at the Shomazzi house in Saratoga Springs saw me today. She yelled something. What was it? Oh yes, she said, 'It's he, it's he.'*

How could she have known? I was totally disguised. The bandanna! The cap! Not enough of me to be seen! Yet she yelled, 'It's he, it's he.' Did the others coming into the room see enough to know me, to recognize me if we meet again? I wonder. Maybe it's time to be cautious.

Going to a drugstore, he purchased hair coloring and sunglasses. Over the next four days, he remained secluded, calling room service for food and newspapers and sitting in front of the television. By the evening of the fourth day, he looked at himself in the mirror. His normally swarthy face, unshaven since the day before the attempted kidnapping, now had a healthy beard and mustache. Taking scissors, he trimmed his hair. Carefully, he applied coloring to his head, beard, and moustache, aging himself with streaks of gray. Donning sunglasses, he smiled. *You're damn good-looking for someone newly born.*

CHAPTER 32

I DO

All was quiet! Stacey, with her ever-present baby smile, was sound asleep, having pleasant dreams that pushed aside the horrors of the night. Martha was in her bedroom reading, and Giant and Windy were taking a final stroll around the building premises and condominium floors to be certain no unexpected visitor was lurking.

Shoe waved good night and walked to his room.

"Good night, Doc! See you in the morning!"

"Before you turn in, Dora, come out here on the porch. There's a sight you have to see."

"Oh, Doc, how lovely!"

The clear black sky was filled with stars, and a full moon cast light on the earth.

"God's artistry to behold!"

"Dora, that's a side of you I've never witnessed. Five, six years, I've known you and never have you given reference to the Almighty. Is there a theological side to you that remains hidden?"

"As I once told you, Doc, I have my secrets. As a young girl, I never missed church services. Even until recently, I went, not too often I admit, to various Christian services to reflect and pray. More than a few passages from the Scriptures are silently spoken daily, with thanks given to the Almighty every night for his Divine presence."

"You can't realize how pleased I am to know this. As a boy, my parents attended mass every Sunday, and I with them. My spiritual foundation was enhanced during my studies and subsequent years of medical practice. To witness birth, the fertilization of an egg; the creation of a fetus; the development of the human body with hands and legs, eyes and ears, heart and brain is extraordinary to me. And then the miracles I've witnessed! Lives restored through medical breakthroughs and surgical procedures! Not just mine but others. People, destined to die by historic precedence, recovered to live many good years. Oh yes, I believe in God. What we have, he has given us.

"Take these last few weeks as an example. The discovery and adoption by you of Stacey, the intertwining of you and her, Shoe and me, Windy, Martha, and Giant! Then, the protective care given to her during these harrowing experiences! All of these are gifts, and those gifts have been provided through his Divine power. I truly believe this. With all my heart and soul and mental power!"

"And the future? Stacey's future? Do you believe she will continue to be guided and protected by the Almighty?"

For a moment, he stood silent. Then he took her hands in his and said, "Dora, he will. But there are things we must do. Shoe has businesses that need his presence. Already, he's devoted more time to us than his people can allow. We—you, me, and Stacey—need to be on our way. We have to make a future for ourselves. We must leave here and disappear. And when I say disappear, I don't mean just for a short while, but for a long time. We need to become nomads, finding a home that will be safe for a period, then moving to another and possibly another if necessary. We must eventually lose forever the people in search of this little girl."

"And just how will we do that? All this moving, I mean! How can we afford it? Sure, I've saved money from what I received from the querants but not enough to travel from state to state and to feed and clothe us in the way we've become accustomed."

"I know you can't. But I can, and I intend to help. During my years of practice, I made good money. Large amounts of money! Money I was able to save and invest! Money, aside from the dollars we've used in recent weeks, that still remains available. Even without your help, there is enough to carry us for two or three years! Possibly longer! Time to get established!

"I'm willing to share this with Stacey and you. But there is something I want in return. I want your name on a legitimate marriage license."

"Doc! Doc, am I hearing what I think I'm hearing? Are you proposing to me?"

"I am, Dora. I'm in love with you and have been for some time. And I love Stacey. As a family, we'll no longer be two people making individual decisions that are suitable for only one or two of us. Instead, you and I will make collective decisions, those that are best for a family. Our family! Together, nothing can stop us."

Dora was dumbfounded.

"I never knew you cared."

"Oh, I do, Dora. I do! Please marry me?"

"Yes, yes, yes!"

And she embraced him, kissing him passionately for the first time.

* * * * *

The following morning, at breakfast, the couple made their announcement.

"I'm delighted," responded Shoe. "This is good for both now and the years ahead. So tell me your plans! Where will you go, and what will you be doing to fulfill your needs and desires?"

Dora and Doc stared at each other with neither making a comment.

"I see! You haven't finalized everything yet. Well, you need to and quickly. Someone obviously has an interest in Stacey. Who that is and whether he is acting alone or with someone remains unknown. What we do know, however, is that the person or persons' intentions are both life threatening and near at hand. In my line of work, I've had experience not only escaping the uninvited but achieving ways to gain what was needed. So if you want some guidance, I'll gladly help. Together, we can discuss what to do and how to do it."

CHAPTER 33

WE DO AND HOW WE DO IT

For several hours, the bearded man sat motionless in his car. Observers might think him asleep; his eyes, masked behind dark aviator sunglasses, remained unseen. Yet they never strayed from the revolving door leading into the building where the Shomazzi suite was located.

Through the door stepped Giant. He scanned both sides of the street—north and south—his stare moving inattentively past the Bonneville. Reentering the door, he returned, leading Shoe, Doc, and Dora. As the Lincoln left the underground garage, it circled up the driveway, stopping at the entrance. Windy, the driver, and Giant opened passenger-side doors for the party.

The observer smiled! *That's it! Go away! Let me finish what I need to do!* Reaching for the door handle, he removed the ignition keys.

"Shit," he mumbled.

The car pulled away with Giant standing alone at the entrance. *Damn! Delayed again!*

Reinserting the keys in the ignition, he whipped the car into an illegal U-turn, causing drivers in both directions to lay angry, hands upon their vehicles' horns.

Giant's attention was attracted, and he watched curiously as the Bonneville followed in the same direction as the Lincoln.

About twenty blocks later, the Lincoln came to a stop, and the three passengers left the car and entered a department store. With parking along the road unavailable, the pursuer's only recourse was to follow the Lincoln. Further down the road, Windy pulled into a Shell Station and filled the tank with gasoline. He watched with interest a Pontiac Bonneville passing the station and pulling into a vacant spot along the curb.

Years of experience, both as a driver and bodyguard, schooled Windy into remaining conscious of his surroundings. After dropping off the passengers at the department store, he drove sporadically, accelerating the Lincoln and decelerating to the frustration of other drivers anxious to arrive wherever they were heading. Yet one pursuing vehicle—a distant Bonneville—reacted similarly to the Lincoln, holding Windy's attention.

Paying for the gasoline, Windy decided to take a sightseeing trip of Miami, meandering for miles along the crowded streets into and out of both residential and business areas.

Meanwhile, Doc, Dora, and Shoe walked across the main floor of the department store, exiting an entrance on the opposite side. Hailing a taxicab, they rode to the county Office for Vital Records and applied for the marriage certificate. Returning to the store, Dora took charge.

"This is a big day in my life, and I'm going to do it right. I'm going shopping for my wedding dress, and I expect you, Doc, to at least buy a new shirt and necktie."

They parted company and, in less than two hours, met at the main entrance, boxes in hand.

"You're going to be so proud of me," exclaimed Dora. "I have this lovely off-pink jacket and skirt with a smashing scarlet silk blouse and matching shoes. You just won't be able to say 'I do' fast enough. And what's in those boxes you have?"

"Well, 'boss,' I did as instructed. In fact, I splurged. I bought a new white shirt, a blue blazer, and a blue-and-gray regimental stripe tie that will go with some decent gray trousers I already have. We'll be a gorgeous twosome." And the three burst into laughter.

Nearly ten minutes later, the Lincoln arrived with the Bonneville not far behind.

"Without turning, know that we're being followed," mentioned Windy.

"How long?" asked Shoe.

"I'm not sure! I caught sight of the car after dropping you off. I'm guessing he didn't follow you because there were no convenient parking spots. So I gave him a tour of the city to keep him from learning what you were doing. From the boxes in your hands, he'll probably think you were only shopping. So now, Boss, what shall we do?"

"Go back home and get Giant! We'll finalize travel plans."

During their discussion, Dora and Doc bantered around a number of cities, finally focusing on two—Chicago and Washington DC. Doc preferred the former because he had practiced medicine there and felt he could renew acquaintances with former colleagues and friends. Dora was in favor of DC, having lived and spent time in Baltimore, Alexandria, and the surrounding areas before leaving her irascible and, at times, violent parents for life on the streets. Yet in spite of her youthful problems, she retained fond memories she never wanted to lose.

After hours of conversation, sometimes explosive and unrestrained, Doc relented to Dora, determined to have a life bonded in harmonious agreement.

CHAPTER 34

THE ESCAPE

Giant and Windy carried luggage down from the suite and packed it in the Lincoln. When the evening turned dark, Dora, Doc, and Shoe exited the building's entrance and walked down the street in the direction of the Bonneville. The tracker visually followed their movements. Behind him, the Lincoln exited the underground parking lot and turned the opposite way, unseen by the assailant.

Arriving at the train station, Windy parked the car and made several trips into the depot, carrying luggage from the car. After storing it in lockers, he went to the ticket window and purchased room accommodations on a morning Silver Meteor departing for the nation's capitol four days later.

On the third day, a justice of the peace conducted the wedding ceremony in the Shomazzi suite. Afterward, Shoe hosted a reception for the newlyweds, his three employees, and godchild in a private room adjacent to the four-star restaurant. Beef Wellington, champagne, a wedding cake, and two elegant wrist watches made the evening unforgettable.

The following morning, the Lincoln pulled out of the garage with Windy maneuvering in and out of the traffic, down unpopular streets, trying to shake—unsuccessfully—the Bonneville. Mired in traffic, the family of three finally reached the station at 8:25 a.m.

Half running to the departing train's platform, they were met by Giant who had taken a taxi earlier, retrieved their luggage, and carried it to their private room. He hugged Dora, bid the three farewell, and walked to the Lincoln, slipping onto a seat behind Windy and Shoe.

The stalker wasted moments parking his car before dashing into the station. Looking on the board, he noticed that one train, the eight thirty, had just departed; a second, the eight forty, was about to leave in three minutes; and a third and fourth train, the eight forty-three and the nine ten, respectively, were announcing their boarding calls.

Racing down corridors and up a flight of stairs, he watched the second train—the eight forty Silver Meteor—pull away from the station. Across the tracks, he watched the eight forty-three close its doors and prepare to leave. Racing to the nine ten, he saw people boarding it and jumped on. Walking down the aisles, he looked for familiar faces. No one he had ever seen was present. Reaching the last car, the doors were about to close, and he exited.

Back at the station, he grabbed schedules and looked at the number of cities the four trains serviced—Tampa, Charleston, Raleigh, Richmond, Washington, New York, Philadelphia, and other cities in Southern, Northern, and Midwestern States. Where his quarry had gone, the assailant had no idea. But one thing was certain. His reputation in finding the baby was in jeopardy. Someway, somehow, he had to locate and destroy the infant.

PART II

INFANT TO ADULT

CHAPTER 35

EXPOSURE

The Silver Meteor approached the Washington terminal with Dora humming in Stacey's ear. She was happy, pleased with what was ahead.

But these good spirits were about to disappear. A crowd of people departed the train with available redcaps seized by more determined and aggressive travelers. With not a baggage handler in sight, the family of three remained alone in an empty car with more luggage than two adults could handle.

"You and Stacey remain here," grumbled Dora. "I'll go into the station and find a redcap."

Minutes passed! Workers with the railroad began cleaning the Pullman for its next scheduled departure. Doc, now anxious to leave, stepped onto the platform looking for Dora. Spotting her with a redcap, he motioned for them to hurry.

He handed Stacey to her mother and said to the redcap, "Take us to a locker where we can stow these bags."

"Why?" asked Dora.

"We don't know where we'll be living, and storing them will give us time to eat and look for someone who can recommend a decent motel. Once we have that, we'll move our stuff in and use the room as our headquarters while we search for a permanent place to live."

"Makes sense!" responded Dora, and they followed the redcap to the lockers.

Removing a fifty-cent piece, Dora offered it to the baggage handler. He looked at her, then at the half dollar and back to her. "Better keep it! You may need it more than me," he responded and walked away.

In the station's cafeteria, they ordered from the menu. Dora then asked to see the manager. The waitress pointed out a man, and the bride walked toward him, removing something from her purse. Doc watched with an amusing smile.

Dora spoke. The man shook his head. Again, she spoke; and again, he shook his head. But Dora refused to take his no for an answer. Instead, she went into what appeared to be a lengthy discussion, pointing to their table. The man finally relented and took what Dora offered.

When she returned, Doc said, "You're becoming proficient at that. Earlier today on the train and now in this busy dining room!"

"Well, Stacey does need to eat, and there's a kitchen and a stove in the back. No reason why they can't heat up some formula for our little girl. Besides, I have a half a dollar to give them."

As they sat eating, Doc, who had been watching people walk through the station, excused himself and approached a policeman. They spoke for several minutes while Doc jotted notes on paper. He then walked to a newsstand and bought several newspapers along with maps of the District and the residential areas of Arlington, Alexandria, and Baltimore.

Returning to the table, he told Dora, "A couple of miles from here is a motel. Supposedly inexpensive but clean. I'll get the bellman this time, and we'll take a cab. If the place isn't up to snuff, we'll find another motel tomorrow. In the meantime, we can study the papers and maps for rentals. Then we'll work out a plan on checking them out. One that is most convenient and least expensive."

The motel was in an older area of the District. Though somewhat less than what Doc wished to offer his bride, the room, though old, was clean. It offered two conveniences in addition to a telephone, air conditioner, and television—a small refrigerator and a two-burner range where formula could be prepared.

Dora, with washcloth and detergent in hand, scrubbed the kitchen area. Although the room had a double bed, there was no crib available, so Dora decided to use a large dresser drawer. She padded the bottom with towels, making a bed for Stacey, one that prevented her from falling to the floor.

"For a short time, this room will do, but I hope we can quickly find a permanent place," she said. Together, they began poring over the newspapers' for apartments and affordable homes to rent. Those of interest were cross-referenced to the area maps.

It was growing dark, and Stacey was asleep for the night.

"Across the street is a McDonalds," said Doc. "I'll get some hamburgers, fries, and coffee. Anything else you want?"

Receiving a no, he left and returned shortly with dinner.

Early the next morning, Doc went to a grocery store and purchased items for breakfast and lunch, as well as formula and necessities for Stacey. He planned to spend the day looking for a place where they could live but realized that one of them would have to remain in the motel with Stacey while the other looked at properties. Traveling and transferring from bus to bus would be the least expensive way but obviously not ideal for an infant needing uninterrupted sleep.

For three days, the two adults traded duties—one baby-sitting, while the other viewed potential places to live. Availabilities in Alexandria and Upper Arlington offered the greatest appeal. Though more expensive than they wanted to pay, the monthly rates were relatively equal to the rentals in Baltimore and the District.

Several major benefits became apparent. The nation's government attracted individuals, both foreign and domestic, who had need for temporary furnished lodgings for one or more months. To accommodate these people, well-appointed, completely furnished apartments were available on a month-to-month basis. These offered Doc and Dora more mobility and short-term "savings" from not having to buy furniture.

An Upper Arlington second-floor apartment with two bedrooms, bath, small kitchen, and a combination of living room and dinette captured their interest. For Stacey, they purchased a crib, layette, and other small necessities. They rearranged furniture in the second bedroom to provide an area for the crib and working space for the baby.

"Now I know what I've been missing all my life," offered Doc.

"And what's that?" inquired Dora.

"A family!" he responded.

* * * * *

An immediate responsibility recognized by the couple involved locating a pediatrician. After placing several inquisitive, answer-provoking calls, Doc found a clinic to his liking. Along with his daughter and Dora, the three met with the principal in charge, Dr. Timothy Bell. Doc asked if he and Dora might sit in and observe the examination. Bell welcomed their presence.

During the exam, Doc studied Bell attentively. He found the pediatrician to be a thorough, caring doctor, lifting and moving the infant as gently as a devoted father. As the procedures were performed, he spoke softly and reassuringly, eliciting the baby's smile which prompted favorable comments. But it was the thoroughness of Bell's procedures that convinced Doc that he had selected the right clinic.

As the examination progressed, Doc posed questions, ones about genetic disorders, possible skeletal abnormalities, congenital heart diseases, and other childhood ailments beyond the scope of this initial examination. Doc knew this but had an ulterior motive. He was judging Bell's answers, gaining reassurance that the pediatrician was the right doctor for his daughter. What Doc failed to anticipate, however, was Bell's mental reaction to his questions.

"I'm curious, Mr. ah"—looking at the questionnaire Doc had completed—"McDonald! Your questions are quite unusual. You wouldn't, by any chance, have had some medical training?"

Smiling, Doc replied, "I have."

"To what extent, may I ask?"

"I was a surgeon. Proctology and cancer-related conditions."

"Was?"

"Yes! Used to be but no longer!"

"Why no longer?"

Hesitating, Doc thought long and hard before answering.

What the hell! It's no secret. Many already know! Besides, holding back may not be in the best interest of our little girl.

Doc quickly reviewed how he had lost his license.

"That's a damn shame. I see your given name is Francis. Mine is Tim, and being two people with similar skills, I'd like you to call me Tim rather than doctor. Which would you prefer? Fran or Francis?"

"Your choice! I've answered to both. However, I must warn that I may not reply quickly to either. For years now, I've been called Doc by everyone who knows me. I'll admit, however, hearing Fran or Francis will be a blessing because every time someone shouts Doc, it brings back some memories that aren't pleasant to relive."

"Then Fran it will be! Mind answering another question?"
"Go ahead! Shoot!"
"If you're no longer practicing medicine, what are you doing?"
"Right now, nothing! The three of us have just relocated to the area, and I'm about to go looking for employment. Where? Doing what? I'm uncertain. But with the cost of living, I need to find something."
"Do you still have an interest in medicine?"
"With all the years I've devoted to my studies and practice, it's become a love I'll never lose. Yet becoming involved will never be. So now, I'm open to anything. Clerking in a store! Waiting on tables! Whatever it takes!"
"Well I hope you find something you enjoy. And speaking of satisfaction, I'm pleased to say Stacey is remarkably healthy. The two of you have taken good care of her. I'd like to see her in two weeks for the necessary inoculations. And if you can be present, Fran, I'd enjoy speaking with you again."
"Count on it, Doctor—Tim, that is."
As the three left the office, Bell stared at the closed door. Reaching for the phone, he dialed a number without hesitation.

* * * * *

After much forethought, the man of many names decided to call the contractor.
The phone rang twice.
"Speak!" the respondent commanded.
"Decided to bring you up to date on some recent events! The package and its carriers have disappeared."
"Disappeared? Not again? Where'd they go?"
"I won't lie to you. I don't know. But be assured, I'll find them. You have my word."
"Horse shit! If you don't know where, how can you be so certain?"
"This isn't the first package I've ever had to locate. And it will definitely not be the last. Always in the past, I've found what I went after. They're like treasures, and I love treasure hunts. I'm good at them, you'll see."
Jensen disconnected the call and sat seething. It had taken a self-restraining iron will not to explode and tell the man how he felt. *Shove*

your sorry-ass promises! How many times are you going to continue to botch this assignment, you fucking failure? Will you ever succeed?

But he didn't say any of those things. Vividly, he remembered their last confrontation and the threats the killer had conveyed. Fear of the man was overwhelming—the extremes he went to in abusing and violating his victims. Now Jensen had two problems: the eliminations of a little girl and the executioner hired to do the job.

CHAPTER 36

THE ROAD AHEAD

Eight days later, Doc, Dora, and Stacey returned to Bell's office. Following the inoculations, the pediatrician asked Francis if he could spare a moment.

"I've set aside ninety minutes before my next appointment, and I'd like to take that time to discuss something with you."

"Ninety minutes? You must have a lot to say."

"I do. But first, have you found any work?"

"Not yet! But I haven't been trying too hard. Since coming here, Dora and I have been looking for an apartment. Getting settled has been our first priority. Why do you ask?"

"Well, I have a proposition. Before telling you about it, you need to know a few things. Things about me and the proposition.

"I have a financial interest in a nursing home called *Comforting Care*. I own 55 percent of it. This clinic, however, limits my time to only superficial involvement at the home. My partner, the other 45 percent of the equation, is a businessman, a certified public accountant. His work with client taxes and their investment affairs limits the time he gives the home as well.

"How long have you been running it?"

"It's a new venture. Less than two years! It's doing fairly well but could and should do better. The limited success is mainly due to the way it's staffed and managed. So far, we rely primarily on fulltime nurses. There are three part-time nonresident doctors, men I've known for years, who are on call, supervise the nursing staff and perform necessary examinations. Obviously, this is not an ideal arrangement. Our revenues are limited as my partner continually reminds me. We need to pay our start-up costs, which are dear, due to my having refused to open with less than the ideal facility. We also need to meet our operating costs, which are prudently managed. And finally, we need to cover any emergency expenses, which have been unusually high. Profit is something yet to be realized. In fact, we're struggling to break even, and I can't afford to lose what I've invested. We have to find a way to make money."

"What's the alternative?" asked Doc.

"You'll discover I'm a gambler. Since meeting you, I've come to a conclusion. You impress me. You and I speak the same language. I need a pair of eyes and ears at the nursing home, full time. I know that. Yet I can't afford to pay for a manager. In fact, I don't even want the staff to know we have an overseer on hand. In our struggles to hold costs down, we've been skimpy on raises. New people, appearing as quasi, nonofficial managers, introduce unwanted questions and potential problems. But we do need an orderly. The nurses are constantly asking us to hire a new employee for janitorial duties. The present man has to be replaced. His work is slipshod, and nurses are undertaking his duties, work that is time consuming, undignified, and beneath their professional training but necessary for the healthcare standards required.

Bell hesitated. And the hesitation led Doc to say, "Go on! I'm listening."

"Well, I'm wondering. Does having a job . . . ? No skip that! Does medicine have such an appeal that you'd be willing to be an orderly with the potential—mind you, nothing promised, merely a potential—that if everything works out, a supervisory position could be in the future? That would allow you to cement a professional relationship with the staff as a co-employee, gain their confidences while surreptitiously observing the day-to-day operations and making certain there are no unforeseen inpatient problems existing. In conjunction with all this, I'd expect you to learn what needs to be improved so that *Comforting Care* will earn recognition as an ideal nursing home where patients receive unsurpassed medical care and attention."

"How can you be certain that I'm capable of what you need done? Oh, I heard you say you're a gambler. But you're placing a great deal of faith in someone unknown, not only by you but to a partner who hasn't even met me. It's possible he won't like me or even want me."

"He will. He's already accepted the idea. What makes our arrangement so perfect is a mutual trust in each other. He knows we need an insider looking into all the cracks and crevices. And he trusts me in finding that person."

"That's just it! How can you be certain? You hardly know me. Maybe the loss of my license goes further than what I've volunteered. You're placing faith and a financial investment in the hands of an unknown. I'd never do that!"

"Not completely unknown! Since meeting you, I've spent hours on the phone. I have more than a few connections with people who can find out what practicing physicians try to hide, including medical men. I've contacted the hospital where you performed the surgery, and I've spoken to physicians and nurses who worked with you. Oh, I've done my homework, and I'm convinced our meeting was meant to be."

"I'm amazed. You surprise me."

"Before you give me a decision, Francis, let's go into more detail about what will be expected by my partner and me and what you'll receive in compensation."

The discussion took longer than ninety minutes, delaying scheduled appointments. Doc was pleased with what he heard, and he accepted the position with new hope and positive expectations that had long since been dismissed from years on the street.

* * * * *

Doc embraced the assignment with an eagerness proving contagious to the staff at *Comforting Care*. Quickly, he became an accepted member of the "family."

Stacey was a happy infant—content with her timely feedings and the doting love of her parents as well as the solitude of her own private room.

Dora, in the beginning, held periodic sidewalk readings in Alexandria, Upper Arlington, the District, and occasionally the outskirts of Baltimore. One of the couple's early investments included the purchase of a pre-owned 1979 Ford F-100 custom pickup, allowing the newly licensed driver to transport her table, chairs, and signs to populated areas where she could engage people's interests in the metaphysical.

Three personally designed signs were attention-compelling attractions that pulled crowds to Dora's table. Each sign depicted a Major Arcana highlighting answers to essential subjects of popular interest. With the completion of a reading, Dora gave her querants several calling cards to distribute to friends who might also want to learn the unknown secrets in their lives.

Through word-of-mouth, Dora's prominence grew, enabling her to replace a sidewalk presence with prearranged appointments in a leased office near the apartment. This private setting gave Doc and Dora a more comforting sense of security not present in the open public surroundings but not the entirely confident safety they ultimately desired.

CHAPTER 37

THE GROWING YEARS

One . . . three . . . five . . . seven . . . .

"It's difficult to believe that in a week, Stacey will be eight years old. "Time is moving so rapidly," commented Dora.

Watching his little girl reach for the Tarot cards, Doc again repeated something his wife had heard him say time and time again. "How fortunate we are. This beautiful little girl will become not only a stunning lady, one breaking many men's hearts but a woman with skills far superior to others."

Of all you possess, my little darling, what have Dora and I contributed? Your beauty—the raven black hair, amethystine eyes, sculptured cheeks, and small curved nose—is obviously a genetic gift.

Stacey removed fifty-six Minor Arcana cards from the deck, shuffled them, and randomly placed each face down on the floor. Turning two at a time, she attempted to pair cards—two aces, two nines, two kings, and so on. When the numbers or face cards were not identical, she would turn them over and select two more. She was testing her ability to recall where specific cards were located, pair, and remove them, clearing the floor in as short a time as possible.

Even that brain of yours is a hereditary gift, but Dora and I can help develop your memory. I promise, Stacey, we'll do everything in our power to see that you excel with your God-given gifts.

"Dora, do you think our little girl has the same fascination with Tarot that you have?'

"Definitely, and don't be surprised if she becomes a reader too. Should that happen, she'll be a good one—better than me! Together, we have readings, and she exhibits the wisdom and intuitive powers vital to an oracle. Yet I'm not going to push her. It's her life to live, her choice to make."

"Speaking of choices, it's time the three of us leave. Grab her bag. I'll pull the truck around to the front."

Twenty minutes later, they parked at a children's training center. Stacey was animatedly happy. It was time to go swimming, and her joy was obvious as she pulled her mother toward the building's entrance.

Inside, she was jumping up and down excitedly, causing Dora to struggle to get her into a swimsuit. Running to the pool door, Stacey dashed through it, shouting to her instructor, "Ms. Thelma, Ms. Thelma, I'm here, I'm here!"

The woman smiled and said, "So you are, Stacey. Now you'll just have to be patient while the other boys and girls get into their suits."

Delay was not what she wanted, but she knew better than to fuss, so she sat at the edge of the pool, kicking the water with her feet.

As similarly aged children assembled, directions were given to them, and each instructor took charge of specific boys and girls. Thelma had three—Peter, Johnny, and Stacey—and the hour began. After they progressed through some required lessons, the youngsters became involved in pool events, assigned according to their skills. Peter, Johnny, and Stacey, along with five others, were selected for advanced swimming instructions. Today, they would attempt to swim freestyle the width of the pool.

Individually, they swam at the shallow end with Thelma walking by the side of each swimmer, stopping that child when it was apparent he or she could go no further. For Stacey, this was no challenge. She smoothly stroked her way from the west side to the east side and then reversed her way, swimming halfway back before tiring.

Smiling, Doc thought, *This athleticism doesn't come from Dora or me. I wonder who the hell your biological parents are.*

On the evening preceding her eighth birthday, Dora was sitting on the living room floor wrapping gifts when Doc entered with a package under his arm.

"That's a mighty pretty dress. She'll look adorable in it," commented Doc. "Be interesting to see whether she favors it over the gift I have for her."

As he opened his package, Dora exclaimed, "Not another badminton racket! That's the fourth one this year."

"Except this isn't badminton. It's tennis. The rackets she's had don't hold up. They aren't made for tennis balls, especially as hard as Stacey's hitting them. Now that she's bigger, she can wrap her hands around this handle. And with the joy she gets in banging balls against that wall outside, it's about time she starts using the proper equipment. My head hurts just thinking of the punishment those balls are taking."

At breakfast the following morning, Stacey opened the presents enthusiastically, leaving the racket until last. As soon as she saw it, she darted from the table, leaving a half-filled glass of orange juice and cornflakes untouched. Out of the apartment she fled, taking the elevator to the main floor.

In the back, behind the building, was a row of garages about thirty feet away from a brick wall. Ricocheting tennis balls off the bricks, she chased the bouncing spheres, smashing them over and over with follow-up shots. She tired quickly and sat on the ground to refresh. Then she attacked the wall again until her energy gave way to another sitting. This up-and-down movement continued until she heard her mother calling her to come and finish breakfast.

CHAPTER 38

WHAT LIES AHEAD?

Fifteen . . . sixteen . . . seventeen . . . eighteen years . . . .

Doc and Dora lived comfortably but not recklessly. For years, no one endangered their lives; the unknown one had seemingly disappeared. Yet the two never relaxed, always alert to who was around.

As Doc predicted, Stacey had become a beautiful teenager. High school seniors and college undergrads strived to win her attention. Yet the opposite sex had little appeal. Her interests were focused on what she did well.

As a member of the Honor Society and striving to remain number three in her class, she devoted much of the senior year to her studies—English, American history, French, physics, and calculus. She also scheduled time to a few preferred activities.

As an accomplished swimmer, she could effortlessly glide across the water, gracefully executing every stroke—freestyle, breaststroke, backstroke, and butterfly. When asked by her high school swimming instructor to join the *Aquatic Ballerinas,* the school's statewide prior year contender in precision swimming, she declined. Another activity dominated her interest—tennis!

Following school one afternoon, Stacey was behind the condominium slamming tennis balls against the brick wall when a resident drove into his parking space and walked behind the garage to investigate the recurring sounds. Fascinated, he stood silently, watching her stroke balls powerfully, alternating forehand and backhand while moving rapidly from side to side, returning balls to the wall.

Sensing eyes on her back, Stacey turned and smiled.

The man stepped forward and said, pointing over his shoulder, "I live here. While parking my car, I heard the tennis balls bouncing off the wall. It attracted my attention, and I came to watch. My name's Snow. Tom Snow."

Stacey smiled.

"I'd say, Mr. Snow, your name is out of place in Florida, the land of the hot sun. But still, it's nice to make your acquaintance. I'm Anastasia McDonald! Call me Stacey."

"Well, Stacey, it's my pleasure. You do indeed have a lethal forehand and backhand. Is a career in tennis a deep-seated passion?"

"Oh, no! This just lets me burn off excess energy. In fact, I've never been on a tennis court or had the opportunity to return balls from an opposing player. It's merely exercise."

Tom Snow looked at the girl in disbelief. While he had played some tennis, golf was more to his liking. But her intensity, her power told him that she had the potential to be really good.

"Well, that's too bad, Stacey! But keep up the practice. It obviously favors your appearance."

And although Tom Snow left, he did not forget the girl.

The following week, during lunch with an old friend, Tom mentioned seeing the girl attack tennis balls with authority.

"Jerry, I want you to meet her. She's unusually good."

"Come on, Tom! The last time we played tennis together, it was obvious that you didn't have the hang of the game. Now, you're telling me you've met the queen of the courts. I think you should stick with golf and real estate! Those you understand."

"You're right! I'm no good at tennis. But I do know talent when I see it, and this girl has potential. Just stop by my place tonight and watch her. She doesn't even need to see you. In fact, she may not want an old man of twenty-nine staring at her. Then, after a few minutes, I'll treat you to a drink. I've got some single malt Scotch that'll knock your socks off. I'll even buy dinner. You're single! You have nothing to do. Come on and humor me!"

"And just how do you know she'll be banging balls off the bricks tonight?"

"Because she always does. Every night this past week, she's been outside for an hour or more chasing the damn things. You have to see her!"

"Boy, there has to be something special about this gal. Why I'm letting you talk me into this, I don't know. Okay. I'll be by your place at five thirty. She better be good!"

That night, Jerry pulled into a visitor's parking spot and found Tom waiting.

"Come on! This way! Let's keep quiet because I don't want her to know we're watching. I want her to be natural."

Standing at the end of the garages and some distance away, the two watched Stacey hit, chase, and return balls ricocheting off the wall. But there was something else about her play Tom had not mentioned. Randomly spaced on the wall were seven white chalk-marked circles.

They were targets that she attempted to hit when returning the caroming balls off the wall.

"You're right, Tom. She's tenacious. Hits the ball with authority and moves rapidly. But it's her accuracy that impresses me. If she did just a couple of things differently, she'd be damn good. At least against a brick wall! Against an opposing player, who knows?"

"But will you do it for me?"

"Tom, she might not even be interested. She should have some say in this."

"Of course, the decision has to be hers. But at least you're willing. Come on! Meet her! And remain casual. I don't want her to think you're coming on to her.

"Stacey! Stacey! It's I, Tom. Tom Snow! Over here!"

Looking around, she saw him and waved. After banging one more ball off the wall, she turned toward the two men.

"Stacey, meet a friend. Jerry Forrest! Jerry, this is Stacey McDonald!"

Smiling and struggling to hold his attention on her eyes and not the rest of her anatomy, Jerry said, "My pleasure, Stacey." And he extended his arm for a customary handshake. "Seems you have a friend in Tom, and he wanted me to watch you attack the ball."

Stacey shook his hand and looked at one and then the other, wondering why the interest.

"I wanted you to meet Jerry. He's not only a friend but a former tennis pro who gave up that career to practice law. But as a member of the *Green Acres Golf and Racket Club,* he teaches members the finer points of the game. I told him about you, and he had to see if I was exaggerating."

"Quite obviously, he wasn't," replied Forrest. "Is it true you've never been on a tennis court or ever volleyed with anyone?"

"Afraid so," she smiled.

"Well, if you're interested, I'd be happy to schedule some time at *Green Acres* and give you a chance to run me around the court."

"That's really enticing, but I can't impose upon you that way."

"Don't be silly! It'll be my pleasure."

CHAPTER 39

DEATH REIGNS

Years had elapsed from the time the "package" had been lost. During the first and second year, Jensen spoke routinely with the hired killer, the man of many names, but each telephone call reported "no progress." While this disappointing news was unacceptable, the hired killer's attitude was more disturbing.

"The treasure's deeply buried," he often said, "and more time's required to locate it."

To these comments, Jensen held his tongue, refusing to voice his thoughts. *You're incompetent; your overrated abilities are nothing more than damnable lies, and now all I receive are excuses and unfulfilled promises.*

But a continuing fear paralyzed Jensen's mouth, and prudence compelled him to swallow his dissatisfaction and stifle the admonishments he wanted to voice.

Over time, the frequency of calls subsided to one and two a month, then to one a quarter and finally to no more than one or two a year. This silence forced Jensen to a decision, one he feared but gambled in making. He violated the assassin's rules with the staggered hiring of two additional firms to find the family of three.

As the days slid into weeks, Jensen began to worry. *Would the man of many names find out?* But he did not. And after several failing months by each company, Jensen paid what was owed and discontinued their services.

He was now free of fears. It had been seventeen years since the attacks occurred, and the family of three had totally vanished. Nothing had been heard about them, and nothing had been heard from them. Jensen was feeling safe. He believed that any early suspicions that once existed were now gone. He even convinced himself that the homeless couple probably never forewarned the girl she had been pursued.

Now that she's an adult, he surmised, *it's unlikely she's even aware anyone has an interest in her. No one will ever discover the hidden secret.* All but the assassin, that is.

The unknown was not easily mollified. To fail was not only unacceptable; it was something unknown to him.

From the time the assignment began, he had retraced his steps to cities where the family had lived—Miami, Saratoga Springs, and the streets of New York. Too often, they resulted in nothing more than excessive costs. The upshot: scheduled travel had to be approved in advance by Jensen, and the approvals required hard facts justifying the trips.

Such a restriction was unacceptable to the hunter. Intuitive trips on previous assignments had proven to be effective, and the man of multiple identities intended to continue doing what his gut told him to be right. However, there was also a second reason—one very important to him. The assassin enjoyed lavish living, and flexibility in travel often enabled him to visit out-of-the-ordinary places where padded expense accounts provided money to cover his extravagant needs.

To circumvent Jensen's policy, the assassin took on additional assignments. One related to a wealthy woman in Chicago seeking revenge on a man who had brutally disfigured her. This new task provided the killer an opportunity to investigate a rumor he had heard about Doc practicing medicine in the city and to allow him to offset the costs related to the time and effort involved in the Jensen case by concealing overcharges on the disfigured woman's account.

The brutality leading to this new assignment occurred several years earlier. The woman had been attacked by a rapist while walking in a park. There, she had been overpowered, beaten to unconsciousness, and dragged into the brush where she was stripped. As the seducer began to penetrate her, she regained consciousness and bit his nose, practically removing it from his face. Out of control, he again thrashed her, removed a bottle from his pocket, and poured acid over her face.

The deviate left her on the ground, naked and agonizing in pain. He disappeared but eventually was arrested, tried, and convicted. After nine years in prison, he received early parole, and in keeping with an open court announcement at the time of sentencing, he went in search of the woman, seeking vengeance.

Learning of his release, the victim became frightened. Through acquaintances, she heard about the unknown one whom she contacted. Determined never to see or hear of the rapist again, the victim was willing to pay for whatever long-term protection he could provide.

Once the target's face became known, the contracted one began his search. He quickly located the subject and covertly began following him to study his habits. But the criminal was naturally suspicious and experienced. Accustomed to the techniques of police surveillance, he effectively escaped detection.

The unknown one became incensed. To safeguard his charge, he placed her under protective custody, day and night. On the third evening, in the midst of a winter snow storm, the acid-pouring rapist, clothed in white, parked his car on a back road, hiked through a wooded area, climbed a six-foot brick wall, and landed in the woman's backyard. Obscured by the snow, he darted and waited and darted again through the yard to a circular metal stairway leading to a second-floor door. The house was dark. Climbing the steps quietly, he withdrew a glass cutter from his pocket and removed a windowpane adjacent to the knob.

Sliding his hand through the opening in the window, the intruder unlocked the door and entered an empty room. From there, he crept down a hallway, stopping at times to look through open doors to make certain the rooms were empty. Finally, he came to a closed door. Silently, the voyeur opened it and saw a body lying in a fetal position under blankets, the head covered by a sheet. From his pocket, the sadomasochist removed a bottle of acid, uncapped the stopper, and crept to the bed, preparing to grab the sheet. From a partially opened closet door, a scream startled the attacker, causing him to jerk around to discover the source of the noise. There stood his intended victim.

Earlier, the blizzard had made the woman's protector wary and cautious. Time and again, he had roamed the house: double checking locks on all the windows and all the doors; reexamining every room, closet, and niche on each of the four floors; and vigilantly studying, from open doors and through closed windows, the surrounding grounds for signs of outdoor activity. It was during the latest trip that he saw, through an upstairs window, the man in white heading to the metal stairway to fulfill a courtroom promise.

To protect his charge, the man of multiple identities awakened the woman and had her hide in the closet. He then took her place in bed, assumed a fetal position to conceal the differences in height and physique, and pulled a blanket and sheet over his body to hide recognition.

The attacker, distracted by the screaming woman, never saw the hand burst out from beneath the covers. It deflected the open bottle of acid, causing the fluid to splash over the aggressor's face. He screamed trying to wipe the liquid from his eyes, and running in circles, he stumbled over an unseen ottoman. No longer under the covers, the man of many names had arisen, fully clothed. He retrieved an iron poker from the tool set adjacent to a bedroom fireplace and struck the intruder's head with the poker, again and again until the man subsided into unconsciousness.

Although saved from physical harm, the woman was emotionally distraught. She was shaking and sobbing, lying curled on the floor. Reaching down and lifting her gently, he embraced the near-hysteric woman and gently rubbed her back.

"Are you all right?" he asked.

She merely nodded and rested her head on his shoulder. Tears dampened his shirt.

"I know this has been difficult, but you need to get hold of yourself. You need to follow some instructions. Now sit up and listen," he ordered.

The woman looked at him, unnerved in discovering an authoritative, brusque side never before revealed. She wanted to compose herself. To have time to emotionally unwind! But from the expression on his face, she knew better than to object. She merely nodded.

Taking this as approval, he spoke. "You have to prepare for the police. When they arrive, I'll be gone. Otherwise, too many questions will be asked. When I leave, dial 911. Then wait for someone to come. Take hold of this poker, and keep it in your hands. If he moves, though I doubt that he will, hit him again. But other than this poker, touch nothing. Especially him or the bottle or anything he possesses.

Just sit still and wait for the police. When they arrive, you'll have to give them a story. You couldn't sleep. You were in the room at the end of the hall watching the snowfall, and you became distracted by someone entering the yard and heading to the metal stairs. You ran to the bedroom, fluffed the pillows under the covers, grabbed the poker, and hid in the closet. When the man entered the room, you saw him take a bottle from his pocket and head toward the bed. Your movement—a sound—something made him turn toward you! When you raised the poker, he turned to defend himself and splashed the liquid on his own face. You didn't know what was in the bottle, but you saw him screaming and wiping his eyes. That's when you hit him over the head with the poker. One blow, two blows, you don't know how many. But he fell to the floor, unconscious. Then you called 911.

"Keep the story succinct. The more you tell, the greater the chance you'll cross yourself up and have to make changes later. So tell your story only once, and be brief. That'll not satisfy the cops. They'll try to probe with questions. Refuse to answer and demand a lawyer. They won't like that either and are apt to pressure you. But stay firm. They're obligated to comply with your request for a lawyer."

"Oh, how I wish you'd be here with the police."

"I can't, and that's best for you. Now, I'm going to leave, but I'll be back tomorrow. After you call 911, you might want to phone a friend, preferably a nurse or an attorney, someone who will remain with you tonight during and after the police arrive. But be certain to call that person after you call 911. Remember! Tell your story only once, and keep it brief. Best you rehearse what you want to say after you make the call but before the cops arrive."

With that, he left the house.

* * * * *

The unknown one returned to his hotel room and thought about the evening. His mind drifted back to his childhood. He had known his mother but not his father. In fact, he had many fathers because his mother enjoyed entertaining a variety of men in her popular bed.

A particular man who was one of his mother's favorites was enjoying her pleasures, and the boy was awakened by her cries of ecstasy. Quickly leaving his bed, he climbed up on a chair and looked through a hole in the wall that separated their two rooms. It was a hole he had drilled months earlier, one that enabled him to watch his mother entertain and be entertained.

But on this night, new and different acts of love were taking place. The boy became aroused, and the chair overturned. The noise attracted his mother's lover to the boy's room where the man learned of the child's intrusiveness.

Grabbing the boy by the ear, he dragged him to the woman's room, removed a belt from his trousers, and struck him repeatedly with the rectangular metal buckle. To this day, scars from that beating cover his back, but the deepest scar of all is the recollection of his drunken mother's laughter as she watched her son scream with pain.

CHAPTER 40

INTRODUCING THE HIGH PRIESTESS OF TAROT

In the beginning, Jerry Forrest agreed to train Stacey as a favor to Tom Snow. However, it soon became apparent that she had ability worthy of his attention, and he willingly reserved court time whenever space was available. This led to a bonding. For Stacey, it grew from an appreciation of the technique and skills Jerry was able to blend into her play; for Jerry, it was a connection reinforced by the young lady's eminent qualities—unique and diversified. Stacey had an intelligent, retentive memory; she was multifaceted—athletic, personable, and enlightened, and she had physical appeal—facial beauty and an eye-commanding figure.

Their first tennis lesson involved lobbing balls back and forth. After several dozen exchanges, Jerry approached his pupil and changed her grip. The softness of her skin and the strength of her hand were not forgettable. More volleys! Pleased with her arm and hand movements, he turned her attention to her feet. Footwork patterns and movements were modified to improve her balance. Yet they had to be instinctive. So he scheduled a long session entailing a variety of shots that forced Stacey to duplicate the patterns and movements learned.

He was impressed. She was a good student and a fast learner, intent on doing what she had been told. Glancing at his watch, he decided to spend the last fifteen minutes of court time demonstrating ways to hit the ball strong and hard, with controlled touch and feel. Finally, their two hours elapsed, and they relinquished the court to others scheduled to play doubles.

"You did well. Can you be here tomorrow? I'm able to reserve the court from two until four." Without hesitation, Stacey agreed to the invitation.

The following day, they resumed hitting the ball back and forth with Jerry intent on seeing her execute what she had learned. He was pleased. He then demonstrated the single-handed and double-handed backhand. To ensure that her technique was correct, he moved behind her, took hold of her arms and hands, and guided the motion and direction of these appendages along with the movement of her feet in the ways he wanted her to address an approaching ball. Then returning to his side of the court, he hit balls, forcing her to use both grips. When necessary, he would offer corrective suggestions on arm, leg, and foot movements, which Stacey would practice to perfection. With improvement to his satisfaction, he hit a variety of shots that forced her to play both the baseline and net. Again, he made suggestions, and she responded.

With twenty remaining minutes before relinquishing the court, he suggested they play a set. He hit the ball easy, testing everything she had learned. Her play was good.

"I'm not available for a few days," he told her. "Thursday is the earliest. Friday and Monday are alternatives. The courts are tied up over the weekend. So pick a day. What's your preference?"

They agreed on Monday at three o'clock.

"At the next lesson, I will offer pointers on serving, coordinating the toss of the ball with your stroking arm. You'll discover a softer, more fluid serving motion. And we'll also work on improving your follow through, making the serves more consistent and powerful."

"I like that."

"One final thing! How about letting me take you to dinner tonight? Kind of a gift for being such a good student, but also it'll give us time to discuss what you've learned and bat around a few questions and answers about your play."

"Fine, on one condition," she responded. "You're not treating me. I'm buying you dinner. You've been giving me the lessons at no charge. Dinner is the least I can do."

"Not tonight! Some other time, perhaps! Tonight's on me."

And it became the first of many.

The lessons continued. He improved her swing, causing her to move fluidly. She also learned how to play the arc using her wrist to create a sharply angled chop stroke. Other additions to her arsenal included perfecting ways to drag and slice the ball. Execution of the tips came easy to Stacey because she had the desire to perfect her game and an athletic ability natural to tennis champions.

In time, Jerry realized Stacey had learned all that he could teach her, and he decided only a live test would prove if she was as good a player as she was a student.

"Next week, *Green Acres* is having a tennis tournament. It's the annual member-guest event. Not only am I allowed to play, but I'm encouraged to do so by management. The club feels my presence will inspire others to take lessons, which will pump up revenues. I'd like you to be my partner in the mixed doubles session. What do you say?"

"Me? I'm only a beginner, someone who is now starting to understand what tennis players have to do to be good. And you want me, a novice, to be your partner?"

"Yes! We'll have to compete successfully from the initial elimination round through the quarterfinals, semifinals, and ultimately the finals. And I expect to play in that final match—with you as my partner. Together, we can win. If you're willing, know that you'll have to spend the better part of a week at the club. Is that possible?"

"Of course I can. But I'm astounded! Other than the few dozen games we've played together, I'm underexposed. You want to win, and you can have the choice of partners, players more experienced and better qualified than me. I appreciate the offer, but do yourself a favor and choose someone else."

"No way! You're wrong. It's true. I can find someone more experienced, one who has played in a number of tournaments. But no one gives me a better chance of winning than you. If you really like tennis and enjoy some challenging competition, you'll side with me. Stacey, don't make me question whether I've been wasting my time teaching you. Don't disappoint me now."

Staring into his eyes and seeing that his words were what he felt, she said, "I'd be honored. One thing, however! My folks are curious about you. No one has occupied my time to the degree you have. I think you'd better come home with me and meet my parents, especially now that I'm a partner and not just a pupil."

* * * * *

Walking into the condominium, Doc and Dora were seen at a table. The wife had corralled her husband into ignoring paperwork from *Comforting Care* in favor of a Tarot reading.

"Mom! Dad! Meet Jerry Forrest. He's the tennis pro who's been teaching me how to play."

Dora eyed Jerry Forrest from head to foot, then back to his face. Nodding, she said nothing. Doc turned in his seat, smiled, stood, and walked over to the guest, extending his hand.

"So there really is a Jerry Forrest!" exclaimed Doc. "Dora and I have been wondering who the man is that can occupy so much of our daughter's time. Pardon my wife's impolite quietness, but she's more comfortable as an oracle of the all-knowing Divine than in mixing with mere mortals."

"Perfectly all right," responded the guest. Walking to the table, he said, "Isn't that the *Chakra Spread*?"

Caught off guard, Dora stammered, "How-how do you know that? Do you read the cards?"

"No, not me. But when I was in college, I went through a stage questioning the improbable—astrology, clairvoyance, telepathy, and other topics including divination. And because of my curiosity, Tarot cards triggered an interest. But I'm afraid I've forgotten the little that I learned eight years ago. Stacey, do you read the cards?"

"She not only reads the cards," interrupted Doc, "she designs them. That deck is one of several she's done. It's a favorite of Dora's. Perfect size for her hands and illustrated to her liking. The Arcana, that is. I assume you remember the Arcana?"

"Oh yes, that I remember. The great secrets of the twenty-two Major Arcana and the everyday lessons of life revealed by the fifty-six Minor Arcana! But tell me, is Stacey as qualified as her mother in conducting the readings and revealing the secrets?"

"Are you familiar with *the High Priestess*?" asked Doc.

"As I remember, it's a Major Arcana. What secrets it reveals, whether upright or reversed, I can't recall. In fact, I may have never known. Why do you ask?"

"You're right. It is a Major Arcana. And it's also the name Dora's querents, the customers on the streets, call her."

"Possibly not for long," interrupted Dora. "I suspect Stacey will someday become the High Priestess. Since she was five or six, she sat through my readings, with the clients' approval, of course, and listened to what the cards revealed. Now she has the inner powers common to that Arcana—the wisdom, the knowledge, the intuition, and the virtue. Someday she'll become known as the High Priestess, that is, if she decides to pursue her God-given abilities. I see her as counselor of counselors, the oracle who touches the all-knowing Divine."

"Mom, that's enough! I'm merely a girl, your daughter, one who likes to swim and play tennis, someone who hopes to get into college this fall and pursue studies that'll be useful after I graduate! Reading cards is a fascination that will always be of interest, but it will not be a career path for me like it has been for you."

The sadness on Dora's face was apparent, and to avoid a disappointing discussion, Jerry asked, "Stacey, have you applied to the college you want to attend?"

"Actually, quite a few! All nearby—Georgetown, George Mason, Trinity, and some Virginia colleges! But so far, I haven't been accepted or rejected by any of them."

"It's still early," volunteered Doc. "She's a good student and has done well on her SATs. She'll be hearing from them soon."

"You might even be able to earn a scholarship once they know how well you play tennis," said Jerry.

"Hold on, Coach! I think you're catching 'The Stacey Epidemic' that my parents spread. We'd better get out of here and go to dinner, or I'll be so full of myself that I won't be able to enter my first class if and when I get accepted."

CHAPTER 41

A PROMISING FUTURE

The Member-Guest Tennis Tournament at *Green Acres* was well attended by registered players and visiting spectators. Members of the club were heard voicing their favorites, and depending on who was speaking, no one other than Mr. X or Ms. Y or Team Z would be crowned the club's Singles Winner or Doubles Champion.

Jerry, because of his coaching and professional status, refused to enter the singles tournament, but his presence in the mixed doubles match resulted in an overflow of onlookers. Many were questioning who his unknown partner was, with few believing her to be a novice. Forrest had the reputation of being highly competitive, and to him, winning was all that mattered.

Members of the club crowded into the stands. Each was determined to judge the unknown's performance and decide whether she was or was not a ringer. The first day's match finished quickly, with Forrest and McDonald the decisive victors. More questions arose! Who was this attractive newcomer?

The quarterfinal match, on the following day, was close but not a hair puller. Forrest-McDonald won the first and third sets but lost the second set four-six.

Victory in the semifinal match came to Stacey and Jerry after losing the first set but dominating in the second and third. Still, opinions regarding McDonald's experience continued to be debated. Some thought she was a professional; others were unsure. Yet one conclusion agreed upon by everyone: Stacey excelled on the court.

The championship match on Sunday attracted a crowd of spectators. People packed the stadium and jostled each other with their continuous jump ups and crowding sitdowns.

In mixed doubles, the player receiving is the same sex as the server; and in this championship match, Stacey was scheduled to serve first. Her opponent, Judy Jenkins, was a player with years of tournament experience. Had she been five years younger, she would have turned professional.

Apprehension at the beginning of the first game was evident on Stacey's face. She stood at the baseline and stared across the net at her opponent. Tossing the ball upward, she arched her back and drove it across the net into the serving area. Jenkins took one step to her left and rifled the return over the net two feet away from Stacey's outstretched reach and well within the chalk lines. Score: love–15. And it continued: love–30, love–40, then game, receiving team.

Jerry walked over to his partner and said, "Relax! You're every bit as good as she is!"

Now receiving, Stacey stared back at her opponent with a challenging look. The first serve was an ace. *Advantage in!* The second serve resulted in a six-volley return with the final shot arcing over Jenkins head and landing within the baseline. Deuce, 15–15! And it continued: 15–30, advantage out; 30–30 deuce; 40–30 advantage in; 40–40 deuce; then advantage in; and finally 60–40, game; Judy Jenkins and Rex Ferguson winners.

While Judy was superior to Stacey, Jerry's opponent was out of the former pro's league. Jerry won his service match handily, 60–15, and the Forrest-McDonald team followed up winning the receiving set, 30–60.

Stacey was now relaxed. When her partner was serving, she played the net superbly. Several chop shots, a cut, and a spinning return put their opponents on the defensive, forcing errors on the balls returned.

The three-set match had shifted back and forth. The first set was won by Ferguson and Jenkins with the second set going to Forrest and McDonald. The third and final set turned into a 6–6 tie, forcing a one-game tiebreak. To determine a winner, one team had to have a two-point advantage over the opposition at the conclusion of the game.

The games seesawed back and forth, reaching 5–5. It was now Stacey's turn to serve from the deuce court. The ball, a mere inch over the net, very fast, and well placed, was returned into the net. Score, 6–5!

Jenkins's serve to Stacey began a series of forehand and backhand team volleys with the final return by Ferguson heading toward Stacey. Retreating rapidly, she moved ahead of the ball, planted her feet, and stroked her shot with accuracy into the far left corner of the doubles alley. It hit precisely within the chalk area, a distant ten feet away from the out-of-position Ferguson.

"In," shouted the umpire. "Winners, Forrest-McDonald, 7–5."

The spectators stood and roared their appreciation. But well into the evening, the previously cited comments were repeated. "Is Stacey McDonald really new to tennis? Her quality of play suggests otherwise."

CHAPTER 42

HIS NAME'S FRANCIS MCDONALD

The day after the attempted attack, the man with many names returned to his client's home. Upon ringing the doorbell, he was greeted by a plump, plain-faced nurse whose features brightened when she saw the handsome stranger.

Asking to see the lady of the house, the nurse replied, "I'm sorry, but Mrs. Donahue is recovering from a difficult night and is not receiving visitors."

"A favor, please! Yesterday, she clearly stated that she wanted to see me." Using the alias by which he was known, he continued, "Tell her Harry Robinson is here. If today is inconvenient, ask when she would like me to return. I don't want to be a nuisance, but she has expressed an interest in my visit today, and I want to satisfy that request."

The nurse left and five minutes later returned with Mrs. Donahue leaning on her arm.

"Harry," the victim welcomed, "do come in. Anna, get the gentleman a cup of coffee. Black, two sugars! Let me have your arm, Harry, and we'll go to the sitting room."

There, the hostess began recounting her experience with the police, stopping only when Anna returned with coffee and pastry. After the nurse left, she continued, mentioning that his "interrogation," as she termed it, went pretty much the way Robinson had predicted. Fifteen minutes into the questioning, she demanded an attorney; however, before he arrived, the detective in charge asked her to repeat her story. She refused. As soon as her counsel appeared, the detective resumed his questioning with replies or refusals based on the legal direction offered.

Following a few questions from Robinson, the conversation turned to more pleasant subjects. Then Anna returned and insisted that Mrs. Donahue go to her room to rest.

"Don't feel that you have to leave now. Anna, refill his cup and chat with him awhile. Call me tomorrow, Harry, if it's convenient. I don't want our relationship to end abruptly."

Mrs. Donahue's invitation pleased Harry. As a nurse, Anna could possibly offer some direction on how to locate the doctor in his other case.

Minutes later, the nurse returned. "I'm glad Mrs. Donahue suggested we talk." Placing her hand on Robinson's arm, she continued, "It gets lonely sitting around while she's resting, and your company will help pass the time. If I may be so bold, just what is your occupation? Obviously, it's something important for Mrs. Donahue to employ you."

"Not too important. I'm a private investigator who was hired some weeks ago to clear up some matters involving her late husband. Sorry, but client privilege prevents me from saying any more other than it's really a small matter."

Patting his forearm, she said, "A private investigator! How exciting! I love mysteries—the excitement, the intrigue, the secrecies."

Harry laughed.

"Don't believe everything you read in novels or see on television. My job can be very boring, more than even yours when the patient is sleeping."

"How depressing. Here I thought you'd engross me with some hair-raising, bloodcurdling past adventures. Now I'm disenchanted," stroking his arm.

"Sorry. I can't offer that. But you may be able to help me with a current matter. Not too exciting, however."

"Oh, I don't mind. If it's not too complicated, I'd be happy to help. What is it?"

"Several years ago, a medical doctor lost his license. I've heard rumors that he was here in Chicago. I've seen a picture of him, but

I don't know his name, his specialty, or whether he was actually in this area."

"And you expect me or anyone, for that matter, to help you locate him?"

"Oh, I don't expect you to pluck a name out of the air. What I am interested in learning, however, is where should I go and what questions should I ask to gather information on doctors who lose their licenses?"

"Sorry, I really don't know. My guess would be to start with the Division of Professional Regulation on license lookup. Or go to the state health department's Web site. But no matter who you contact, you're going to need a name, something that will identify the person."

"You're probably right. I just don't know enough about him to know where to look or what to ask. I've heard he has a vast knowledge of medicine and know he's a short guy with a distinguishing walk. A hitch step! But that's not much to work on, is it?"

"A little guy with a hitch step? It can't be?"

"Can't be what?"

"Francis McDonald!"

"Francis McDonald? Who's he?"

"He was one of the most respected physicians around, a doctor specializing in the diagnosis and treatment of disorders in the colon, rectum, and large intestine. He had a huge practice, especially with people fearing colon cancer. During a routine operation, he failed to see a polyp that became malignant. The patient was a socialite, a wealthy contributor to charitable events. She died, and both the hospital and Fran were sued. The case was reviewed, but the hospital didn't support him. He was screwed, royally screwed."

"You seem to remember a great deal about McDonald and the case. How come? It had to happen twenty-five, maybe thirty years ago."

"Oh, I remember all right. I worked for Fran. And for several years after that, he sent me cards on my birthday and Christmas. He was very kind to me."

"Do you, by any chance, remember where he was or where he is today?"

"No! Even back then, I didn't have an address. The cards were always postmarked New York City but no return address. And then, a couple of years ago, they stopped coming. But I do have a picture of him. Too bad I don't have it with me."

"Would you mind if I followed you to your house? I'd like to see what your Francis McDonald looks like."

For a moment, she hesitated.

"What's the matter?" he asked.

"Just why do you want him? If my Francis is the guy you're looking for, I won't be party to getting him in trouble. I owe him too much."

"You needn't worry about that. A lady, my client, was walking home one night and suffered a heart attack. She fell over and stopped breathing. This stranger, possibly your Francis, was present and gave her CPR. By the time she regained consciousness, a policeman who witnessed the incident called an ambulance. After it arrived and the woman was placed in the vehicle, the Samaritan disappeared, leaving no name or any identification. People witnessing the CPR said they believed him to be one of the homeless who roamed the streets of New York. And if that's true, the woman wants to reward him."

"Homeless! Walking the streets of New York! That can't be. It mustn't be. Yes, follow me. I'll give you the picture and by all means, find him."

"I intend to. And whether they are or are not one and the same, you can keep the picture. All I need is to see the face."

* * * * *

The nurse's home was exactly as the man of many names pictured it—small, five rooms, neat, but not pretentious.

As she unbuttoned her coat, Robinson's hands moved up her arms, across her shoulders, to the lapels of the garment. He politely removed the wrap.

Anna turned and pressed her arm into his chest. Staring into his eyes, she thanked him and carried the coat to the closet.

The visitor watched her every move.

With her back facing him, she hung the coat, allowing her free hands to rise to her neck and hesitate. He noticed a slight movement of her arms, but why, he did not know. Then her hands continued to the overhead shelf, and she removed a box. Turning, she brought the carton into the room and placed it on a table. She bent forward to finger through the papers in search of the picture. Pearl buttons on her blouse had been unfastened and her bra-covered cleavage was partially exposed.

Looking at her guest, she saw his eyes admiring the view. She smiled, retrieved a photograph, walked to the sofa, and sat down. She leaned a breast into his arm and pressed her thigh against his leg. Handing him the picture, her free hand dropped to his knee.

"This is the latest picture I have, and it's an excellent likeness of how he looked when we were together." On the back was printed, "Happy birthday, Anna! Hope all is well. Francis."

At first, the man of many names shook his head, disappointment in his eyes. *This is not the Doc I'm looking for.* But as he continued to study the picture, his expression slowly changed. *Damned if it isn't he. Not the scraggly, out-of-shape, unkempt Doc I know, but a neat, well-dressed man of distinction. How you've changed. Is it possible, now years later with some money in your pockets, you once again look like you did years ago? And what about Dora? Has her appearance changed too?*

Suddenly, his thoughts returned to the present. Anna's hand was slowly moving to the midpoint of his thigh, and she said, "Is that the man you're seeking? Let's discuss it. And while we do, we'll have some wine and talk . . . about him . . . and . . . other things. I'm certain there are many interesting things I can learn from you. In fact, there's much I want to know, to see, and to show you," she offered in a low, husky voice.

He touched the back of her head and pulled her face to his. Pressing his lips to hers, he glided his tongue across her mouth. She opened her lips to receive it, and he drew her thigh-holding hand further up his leg, stopping short of where she had expected it to go. As they continued the kiss, he placed one hand on the front of her throat and slowly glided it down to the opening of her blouse. Slowly . . . attentively . . . he buttoned the two-pearl fasteners.

Withdrawing his mouth from her, he kissed her forehead and stood. "As much as I would enjoy talking with you . . . and enjoying the other treasures you're willing to offer, I must leave. Other pressing matters!" At the front door, he felt the intensity of her stare stabbing him in the back.

* * * * *

Sixty minutes later before takeoff, he motioned to the bartender for a second Scotch.

An eventful day! I've finally discovered the man I'm looking for—the man I'm about to find. Thirty, possibly sixty days, but no longer. Then Francis

McDonald, you'll be mine. You're about to make me very happy. And you, Mrs. Donahue. You're happy too. But what about Anna? What an alley cat! Reminds me of you, Mother. Where ever you may be? High in the heavens or deep in a fiery hell! I only hope you were watching. Then you'd have seen me turn my back on Anna just as I turned my back on you—years ago. All alley cats deserve to be rejected while other animals need to be found.

Sipping his drink, he opened his crossword puzzle book and looked at one across. *A word for a ratter, a domesticated mouse catcher.*

Laughing, he printed the answer: *CAT.*

CHAPTER 43

A CUSTODIAN WITH INFLUENCE

From the day Francis McDonald entered *Comforting Care,* he began winning the staff's approval. He was not only zealous in fulfilling his custodial duties; he became the nurses' helpmate in caring for their patients. The years of aimless living were finally behind him. He had returned to medicine, his first love.

Dedicated and conscientious, Francis was willing to do what was necessary—for the nurses, the patients, and even the visitors. Affable and even tempered, he seldom objected to any requests. His responsibilities grew over the years, outdistancing the custodial duties for which he had been hired. Many tasks were assigned, others requested, and more than a few silently volunteered. He discovered the not so obvious—things overlooked, things incorrectly handled, and things neglected because the correct procedures or necessary equipment were unavailable.

When an improvement could be achieved by simple modification, he went ahead and made it—unannounced. At first, the improvements were minor and went unseen. But in time, the two head nurses, Jean White (early morning to early evening) and Sally Longstreet (early evening to the following morning), noticed things—alterations and enhancements too major to go undetected. After several private conversations, they cornered the custodian and pried out of him confessions to his actions. They demanded to know how he had the foresight to recognize the need and the ability to implement what was required. So he became forced to reveal he had been a doctor on staff at two major hospitals in Chicago before losing his license to what was officially deemed negligence and incompetence.

The nurses could not believe what they heard. Their instincts led them to feel he had been unjustly "convicted" and were so upset they met with Timothy Bell the following day and argued that the home should utilize McDonald's medical knowledge in ways more advantageous than as a mere custodian. They told the owner about changes McDonald had implemented, which led Bell to question Doc whether there were other deficiencies or inadequacies requiring correction. Citing a few necessitating major financial commitments, the principal looked at his employee with great respect. Excusing the nurses, they returned to their duties.

"Francis, if you'd been involved in the decision making at the time *Comforting Care's* first hole was dug, how different would the home be from the one we now have?"

"Tim, that's an unfair question. Times are different. Possibly, I would have suggested a couple of things, but overall, it's a sound facility."

"In learning what Jean, Sally, and you have been saying, I think it's time for my partner and me to utilize your expertise with some future plans we're considering. However, what I'm about to say must remain confidential."

"You needn't caution me, Tim. I don't volunteer things I hear unless told to do so."

"Good, that pleases me! *Comforting Care* is finally turning a profit. We're optimistic and are, therefore, planning to expand. We have three sites in mind—one in West Virginia, a second in Maryland, and another in southern Virginia. Our intention is to take on two of the locations, not three. With the plans my partner and I are developing, we believe we can staff and financially operate only two more. I'll be reducing my pediatric practice to devote more time to the venture and Charlie's cutting back from his firm as well. In other words, we're going to concentrate on the nursing home business. I believe, from what I've seen and from what I'm hearing, that we can enhance our chances for more rapid success by bringing you into the inner circle. In other words, pick your brains regarding the three locations along with how you would design, equip, and staff the two selected. This means making you a partner with executive responsibilities and a significant salary enhancement. What do you say?"

"I like it. But better yet, what will Charlie say?"

"Oh, he's not only in favor of it but encouraging it as well. Don't underestimate him. He keeps an eye on *Comforting Care* and overlooks nothing. But understand this—like the two of us, your responsibilities are about to change. You'll be traveling a great deal. Making onsite examinations! And based on your thoughts, we'll finalize decisions and assign responsibilities. Charlie will do the budgeting, bill paying, and control the money spent. I'll deal with the general contractors. You, with Charlie's and my input, will order and schedule the arrival of kitchen, pharmacy, and patient medical equipment. That'll be a large undertaking, and the timing will require all three of us to be involved."

"Tim, I've been away from this business for many years. In my recent short exposure, I've learned many new things. For me to do what you want done is going to require my visiting manufacturers, suppliers, and possibly even some other nursing homes just to see what's available. That requires time."

"True, but if you weren't doing it, Charlie and I would be. And frankly, we're more ill-informed than you. I'm counting on your knowledge of hospitals and your willingness to personally bury yourself in this assignment as critical to our success. You'll be traveling away from Dora, Stacey, and your Upper Arlington apartment for the better part of this year and most of next year. Will that be a problem?"

"No, I can handle that. Stacey will be in college, and if you have no objections, I'd like to have Dora travel with me, on occasion and at my expense, of course. She won't be in the way. In fact, she'll want personal time to remain busy with her cards. New surroundings and new querants are her life, and the more invisible I am, the happier she is."

"Good! Let's go see Charlie and finalize a package for you."

CHAPTER 44

CHOICES

The letters arrived! Stacey was accepted by all seven colleges to which she applied. Yet her decision was easy. Georgetown was her preference, and she looked forward to being a freshman in September 2003.

She foresaw a future in business, and her undergraduate years would include a blending of liberal arts and business courses—English, history, general psychology, theology, accounting, statistics, principles of marketing, strategic management, and electives. Add to these the excitement of living on campus, making new friends, and getting involved in one or two student organizations.

But one thing not immediately high on her list was tennis. The university had a competitive women's team, yet Stacey's racket was destined to gather dust on the top shelf of her closet. There were only so many things she was willing to undertake during her freshman year, and some things had to remain second to her studies.

As her first year progressed, she held fast to these plans. New friends gravitated to her, and while she was popular with girls, boys were always around. She had what they liked—beauty and a warm, friendly personality. While she dated, she refused to get involved, seeing many without encouraging any. And besides, there was always Jerry Forrest. He phoned frequently, and more than infrequently, he came to the campus to drive her into the city for dinner, movies, dancing, and merely social time together.

With the coming of spring and her studies progressing well, Stacey finally relented to Jerry's often repeated request. With cloth in hand, she removed the tennis racket from the top shelf, wiped away the dust, and reserved an outdoor court for two.

It had been one year since they had played together. She was excited yet apprehensive. *How rusty am I? Will I remember what he taught me? Will I make a fool of myself?*

She threw the ball into the air, arched her back, and drove the sphere across the net. It fell into the service court, and she responded naturally, placing her return shot into a space vacated by him. She was pleased. She had not lost her touch, her balance, or her accuracy on the ball's hit. Once again, an exhilaration from the sport she loved flowed through her body.

In an adjoining court, two girls stopped playing and watched them. Jerry was skillfully placing the ball around the court, forcing Stacey to respond with sharply angled chop shots, slices, two-hand backhands, and other techniques he had taught her. Finally, after finishing the game, one of the girls in the other court came over and introduced herself to the pair.

"I'm Janet Walker, and my friend here is Joan Shaffer. We've been watching you and would like to know if you'd care to play a set of doubles."

Stacey hesitated, and Jerry quickly responded, "We certainly would."

Joan was first to serve, and as the ball moved around the court, Jerry, who in the beginning downplayed his ability, began hustling. The girls were good.

When the set was over, Jerry congratulated them, saying, "Thanks for suggesting the match. You two are doggone good. I haven't run that much in nearly a year. It was fun, and again, thanks for the invitation."

"You're welcome. But frankly, we had an ulterior motive in asking you to play."

"Oh! What was that?" he inquired.

"Janet and I are on the Georgetown Women's Tennis Team, and when we saw how well Stacey was doing, we wanted to have firsthand experience with her. I assume you are a student here?"

Stacey nodded. "My first year!"

"Well, why haven't you come out for the team? We need girls with your ability."

"I've been tempted, but my priorities have been my studies, and tennis was put on hold."

"We understand. It's good to concentrate on your classwork, but next year, you need to consider sharing your tennis skills with the University. Janet and I won't take no for an answer. In fact, we're going to mention your name to our coach. When she calls, and she will call after she hears what we say about you, give her the time of day. Visit her office. Find out about the team. If, after speaking with her, you continue to avoid tennis, I won't understand, but at least I'll know I've given the school my best shot."

Within a week, Stacey heard from the coach. They met, and near the end of their conversation, Stacey was asked to hit a few balls. They volleyed for a while, and then Stacey was challenged to several games. At the conclusion, she was asked to try out for the team, and she did.

During her sophomore year, she practiced with the team but never traveled to any other university for a dual meet. This changed in her junior year, and by her senior year, she was a respected and often star performer in match games against rival colleges.

As a member of the tennis team, she gained new respect. More and more students wanted her company, and this flourished when another talent was revealed.

One evening, during her junior year, she and a friend, Angie Blakely, were studying together. A discussion arose on a theorem, and Stacey began looking for the answer in one of her classroom notebooks. Searching for a specific spiral steno book, she scattered items from a drawer on the top of her desk.

"What's that, Stace?"

"Tarot cards," she replied.

"Can you read them?"

"Sure, ever since I was a little girl!"

"Am I glad I know you! I'm fascinated by the secrets those cards reveal. I've been read to a half-a-dozen times but not recently. We've studied enough. Close the books, and let me shuffle those cards. I want a reading. I want to know if Bobby really likes me as a person or is merely trying to get into my pants. Please, please! Read for me."

And the word spread: *"Have you heard? Stacey McDonald has an ability to contact the all-knowing Divine."*

Then more publicity! Somebody secretively affixed to her study room door: *The Realm of the High Priestess of Tarot,* unknowingly identifying the girl by the title her mother once predicted.

Whatever purpose the wordsmith had in mind—whether to inform, question, embarrass, mock, or proudly acknowledge Stacey's skills—her ability as a reader was no longer a quietly kept secret. Across campus, her presence prompted instant recognition from students and members of the faculty whom she had never met. Occasionally, someone would make an unkind remark, yet the normally private young lady always remained gracious, diplomatically sidestepping what had been said.

In June 2007, Stacey, at the age of twenty-two, received her Bachelor of Arts degree, whereupon she applied to and was accepted by Georgetown's McDonough School of Business. Her objective: to earn a Master of Business Administration Degree. Two years later, in the spring of 2009, she received that degree, possessing command of the academic fundamentals required for a career in corporate business development.

PART III

THE ARCANA

THE SECRETS OF TOMORROW

CHAPTER 45

TIMES, DATES, HAPPENINGS

Wednesday Night, September 9, 2009, 8:17 p.m.
It was a cold, crisp evening, the temperature 22 degrees. A shooting star, streaking across the sky, gave momentary light to a starless, ebony heaven. Midway across an empty lot, one single car was parked. A man, leaving an empty office building, moved rapidly toward it, following a glowing beam from his handheld flashlight.

At the driver's door, he set his briefcase on the ground and withdrew car keys from his pocket. From behind, a wire dropped in front of his face and tightened around his neck. He gagged, his arms moving wildly to the front and side. Suddenly, as quickly as the movements began, they stopped, and Francis McDonald inhaled his last breath of air.

Now to confuse the cops with the thought that your death is related to the super natural, thought the killer. Removing Tarot cards from his pocket, the strangler fanned the deck and glanced at the pictures.

Who can believe this crap?

At random, he picked a single card and jammed it into McDonald's mouth, the lower part hidden behind clinched teeth, the upper half exposed for all to see. It was the *Judgment* card, a Major Arcana. Smiling, he began jogging to his car several blocks away.

Wednesday Night, September 9, 2009, 9:45 p.m.

A key slid into the lock of the apartment door. Dora's hand reached through the opening and flipped on a switch controlling the living room lights. Walking to the kitchen, she placed a bag of groceries on the counter and then went to the bedroom where she tossed her coat on the bed.

Leaving the room, she headed back to the kitchen unaware that the closet door was slightly open. In the kitchen, she filled a cup with water and pressed a teabag to its bottom before placing it in the microwave.

From the bag of groceries, she removed a lemon, halved it, and cut a slice from one of the sections. Going back to the microwave, she watched the cup come to a boil, removed it, and squeezed the lemon and pulp into the brew. She took a sip and was satisfied.

Dora then returned to the living room and lowered herself into a chair, facing a card table where she placed the tea in one corner. In the center of the table were four cards facing down in a *Law of Attraction Spread*.

Looking at her watch, she whispered audibly, "Well, Doc, in another twelve minutes, you'll be home, and we can resume this reading. I'm curious what the future holds. Hopefully, there are no ugly surprises or bad days ahead. I'm excited to learn what our first step is to be."

Placing her elbows on the table, she rested her chin on two overlapping hands and smiled. *The recent months couldn't have been better. I'm so fortunate. A loving husband, a wonderful daughter, and a beautiful home. Everything is perfect.*

So absorbed in her thoughts, she was unaware of the stranger silently moving toward her. Then suddenly, her head snapped backward. Someone's hand was pulling her hair. Frantically through wild eyes, she saw the violent face of an unknown man.

"Dora, Dora, Dora. How you've changed. So much more presentable . . . much more neatly groomed than during your days on the streets. In fact, you're even attractive. I wonder how much of this is due to the cards, the money they've provided to you the oracle and counselor of people's hidden secrets. Ah yes, Tarot! It does have power. But did it forewarn you of this?"

Passing slowly before her eyes was the blade of a knife.

"Consider this a gift from Frisky Fingers Freddy, for the switchblade was once his. And after I find your Stacey, this same knife will taste her sweet blood also."

With a swipe, he slit Dora's throat from one side to the other.

Wiping the blade on her blouse, he searched every room, inspecting the contents of various drawers. Finally, he found what he wanted—a scrap of paper with two notations: Stacey's name and telephone number.

In front of a wall mirror, he noticed drops of blood on his face and yellow rain slicker. Removing the coat, he turned it inside out and rolled it into a tight bundle. Entering the bathroom, he removed surgeon gloves and rinsed his face. Then he dried himself with a hand towel and wrapped the towel around the raincoat and gloves.

He walked to the kitchen and removed potato chips and peanuts from the grocery bag. Opening the front door with handkerchief in hand, he flipped off the light and secured the inside lock.

Miles outside of DC, he headed east to the Chesapeake Bay and then north toward Sparrows Point, Maryland. Along the way, he came to a stop and threw the raincoat and towel into the bay. Continuing on, he gave thought to how, after twenty-four years of searching, he had finally located Doc and Dora.

Five Days Earlier, September 4, 2009, 2:32 p.m.

It had not been thirty or sixty days as the hunter had anticipated when he learned about McDonald from Anna. Instead, it had been months before McDonald was finally located, all because of mistakes—clues that proved useless, leads that headed to dead ends, and hunches that never paid off. Simply summarized, a lot of worthless information.

He had traveled thousands of miles throughout the Midwest and the Northeast. Only the airlines profited. And now, once again, based on nothing more than *I've got to do it,* the man returned to Chicago. It was his eighth visit to the Windy City.

Previous attempts in locating doctors and nurses familiar with Francis McDonald had been unsuccessful. Too many years had elapsed for the present generation to have either known or to have heard of the colon cancer physician. And, as in the past, these most recent two days were uneventful. But the hunter refused to give up, to lose hope. Possibly one or many reasons drove him—the hatred of failure, the fear of a diminished reputation, the challenge of new and more intense competition; a gloating Jensen; the loss of a sizable reward; or simply pride.

So once again, he began visiting more clinics—so many he had lost count—clinics that specialized in a variety of ailments and diseases—cholesterol, hypertension, sleep apnea, obesity, diabetes, and other disorders. Entering this one, the third one of the day, he requested to see the proctologist. Told by a receptionist to sit in the waiting room, he began leafing through a number of health-care magazines presenting articles on a variety of health-care issues.

One article of interest featured nursing homes and extended care facilities. Becoming impatient for the doctor to appear, he nearly overlooked the information he was seeking. Flipping pages, his mind caught up with a picture his eyes previously saw, and he turned back several pages to study it. There, visible for all readers to see, were the faces of a successful team responsible for operating three and on the verge of opening a fourth convalescent facility: the principal-in-charge, Dr. Timothy Bell; the treasurer and CPA, Mr. Charles Ellenberger; and the chief operating officer, Mr. Francis McDonald, a man, though older, but the man in Anna's picture.

As he scanned the article, the assassin learned the locations of each of the facilities along with an address of the executive office building. Dropping the magazine in his briefcase, the visitor abruptly left the clinic without mentioning to the nurse in charge that he was going.

CHAPTER 46

THE FUNERAL OF THE WELCOMED AND NOT WELCOMED

From his hotel room, the assassin dialed a District of Columbia telephone number on the paper found in Dora's apartment.

"*TH&E,*" the receptionist answered.

"*TH&E*! Who is TH&E?" asked the caller.

"*Thoman, Holmes, and Ettinger International Consultants,*" replied the operator.

"I believe Anastasia McDonald is employed with you. Am I not correct?"

"You are, sir!"

"Will you please put me through to her?"

"I'm sorry, sir, but Ms. McDonald is traveling with Mr. Thoman. She'll be away from the office for a few days."

"Then give me a forwarding number. I need to speak with her."

"I'm sorry, sir, but company policy prevents me from divulging locations of personnel on assignments. However, I'll gladly take your name and number and have her return your call the next time I speak with her."

Surprise appeared on the operator's face when the call was abruptly disconnected.

Yet there was one person who knew where Stacey was. At 9:00 p.m. London time, Jerry Forrest placed a long distance call to her hotel room.

"Hi, Stace!"

"Jerry! What a pleasant surprise. Something told me to get back to the room early. Truly a premonition!"

"Honey, I've got some dreadful news. You better sit down."

Although he tried to soften the tragedies surrounding her parents' deaths, all he could hear against the avalanche of tears was "No! Dear God, no! Tell me it isn't true!"

Jerry endeavored to ease her pain, but the heartbroken daughter could only sob, repeating over and over her regret in not being with them when needed. Finally, she willed her composure, and together they made plans. She would board the first flight to DC, and he would make preliminary funeral arrangements. On her arrival, she would provide a list of people to be notified, and together they would contact individuals in the District, New York, Florida, and elsewhere. Burial was scheduled to take place in five days.

Jerry worried about seeing Stacey the following day. By then, she would have given thought to her parents' deaths and would want details about the investigations, and how they were progressing. Currently, the police were clueless. Other than knowing how the two died, there was no evidence pointing to why or by whom.

The first person Stacey called was her godfather, Vincent Shomazzi. Giant, Windy, and other Shomazzi employees contacted homeless people living in the streets of New York and told them that a bus, chartered by Stacey, would provide transportation to those wishing to attend the interment in Alexandria.

Through Jerry's connections, arrangements were finalized for a memorial service to be conducted by a minister at a nondenominational church with the bodies buried side by side in a mausoleum. The mourners would then walk to a nearby building where they would recall memorable events and experiences while dining on food and beverages available.

Attendance overflowed. There were medical personnel and ambulatory patients from *Comforting Care,* violent-looking men from Shomazzi's enterprises, and well-tailored individuals from Jerry's law firm and *TH&E*. But of all who were present, one misplaced, nonconforming group of individuals stood out from the rest. They were eighty-three homeless people from the streets of New

York—shaggy men with faces raw from scrubbing, dressed in trousers and mismatching jackets with garish-colored wool fabric shirts buttoned to the collars, and proud women attired in outdated dresses, hats, and gloves reeking with more than a dab of cheap cologne. Yet this crowd of individuals, joined together and separate from the others, beamed the proudest, being present at their closest friends' final farewell. Yes, an eclectic group but warmhearted and compassionate.

Still there remained one more very happy person—a confident, uninvited guest who was slipping among the crowd striving to remain unnoticed. He was the man of many names.

Although my disguise, the beard and highlighted hair worn after Martha recognized me, has long been gone, who can identify me now? No one! It's been years since Saratoga Springs and Miami, and now I need only a little time. For Stacey, you are about to join your mother, father, and all the others who had the misfortune of being involved in your not-to-have-been life.

But this time, the assassin's optimism was premature. The ever-alert Windy was intently watching the crowd, and one individual, lurking inconspicuously among the people, captured his attention.

I'll be damned. Look who's here. That's the guy Dora sketched. The one Martha described. His being here can't be good.

Windy followed at a distance. The man of many names went to the parking lot and entered a car. He got involved, looking through a satchel and talking on a telephone. Windy dashed back to the building where people were mingling. He motioned to Giant who stood head and shoulders above the crowd. Together with Shomazzi, the three huddled. Windy described what he observed.

Shoe ordered the two to detain the man and prevent him from getting near Stacey.

"In an hour, my goddaughter is returning to London, and I not only don't want him anywhere near her, I don't want him learning of her plans. Pick him up and bring him to me. His presence bothers me. We need to talk. For all I know, he may be key to Doc and Dora's deaths."

But the assassin was no amateur. He was well trained. Alert to people and events around him, he waited patiently, observing the restaurant's entrance. When the oversized man and the inconspicuous smaller one appeared and headed toward the parking lot, the man of many names watched. The smaller one stayed focused on where he was going; the bigger man, less composed, turned his head in the direction of the assassin's car and stared.

Time to go! Once again, Stacey, you remain alive. But what about tomorrow or the next day? You can't escape forever. And when I meet you, and I will, the fun begins. And away he drove.

When Shomazzi learned he had been outmaneuvered, he was enraged. He demanded that Stacey and Jerry accompany Windy, Giant, and him to Dulles International where they watched her safely board the plane to London.

CHAPTER 47

PRESENT, ABSENT, PRESENT

Shomazzi was not the only one infuriated. The man of many kills was also incensed. This lack of success was a first. Mistakes were becoming a festering irritation. He had devoted years to the job—unacceptable years. He could not—he would not allow the assignment to fail; it demanded results, rapid results.

Yet his leads had all become dead ends. He did not know where Stacey McDonald lived or how to find her. He had only one option, and while it had proven worthless so far, it required—by necessity—his attention.

Two times during the week, seven times in the past month, he had dialed *TH&E*. Once again, he tried.

"Anastasia McDonald, please?"

"I'm sorry," the operator replied, "she just left the country."

"Just left? When?"

"Actually, yesterday! And we're not expecting her back for some time."

"Yesterday? I spoke to you four days ago, and you told me she was away. Now, you're saying she returned and left again in less than a week?"

"Yes, sir, I am."

"Come on, lady, you've got to be kidding. No one, traveling as extensively as she does, flies in and out of the country without staying at least a week."

"Around here, we have a saying. 'There's Stacey. Don't wink, don't blink, catch her, or she'll be extinct.'" The caller slammed his telephone in the cradle.

What am I to do?

Pacing, he tried to think of a plan. Walking to a mini bar, he poured a double shot of ten-year-old single malt Scotch over ice. As he sipped, he continued to think. He moved to a chair and sat, staring at a blank television screen. Slowly, his expression changed, and a smile appeared on his lips.

A long shot but possible!

The wall clock struck four. Going to his bedroom, he slipped out of his jeans and flannel shirt and dressed for a night on the town. Putting on a turtleneck sweater and slacks, he went to the garage and drove to a parking lot across from *TH&E*. It was five o'clock, and the office staff was either leaving for home or planning on having an enjoyable Friday evening in town.

He watched, looking for someone he did not know and had never seen but was certain he would recognize. Finally, he saw her; she was one of four. Three of the women were attractive, animated, and bubbling in conversation. The fourth was plain, quiet, yet happy to be a part of the group. They continued walking while the casually dressed one followed at a distance.

Nearly seven blocks later, they entered a cocktail lounge, *This Side of Heaven*. It was happy hour, and crowds of young people were pushing through the door. The place was mobbed. The unknown one entered and began searching for the four women. Many of the tables were taken. Dancers with creative steps and motions were gyrating to loud, live music, and people standing two and three deep from the bar were shouting for drinks from four busy bartenders.

Scanning the room, he located the four women. Each was holding a glass of wine with the three pretty ones teasing a bunch of guys drifting to and from their table. The plain one lacked attention.

The stalker ordered a beer, stood off to the side, and nursed it while watching his quarry. After twenty minutes, the apparently disappointed gal rose from the table, said good-bye to her friends, and headed for the door.

Stepping up behind her, he said, "I hope you're not leaving?"

She stopped, turned, and looked in disbelief at this handsome stranger.

"Are you speaking to me?"

"I am! And as I said, I hope you're not leaving."

"And why should that matter to you?"

"Because I've been watching you, and I feel we have something in common."

"In common! You're kidding. We've never met! Never seen each other before, and you think we have something in common. How can that be?"

"Well, I noticed you sitting with three ladies. Friends, I suppose. Guys kept flowing to and from your table, and in this mad house, only you and I seem to be left alone. Yes, I'd say we have something in common."

"Well, thanks for sharing that observation with me."

Turning, she stepped forward to leave, but he took hold of her arm. "Please! Forgive me. I didn't mean to be callous. I'm just lonely and want someone to talk to. Nothing more. Won't you give me a moment? That table there is mine. Let me buy you a drink! Give me five minutes of conversation, and if you become bored, leave. Nothing distasteful can occur in that short time, and just possibly you'll enjoy my company."

Staring at him a moment, she said, "Fine. But for only five minutes!"

Once seated, he waved to a waitress and ordered a glass of wine for the new acquaintance. "Five minutes doesn't give us a great deal of time to really know each other, but we can at least begin with our names. I'm Jeff, Jeff Taylor," he lied. "And what may I call you?"

"Jane Wayne!"

Appropriate, he thought! *Plain Jane Wayne!*

"Well, Jane Wayne, you have about three minutes to mesmerize me with all the enchanting details of your life! So why don't you begin?"

She laughed. "Guess what! Your three minutes are already up. There's nothing enchanting about my life."

"No! No! No! I don't believe that! There's something enchanting in everybody's life. All one needs to do is relive one moment by recalling it. Then you'll discover that there is not just one thing but many things."

"Well, maybe for others but not for me."

"Let's play a game. Call it *Discovery*! I'll ask a simple question, and from that question, your answer will prompt all kinds of pleasant memories."

"Good! We'll try your game, and then you'll see what a humdrum life I live."

"Okay! Let's see? Where do I begin? How about where you work? What do you do for a living?"

"Congratulations, Jeff Taylor! You couldn't start with a bigger bummer. I'm a Recommendation Collaborator at *TH&E*"

"How about that? And a good one, I'll bet! Probably because of you, that international consulting company is able to present recommendations in an articulate, easy-to-implement, stimulating format."

"You're familiar with *Thoman, Holmes, and Ettinger*? I'm impressed. Few people have ever heard of the company. How do you know about it?"

"Actually, I don't know that much. Sometime ago, I met a young lady who works there. She couldn't say enough good things about her employer."

"Remember her name?"

"It was a while back. Although we talked for nearly an hour, I've had no reason to remember her until now. What the devil was her name? Give me a moment and let me think."

Sipping his beer, he stared at the table top. Finally, he said. "Her first name was unusual. Not a common Mary, Ann, or Joan! Something more unique! Something like . . . like . . . Casey! But . . . no . . . that wasn't it?"

"It wouldn't have been Stacey, would it?"

"That's it. Stacey! Does she still work there?"

"Does she? In the short time she's been with the company, she's brought on three new clients and helped develop solutions for others, all contributing favorably to the bottom line. Now, if you want to play *Discovery* with someone, she's the one. She's bound to have more fascinating memories than any person I know."

"Quit that! I'll bet if she were here, she'd be complimenting you on your contribution to her proposals and the impact it had on their acceptance."

"Possibly! Sharing accolades is her style. But it's unnecessary."

"You sound . . . not envious, but . . . idolizing."

"Why shouldn't I? She's intelligent and conceptual with beauty and personality! And besides, she has the opportunity to travel the world, visit exotic cities, and wear clothes that I envy! You should see her apartment. I'd give my teeth to have it. Stacey's a one and only."

"Admittedly, the fact that I even remember her confirms that she leaves a favorable impression. But you have her on such a pedestal, I wonder if it can support her? Let's just take one of those accolades. Her apartment, for example! What's so unusual about it?"

"Well, if you were ever in it, you'd discover beauty unlike anything I've ever seen. Furnishings, carpeting, pictures, accessories—a plethora of things that make me green with envy. And all this is in one of the finest gated communities in the area."

"This city has a number of those."

"But none superior to *The Quad*."

"I hear that's a beautiful place. But enough about Casey or Stacey or whoever. Let's talk about you, and some of your enchanting secrets."

Suddenly, Jane's attention was drawn away from the man of many names.

"What's the matter?" he asked.

"My friends. They're leaving. Best I go too. That way, I can split the cab fare home. Jeff, thanks for keeping me company. I hope I see you again. Give me a call at *TH&E* Maybe we can have coffee together?"

"I'll do that, Jane."

Standing, he gave the woman a hug, his fingers circling the back of her neck. Quickly, however, he dropped his hand before squeezing too hard.

CHAPTER 48

THE QUAD AND MORE LIES

Tuesday, November 17.

A security guard carrying a clipboard walked to the black Chevrolet door and asked, "Who do you wish to see, sir?"

"Actually, I'm new to the District. Recently transferred here and was told this is the place to live! Do you have an onsite leasing office?"

"We do. You continue straight ahead to Homestead Road. First street on the left. Turn, go about one hundred yards, and you'll be at the office. However, I need to give you a pass and jot down your name and license number on my sheet."

"Harry Hopkins," the man of many names lied. "This is a rental, and you'll have to check the plates for the number. I don't remember it. Later this afternoon, my wife will be arriving by plane, and I'll have to leave to get her. If this complex is appealing, the two of us will be returning. Can I keep the pass when I leave, or do you need to assign a new one?"

"No! You can leave and return as often as you like, as long as the visits are today. On your last trip out, put the pass in the drop box on the other side of this station."

Completing his notations, the security guard waved the visitor onto the premises.

Arriving at the office, he was greeted by an attractive woman.

"Welcome to *The Quad*. I'm Brenda James. I understand you're new to Northern Virginia, Mr. Hopkins."

"My, you know my name and that I'm not from around here. Am I that obvious?"

"No." She laughed. "The guard called ahead. We've had a couple of unwelcome visitors who tried to sneak in. To avoid that, we take precautions."

"Already I like what I am learning. So don't disappoint me. Tell me you have some vacancies to show."

"We do, indeed. A few, not many! What do you know about *The Quad*?"

"Actually, nothing other than what one of your residents told me. And she merely wet my curiosity. So tempt me!"

"That I will do! *The Quad* is a planned living community for families. Its name comes from the four sections that comprise it, and those four sections give it a distinctively unique milieu. The sections are differentiated by points on the compass—north, south, east, and west. Depending on where you are headed, the residence or building number is preceded by an *N, S, E,* or *W,* and no two sections are alike. Three of the sections—North, South, and East—are residential. West is commercial. It has a major supermarket chain store and two delicatessens: an independent retail pharmacy; three four-star restaurants; a department store, women's and men's apparel shops; a jewelry store, theater, several gasoline service stations; and a few specialty shops.

"North faces Washington DC; however, the capitol and monuments are too far away to be seen. Within North, there are twenty-two nine-room homes—two unoccupied, thirty-one townhouses, and eighty-seven apartments. The architecture is authentic Georgetown and caters predominantly to elected or appointed officials and high government service personnel.

"East attracts the younger, athletic set. It's the most spacious, and the residences face either tennis courts, an eighteen-hole golf course, or the Chesapeake Bay for the sailing buffs. This area has only thirteen homes, twenty-four townhouses—one unoccupied and one hundred and forty-five apartments, with two available. The architecture is more contemporary.

"The final area faces south toward Virginia, and its architecture is Williamsburg Colonial. There you will find predominantly homes and townhouses, a lesser number of apartments, currently with no availabilities.

"Before discussing the areas of appeal, I'm curious. Are you married?"

"Why?" he asked with a smile. "Are you looking?"

"No." She laughed. "As you can see, *The Quad* has only a few vacancies at this time, and while we have single male and female residents, the vacancies more adequately accommodate married couples and families."

"Oh, I'm married. A short time, less than two years! My wife is arriving by plane this afternoon, and if *The Quad* has appeal, I'll be bringing her here. If your time permits, I'd like you to show me around, so that I can describe it to her."

"I'm yours, though not permanently." She laughed. "My car's out back, and since I am familiar with what's available, I'll chauffeur. We'll visit the residential areas first and leave West, the shopping area, until the end. You observe and ask any questions that come to mind."

While driving, Brenda asked, "You mentioned an acquaintance living here. Who is that?"

"Anastasia McDonald."

"Oh, Stacey! She's one of my favorite people. Her apartment is in East. How do you know her?"

"Why I . . . . But first, tell me something. Your mailboxes are placed at the beginning of the roads leading to the residences. Obviously then, there is no at-home delivery?"

"That's right. These groupings facilitate postmen's handling and have proven not to be an inconvenience to the residents. As people either leave or arrive, they pass their individual boxes and conveniently mail or retrieve letters."

"But I notice many boxes have only a number, no names. Doesn't that cause some mishandling?"

"Not really! Some of our tenants do not want their addresses to be known, and we at *The Quad* honor those privacies. Having your name on your mailbox is your option. Insert your name in the slot provided or rely on the postman's ability to deliver the mail to a numbered box only."

"Fine, I'm sure it'll cause no problems. Just curious."

However, there are thirteen boxes in East without names, and one of those belongs to Stacey. Looks like I'll be doing some snooping.

After visiting each area, the man of many names mentioned, "My preference leans to East. My wife and I are pretty athletic and like to be around young people. You mentioned that there are two vacant apartments and one available townhouse."

"Would you like to see them?"

"Yes, if it's no trouble?"

"Please, Mr. Hopkins, it's my job."

As they walked through the units, he studied the layouts carefully. "Tell me! Are the floor plans for all the apartments and townhouses similar?"

"North, South, and East have identical floor plans within their respective areas but differ from one subdivision to the others architecturally. Construction costs, being what they are, provide some economies when we can duplicate plans."

At West, laborers were working hard with an outdoor amphitheater on a spacious green surrounded, at a distance, by retail outlets and other businesses.

"Appears you're getting ready for something exciting?"

"Indeed, we are. Every Thanksgiving, *The Quad* conducts what is known as *The Spectacular*. On Thursday, Friday, and Saturday evenings, this year, we'll be holding three different events. Thanksgiving night, a group of local actors and actresses will perform in a two-act play involving a war between the *Mayflower Pilgrims* and the *Indians*. This will be followed by the signing of a peace treaty and a Thanksgiving Day feast for all attendees.

"On Friday night, historic speeches and events that occurred from 1621 through 1864 will be reenacted, including Abraham Lincoln establishing the last Thursday in November as the celebrated Holiday. Then on Saturday evening, a local symphony orchestra and accompanying vocalists from the stage, screen, and opera will provide three hours of music guaranteed to excite every patriotic fiber in a person's body."

"And *The Quad* underwrites all these costs?"

"No indeed! Attendance to each event requires the purchase of a ticket, and that income goes toward covering expenses—insurance, costuming, set design and decorations, advertising and promotion, to name only a few. Payroll alone—actors, vocalists, musicians, security, and maintenance personnel—is significant. There's no way *The Quad* could underwrite this spectacular let alone the other two scheduled: Memorial Day and Christmas."

"Can the reward be worth the risk?"

"Previous productions—and this is the fifth one—have been more than satisfactory. *The Quad's* reputation and presence in the community have benefitted, and we've made a few dollars on each, so far."

"But what an accounting nightmare it has to be. Scheduling the work and incurring advance expenses before even the first ticket's been sold—must cause someone sleepless nights?"

"Oh, we have a highly capable accounting department, and considerable advance planning goes into the budgeting. In fact, Stacey, who's responsible for all production, has earned some unflattering titles. 'Budget Bitch' and the 'Good Riddance Priestess,' immediately come to mind."

"'Budget Bitch!' 'Good Riddance Priestess!' How do they apply?"

"Well, you've undoubtedly heard that she's been referred to as a High Priestess, the result of her ability to interpret the meaning of Tarot cards read. Well, 'Good Riddance' has now been added to the 'Priestess' because she's also known to make last-minute changes in programs conducted in order to keep in line with the budget. Consequently, the titles."

"She's obviously an amazing lady. To travel internationally, as much as she does, and to handle these projects as well . . . It's mind boggling."

"You're right. I know I couldn't. But then again, I'm not as well organized or as capable an administrator as she is. In both areas, she's the best I've ever known."

After nearly two more hours of travel and indoctrination to *The Quad*, the assassin thanked the office manager and promised to return with his wife.

CHAPTER 49

"THE WIFE"

As the man of many names left *The Quad,* he passed the drop box without leaving the admission slip. Continuing along the winding road, he drove several hundred yards and parked the Chevy. He then trotted back to the security guard shed.

The access and departure roads were separated by landscaped colorful gardens. Bordering the outer edges of the roads were trees of many varieties. He remained unseen, shielding his approach behind the trees.

Opposite the shed, he waited but not long. Two cars accessing *The Quad* approached the entry gate on the opposite road. As the guard left his post to gain information from the driver in the first car, the unnamed one ran to the opposite side of the shed and entered through its door, crouching low not to be seen. On the desk were three stacks of yellow admission tickets, one pile completed with the current day's date, the second with the following day's date, and a third pile of blank cards. Helping himself to some unmarked ones, he retreated through the door, walked rapidly back to his car, and put the passes in a briefcase.

Returning to his hotel room, he dialed the phone.

On the first ring, he heard, *"Lasting Memories!"*

"Hello, Carmen! It's a pleasure hearing your voice. This is Client 13."

"Oh, no! The pleasure's all mine. It's been a long time since we've heard from you, Mr. 13. How have you been?"

"Couldn't be better! Is Joy available?"

"Always for you! One moment please!"

"Joy Times!"

"Hello, Joy! It's I, 13."

"So it is. What a pleasure! Chandra will be delighted."

"Sorry, Joy. Not this time. I've a special request."

"Special? Not Chandra? I never thought I'd hear that from you?"

"Actually, Joy, I'm not looking for personal pleasure this time. I need a special escort. A woman forty to forty-five. Striking. Cultured. An actress who will be playing a role."

"What have you in mind, 13?"

"Nothing you need worry about! Provide the woman I want, and charge me twice the normal fee. And if she performs as well as I want, I'll reward her handsomely."

"You're being very secretive. If it were anyone else, I'd recommend other agencies to call. But for you, 13, because you are who you are, I'll provide such a woman. Antoinette's her name. Where and when do you need her?"

"Soon. An hour from now, two at the most. I'll drop by and pick her up. One other thing. Have her wearing a classic lady's suit, elegant blouse, nylons, and attractive high heels. I'll apprise her of her role. Nothing kinky. In fact, nothing sexual. She merely needs to be an articulate, well-bred showpiece."

Ninety-five minutes later, he met Antoinette.

"I'm impressed!" he told her. "If you speak and perform as well as you look, you'll earn a very handsome tip."

"To say you have my attention is an understatement. From what I've heard about you, 13, I am not only honored but intrigued. Tonight's nonsexual engagement is something new for me. Yet more beguiling is what's left unsaid, what's implied. Obviously, this night is likely to be something I've never experienced. So I am all ears. Tell me what this actress is supposed to do?"

"You're to be my wife but in pretense only. Tonight, I am Harry Hopkins, and you're Antoinette Hopkins. Do you have a pet name? Or a nickname?"

"Friends call me Toni."

"Toni, it will be. Here, put on this silver wedding band. Hopefully, it's not too large."

"Fits fine! I have big hands."

"Are you familiar with *The Quad*?"

"I've heard the name but know nothing about it."

"It's a planned residential community. In less than one hour, we're going to be seeing a leasing agent. Brenda James!

"We're going to be looking at some vacancies in three sections that they refer to as North, East, and South. I want you to be particularly interested in two apartments in East, a one-bedroom and a two-bedroom unit. While single people live at *The Quad*, management seems more interested in leasing to married couples, with and without children. My guess is they've had some problems—noisy parties, roughhousing, and possibly structural damaging by the singles. It's important to me that they are willing to accept me as a tenant. So your presence, your favorable impression is a quality important to my being approved."

"What happens after you move in, and I'm no longer around?"

"I'll find acceptable excuses. You travel. We've separated. Whatever. I'll worry about that later. All that is important now is for you to help sell us as a couple."

Arriving at *The Quad,* Toni and Harry were warmly greeted. They visited vacancies in the various sections with Brenda's attention directed more toward Toni than Harry. And the actress responded magnificently, frequently guiding conversations to Harry that allowed him to pursue information of importance.

In the apartments at East, the "wife" made inquiries that a prospective female buyer was likely to ask. While a number of the questions were of little value to the assassin, one regarding a nonobvious crawl space, that Toni discovered, appealed to the killer's interests in hiding.

Upon completing the tour, Brenda James offered her first sign of encouragement. "This has been a gratifying visit. I hope, Toni, you and Harry decide to live here. It takes couples like you for *The Quad* to maintain the reputation and respect required."

As the lady of the evening slid into the car, Harry said, "Toni, you were outstanding. Besides your normal fee, I'm giving you a one-thousand-dollar-bonus, plus dinner in one of the restaurants at West." Two hours elapsed, and the meals were finally finished with the two agreeing that the restaurant was worthy of its four-star rating.

Back at *Lasting Memories,* Toni asked the man of many names to park his car around the corner of the building.

Shutting off the ignition, he turned to her and said, "Again, my thanks. I couldn't have asked for more."

To this, she replied, "You possibly don't know this, but you're a mystery to all of us inside. Chandra has gushed about you so much that we've become jealous. I have no idea how exciting you may be in my bed, but your handsome appearance, your demeanor, and your generosity tonight is deserving of a gift from me."

Reaching over, she unzipped his fly and moved her face to his lap. Later, stroking him a moment longer, she looked into his eyes and said, "If Chandra is ever unavailable, call me." With that, she left the car.

CHAPTER 50

FINDING STACEY

In the hotel room, the tracker replaced his afternoon apparel with a turtleneck sweater, trousers, sport coat, felt hat, and tennis shoes—all in black. From under the front seat of his car, he removed a pair of Montana license plates and substituted them for the rental plates.

At *The Quad,* he entered another security gate and flashed the original admittance card. Then he drove to the East and scanned the mail boxes for a woman's name. Finding one, he proceeded to an upper-level apartment and knocked on the door. An elderly woman opened it.

"Is this Stacey's apartment?"

"No, young man, it isn't."

Comparing the number on the door with one written on a slip of paper, he said, "Gosh, I'm sorry. I must have written down an incorrect number. Do you by any chance know a Stacey McDonald?"

"I do."

"Would you mind telling me where she lives? I'm already ten minutes late and don't care to keep her waiting any longer."

"I'm not certain of her apartment number, but I believe she lives one or two roads down from here. Go out this road and turn right. Wish I could be of more help. Sorry."

With that, she slammed the door in his face.

At the next road, he tried the same approach. No one answered the doorbell. At another door, the person who answered had never heard of the woman.

As he walked to his car, he saw an elderly lady, in the next driveway, struggling with a bag groceries.

"May I be of help?" he asked.

She looked into his smiling face and said, "I'd like that. There are four more bags on my backseat."

He retrieved two, carried them to her kitchen, and returned for the others. As he entered her home, the woman was removing her coat and hanging it in the closet. Passing her, he placed the two bags beside the other three.

"You don't know how much I appreciate your help. I'm getting too old and too weak to manage all that weight."

"I'm glad to have been of help. Hopefully, you can do a favor for me in return."

Her smiling face turned solemn.

"What is it you want?"

"Stacey McDonald asked me to meet her tonight, but I apparently wrote down the wrong address." Removing a slip of paper from his pocket, he continued, "I thought she lived in the E200 section, but after stopping there, I learned I was mistaken and was directed to the E600s, instead. You wouldn't by any chance know which apartment is hers?"

Once again smiling, the woman said, "I certainly do, but I thought she was out of town. Guess I'm wrong."

Going to the front, she pointed to an upper apartment across the road. "She lives in E648."

"And here I wrote down 248 rather than 648. No wonder I couldn't find her. Thank you very much."

"Anytime! Tell Stacey I think you're very nice."

It was five fifty in the evening, and the homeward-bound vehicular traffic was increasing in number. Deciding to wait for a less busy time, the "nice man" drove to the guard's shed and dropped the admission ticket in the box.

Thursday, November 19

Fifty hours had elapsed since learning where Stacey lived. It was late, and the prewinter season night—cool, dark, and free of moon and stars—was ideal for visiting a vacant apartment. Other residents, keeping warm and comfortable in their dwellings, were unlikely to notice a stranger prowling around the area.

The security guard, after examining the yellow admission pass, waved him through the gate. At her apartment, the intruder saw a lighted table lamp, but it gave little thought, confident it was only a warning to outsiders of the occupant's presence.

He continued to the E700 section and parked in a visitor's spot. Then, he proceeded on foot through a passageway separating E704 and E705. From behind these units, he moved rapidly over a grassy area to the rear entrances of apartments E630 through E639. One floor up were the backdoors to the single-bedroom apartments, E640 to E644, a supply room, a passageway to the front entrances, and the backdoor entrances to the two-bedroom apartments, E645 through E649.

Quietly, he ascended the stairs to E648. Knocking on the door, he waited. No activity! He removed keyhole picks from his pocket, unbolted both the door lock and dead bolt and then unfastened a chain. Immediately, he disarmed the alarm.

There's no safe haven from me, Stacey.

Beyond the door was a hall leading from the rear entrance to the front door. To the intruder's left were four doors: one leading to a laundry room complete with washer, dryer, and stationary tub; the second to a master boudoir with a connecting bathroom to the guest's bedroom and its private hallway entrance; and finally, the fourth door leading to a spacious living room complete with visitor's lavatory.

To his right were another four doors: the first leading into a storage area; the second to a well-equipped kitchen with access to the dining room and its entrance to the hall; and finally, a fourth door leading to Stacey's den and its architectural opening into the dining room. The design of the floor plan gave a tenant the option to either close off or leave open a viewing access from the kitchen through the dining room into the den.

Of particular interest was the storage area. Within the room was a sizable wire cage, shelving on two walls, and an open floor area with boxes neatly stacked, the contents identified. Stepping around the boxes, he walked to the end of the cage and squeezed through a space separating it from the wall. Behind the cage and continuing the length of the enclosure was a narrow three-foot-wide aisle similar to Toni's discovery in the other apartment. Several empty two-drawer file cases were abandoned there, leaving space for him to hide and wait.

He then examined the bedrooms, spending time in Stacey's room opening drawers, fondling and smelling bras, panties, and other garments of interest. The kitchen received cursory attention with only the knives being thumbed for sharpness. From there, he walked into the dining room with its custom-made table, matching chest, fabric-covered chairs, and corner cabinet displaying china and crystal.

At the den, he was surrounded by books. In one wall section, behind fake book bindings, was a hidden bar. From a shelf, he removed a glass, partially filled it with ice, and poured over the cubes several ounces of Johnny Walker Black Label. While sipping the drink, he went to her desk and rummaged through the drawers for correspondence and personal notes. There, he found what he needed—her returning airline flight, date, and time of arrival. Reentering the kitchen, he rinsed the glass and returned it to the bar.

Satisfied with what he learned, he proceeded to the living room. There, his eyes grew narrow and intense. To an observer, the explanation would be an appreciation for the room's completeness—subtle posh carpeting essential to the antique furnishings and modern-day pieces, enhanced by wall-hanging masterpieces on patterned fabric, crowned by sculptured molding, and personalized by a television-stereo system and electric fireplace.

However, such an explanation would be inaccurate. The intruder's eyes were livid. In a corner location, beneath a lighted wall sconce, was a card table—Dora's card table. Displayed were two photographs, one of Doc, the other of Dora. Their faces were slanted forward, their eyes studying a silent message. On the table, Tarot cards lay in the *Law of Attraction* spread, an uncompleted reading Dora had planned for Doc on the night they were killed.

Irate, the intruder charged the room, grabbed a leg of the table, and hurled it with its contents into the center of the room. He stood motionless, never to know what the cards revealed. Gradually, his scowl turned to a smile. The clutter, the destruction of the shrine, was gratifying. He laughed heartily, practically dancing to the rear entrance. He rearmed the alarm, replaced the chain, and engaged the locks, never losing the smile on his face.

At his car, he gave thought to the visit. *No one, Stacey, creates a lasting tribute to people I dispose of. If I were able, I'd even eliminate every memory every survivor had of the needless people I've rid the world of. But with you, Stacey, I'll be able to accomplish that. How? Because your days are numbered. You haven't time to reflect on Doc and Dora. Or to enjoy life at The Quad, TH&E, or any other place that gives you pleasure. No, Stacey! Your mine, all mine!*

Once again, he began to laugh—long and hard—all the way to the exit gate.

CHAPTER 51

SURPRISE—YOU HAVE VISITORS

Sunday Morning, November 22, 2009

The assassin was scruffy, his face unshaven, trousers and jacket wrinkled, and a loose tie hung around his neck. He had spent the night in the airport walking, reading, and napping. The previous evening's scheduled arrival from London Heathrow Airport had been delayed. Yet he remained calm unlike others in the waiting area.

A light at the gate flashed, and he heard an announcement reporting the arrival of Stacey's plane. After jotting down two more words in the *Washington Post* crossword puzzle, he saw travelers heading his way.

Remaining seated, he waited. Finally, she appeared, and he rose, placing the folded paper under his arm. He reached into his pocket and smiled. His hand clutched a souvenir—Frisky Finger Freddie's switchblade.

Minutes from now you'll taste the sweet blood of another victim, he mused. *The intended one! Twenty-five years late in coming.*

As he headed toward her, she stopped, turned, and looked at the passengers behind her. A man, waving his arm, had apparently called her name. She was too distant and the crowd too noisy for the assassin to hear what was said. She waited. When the man reached her side, the two proceeded together to the escalator.

The assassin originally intended to follow his prey to the lower level, stab her when she walked with the crowd to customs, and casually leave during the confusion. Now, his plans needed to change.

Moving quickly, he rudely pushed his way in front of two elderly women and descended the escalator behind Stacey and her friend.

"Where are you going?" he heard the man ask.

"The office!"

"That makes two of us. Is your car here?"

"No, I came by cab. Cheaper than eleven days in long-term parking and more convenient."

"Good! I've reserved a stretch, and the driver will be at the carousel. Give him your luggage tickets and ride back with me to the shop."

The assassin stepped back and watched the man beckon the chauffeur and point out their luggage. The driver took Stacey's bags, and her colleague carried his own to the short-term lot.

Damn, another delay. But I'll get you, bitch, and it'll be soon.

* * * * *

Two nights later, the disappointed one pulled his car into a visitor's parking space in full view of E648. Other than her living room security light, the apartment remained dark. Restless, his mind traveled back to the last visit.

I wonder, Stacey, what you thought when you arrived home from your trip and found "Mommy, Daddy," the cards, and table strewn across the living room. Bet you didn't sleep well that night. Well, tonight you won't be sleeping. In fact, you'll never sleep again.

Content and happy, he reached for his crossword puzzle book and waited.

Finally, a party of four arrived. Stacey unlocked the front door, and they all moved into the den. Taking orders, the hostess proceeded to serve wine and cocktails. Through binoculars, the assassin watched the activity.

The hostess left the room with one of the men but quickly returned with a folding card table, while the man carried four folding chairs. Setting up the table, a chair was placed at each side, two close to the table and two somewhat removed from it. Out of the desk drawer,

Stacey retrieved something. The uninvited visitor, having previously inspected the drawer, smiled.

Good, a reading! That'll give me all the time I need.

Again, he was correct. The female guest, sitting across from Stacey, shuffled the Tarot cards.

At the direction of the hostess, the guest cut the deck with her left hand and placed the cards in three stacks, right to left. With her left hand, she retrieved the pile on the left, placed it on top of the center pile, and then transferred the larger group to the remaining pile.

From the pile, the guest selected a card and placed it on the table. Conversation was exchanged between the two. Following questions and turns by the querent, Stacey read the cards and positioned them in one of the twelve spreads of choice. After four turns, the woman turned to one of the men, clutched her chest with both hands, and spoke with what appeared to be great joy.

While this was occurring, the stalker left his car and ran through the passageway to the other side of the apartments. He quietly ascended the steps, two at a time. At the upper level, he moved to the back of E648. Through a window in the door, he could see lights at the far end of the hallway. Quietly unlocking the door, he entered the apartment and moved silently into the storage room, stepping cautiously around the boxes to the opening between the back of the cage and the wall. He moved one of Stacey's file cabinets near the entrance, and there he sat.

The visitors finally left, and Stacey began rinsing the glasses and plates. The unknown one continued to wait. Patience was a habit mastered over the years, one that helped arouse him as he waited to disperse the evil he delighted in giving.

The clock struck one. All was quiet. Flashing the beam from a penlight, he cautiously left the storage room. Darkness was everywhere. It was his ally. Proceeding down the hallway, he moved into her open bedroom. It was empty.

From the door, he saw a shallow light cast on the carpet outside the entrance leading to the den. Crossing the hallway to the kitchen, he looked through open doors to the den. Stacey sat at her desk, her profile visible to him. She would write, stop, and think then resume writing.

Tiptoeing into the dining room, he carefully watched her every movement, his eyes never leaving her face. He rubbed his hands together and cracked his knuckles. From his pocket, he removed the knife, pressed the button on the handle, and a seven-inch blade sprang out. Resting the sharp edge against his lips, he smiled. He stared. No other motion, no other sound. Only the intensity of his steadfast gaze.

Slowly, she turned. Less than twenty feet away stood a man, an unknown man. One with vicious dark eyes, a cold, cruel smile, an open knife tapping against his lips. An eerie laugh penetrated the silence.

What caused Stacey to look? A mental warning? The intensity of his stare? She would never know. She would only react. Leaping from her chair, she dashed to the front door and threw it open. The alarm, engaged when her guests left, sounded loud and long through the sleeping community. Lights in the six hundred dwellings illuminated. Front doors opened. People in night clothes, robed and unrobed, appeared in doorways. Stacey stood with her back to the handrail, screaming. The intruder had only one option. He ran down the hallway, out the rear entrance, down the stairs, to his car. Quickly, he left the parking area.

The roads turned active. Security cars rushed to the E600 block. The intruder had several decisions and again made the correct one. Instead of driving to the front gate, he went to West, the commercial section. Night shift laborers were working to finalize the stage, arrange the seating, erect the lighting, and cordon off areas where battles were to be fought. Preparation for the Thanksgiving Weekend celebration was nearing conclusion. The intruder parked among hundreds of workers' cars, making detection of one more unpretentious vehicle difficult to spot.

Tired, he pulled his topcoat tightly around him, lay down in the backseat, and closed his eyes. But sleep eluded him for nearly an hour. Whether it was the cool November night or the disappointment in not finalizing what he wanted to do or the possible discovery and ultimate failure in the assignment, he was uncertain. Yet the fear in Stacey's face, as it reappeared again and again in his mind's eye, brought a smile to his mouth, one that remained even through the overdue slumber.

Hours later, he awoke. All was quiet. He started the engine and drove away with the workmen who were finishing their shifts. No one followed him. No one questioned him. Once again, he remained undetected.

CHAPTER 52

THE FINALE

Vandalism and residential burglaries are not infrequent. While they draw local exposure, the coverage is neither front-page news nor more than an aside to the audiovisual media. Yet Stacey's intrusion received prominent attention from the *Washington Post, Washington Times,* local networks, and several tabloid publications. The reason: it was not the typical break-in at a customary neighborhood home or standard office building; it occurred at *The Quad*. And Anastasia McDonald, the resident, was an attractive staff member at *Thoman, Holmes, & Ettinger International,* a woman who also happened to be in charge of the Thanksgiving Weekend Spectacular at *The Quad*. All this provided ammunition for reporters' stories, some factual, others unsubstantiated.

One specific article brought lasting coverage. It was entitled "Is It in the Cards?" Stacey's empowerment in explaining the secrets of the Arcana had been discovered when former querants were interviewed, and her "stardom" blossomed when it was revealed that she was more than merely a reader; she was considered by some to be a High Priestess of Tarot.

This publicity was unwelcome and impeding. People, particularly residents at *The Quad,* approached her again and again, seeking either audiences or answers to meaningless questions. And while she endeavored to minimize any clairvoyant abilities and remain focused on other primary responsibilities, total escape was impossible. The weekend event demanded her presence, and a following trip to China, on Tuesday, could not come quickly enough.

In the meantime, eyes followed her everywhere, including one pair never far away. The assassin's supply of admission tickets to *The Quad* gave him access when desired; and disguises concealing facial features, along with garments belying his physique, enabled him to remain unworried when conspicuously in the open. Together with his knife, confidence was his ally.

Immediately after the break-in, Jerry Forrest assigned his law firm's chief investigator, Hank White, to be Stacey's guardian.

At first, she rebelled, but Jerry persuaded her, saying, "Do it for a short time. When things quiet down, you can be on your own, but for now, go along with what's good for you. I'd never forgive myself if something ominous happened. Humor me, Stace! Please?"

Whether it was the passion of his plea or the demands before her, Stacey agreed. Too much was on her plate to waste time arguing against something that was in her best interest. She needed to finalize the weekend performance and have it behind her.

I'm Proud to Be an American
A Thanksgiving Weekend Spectacular at The Quad
Tickets Available to All

Banners, posters, and local advertising gave the event area-wide exposure without overselling the production.

Thursday night's opening exceeded expectations. Battles between the Pilgrims and the Indians, the signing of a peace treaty, and a Thanksgiving Day feast delighted the audience. But this was merely the beginning. Nonticket holders were racing to open windows anxious to attend the Friday and Saturday night performances that would include important Americans making historic speeches while reenacting events spanning the years.

* * * * *

Behind closed curtains on Friday night, four trumpets blared, accompanied by the soft-sounding strings of seven violins. Then the brass, percussion, string, and reed sections of *The Quad's* one-hundred-and-ten-piece orchestra blended in.

Late audience arrivals ran around in search of places to sit but found that all the seats were occupied, and the only spaces available were open areas on the ground not cordoned off for the actors' skits. These empty spots were rapidly taken with blankets brought by the last-minute crowd, hoping to be within eye and ear distance of the performances.

Suddenly, the orchestra stopped playing. A hush fell over the audience. Then there was pandemonium, overlapping, unrecognizable conversations communicated behind closed curtains. As the draperies parted, the source of the uproar became visible. Men were shouting; the dialogue was intense; emotions were peaking; and the conversations clashed.

"Remember Lexington," shouted one voice above all others.

"And don't forget, it was the British who fired the first shot," interrupted a hardliner.

"But what about the damn British ships? Those anchored along our coast?" screamed another. "What are we going to do about them?"

"The navy be damned," objected a responder. "It's the Redcoats, we need to fear. They're already on our land, in our towns, killing Americans, and causing untold damage and corruption that will take years to clean up."

And the shouting continued, most voices ignoring others; many informants interested in only what they had to say, not what others were saying.

"Order! Order! I insist on order. Quiet all of you. Sit and act like the men of honor you're supposed to be. Not an out-of-control mob," shouted the president, "Peyton Randolf."

Gradually, the voices hushed. "John Hancock" leaned back in his chair, his eyes searching the crowd. "Benjamin Franklin" merely shook his head. And a closely seated "Thomas Jefferson" stared down at folded hands. Others, those delegates representing their colonies on this May 10, 1775 meeting of the Second Continental Congress, remained chastised.

"Now, if we are to do what we need to do, as appointees of the colonies we represent, then we need to act and to behave like civilized leaders. There's much to be discussed—the adoption of the Declaration of Independence, the raising of armies, the planning of tactics, and more, much more.

And the meeting progressed. Interspersed among the vocal complaints were objections to the acts of the British, those that were disrupting the economy and the independence of the colonies—the Sugar Act, the Currency Act, the Quartering Act, and the Stamp Act. And although the delegates maintained their self-control, it was evident that their animosity toward the crown was unyielding.

Darkness descended on the stage, and silence followed. Moments passed. Then a soprano, accompanied by *The Quad's* orchestra, inspired the audience with Irving Berlin's *God Bless America*:

> *"While the storm clouds gather far across the sea,*
> *Let us swear allegiance to a land that's free.*
> *Let us all be grateful for a land so fair*
> *As we raise our voices in a solemn prayer . . . ."*

Complete silence followed. Then applause, a resounding applause. Spotlights illuminated the darkened stage. Two people appeared: a standing "George Washington" speaking to a seated "Betsy Ross." Handing her a piece of paper, he commissioned the lady to make the first American flag.

As a banner of thirteen stars and thirteen stripes rose on its staff, a coral group sang:

> *"O beautiful for spacious skies,*
> *for amber waves of grain;*
> *for purple mountain majesties*
> *above the fruited plain!" . . . .*

With the final notes of *America the Beautiful*, the floodlights diminished and others brightened. A battle raged on the off-cordoned grounds. Redcoats retreated; the Continental Army charged. A salvo of canon and rifle shots were fired; explosions and smoke filled the air. Alternating lights, individually illuminated, isolated portions of the grounds, focusing on different scenes—groups of wounded and dead soldiers and units of Minutemen advancing against armies of Redcoats.

More changes in lighting and focus. A captive Continental Army Captain, surrounded by the British, was heard to say courageously and with conviction, *"Almighty God! I know not what course others may take, but as for me, give me liberty or give me death."* The ovation for "Nathan Hale" was that of a proud American audience.

Then a drumroll. More gunfire. Screaming voices and agonizing calls for medics pierced the scene. Two buglers—one near at hand and resounding, the other more distant and echoing—played taps.

The setting faded to the evening's natural darkness. The heaven burst forth in brightness. Fireworks lit the sky. Minutemen were seen stalking, routing the Redcoats. The direction of the war was turning. Mothers and fathers, youngsters and soldiers paraded joyfully to the spirited music of a fife and drum corps. Peace was finally declared, and Great Britain acknowledged the new nations' victory with a spirited portrayal of the Peace of Paris.

A standing audience applauded its approval. Conversations began. People anticipated the following night's production.

* * * * *

Saturday's performance opened to a "paperboy" shouting, "Extra, extra! Buy your paper here. Read all about the nation's commerce, its economy. Learn the problems facing us. It's all in this paper, and the price is only two cents. Read and learn. Extra! Extra!"

Cameos portrayed a waffling postwar economy. Exports and imports with Great Britain remained lower than the prewar years. Trade with a restricted West Indies deprived the country of a major market. A partial offset came from shipments delivered to other European nations, China, and the Pacific Northwest.

On stage, "farmers, hunters, manufacturers, and merchants" bartered over the exporting of native items exhibited—tobacco, furs, wheat, lumber, and cotton. But it was the dialogue and acting that told the story. With China, a new customer, exporting flourished. But half-filled ships destined for Britain were delayed, and those scheduled for the restricted West Indies remained anchored at the piers. Other ships, partially filled, sailed to any location demanding goods.

In time, conditions changed. Foreign trade and domestic commerce grew. The economy strengthened. Improvements were highlighted on a large screen with pictures filmed. Key to the reversal were major accomplishments—the completion of the Erie Canal, increasing domestic freight shipped east and west over the five Great Lakes, and a tonnage of goods handled by the merchant marines from ports along the Atlantic and Pacific coastlines. American products—cotton, wheat, flour, beef, pork, and technological advancements—were in demand.

Abruptly, the screen went blank. Nothing was seen. Then gradually, very small, difficult to read, years appeared—1861 to 1865. Slowly, the years began to grow . . . and to grow . . . and to grow until they became so large they over flowed the screen.

Darkness followed. Then a boy, under a spotlight, walked on stage. It was the newspaper boy, reappearing and shouting, "Extra! Extra! Read all about the nation divided. The North against the South."

Depicted by cameos, different circumstances came into view. A large screen presented photographs of the Monitor and Merrimac, along with story-book snapshots of important battles—Shiloh, Antietam, Fredericksburg, Vicksburg, Chattanooga, Petersburg, and Atlanta.

The screen again went blank. Another spotlight focused down on a tall bearded man, dignified and solemn. From his lips, for only seconds longer than two minutes, he recited two hundred and sixty-eight words—self-written words—words that are among the most frequently referenced, finest articulated words ever spoken by an American:

> *"Fourscore and seven years ago our fathers*
> *brought forth on this continent a new nation,*
> *conceived in liberty and dedicated to the*
> *proposition that all men are created equal.*
> *Now we are engaged in a great civil war*
> *testing whether that nation or any nation*
> *so conceived and so dedicated can long endure . . . ."*

Faint whispers of an emotionally inspired audience spread throughout West as "Abraham Lincoln" concluded his Gettysburg Address.

More darkness, another spotlight! The narrowly focused beam angled upward on four men, center stage. The audience hushed. One man, the lead, began to sing, *"Oh, say, can you see, by the dawn's early light . . ."* From his left, a baritone harmonized. *"What so proudly we hailed at the twilight's last gleaming . . ."* Then a third, a well-groomed tenor voice, complemented the two with *"Whose broad strips and bright stars thro' the perilous fight . . .,"* led to the fourth, a cultured bass voice, joining the trio through to the conclusion of the *National Anthem*.

The audience, on its feet from the moment the lead began singing, faced a fifty-star American Flag and sang along with the quartet, their hands respectfully over their hearts.

Lights again brightened the stage. Seated around a table were four American patriots. Three were quiet and listening. The fourth began to recite:

> *"We the People of the United States,*
> *in order to form a more perfect Union*
> ....
> *do ordain and establish this Constitution*
> *for the United States of America."*

Everyone, performers and audience together, remained quiet, giving thought to the Preamble of the Constitution of the United States. The stillness was broken by a choral group singing:

> *My country, 'tis of thee,*
> *sweet land of liberty,*
> *of thee I sing . . . .*

At the conclusion of *America,* another prominent American appeared on the screen as the final moments of *I'm Proud to Be an American* neared its finale. The American, John Fitzgerald Kennedy, was heard reciting a line from his inaugural address:

> *My fellow citizens of the world*
> *Ask not what your country can do for you—*
> *Ask what you can do for your country.*

The screen darkened; perimeter lighting illuminated the entire grounds. A standing audience began to shout, "Stacey, Stacey, Stacey."

To the side and behind the curtains, the producer was prepared to walk on stage. But she hesitated when other cries for her appearance were voiced. "Priestess, Priestess, Priestess." Slowly, she shook her head and quickly sent signals to the conductor and a vocalist to conclude the three-day performance with another inspirational favorite:

> *"O Columbia, the gem of the ocean,*
> *The home of the brave and the free,*
> *The shrine of each patriot's devotion,*
> *A world offers homage to thee . . . ."*

As the final words and notes were heard, Stacey appeared from the left side of the stage, bowed her head, and quickly retreated behind the curtains. The applause continued for her reappearance, but she never returned. Instead, she left the area and headed back to her residence.

Fireworks lit up the sky. The curtain fell. *The Quad's Thanksgiving Spectacular* was over.

* * * * *

While the performance was nearing its end, Jerry Forrest's investigator noticed two men taking an unusual interest in the apartments at E600. They were not the typical visitors. Their movements indicated a behavior refined through training and practice. Jerry telephoned for backup. Together, two investigators covertly began watching the unknowns.

Since the intruders were not novices, they became aware of being watched and developed a plan. The larger of the two visitors roamed around the apartment complex, both front and back. His partner entered a car and drove away. Waving to the departing driver, the big man retraced his steps toward the last apartment, E639. Before arriving there, he was confronted by the two investigators.

The one in charge asked, "Sir, mind telling us what you're doing here?"

Glancing from one to the other, the big man noticed that they were six feet away from him and four feet apart from each other. While the stranger was a good four inches taller than either of the two and outweighed both by nearly thirty pounds, he was not foolish enough to make any abrupt moves, especially with their hands in their pockets.

"I'm waiting for a friend," he replied.

"And who might that be? And just why are you and your friend here?"

"Unless you're security guards with *The Quad,* and you don't appear to be wearing uniforms, I don't see a need to answer those questions. In fact, I imagine I have as much right in being here as you have."

"Watch your mouth, big guy! Now, I'll ask you again. And I'd suggest you answer me politely. Why are you—"

From behind the two investigators, a voice said, "Raise your hands above your heads, gentlemen, because I have a very itchy finger."

The lead investigator jerked his head around and was looking into the face of the man who had driven away. In one hand was a Glock 9mm handgun. Slowly, the two men raised their hands.

The big man grabbed one of the investigators, slapped a pair of handcuffs on his wrists, and pressed his foot into the back of the investigator's knee, forcing him to the ground. The second man felt something hit his head and suddenly went unconscious.

Speaking to the conscious man lying on the ground, the little one said, "Rather my answering you, why don't you instead tell us what you're doing here?"

The investigator remained silent.

"Giant, find Stacey and bring her here. Maybe she can shed some light on who these characters are?"

"Stacey? Anastasia McDonald?" asked the investigator.

"And what if it is?" asked the little one.

"What's she got to do with you?"

"When she gets here, she'll tell you. Now, Giant, go find her."

Twenty minutes elapsed before Stacey arrived.

"Windy, what's going on? First, Giant surprises me, and now you."

"Mr. Shomazzi saw the articles in the *Post* and *Times*. He thought you might need protection, so we were sent. It's good to see you, Stacey. It's been a long time."

"Who are these lugs?" asked Hank White, Jerry's chief investigator.

"They're associates of my godfather. Giant, remove those cuffs, and the four of you follow me to my apartment. After this evening, I need a glass of wine, and I'll gladly pour one for each of you as well."

Across the parking area, the unknown one stood covertly observing the entire proceedings. *Three I know, but who are the other two? And why are they leaving together? Something's strange, and I have to find out what it is.*

CHAPTER 53

ADVICE

It was nearly five o'clock on Sunday afternoon. Stacey stirred, stretched, and looked out her window at snow falling gently to the ground. She smiled. She not only enjoyed the winters, but the thirteen hours of sleep had fully refreshed her.

On Saturday night, she had been exhausted. The program had been demanding, and the invitation to have a friendly glass of wine with her protectors became two and then three before everyone left. Her movements to bed had been interrupted by a call from her godfather. His nonrequested and not-to-be-interrupted advice lasted two and one-half hours. At four o'clock and finally in bed, she was now uncertain if her eyes had closed before or after her head touched the pillow.

During their long-distance conversation, dozens of questions had been asked, and her abbreviated answers combined with a number of "I don't know" led Shomazzi to one conclusion; he would arrive at Ronald Reagan National Airport on Sunday night at seven o'clock.

"I'll be picked up by Giant and Windy. When I get to your place, make certain that Forrest and his two investigators are there. I want to meet them, especially the lawyer."

* * * * * *

From a prompt seven o'clock until twelve-thirty that night, the seven talked. Shomazzi made it clear that he was not going to allow anything to happen to his goddaughter. And although he took charge of the meeting, information solicited and questions asked were not always answered to his satisfaction, especially those involving the intruder.

"Forrest, you can keep these two bulldogs of yours on the scene, but I want the three of you to understand something. Giant and Windy are her personal guards. Don't interfere with them.

"Stacey, I want you to move out of this joint. Obviously, the security is lax, or else this door crasher, Forrest's two private dicks, and Giant, and Windy wouldn't have bypassed the gate so easily. You need to be where you can be safe."

Stacey listened but said nothing.

"Windy, find out who that meddler is. Then we'll decide what to do with him!"

"Hold on, Mr. Shomazzi! None of us, especially your goddaughter, is going to be party to some vigilante scheme that takes the law into your hands. I won't allow it. You want your jokers to shadow and protect Stacey; that's fine with me. But there's a limit as to what that protection will be. Am I being clear enough for you to understand?"

Shomazzi looked at the lawyer with new respect. Forrest had been quiet during the better part of the prolonged meeting, asking a few profound questions and offering some thoughtful observations. But until this moment, he had remained somewhat subservient to the older man, sitting back and sizing him up. This outburst gave the lawyer spine.

Staring silently at Forrest, Shoe finally said, "Okay! I'll accept that for the time being. The seven of us will work together as a team. Keeping everyone informed. Not making any independent major moves. You, your guys, me, or my men. But if something bad is about to happen, we damn well communicate among ourselves before the fact. In the meantime, Stacey, I want you out of here. And pronto! Giant! Get the car. I need a couple of hours sleep before boarding the plane home. Stacey, come into the next room. Alone!

She entered the room and sat down beside Shoe.

"Tell me about this Forrest! What's he to you? I know he's your tennis teacher and longtime friend! But is there more to your relationship than that? Something in the future? Something you haven't told me? Romance? Marriage, maybe? Anything like that?"

"No, Shoe, nothing like that! I see him often. We're close and pal around together. But nothing more! His work and my work are our priorities."

"Well, maybe it's about time you start examining those priorities. I like him, and I think he likes you. Don't lose something you'll later regret."

With that, the man kissed his goddaughter on the cheek and shouted, "Windy, time to go."

CHAPTER 54

A DECISION!

It was Sunday night, and everyone had left. Stacey was alone, deep in thought—confusing thoughts, uncomfortable thoughts, unanswerable thoughts. This was unusual. Normally, when she was troubled, she was able to develop solutions. And though she never admitted it, she enjoyed the challenge in overcoming resistance. Failure was an option she never accepted. Whether it had to do with her education, her tennis, her swimming, or her career, she always expected to be an achiever.

But this was different. This had to do with her emotions, her heart, her feelings, her personal life. She sat staring at the bare desktop, mentally wrestling with the things she had been told. Her mind kept returning to what Shoe had said. His two pieces of advice: "Find somewhere else to live," and "don't lose something you'll later regret."

The first, "find somewhere else to live," was not difficult. In fact, relocation was a viable option. She had been thinking about leaving *The Quad* ever since the break-in. Where she might go was an uncertainty, but the possibilities were numerous. In fact, a move was both exciting and settling. She could leave surroundings that had proven to be less than safe and enjoy a personal life away from the demands of *The Quad's* holiday spectaculars. *Over Thanksgiving, I proved to myself I could supervise a successful production. I don't need those exhausting demands anymore. It's time for me to enjoy living.*

But Shoe's second piece of advice, "Don't lose something you'll later regret," has me deeply concerned. I like Jerry. He's seldom away from my thoughts. Could I marry him? Yes, he possesses every quality I admire in a man—considerate, intelligent, handsome, and caring. But how does he feel toward me? Am I merely a friend to be around, an attractive companion, a non-embarrassment, or perhaps merely a student? Do I love him? Oh, I may. But love is new to me. Something I've never had. I don't know what it really is or how one should feel. I only know he's constantly with me. Sometimes physically close, other times mentally. Oh, Mama Dora. How I wish you were here. I need authoritative advice. I need your counsel and the counsel of Tarot.

CHAPTER 55

RELENTLESS

Monday, December 21

Gratification arising from Thanksgiving's three-day festivity was now history. Yet there was hope for it to be a forerunner to future extravaganzas. And the break-in at Stacey's apartment had also become a thing of the past, something never to occur again, so management and its security promised.

On the surface, all was quiet; things appeared to be normal. All but one thing, that is. The man of many names was enraged.

Bitch, you continue to escape me. Twenty-five years. You'll rue every one of those days. When I get my hands on you, and I will, you'll suffer. Oh, how you'll suffer. There are many who are no longer around to talk about their experiences, people who have slowly, very slowly felt pain, my pain. But no one has suffered the way you will suffer. And I'll enjoy every moment of it.

With the yellow admission ticket on his dashboard, the killer was waved through *The Quad's* gate, and he drove unerringly to the E600 section. Having spoken to the operator at *TH&E*, he knew Stacey was away. But he did not care. In fact, he had no intention of entering her apartment. His mission was entirely different, an activity that would place her at his fingertips, anytime he desired.

After parking in a visitor's space, he walked to a car with the license plates SMD, a burgundy Coupe De Ville. Picking the lock, he entered the car and checked the registration card to be certain it was Stacey's convertible. Quickly, he inserted a GPS tracking device. He went back to his Chevrolet, left *The Quad,* and turned on his control panel. A map revealed the Cadillac's location.

Monday, December 28

Twice a day, for the entire previous week, the killer checked his tracking device. The car remained where it was parked. Then on this day, her convertible began to move, and the assassin began to follow.

She drove to *TH&E* where she remained for five and a half hours. Leaving, she walked to a corner deli, grabbed a bite, and returned to her car. He followed her, at a distance, to a realtor's office where he lost her. Unknown to him, Stacey and a saleslady left the building through a back door where they entered the agent's car. Hours later, the two returned, and it was not until then—after the saleslady parked near Stacey's convertible—that the tracker realized his intended victim had departed with the agent.

When the two women separated, Stacey returned to *The Quad,* and the tracker called it a day.

Entering her apartment, the telephone was ringing.

"Hello," she answered.

"Stacey, am I ever glad to hear your voice. I was worried."

"Hi, Jerry! Worried? Why?"

"I knew you were scheduled to land this morning, and when I didn't hear from you, I began to make calls. Several to the apartment, with no response! Then to the airlines, where I learned your plane had arrived on schedule, hours earlier. Then to *TH&E*. But you weren't at the office, and the operator wasn't sure if you would be."

"I had some errands to run, and I know this week will be hectic, so I decided to get them behind me."

"Well, tell me, how'd the meetings go?"

"I think well, but the final decision about activating my recommendations will remain unknown for a while. The Chinese don't rush into things, especially things new and untried. However, as I left, the chairman thanked me and expressed an interest in several of the recommendations. I was flattered. And if he does agree with them, it's going to mean more time in the Far East."

"To say nothing of the money *TH&E* will earn!" added Forrest.

"True! And while I have you, Jerry, mind if I ask a favor?"

"Not at all! What is it?"

"I want to show you something. It'll take a few hours!"

"Fine, if it's not today. I'm up to my neck and running against the clock."

"Even if you weren't, you couldn't see it today. How about tomorrow?"

"Perfect, as long as it's after ten thirty. I have a breakfast meeting."

"I'll pick you up at your office."

"No! It's better to let me drive in case the meeting runs longer. How about my picking you up at your apartment? Around eleven. If there's a change in the timing, I can call you there."

"Sounds good. I'll see you in the morning."

And they hung up.

Jerry then placed a call. After two rings, he heard, "Yes!"

"Hi there! Just wanted you to know Stacey's back. I'll be seeing her in the morning."

"Thanks! Be certain to keep me informed."

Pressing down on the disconnect button, the man called then dialed his phone.

"She's back!"

"I know! I've seen her."

"Are you at her place?"

"Outside in the car, but she doesn't know it."

"Good! Keep it that way, but don't let her out of your sight."

"I won't, Mr. Shomazzi." And Windy hung up the car phone, continuing to make his unseen presence invisible to everyone.

CHAPTER 56

STACEY'S UNACCEPTABLE DECISION

In the morning, Stacey slid into the seat beside Jerry and gave him a hug and a kiss on the cheek.

"Where to?" he asked.

"Go out the gate and turn left on the main road."

As he pulled away, Windy sat patiently watching for movement around the parking lot. When nothing happened, he followed at a discreet distance, watching cars ahead of him but behind Forrest. As cars either turned off the highway or overtook the traveling pair, he settled back for a relaxing ride.

Half an hour later, the attorney parked at a curb on Rocky Mountain Pass.

"Look at that house, Jerry. Isn't it lovely?"

"Very impressive and quite large! So what?"

"I'm buying it."

"You're what?"

"I made a deposit yesterday. Once I've been checked out and the closing is finished, it'll be mine. Not immediately! The owners want occupancy until late March, possibly even early April. But for this house, I can wait."

"Stace, I don't understand. I know Shoe wants you out of *The Quad,* but you never mentioned buying a home. Especially one as big and stately as this one! And so isolated! Are you certain this is what you want?"

"Absolutely! Wait until you see the inside. Then you'll understand."

"I'm not certain I will. At *The Quad,* you're nearer *TH&E.* You're surrounded by people you know. You have a security system in place. Out here, you're unprotected, alone, separated from your neighbors. You know someone's after you, just like he or someone else was after your parents. Why, who knows? But we do know your life is in danger just as their lives were. Living out here makes no sense."

"Jerry, you're right about someone being after me. And true, I don't know why, but I refuse to live in fear to be constantly looking over my shoulder. Obviously, *The Quad* hasn't been Fort Knox. Look how easy it was for the intruder to get through the gate. With an alarm system in place, this house will be safe. And in the meantime, I can enjoy living in a marvelous house with spacious, beautiful rooms. The layout's grand. And from the back deck, I can sit, sip a glass of wine, and enjoy the beauty. This is what I want, and this is what I intend to have."

"Wait until Shoe hears this. He won't be happy. When he suggested you leave *The Quad,* I'm sure he didn't have an open frontier in mind."

"Open frontier? Come on, Jerry. Sure, it's on a large piece of property with lots of trees, but this is a populated community. The neighborhood is charming. These people will become my friends, and I'll be safe. I intend to take care of myself. Now, follow me. Jenny Parsons, the owner, knows I'm bringing a friend to see the house. She's waiting. Get ready for the sight of your life."

As they headed up the walkway to the front door, Windy dialed his car phone.

"Mr. Shomazzi, I'm in northern Virginia on a road called Rocky Mountain Pass. Forrest and Stacey have been here for a few minutes talking. They've left his car, and they're walking into a house. I'll continue to watch, but I can't be sure I'll learn anything more."

"Don't worry, Windy! I'll call Forrest later and learn what's up. For now, keep an eye on them. I don't want that killer anywhere near her."

In the early evening, Vincent Shomazzi telephoned Jerry Forrest at his residence. When he heard of Stacey's decision, he was livid.

"Why in the hell didn't you talk her out of it—convince her the decision is careless, insane, and life threatening?"

"Oh, I tried. But she was adamant."

"Well, we'll see. She always listens to me, and she'll listen to me now. She'll change her mind."

But she didn't. Two hours on the phone with convincing arguments, high-pitched objections, and emotional pleas did not change Stacey's decision. The house was going to be hers.

CHAPTER 57

THE CAT AND THE MOUSE

The following morning, when Stacey left her apartment, the man of many names—several blocks from *The Quad*—picked up her movement on his GPS monitor. The direction, while toward him, was away from both *TH&E* and the airport.

At a stop sign, near the road on which she was traveling, he waited. Moments later, the Coupe De Ville passed. He edged forward, but he was forced to again stop as moving traffic prevented him from entering the road. When the seventh car passed, he muttered, "Hello there!"

The driver was Windy.

Now this is getting interesting, he thought. *First, the girl, now one of her guards. Where are they off to? Well, it won't be long before I know.*

As the unknown one entered the highway, he kept Windy's car at a visual distance while Stacey's car, farther ahead, was being tracked on the monitor. All three left the District and traveled into northern Virginia. Nearly twenty miles later, the monitor showed the Cadillac turning and coming to a stop. Then the tracker observed the little man pulling his car to the side of the road.

Curious, the man of many names remained in the parade of cars and continued down the road beyond Windy. At a street opposite the driveway on which she was parked, he turned and laughed.

"How appropriate! Destiny Lane!"

Parking under a willow tree, he observed Stacey being greeted by a woman at her front door. His subject entered. Twenty minutes later, she exited the house, got into her car, and drove back in the direction she had come. Almost immediately, Windy turned into the same driveway, backed out, and followed Shoe's goddaughter up the road.

The stalker started his car and headed to the intersection of Destiny Lane and Rocky Mountain Pass. On the property visited, a realtor's sign announced *Sale Pending*. Dialing the office from his car phone, the assassin responded to the answering agent saying, "Young lady, my name's Jesse Turner. You have a home listed that a friend of mine is thinking of buying. And I'm wondering if it's still available."

"Be glad to help. What is the address, please?"

Responding, he waited while the woman checked her computer records.

"I'm sorry, but an offer has been made on that house. However, if your friend stops by, I'm certain we can show the person something else that is suitable."

"That's a good idea. One other thing, though. I've been out of town, and it's possible she's already made an offer without my knowing it. My friend is Anastasia McDonald. Could you check your records to see if she's the buyer?"

"Why yes, she is."

"Oh, that's great. I'm so pleased for her. She was really excited when she saw the house. Thanks for your assistance."

And the killer disconnected the call.

As he was about to leave, he watched a car backing out of the driveway. As it turned onto Rocky Mountain Pass, the observant one recognized the driver. It was the woman who had invited Stacey into her home.

Once the car disappeared, the man drove onto the driveway and walked to the front door. He rang the bell and waited. No one answered. Leaving the porch, he walked to the back door and picked the lock. Without hurrying, he studied every room and opened every door. After an hour, he knew the interior layout as well as the home in which he had been raised.

Leaving by the back door, he studied the yard—front, back, and sides. From what had apparently been the master bedroom, he had observed a large oak tree, and now, standing at its base, he examined it. One large limb, apart from the others, angled toward the bedroom window. It held his staring eyes. He smiled, left the yard, and drove back to the District.

CHAPTER 58

THE CAT SCANS

Now is the time, little lady. Now is the time. I know where you are, and I know where you intend to go. I merely have to decide when and where. And to do that, I'm going to become your shadow, an invisible shadow to you and to that little man who is constantly near you. For the next few days, I'll study your movements, your routines. I'll know what you intend to do before you even do it. Oh yes, lady, I will be around . . . constantly around . . . though out-of-sight to you.

And the man of many names began tracking his victim's movements from the time she awakened until she went to bed. The first day was easy—in her car at seven thirty in the morning with a seven-forty-seven stop at a small diner for breakfast. Her figure-flattering meal was orange juice, a bowl of oatmeal, one piece of dry whole wheat toast, and black coffee. He knew this because he sat disguised, watching from a distant counter. The next stop, her office at 9:13 a.m. Inside until 11:52 a.m., and then a cab ride to an exclusive French restaurant for a luncheon meeting with two clients. Her meal was unknown since he could not see it from the bar where he slowly nursed three beers while devouring free nibbles from the counter. Back in the office at 2:17 p.m. where she remained until seven that evening. Out the door and back to *The Quad* by 8:18 p.m. A semi jackknifed, delaying her return.

Windy's presence was never a problem. When she was in her car, the stalker followed at a distance. When she was in a restaurant or her building, he remained outside and away from the guardian. And when she returned to *The Quad* that night, he never entered. Why risk being seen by the Shomazzi employee? Instead, he remained on the main road, outside the closed community, waiting until ten thirty before going home. After all, he needed sleep just like her.

The second day was similar—in her car at seven thirty, seated in the diner at 7:51 a.m. for identically the same breakfast, and in the office by 9:05 a.m. The noon meal was different. No customers, so a "quickie" at a nearby deli. She was back to her desk forty-seven minutes after leaving the building where she remained until 6:15 p. m. That night, she met Forrest at a cabaret where they enjoyed each other's company until 11:19 p.m. Then they parted company, and she drove to *The Quad*.

The third day, the stalker left his hotel at the same time; and when he turned on the monitor at 7:10 a. m., he discovered that Stacey was already at the office.

Before he arrived at *TH&E,* the monitor revealed the Cadillac moving in the opposite direction. Giving chase, he arrived at the airport in time to see her entering the front gate for an early morning flight. Where she was going and how long she would be gone, he did not know.

This incident was the first of many unexpected changes indicating the woman had a very flexible routine. She was too involved with too many activities—client conferences, foreign travel, early outside planning meetings for *The Quad's* Memorial Day celebration, periodic dates with Jerry Forrest, and soon her move.

Finally, the assailant made a decision.

I'm going to have to follow you secretly, avoid the goon who's always at your back, take advantage of the situation, and attack you without a preplan. Something I normally avoid.

Days later, she returned and again caught him by surprise. The morning after arriving home, she took a 6:30 a. m. taxicab rather than her car to work and left later by another cab for a return trip to the airport. The Chinese wanted to move forward on the consulting agreement.

A full day elapsed before the unknown one learned that Stacey had left the country. His source of information, the Recommendation

Collaborator with *TH&E*, Jane Wayne, whom he had befriended at *This Side of Heaven*. While she did not know when Stacey would be back in the country, it provided him time to finalize another contract that led to an unappreciated wife's departure to join her parents in heaven.

CHAPTER 59

THE CAT MOVES

Stacey's trip to China was prolonged. For nearly five weeks, she traveled throughout the country visiting Shanghai, Hong Kong, Chongoing, and other cities. With the aid of an interpreter, she learned some mandarin and, through observation, became proficient in many customs and habits of the Chinese. But her greatest accomplishment was the persuasive impression she manifested with the decision makers.

She returned to *TH&E* for the presentation of her recommendations and final report to senior management. After some modifications, she traveled back to Shanghai, with a managing vice president, to offer her company's agreed upon plan of action. This led to a contract being consummated and resulted in Stacey remaining in China for three additional weeks to help implement what *TH&E* had promised.

It was now early March, and Stacey began making buying decisions on some furnishings for her new home. The sale had been finalized, and occupancy was to take place at the end of the month. Although cautious, she remained unaware of the ever-present pursuer and often scurried around town, when time permitted, without informing Shomazzi or Windy.

One evening, she hastened to a furniture store located in a mall. It was an hour before closing. Parking on an upper level, she hurried to a stairwell and descended one flight to the passageway leading into the mall.

The assailant followed. The stairway was dimly lighted. Pleased, the stalker walked down two flights and waited. There he slipped on a slicker and a pair of surgeon's gloves.

Never taking his eyes off the door, he reached into a pocket and clutched Freddie's knife. His thumb slid unconsciously forward and backward over its handle. Becoming aware of what he was doing, he removed the knife and clicked the button repeatedly, watching the blade spring into action.

At nine, the stores closed, and the remaining patrons began leaving for their homes. The stairway door swung open and shut, intermittently. The assailant looked carefully at each exiting person. Finally, Stacey appeared.

Clicking the button one last time, the blade sprung open, and the killer proceeded quietly up the stairs. Near the landing, the door again opened, and three women, excited about their purchases, spoke animatedly.

Sliding the blade back in its shaft, he pocketed the knife before pushing one woman aside. A second woman, short but stout, grabbed his sleeve and said, "Apologize, you rude creep."

Turning his head toward the woman, he grabbed her hand and twisted it back to her wrist. His black eyes stared menacingly into hers. She screamed and moved her free hand to her mouth, and tears filled her fear-stricken eyes. Applying pressure to her hand, he suddenly released it, saying nothing, and he dashed through the door. Stacey was nearing her car when he began running toward her. He jumped back suddenly. A vehicle with three teenagers shot by him, laughing. "Watch out, old man, or you'll be sitting on your big fat ass."

By then, Stacey was in her car and driving home.

* * * * *

The following weeks jumped from hectic to normal to hectic. She was occupied, surrounded by office personnel for guidance on projects, reassigning her responsibilities at *The Quad* for the forthcoming Memorial Day presentation, making last minute purchases for her new home, scheduling the packing and move to Rocky Mountain Pass, and—when time allowed—enjoying the company of Jerry Forrest.

While all of these were taking place, Windy and Giant were visibly close, and the unknown one was nowhere to be seen.

During the week of her move, she received a call from Joan Shaffer, one of the two girls who had opened doors at Georgetown enabling Stacey to meet the tennis coach. Throughout college, Joan, Stacey, and Janet Walker, the second girl, remained close. Following graduation, Stacey and Joan cemented their friendship further with frequent phone calls, intermittent letters, and occasional visits.

"Hi," said Joan. "It's been a while since we've been together, and I've a great idea, one certain to be fun. I hope you like it and have time to keep me happy by taking advantage of it."

"Well, get to the point, girl, or any time I might have will disappear with your prattle."

"Same old Stace, being a smart ass. But I don't mind. In mid-June, I'm going to Bermuda for a week. I've got a room at this fancy hotel at Elbow Beach, and I can upgrade to a suite. The weather will be unbelievable. The water warm and clear. But better than that, we can enter *The Bermudian*."

"What's *The Bermudian*?"

"Stace, do you live in a vacuum? It's a tennis tournament with named players from all over the world. I've already entered the singles, but I'd like you to be my partner in the doubles. Will you, Hon? Will you?"

"It does sound like fun. I've been working my butt off and have vacation time coming, but I haven't played tennis in months."

"No excuse! We're talking nearly ten weeks from now. Get that good-looking lawyer friend of yours to chase you around the court . . . playing tennis, that is. In no time, you'll be as good as ever."

"It does sound great. Send me the particulars on the dates, hotel, and whatever else I need to know, and I'll make arrangements."

CHAPTER 60

AN UNEXPECTED SURPRISE

Now that the move was complete and her consulting assignments were under control, Stacey looked forward to Bermuda. Agreeing with Joan's suggestion, Stacey asked Jerry to help sharpen her game. They played thirty-eight sets over the ten-week period, and the student once again regained her previous skills. Feeling confident, she signed up for both the singles and doubles tournaments.

The day of departure, Stacey hopped on a plane to Boston's Logan Airport rather than flying from Washington. There she met Joan, and together, sitting side by side, the two relived their experiences.

It was important to get relief from the anxieties and time-consuming activities that were a part of Stacey's life, and Joan was the ideal person to know her needs. She was more than a friend; she was a confidante whose thoughtful mind and intellectual suggestions were respected.

After settling into their hotel suite, the women decided to see the island. With automobile transportation limited to taxicabs and limousines, other choices of travel were buses, bicycles, and mopeds. Adventuresome, they each rented a moped and skirted the island, taking in a few sights—a botanical garden, a fort, and some historic houses. The afternoon hours were too limited for more sightseeing, and visits to the crystal caves, beaches, forts, and other gardens had to be delayed for another day.

Returning to the hotel, they dressed fashionably and went to the *Lido* for fine wine and a savory dinner before calling it a night.

In the morning, they visited the tennis courts where *The Bermudian* would be held. With the tournament starting the following day, no one was allowed on the courts, so they inquired about other courts where they could practice.

Joan was competitive and never intended for her friend to enjoy an easy game. Placing balls in out-of-position locations near the net and back close to the baseline, she was determined to have Stacey burnout. But Stacey, a physical conditioning buff, did no more than pant occasionally. She refused to tire. As their practice progressed, she appeared to gather strength and a second wind. At the conclusion, Joan was the winner, a tired winner: 6–3, 4–6, and 7–5.

The girls left laughing, arms over each other's shoulders. "We will be victorious," they shouted for the startled players in the adjacent courts to hear.

Finally, opening day arrived, and male and female contestants from Asia, Australia, Canada, Europe, and the United States were assigned to several stadiums since no one facility could accommodate all the men and women entering what was recognized as the Ruling Tournament of Tennis. Because of this distinction, spectators painstakingly made certain their tickets were at the courts featuring their favorite players.

The singles competition was scheduled to be played first, followed by the doubles tournament later in the week. As competitors were eliminated, the courts available for play were reduced, leaving only the largest spectator court for the semifinal and final matches.

Joan and a group of women players were assigned to one flight; Stacey and another group of women were in a different flight. Matches were scheduled, and sets were completed. Winners advanced, and losers went home. Stacey and Joan, both victorious, moved ahead.

It was the day of the quarterfinals, and the bleachers were filled. Stacey was scheduled to play at eleven with Joan and her opponent taking over that same court after Stacey finished.

As expected, the match became a nail-biter. Stacey's opponent had years of competitive experience and gave the younger player an arduous contest. The first set went to Stacey's opponent, 6–4. After twelve games in the second set, the score remained 6–6, requiring a tiebreak game. To win the set, the victor had to have at least two points more than her opponent. Otherwise, more tiebreak games would be played until one player had achieved the two point advantage.

Stacey held a 6–5 advantage. She needed to win her serve to gain the required two-point differential. And she did, scoring an ace. Whether the serve unnerved the opponent, or losing the set demoralized her, or the physical demands required simply tired the older athlete, no one knew, but the player became an easy adversary for Stacey who won the third set, 6–1.

When the final set had reached 5–1, a man, seated next to a woman in the third row, rose and walked to the chain-link fence. After extending a handshake to the loser, Stacey walked from the net to a bench, sat down, and began toweling off her arms, hands, and racket.

The man carefully eyed Stacey from head to foot, taking a moment to stare at her thigh.

"Ms. McDonald, would you mind indulging an old man?"

Smiling, she stood and walked to him.

"I'll certainly try if I'm able. What can I do?"

Rolling his program into a tube, he said, "Years ago, I was a pretty fair tennis player. And watching you play, yesterday and today, I wish I had had the opportunity to have you as a partner in my younger days. You're very good."

"Thank you," responded the grateful Stacey.

Sliding his program through the fence, he continued, "I'd be honored if you'd be so kind as to sign my program. I intend to be here tomorrow cheering you on to victory."

"With that promise, I'm the one who is honored. But now you're forcing me to let you in on a secret. This is a first for me. No one has ever asked for my signature before, and because of that, I have no pen. May I borrow yours?"

Reaching for his pen, he laughed. "How thoughtless of me! Shows how old I am, forgetting that pens aren't among the required pieces of tennis equipment."

As Stacey opened the program, he said, "Beneath your picture, if you don't mind."

"And for whom do I have the pleasure of signing this?"

"Merely 'WJ.' That's what everyone calls me."

"Well, thank you, WJ. You've made this win all the more important for me."

And as they parted, the older man returned to the seat next to his female companion.

Unfolding the program, he sat, staring at the autographed picture. The woman leaned to her side and read the notation:

> To WJ,
> My first fan!
> Stacey McDonald

The woman looked at the man. Carefully, he folded the program and placed it in his inside-coat pocket. Then he stared at the court. Joan and her opponent were entering the playing area.

Interrupting his concentration, the woman asked, "Are you going to watch this next match?"

"Indeed, I am. Joan Shaffer and Stacey McDonald are close friends, and I'll be very surprised if they're not opponents in the final match.

"Well, you watch it. I'm hot and thirsty. I'm going for some lemonade. I'll either meet you here or at the gate where we entered."

Finding an empty table near the lady's locker room door, the woman sat down and ordered a pitcher of lemonade along with two glasses. Filling one, she took a sip and waited for the door to open. Minutes passed, and finally a woman appeared.

"Anastasia McDonald," she called out.

Stacey looked at her, waved, and began walking toward the tennis courts.

"Anastasia! Stacey! Please, a moment of your time?"

Nowhere on the program did the name Stacey appear, and this woman's reference to it caught her off guard and curious. She altered her course and came to the table.

"Please! Won't you be seated for a moment? Have a glass of lemonade. I have something to tell you, something I cannot believe. And it has nothing to do with tennis."

Stacey was puzzled.

What can this stranger tell me?

"You have my curiosity. I don't believe I've ever met you before, yet you know me as Stacey. How can that be?"

She sat down, crossed her legs, and pulled one leg of her tennis shorts down over a birthmark on her thigh. The woman noticed but disguised the observation by filling Stacey's glass and handing the lemonade to her.

"Oh, the answer to that is simple. By the way, I'm Maggie Muldoon. I happen to be the companion . . . maid . . . housekeeper to the man who asked for your autograph earlier. He showed it to me, and that's how I learned your name.

"And now you want to meet me. I'm flattered."

"Oh, I'm not the tennis enthusiast that W. J. is. I'm curious, however, if you believe in coincidences?"

"Coincidences? To some degree. Why do you ask?"

"You have a remarkable resemblance to a woman I once knew. A very close and dear friend!"

"Common resemblances aren't unusual. I've had a few people, not many though, who have told me I look like someone else. It happens to a lot of people, don't you think?"

"True, but this resemblance is more than a close similarity. It's as though you are sisters. I regret not having a picture of her with me because I know you'd be amazed.

"By any chance, do you swim?"

"Swim?" Stacey laughed. "You have a way of asking unusual questions. I used to. Quite a bit, in fact! I like to exercise, and it keeps me in shape. But I haven't been swimming for some weeks. Too many things going on in my life! Is it important?"

"Merely another coincidence! Your look-alike was an excellent swimmer. But she drowned. Not far from here, in fact. It's something I've never been able to understand. Not someone who could swim like her."

"Was it recently?"

"Oh no! Some twenty-five years ago! That's one of the reasons I was so startled when I first saw you. Mind my asking your age?"

"Twenty-five."

"Unbelievable! Another coincidence! You don't live here, do you?"

"No, in a small town outside of Washington DC!"

"I live here and wish you did too. If you don't mind, do me a favor and give me your address. I want to send you a picture. Possibly it will be the beginning of a friendship."

"You're a convincing soul. With the interest you've taken in speaking with me and your persuasiveness, to say nothing of the coincidences, I'd be making a mistake if I didn't see my look-alike. Here's my address."

Parting company, Stacey returned to the court in time to see Joan defeat her opponent.

CHAPTER 61

POSITIONING THEMSELVES

At his Bermuda home that evening, Walter Jensen dialed a private number.

"Who's this?"

"A voice from your past," Jensen responded.

"Walter! It's been a long time. But I haven't given up. In fact, your package is very close to being retrieved. Soon, the contract will be fulfilled. You'll be happy, and I'll be richer."

"Close to being retrieved? Do you mean physically close?"

"Well, not exactly! The package is sent all over the world. The company controlling it is always sending it someplace. Seems the package is quite valuable."

"And just where in the world is it at this moment?"

"Unfortunately, I don't know. I know it left the States, however, when it returns, I'll have my hands on it."

"Instead of waiting for it to return, why don't you go fetch it?"

"I would if I—"

"Quit making excuses! I've been listening to them for more than a quarter of a century. I've heard about your holding the package and giving it up and later locating it then being outwitted and losing it. Now, I'm going to help you because I want this package shattered."

"You're going to help me? And just how are you going to do that?"

"Because I'm less than ten miles from it at this very moment!"

"Ten miles! Where in the hell are you?"

"At my home on the island. And the package is being seen every day by more than a thousand people. You know the island. You've been here before. Possibly you even remember the reason why. Twenty-five years ago!"

"I remember."

"Well, get your sorry ass over here! Tomorrow! The following day at the latest! The place where it's being viewed will be closing down in three days, and I don't intend to wait another twenty-five years while you go looking for it."

And he slammed down the receiver.

By god, he seethed, *I can't wait until I get my hands on your bitch. Once you've paid me, Jensen, you'll find out what it's like to piss me off. Your days are numbered."*

* * * * *

After finishing a quick dinner, Joan and Stacey returned to their suite. Each was tired, but only Joan went immediately to bed. Stacey, instead, curled up on the couch and thought about her afternoon conversation with Maggie Muldoon. Many questions and a few answers came to mind.

Why this interest in me, Maggie Muldoon? Do you have knowledge that will help me uncover the secrets in my life—those secrets unknown to me? And if I listen to you, can I trust what you say? Will it be the truth?

Well, that's a decision I have to make on my own. One thing is certain, however. I need to keep all my options open. If I never hear what you want to tell me, then I'll always question what I missed. And besides, you're the first person to ever hint at anything about my heritage, my unknown background and beginning. Possibly, I won't like what I'm told, but I've got to find out what you know. What the connection is, if any, between my look-alike and me.

CHAPTER 62

THE FOURTH COINCIDENCE

On the day of the semifinals, Stacey went courtside to face her opponent. Walking through the gate, her attention was drawn to the third row of the bleachers. There sat WJ and Maggie Muldoon. He stood and applauded; Maggie smiled and waved; Stacey affably bowed her head.

The preceding night had not been good. Stacey had slept fitfully, awakening to dreams of strangers approaching her—a woman smiling with mistrust in her eyes and a man attempting to overtake her with vengeance in his movement.

Finally, when out of bed, the morning proved no better. She nibbled at her breakfast, was unusually silent to her roommate, and walked throughout the suite aimlessly. She was filled with haunting, unanswered thoughts from the night before.

But following her opponent's first serve, her mind focused on the tennis ball, and she became absorbed. Her play was overwhelming. In two quick sets, she defeated the woman: 6–2, 6–love. She was now a semifinalist.

After a quick shower, she sat in the bleachers opposite WJ and Maggie, watching her good friend defeat her opponent in three sets. Two days later, Stacey McDonald and Joan Shaffer would face each other for the trophy. But until then, they intended to enjoy Bermuda and see the "treasures" that had not yet been visited.

* * * * * *

Finally, the tourist attractions of Bermuda had been seen. But now it was another day, the day that would justify whether the trip was meant to be, the day that one of these two friends would learn who was to be crowned the women's singles champion in the Ruling Tournament of Tennis. Each was a finalist. But to receive the crown, one had to win three out of five sets, with each set destined to being a grueling one.

Beside the formidable opposition, the temperature was 101 degrees with the overhead sun, on a windless day, bearing directly down on the contestants. The heat off the surface of the court traveled through the soles of the tennis shoes to the bottoms of the players' feet, while perspiration ran down their arms and off their hands to the handles of the rackets. Hours of running caused exhaustion, the cramping of muscles, and the disappearance of energy. But the competing players, the two men and two women, had heart; each struggled to endure and win.

For the women, it involved fifty-one games with the first set ending 6–4 in favor of Joan; the second 6–3 for Joan; the third (a tiebreak) going to Stacey 7–5, followed by another 7–5 tiebreak for Stacey; and then a final 6–2 win for Joan over a game but tiring opponent.

At the net, the girls embraced, and Joan said, "I was lucky. But I promise you a trophy too. We'll win the doubles tournament with ease."

Walking together to the locker room, Joan continued, "After we shower, let's get all dolled up, go to that restaurant we've been talking about, and have a relaxing dinner. But before eating, I'll treat you to a margarita . . . or two . . . or three."

"Sounds great, but hold off for an hour or two. Instead of showering, I'm going for a dip. Since arriving, I've been wanting to test that ocean, and I've never been so hot as I am right now. I can't think of anything more refreshing than a relaxing swim."

"Relaxing! Going out and fighting the current! You have to be kidding."

"Not on your life! To enjoy the water, you don't have to move your arms. You can merely float on your back, and that's all I intend to do."

Stacey stepped into her bathing suit, grabbed a towel, and walked to the water. Dropping the towel, she dove into the blue Atlantic gracefully skimming over the surface. After a few minutes, she stopped, tread water, looked to the shoreline, and gauged her distance. To her left, a brilliant flash reflected off the ocean's surface. Quickly, it disappeared. Thinking nothing of it, she began floating on her back—a light flutter kick and an occasional movement of her hands, outward from her body and back toward it. She was buoyant, happy, and relaxed.

But the earlier flash was more than an aberration; it was the reflection of the sun off a scuba diver's oxygen cylinder. The swimmer descended five feet beneath the ocean's surface and breaststroked his way to the floating Stacey.

What a life! This beautiful island! A good friend! Exciting tennis! And now, this refreshing oce—

Suddenly on her left, an arm appeared out of the ocean and fell across her waist. Fingers seized her side while a second hand pushed against the back of her right shoulder. Stacey flipped on to her stomach. Whether it was her swimmer's instinct or her Creator's influence, the seized woman filled her lungs with air before submerging into the water.

The attacker struggled to take control, attempting, at the same time, to maneuver his body over Stacey's back. But the athlete refused to be docile. Well-conditioned and physically fit, she resisted. Her unrestrained arm movements and twisting body prevented him from overpowering her. Impatient, he unintentionally reacted by laying his chin on her shoulder, a reflex to be later regretted. Stacey's fingers grabbed hold of the open-circuit hose and mouthpiece feeding oxygen to his lungs. She yanked the lifeline from his lips.

Choking, he released his arms, and Stacey turned on her back, tucked her knees to her waist, and extended her legs against the attacker's chest, pushing him backward, forcing more water into his open mouth. Kicking his feet, his fins brought him to the surface. Choking, he coughed and spit, straining to clear his throat of the salt water. Finally relieved, he searched for his victim. Fifty yards away and knee-deep in water, Stacey was running to the shore.

The attacker's thoughts wandered. *Damn you, bitch. Once more you win. But never again! You showed me something now, something that will change the way we play my game the next time we meet. Beneath that exciting body is a strength I never foresaw. So the next time, I'll be prepared. When we meet, I'll first beat you unconsciously. Then I'll use my toys, my passion playmates, and shackle you in a spread-eagle position, your wrists and ankles chained to four stakes. Slowly, very slowly, I'll strip away your clothing and stare at your hidden treasures, devouring visually all the curves and openings you possess. Then I'll fondle, kiss, and tongue each of those treasures before entering you again . . . and again . . . and again.*

Clutching his groin, the deviate smiled. *Ah, Hoss, my plans arouse you. What thrills you and I will enjoy. Too bad these will be the last pleasures the McDonald broad shares with anyone else. For when we finish, I'll fulfill my promise to Dora. I'll take Freddie's knife and my forceps slitting and ripping Jensen's illegitimate into hundreds of pieces before scattering them countrywide. No souvenirs for me. Only memories! Long, long, lasting memories!*

Discarding his tank, the man of many identities swam away.

On the beach, Stacey dragged herself to the hotel, falling at times before reaching the oceanside entrance. Inside, guests, bellmen, and registration clerks watched the fatigued woman stumble through the lobby, dripping water and sand on the marble floor.

Before anyone reached her side, she made it to the bank of elevators where she slid her hand between the frame and the closing door. Automatically, it reopened. Staggering in, she fell to her knees; and an older couple, attired for an evening's entertainment, looked at the sobbing arrival.

"My dear, are you all right?" asked the caring lady.

Stacey, short of breath, merely nodded, saying nothing as she blindly reached behind her, searching for the panel of floor buttons.

"Allow me," offered the man. "What floor do you want?"

"The . . . p-pen . . . penthouse, pl-pl-please!"

As the door opened, the man helped Stacey to her feet, and he and his wife stood in the open doorway watching the newcomer totter from side to side down the hall.

At her door, Stacey banged her fist and sobbed, "Please, Joan! Please be inside!"

Pounding again and again, the door finally opened. "Forget your key, Sta—? My god, what happened to you?"

Embracing her friend, the dinner dress Joan was wearing turned wet as she took hold of Stacey and helped her into the living room. "Get out of that suit," she ordered. "Lie down on the sofa. I'll get you a towel and bathrobe."

With blow-dryer and brush in hand, Joan worked on Stacey's hair. The exhausted roommate began to say something, but Joan interrupted, "Not now! Later!"

Finishing, she went to the minibar and mixed Stacey a sweet Manhattan.

"Drink it slowly. Then take a nap. Later, you can tell me what happened."

After Stacey awakened, she told things never revealed, stories about her godfather and his protection, the deaths of her parents, the break-in at *The Quad,* and now, the attempted drowning. But Maggie Muldoon was never mentioned.

"What are you going to do, Stace?"

"Continue to live! I refuse to let this scumbag control me and be in charge of my life."

"I admire your guts, girl, but I question your sanity. You need to be safe. Tell your godfather or Forrest what happened so that someone can assign guards to protect you."

"For how long? A week, a month, a year, all my life? I can't do that. I won't do that. This madman doesn't have me yet, and he never will. I won't allow it."

"That sounds so courageous. But look at you! Look at how you reacted to this near drowning! You were frightened . . . frightened out of your mind. You can't exist that way. You'll lose your health and your sanity. You need protection. You need to have this murderer put away. At least tell Jerry! Get his help!"

For a while, Stacey remained quiet. Finally, she spoke. "I'll see!"

Shaking her head, Joan obviously disagreed.

"Okay! Have it your way for the time being. But know this! As much as I regret you're not having a trophy to carry home, you and I are going to drop out of the doubles tournament tomorrow. Instead, we're going home, immediately."

Stacey did not disagree. The island was lovely, but she wanted to be in her new home, away from the threat and away from the memories.

CHAPTER 63

NO ONE'S SAFE

Arriving at her home on Rocky Mountain Pass, Stacey parked in the garage and rapidly climbed the back steps. Then she began to take her time, walking slowly through every room, touching objects, cherished ones and trifling ones. Finally, she sat quietly and gazed appreciatively at what surrounded her.

It's good to be back. To be with all the things I have. Thank you, Lord, for watching over me. Taking care of me. And letting me continue to enjoy life.

Finally, she returned to her car and retrieved groceries purchased on her return from the airport. After putting them away, she walked to her bedroom, kicked off her shoes, and dialed the telephone, twice.

On the second call, she heard, "Forrest here! Who is calling, please?"

"Though you sound officially stiff, you don't know how good it is to hear your voice."

"Stace! Are you back? Tell me you're home!"

"I am. Here in my house, talking to the second person I've called since arriving. Had to check in with my boss first."

"Always second. The story of my life. But it's sure good hearing your voice. Tell me! How was Bermuda? Did you have fun? And the tournaments? Did you win a trophy?"

"Slow down, lawyer! This isn't a cross examination. If you'll give me a moment, I'll bring you up-to-date."

Over the next fifteen minutes, she reminisced—the beauty of the island, the accommodations of the hotel, the restaurants, beaches, activities; and the singles competition which he questioned in detail. The only thing omitted was the attack in the sea.

"What about the doubles tournament? When will I get to see your trophy? I know Joan and you destroyed every other pair."

"We decided not to enter."

"Not enter? Why?"

"A number of reasons. It was dreadfully hot. We were tired from the singles matches. They wasted us. Besides, I wanted to see you. I missed you."

"Come on, Stace! As much as I like hearing that, Joan and you are too competitive to just drop out. Especially with the odds of your winning being so great. What aren't you telling me?"

"Lawyer, that career of yours is turning you into a skeptic. Neither Joan nor I regret not competing. And I hope you won't make me deplore that decision with constant reminders. Instead, if you're really glad that I'm back, meet me for dinner at that fancy new French restaurant, and I'll let you buy."

"You're on! But let me pick you up. You must be tired after your long flight."

"No, I want my car, in case my boss calls. Earlier, he mentioned a problem with the Chinese and wanted to hear my thoughts in the morning. However, knowing I'm now back, he may change his mind and want to meet tonight. He's always in a hurry."

* * * * *

Earlier that morning, at 8:00 a.m., the assassin went to the tennis admissions office, purchased a ticket, and walked to the upper row of the bleachers behind and out of the view of Walter Jensen. Partially disguised, he felt secure, unlikely to be recognized by Stacey McDonald or others during the doubles tournament scheduled at ten.

While side-stepping in front of other spectators on the way to his seat, an announcement over the public address system was heard.

"The second doubles match scheduled later this morning will not be held. Joan Shaffer and Anastasia McDonald have withdrawn from the tournament."

A disappointing and vocal outburst drowned out other words offered.

Continuing past the remaining seated spectators, the killer reached the aisle and walked to the main concourse. From a public phone booth, he called the hotel where Stacey was staying and learned she had checked out. Returning to his hotel, he telephoned the airport and booked passage on a late-afternoon flight.

When he arrived at his hotel outside of DC, it was 7:35 p.m. Entering his room, the phone was ringing. "Yes!" he responded.

"Finally, you're back!" snapped Walter Jensen. "I've been trying to reach you all day. On the first half dozen calls, all I received was ringing. Finally, the desk clerk told me you checked out and where you were headed. But enough of that! What about the package? It didn't show up where it was supposed to be. Does that mean you finally located it and did what you had to do?"

"Not yet!"

"Not yet! Why the hell not?"

"Complications!"

"Complications. You're supposed to be a master at handling complications. Instead, all you seem to do is fail. To think of all the years and all the money I've paid in covering the expenses that have led only to fuckups! What a waste. Answer this if you can. Have you another plan? Better yet, do you honestly think you can do what you're supposed to do? And if so, when? Enlighten me!"

"I know exactly what I'm going to do. And it won't be long before your precious package is handled the way you want it to be." Slamming down the phone, he cut off the man, refusing to hear more complaints.

Staring at the phone, his eyes were livid.

In no time, this assignment will be over. But the real pleasure comes from the job that follows. It won't be as lucrative; in fact, it will be totally free. But what satisfaction it will give me? No longer will I have to put up with your horseshit.

Annoyed but no longer sleepy, he decided to close out the contract that night. He changed to a black cotton turtleneck shirt, black trousers, and black tennis shoes. At his car, he turned on the GPS monitoring system. Stacey's Cadillac was not at home but parked at another location.

Not quite nine. Hope she'll head home. Think I'll go there and wait.

CHAPTER 64

ONCE AGAIN

Quietly, he sat in his car under the willow tree on Destiny Lane. Stacey finally arrived home and entered the house. The man of many names filled his backpack with the toys he planned on introducing. Donning the *Remember Me* head mask, he got out of the car and inadvertently slammed the door. Irritated at making noise, he remained standing staring at the house. No movement, no reaction within.

He slid his arms through the straps of the backpack and jogged across Rocky Mountain Pass, moving among the trees on the western side through the backyard to the eastern side of the house. Arriving at the oak tree opposite her bedroom window, he scaled to a protruding limb. Within the window, he saw the frightened woman staring back at him.

Just wait, my dear! You have no idea of the horrors you face and the fun I'll enjoy.

Grabbing the limb, he began swinging his body back and forth, gaining momentum to fly five feet through the window.

With a crash, he was in, off balance but moving toward his prey. Unexpectedly, his feet flew out from under him, and he struck a table with his head and shoulder. Little crystal balls under a cloth were rolling across the floor. Shaking his head, he jumped to his feet and darted after the woman. Again, his feet stepped on unseen balls, causing him to hit the floor a second time with jolting impact. Rising and cursing the woman, he left through the door she had exited. Moments were wasted, first with the falls, now with misdirected movements in the hallway, trying to discover the way she had gone.

Finally, he saw where she had fled, and he followed down the back stairs, his long legs gaining on her. A short distance away, she pushed open and slammed shut a basement door, running as fast as her feet would move.

Coming to the closed door, he slid to a stop before opening it. Through the door, he entered a well-lighted garage. Only lawn and snow removal equipment, a storage bin, and wall-hanging rakes, shovels, brooms, and paraphernalia prevented the room from being empty. At the opposite end, the garage doors were open. Sprinting into the yard, he stopped and slowly moved around looking for the intended.

From his backpack, he removed a five-cell flashlight and flooded parts of the yard with light. Nothing! Moving to his left, he searched the western side of her house, peering in the trees. Again, nothing! As he reached the front yard, he stopped and looked straight ahead. A sound! Remaining still, the sound gradually grew louder. It was a siren! Two sirens! Turning off the flashlight, he darted to his car on Destiny Lane, entered it, sat back, and waited.

Within minutes, two police cruisers and a sedan pulled into the driveway. Four policemen and Jerry Forrest stepped out of the cars. A sergeant ran to the Cadillac and opened the unlocked door. Empty! A second officer was on the front porch trying to turn the unmoving doorknob.

Congregating, the sergeant gave orders. Two of the policemen and Jerry went to the left side of the house; the sergeant and remaining policeman moved to the right. As they disappeared around the back corners, the man seldom seen started his engine and drove, without headlights, to Rocky Mountain Pass. Going right, he continued a block before turning on his lights and accelerating into the distance.

Meanwhile, the party of five assembled at the open garage doors and entered the house.

"The basement door's open," exclaimed Jerry.

"Charley, Pete, you follow me into the house," commanded the sergeant. "Rusty, stay here with Mr. Forrest!" Drawing their weapons, the three headed for the steps.

"Jerry," Stacey shouted. "Thank God you're here."

Turning, the group faced a swollen-eyed woman standing in an open storage bin, purse in one hand, cell phone in the other. Jerry ran to Stacey and wrapped his arms around her shoulders. She buried her tear-covered face against his neck.

The comfort of Forrest's embrace and the presence of the four police officers settled the terrified woman.

"You three," ordered the sergeant, "search the house. See if the perp's still here. Ms. McDonald, let's go upstairs and talk. Anything you can tell, along with a description, will help us find him."

In the kitchen, Jerry poured a glass of wine for Stacey. "Sergeant, care to join her?"

"Thanks, but no!" replied the sergeant. "The four of us have two more hours of duty, and my enjoying, what looks like good wine, wouldn't be too smart."

In response to being prodded, Stacey told of the break-in and the chase.

"This isn't the first time," interrupted Jerry.

"True! Recently, a man got into my apartment at *The Quad,* and when I was an infant, someone—possibly he—attempted to kidnap me."

"Why?"

"I wish I knew. But I have no clue, no idea."

"You say 'a man' broke into your apartment. Was it this man?"

"I believe so, but I can't be certain. This man was masked." Then she proceeded to describe the *Remember Me* disguise.

"My gut tells me it's the same one. I can't explain why anyone would be after me, especially someone I don't even know. But two men? It makes less sense."

"Unless they're working together," offered the sergeant.

"Stacey," Jerry added. "Tell the sergeant about the attack several days ago."

Staring at him but saying nothing, he continued, "The one in Bermuda!"

"How do you know about that?" she asked.

"Joan called to find out how you are. During the conversation, I questioned why the two of you left the island without entering the doubles tournament. She enlightened me on the real reason for your departure. The attack in the ocean."

"Attack in the ocean?" asked the sergeant. "Tell me about that."

Describing her physical battle with the man, she concluded by saying, "This masked madman tonight is probably the same person.

At least I think so. The height, physique, and athletic ability are too similar. And while I didn't see the face behind the *Remember Me* mask, I did see the face of my ocean attacker. And he was the same man who broke into my apartment at *The Quad*."

"There's little doubt in your mind that these guys are one and the same?"

"All but the attempted kidnapping when I was a baby! I can't be certain of that."

"We have an artist . . . someone who can replicate facial and hair descriptions. Do you think you can describe the man?"

"Definitely! I'll never forget his face."

Pete, Rusty, and Charlie reappeared. They did not find the intruder but proceeded to describe Stacey's bedroom. This led to questions regarding the broken window, table, and glass balls on the floor. After answering these questions and others, the sergeant concluded the investigation for the time being.

As he was leaving, he said, "A suggestion, Ms. McDonald. Don't spend the night here, especially with that broken window. Stay with a friend or in a hotel. Somewhere safe."

Finally alone with Stacey, Jerry said, "I know just the place. My house! You get the bedroom across the hall from me. You'll definitely be safe. I'll keep my door ajar, and because I'm a light sleeper, you can shut your eyes knowing no one's going to bother you. How's that sound?"

"Oh, Jerry, you don't know how much I appreciate that. I don't want to be alone, not tonight. Having you close will be comforting."

Stacey left her convertible at the house and rode with Jerry to his home. It was nearly morning, and both were tired.

"Get a good night's rest," he advised. "We'll wake up when we wake up, and we'll call our offices then. Tell your boss you'll be in later. A couple of hours missed will not bankrupt either company. For now, a good night's sleep is all that's important."

In bed, Jerry lay staring at the ceiling. He was thinking of the times when he didn't have his cell phone with him. Fortunately, this was not one of those occasions. As soon as he had heard the distress in Stacey's voice, he dialed 911, and the police responded immediately. Everything worked out well. If it had not, he knew he would never forgive himself.

Slowly, his door opened wider, and light in the background, from the room across the hall, silhouetted Stacey. She was standing in bra and panties.

Rising, he watched her enter, coming to his side. "Jerry, I don't want to be alone. Hold me in your arms. Let me sleep with you."

Puffing up the pillow, he pulled back the covers. She looked down at a bare, muscular chest, stomach, and legs-covered pajama bottoms. Crawling in beside him, she was trembling. Was it from the attack or from the nearness of his body?

Embracing her, he pulled her closer to him. He stared into her swollen red eyes and kissed them tenderly. His fingers touched her head and stroked her hair. Then he slid his fingers to her cheek and caressed it. Lifting his face inches from hers, he looked down on her lovely face and smiled with endearment. Slowly, he moved his lips to hers, and they met and remained, each pair in no hurry to leave.

"Make love to me, Jerry! Please, please make love to me," she whispered.

Again, his closed mouth touched hers. Slowly, their lips parted; their tongues met. Excitedly, passionately, they moved together.

His hand slid down from her shoulder to the bra strap. He unfastened it adeptly. His free hand moved underneath the cup, and he gently caressed her breast. Simultaneously, they removed there lower garments and joined together as one.

* * * * *

After awakening the following morning, they called their offices and gave excuses for their absences. Then, remaining together, they shared untold secrets, interrupted with kissing and caressing. Later, they showered together, each exploring the other's body. Aroused, they made love under the warm-flowing shower water. Toweling each other dry, they dressed.

From in front of the mirror, Stacey asked, "Honey, bring me the lipstick from my purse."

Entering the bathroom, he said, "I found this letter. Is there a reason why it's unopened?"

"In all the excitement, I forgot about it. I'll read it in a moment."

As she headed into the kitchen, she exclaimed, "What a host! A night and morning of unsurpassable love! A shower with a handsome man who washed me from head to toe. And all of that is followed by a breakfast that smells and looks divine! I'm in heaven."

After taking a sip of hot coffee, she opened the envelope and gasped.

Moving to her, he inquired, "What's it say?"

"Look for yourself."

There were two pictures and a letter. One photograph portrayed a beautiful lady in her early thirties, someone identical to Stacey. The other was a man, bending his back with arm extended, preparing to serve a tennis ball. The letter was brief.

> My Dear Stacey,
>
> It was disappointing to learn that Joan Shaffer and you decided not to enter the doubles tournament. I carried to the court that day the enclosed photograph of your "twin." Also enclosed is a picture of WJ when he was much younger. Study the photographs closely. We need to talk. There are things you have to learn. I am planning a visit to New York in a week. Possibly you can meet me there? You won't regret it. In fact, it might well influence your life.
>
> Call me.
>
> Your friend,
> Maggie Muldoon

"Who's Maggie Muldoon, Stace?"

Stacey explained about their meeting and the coincidences bonding Stacey with Maggie.

Jerry asked, "Other than the resemblances of you and this woman and of WJ's tennis interest, what else needs to be studied?"

"I'm not certain."

"Well, there's obviously something she wants you to see."

"These pictures, along with the letter, they . . . make me wonder. Her persistence has me curious. Just possibly she knows something about my life that I don't know. I'm going to call her and meet her in New York. I hope you'll come. We can have a fun-filled few days together."

"Plan on it! I'm working a case that has some people living there, people that I need to see. You can meet privately with Maggie Muldoon and find out exactly what she knows while I'm doing my thing."

PART IV

ANOTHER BEGINNING: A FINAL ENDING

CHAPTER 65

DISCOVERY

It was mid-afternoon, and Stacey entered Maggie Muldoon's room at the Marriott Marquis.

"Forgive me, but I want to call you Sara. You look so much like her."

"Well, at least now I know the name of my double."

"How thoughtless of me! I hadn't told you that, had I? Well, there is much for you to learn, and we might as well start with her name. She was born Sara Ferguson. But she married Walter Jensen Jr. who was, at that time, vice president of sales at Jensen Manufacturing International."

"Oh, I'm somewhat familiar with the company. Several months ago, it became a client of one of my associates at *TH&E*."

"*TH&E!* What's *TH&E?*"

"A consulting company. *Thoman, Holmes, and Ettinger.*"

"Several months ago. That's interesting. Would you by any chance have been involved in the agreement?"

"No! Why do you ask?"

"It was around that time that Walter Jensen Sr., the president of Jensen, began taking an interest in you. Through tennis, that is. But I'm getting ahead of myself. Let me tie this together. As you know,

I am the traveling companion of Walter Sr. Besides that, I've also been the family maid and housekeeper. And when I say those things, I mean only those things. No other relationship ever existed. I've done those things for nearly thirty years, having been responsible for maintaining the Jensen homes in New York and Bermuda."

"Obviously, you know many things about the family."

"Indeed I do. When Virginia Jensen—known as Ginger to her friends—came down with amyotrophic lateral sclerosis, Lou Gehrig's disease, I cared for her. Up until she died. In fact, I insisted that her final days be spent in Bermuda because that's where she wanted to die. Unfortunately, another tragedy occurred prior to her death—the drowning of Sara Jensen."

Stacey carefully listened but said nothing.

"Sara was unlike the family. She had been raised in Canada, and probably because of our mutually modest beginnings, she took a liking to me and confided things she had never told anyone else.

"As a young girl, she was not only a good student but an ambitious one. After high school, she left Canada to become a secretary. She moved to New York and enrolled in a two-year training course. After graduating, she landed employment at Jensen Manufacturing in the secretarial pool. At first, she circulated among a variety of executives, seniors, and juniors, those needing someone who could type fast and take accurate shorthand. She was doing quite well, receiving favorable reviews and above average salary increases. Then one day, the secretary to Walter Jensen Jr. became ill and remained home for several days. Sara received the assignment to fill in. On the first day, nothing unusual occurred. But on the second day, probably due to her aspirations, she dressed more conspicuously—a tight white cashmere sweater, an above-the-knees white skirt, and black stockings.

"When she told me this, she laughed. Sara wanted to attract and hold the attention of this handsome single heir apparent to the presidency. And she did. At first, he found it necessary to enter and reenter her office, walk behind her chair, touch her shoulders, and issue unimportant assignments. Possibly tiring of these trips back and forth, he began calling her into his office where he would have her sit across from his desk, sometimes taking dictation, other times carrying on useless conversation. Realizing the interest she was generating, she began to dress more provocatively—tight blouses open suggestively at the neck and skirts with slits running along the thigh.

"The third day, he asked her to work late, and at six thirty, he offered to buy her supper. They ate at an elegant restaurant and enjoyed a meal unlike anything she had ever eaten.

"And this continued, even after his regular secretary returned. He devised work requiring secretarial assistance and even occasional weekend assignments at the office. Then an industry-wide tradeshow was held, and he arranged to have her accompany him to 'facilitate writing orders.' On the second night, dictation took place on the pillow, and not long thereafter, Sara and young Walter were married.

"Their union met with the approval of both Walter's mother and father, but for two different reasons. Virginia Jensen adored Sara. She was like a daughter. The two were constantly together with one not doing enough for the other. However, the father's interest was not paternal. He had a reputation as a philanderer, and the attention he gave his son's wife apparently went unnoticed by Virginia and young Walter."

Maggie's tone and cadence changed. She spoke quietly, quickly, and critically.

"Now, what you will hear is what I've pieced together from things I observed, statements overheard between senior and junior, and conversations Sara shared with me in confidence.

"One Friday evening, Walter Sr. advised his son that an important client had asked him for an opinion on whether the Jensen Corporation could provide materials to accommodate manufacturing enhancements under consideration. He went on to say that the request had been asked earlier that day, and while he reviewed the documents and had the necessary answers, time would not allow him to finalize a formal response and an accompanying contract, both required on the following Monday.

"Jensen told his son that his executive secretary was away for the weekend, and he needed a secretary he could trust. The required paperwork had to be closely guarded so that competition would not learn about what was being offered and attempt to underbid.

"While this discussion was taking place, I was serving the two men cocktails and snacks. I recall the senior Jensen, saying, 'I'm in a dilemma. Finding a trustworthy secretary at this late date is difficult, at best. And our ability to supply these requirements will certainly add handsomely to the bottom line. I'm telling you this because I have a big favor to ask of both you and Sara. Do you think she'd be willing to work this weekend? I'll buy her that Mercedes she's been wanting. And if she doesn't mind, will you? I'll need her for at least two days and possibly three. I want us to get away from here, someplace quiet with no distractions. How do you feel about that?'

"Of course, it was all right with Junior, and after learning about the car, Sara was elated. So early Saturday morning, Sara and her father-in-law put overnight bags, a typewriter, paper, product manuals, and other essentials in the big car and drove to a hotel in the Adirondacks where Senior had booked a suite.

"According to Sara, for two days and the first night, they worked hard, finishing by early evening on the second day. On the morning of the second day, when Sara was typing the final documents, Senior had the hotel staff rearrange one of the rooms in the suite to accommodate what he referred to as an appreciation dinner. A table complete with candles, bone china, silverware, and crystal was set in a subdued, intimate interior with champagne and lobster served by the hotel staff. Following the evening meal, Walter ordered a liqueur which was served at the time Sara went to the restroom. When she returned, he toasted her with a gracious thank-you speech, and together, they sipped the cordials. In a few minutes, Sara began feeling numb."

Stacey sat, spellbound, engrossed by every word.

"Sara's speech began to falter, her coordination disappeared. She remembered Walter coming to her side, asking if she felt all right and tenderly touching her forehead. Then his behavior changed. He abruptly kissed her, and his hands began to explore her breasts and thighs. She was unable to ward off his advances. She couldn't even say no. She was out of control. Then, she lost track of what followed. Possibly, she blacked out, for the following morning was the next thing she recalled. She was naked, lying on her bed under a sheet. She was weak, light-headed. Her clothes were strewn around the room. It was as though she had sex but could not recall it. She was unable to move. Remaining still, she finally fell asleep."

"Oh my lord," murmured Stacey.

"Later," Maggie continued, "Walter entered Sara's room with a tray of orange juice, eggs, toast, and bacon. Placing the food beside her, he said, 'I trust you'll keep our little secret to yourself. In addition to the Mercedes, I'm giving you this.'

"He handed her a box from a jewelry store near the hotel. She opened it and saw a gold bracelet inlaid with rubies and sapphires. 'Consider the car as a gift for the secretarial work and the bracelet as a thank-you for your feminine charms.' She threw box and bracelet at him. 'Just remember,' he stormed, 'your life will not be worth two cents if Ginny, my son, or anyone hears of your uncontrollable advances.' With that, he left the room.

"On the ride home, Sara remained in the backseat, saying nothing. Upon arrival, she acted with civility, attempting to hide from others the animosity she held for the senior Jensen.

"Then three months after the return, she flew to Canada, saying she had to visit ailing parents. But the suddenness of the trip and the coolness she had exhibited led young Walter and Ginny to believe she was unhappy, and they feared her leaving was the first step toward a divorce. The fact was, she had missed her period and was returning home to have a baby, a baby she could not explain to her husband because they had, for some time, been celibate.

"When she finally returned to Bermuda, she was without the baby, and no one other than her father-in-law knew she had a child."

"What happened to the infant?" interrupted Stacey.

"I'm coming to that. Before she left Canada, Sara called her father-in-law and told him of a daughter, his. She demanded help. Along with Peter Grouse, Walter's chauffeur, the two drove to Canada where Sara and Walter met privately. At first, the conversation was distant with Walter refusing to believe the infant was his. Then it grew argumentative. Finally, he accepted her story, probably, I'm assuming, to keep the truth from ever being learned. He told her he knew of a couple who wanted a baby to love, and through them, he would provide for the infant's future. Also, he promised to compensate Sara for the difficulty and suffering she had endured.

"Sara, wanting the best for her daughter, believed Jensen. She was hopeful the baby would be cared for. But that hope was an uncertainty, for Sara never learned what really happened to her daughter. In fact, other than Walter Senior, and possibly Peter Grouse, no one knew. Until recently! When I met you in Bermuda!"

"You're saying the baby is me?"

"As difficult as that may be for you to accept, I am certain of it. I'm convinced you and the baby are one and the same."

"Why? Because we look alike? Or because of three or four other coincidences? All of which might be meaningless!"

"No, because of one undeniable proof."

"And what is that?"

"Did you examine the photograph of Walter playing tennis?"

"Yes, but there's no physical resemblance between us!"

"It isn't a physical resemblance. It's something else! Have you the picture?"

Nodding, Stacey handed it to the woman.

"Look here!"

Maggie pointed to a mark on Jensen's thigh, large enough to be seen but too small to be identified. Normally covered by his tennis shorts, it was exposed with his stretching reach to serve a tennis ball.

"When we were seated in Bermuda, outside the locker room having lemonade, I noticed a birthmark on your thigh."

"You're observant! So what? Many people have birthmarks!"

"Not one that looks like a woman's face!"

"You really *are* observant! My mother was a Tarot reader, and when I was young, she often told me that the face on my thigh was that of a High Priestess, one of the twenty-two Spiritual Principles of Life portrayed as a Major Arcana in every Tarot deck."

"Well, I know nothing about Tarot decks, Major Arcana, or High Priestesses, but I do know that the face on your thigh is identical to the woman's face on Walter Jensen's thigh. I've seen both often enough. That's no coincidence. That's an inherited trait."

Stacey sat back, amazed at what she had heard. Many questions whirled through her head. Unanswered questions! Disturbing questions! Answers to which would have a bearing on her life, the part already lived, the future remaining before her.

The two spoke a little longer with nothing new added. As Stacey was preparing to leave Maggie's room, she reached out and embraced her hostess.

"Thank you for taking the time and having the interest to share all of this with me. At some time, my awareness to all of this will become known to my . . . to Walter Jensen. That can do you no good. What will you do?"

"After meeting you, I spent a great deal of time wondering whether I should tell you. And of course, my thoughts considered Walter's reaction. But the more I thought about Sara and the love I've had for her, I decided it was necessary for you to hear what I know. Sara would want you, her daughter, to know the truth.

"I've discussed this with Gerard, and we've decided to leave Walter Jensen. Aside from his animosity, nothing will happen. In fact, he'll be glad to have us out of his life and out of his presence. My only concern is with the son, and how he'll react. Yet whatever the consequences may be, the father caused them, and I refuse to punish myself for his sins."

That evening, Stacey related everything she had heard to Jerry Forrest, the one person she trusted and in whom she could confide.

Upon hearing the story, he called Hank White, the law firm's chief investigator.

"Stacey and I are in New York. We're returning tomorrow with information that's not only disturbing but enlightening to her recent experiences. I want you to meet me at *Luigi's*. Reserve a private room at six thirty for seven people. Bring Diane with you."

Then he telephoned Shomazzi and asked him to bring Windy and Giant to *Luigi's*. With them being some distance from New York, the godfather wanted to know why and was not easily pacified with "it's too involved to be discussed over the phone."

They argued. Finally, Forrest said, "Okay, don't come! You live out your days hating yourself if something tragic happens to your goddaughter. The one you supposedly love! I'll try my best without you."

Then Shomazzi relented and assured him that the three would be at *Luigi's* by six thirty.

CHAPTER 66

ON THE OFFENSIVE

Shoe, Windy, and Giant were seated at *Luigi's* when the other four arrived. Before they even had a chance to greet each other, the old man snapped, "Who's that woman?"

"Meet Diane Whittingham! She's a fellow investigator and partner of mine," replied Hank White.

"Why do we need her? We already have Windy, Giant, and you. That's more than enough eyes and ears to sniff out this dog."

Before Shoe commented further, Jerry interrupted saying, "When you've heard what your goddaughter has to say, I think you'll agree that a female investigator is a well-advised addition. Especially someone who is as competent as she is! Diane, meet Vincent Shomazzi and his two associates, Giant and Windy.

"Stacey, let's skip these side comments and get to the substance of this gathering. Tell everyone what you've learned."

For nearly an hour, Stacey held their attention, explaining who Maggie Muldoon was, her relationship with Walter Jensen, and everything that Maggie had told her.

At the conclusion, Stacey added, "I'm devastated. I was raised, loved, and protected by two people who I thought were my parents. I even have a birth certificate confirming their parentage. Now I learn that I was not conceived by them but rather by a woman who I never met, one who was raped by a perverted individual and then abandoned. So how did I end up with Dora and Doc? How can I have this certificate? And other papers too? How can this be?"

Shoe raised his hand and spoke softly.

"Dora's discovery of your infant body should have been told to you years ago. Unfortunately, it wasn't, but they shared the story with me, and here's what I learned."

He began with Dora seeing the chauffeur carrying a package into a New York alley and returning empty handed. When he drove the car away, Dora entered the alley and heard a whimpering from inside a dumpster.

"My god," cried Stacey. "I was discarded with garbage. What else am I to learn?"

"Be thankful for her curiosity, my dear. It saved your life and gave you two people who loved you more than anything else they ever had."

He continued, saying, "You're constant crying caused Dora to believe you were very sick. So she went searching for Doc, the only person she knew who might be able to care for you. As it turned out, you were merely hungry and uncomfortable with a dirty diaper. But because of you, Doc and Dora fell in love.

"With regard to your birth certificate and the other papers, I'm responsible for them. When I heard the story, I convinced them to give you an identity, one that would prevent others, as well as you, from questioning your roots. I contacted a forger, and he prepared the papers. Then Doc and Dora married each other, justifying your being their daughter."

"You mean I forced them into a marriage?"

"No, you never did that. You did much more. You brought two lonely people together. The love they had for you grew into a true and lasting affection for each other. Always be grateful, Stacey! You not only brought them happiness, you gave them a daughter who meant everything to them."

"Oh, I'm grateful! I love them deeply and always will. But these forgeries, how do I deal with them?"

"Don't worry!" interjected Forrest. "Let me examine the documents. I'll see that they're authenticated, legally."

"What about my attacker? And Jensen? What's to become of them?"

"From what you were told about Sara's rape, it appears," interjected Diane, "that Jensen gave her what is commonly known as a 'club drug' or 'easy lay' drug. In other words, a date-rape tablet. Trying to find how and where he got it, so long ago, will be difficult, likely impossible. But it's a straw that, if found, may help to prove his complicity, at least more than a mere birthmark."

"Besides, the story gives us a foundation," commented Jerry. "It opens 'doors' that need to be checked, hopefully doors that will lead to the person who's been after you."

"What I don't understand," interrupted Shomazzi, "is why that Muldoon woman stayed with the Jensen's after she learned of the rape."

"I wondered about that too," interjected Stacey. "And she explained it quite simply. Virginia Jensen's debilitating disease had worsened, and because of the love and respect Maggie had for her patient, she couldn't leave. When she finally died, Maggie admitted that Gerard and she were accustomed to their lifestyle and put off picking up stakes and leaving. But after meeting me and becoming convinced I was Sara's daughter, she felt Sara would want me to know the truth. So Gerard and she decided to tell me and risk the consequences by leaving and knowing Jensen would discover her involvement with me."

"Whatever the reason," commented Jerry, "it's what it is, and now it's over. Let's ignore that and think about the future. It's time for us to go on the attack. I'm open to suggestions."

"Jerry, I may have an idea," responded Hank. "It depends on something, something that's troubling me. But if I'm right, Diane and I will propose a plan that can turn this entire thing to our advantage. Give us a day, and let's meet again tomorrow night. Then we can finalize what we need to do."

CHAPTER 67

THE RUSE

The following day, two cars—Giant and Windy in one, Hank and Diane in the other—were in the parking lot across from the *TH&E* building. The preceding evening, Stacey had outlined her plans for the following day, and each of the four knew she was having a luncheon appointment with a prospective client followed by a visit to another client's office at 2:30 p.m.

Knowing the routes and addresses to where she was going, Giant and Windy were assigned to follow the first car and Hank and Diane the second, if one was available. The location of Stacey's Cadillac was not of great interest, but any other car shadowing her was.

At precisely 11:40 a.m., Stacey's convertible pulled out of the underground employee parking lot and merged into the moving traffic. No vehicle left the curbs, but one car in the public parking lot, a black Chevrolet, started its engine and headed to the exit gate. After paying the attendant, the driver turned on the road in the direction Stacey had gone. Giant and Windy followed. At the first intersection, the Chevy stopped for a red light. Stacey's car was nowhere to be seen. When the light changed, the Chevy moved forward. Giant and Windy at first assumed the car to be merely another departing vehicle until it picked up speed and began passing traffic. Veering in and out of lanes and racing through yellow lights, Shomazzi's men fell well behind and lost sight of the black car.

In the meantime, Hank and Diane left the lot and traveled to where they knew Stacey was headed. Twenty minutes later, they saw the black Chevrolet and then the second car.

Each was parked a block apart. Hank and Diane drove past the Chevy and approached the side of the second car, motioning Windy and Giant to follow. Another block down the road, each car pulled to a stop.

Exiting his car, Hank walked back as Giant turned down his window. "Were you able to follow him all the way?"

"No, we lost him," admitted Giant. "We were doing all right until he began to speed and ignore the red lights and crossover traffic. We didn't catch up to him until we got here. He's back there in his car."

"Was he always in sight of Stacey's car?"

"Can't be certain, but I don't know how he could have been. Road repairs along the way slowed the traffic for a spell. When you got past the workmen, the road opened up, and you could travel fast. If Stacey hit the pedal, she should have lost him. She was well ahead before reaching the work area."

"Thanks! You go back to where you were parked. Stay with Stacey, and give her protection. If the Chevy and Stacey get separated, forget the guy. We'll follow him. He's got my curiosity."

When Stacey had finished with her client meeting, she drove to Rocky Mountain Pass. Giant and Windy followed. The driver of the Chevy lost interest and drove away in another direction. Hank followed at a distance always keeping the Chevy in sight. Nearing dinnertime, the pursuer stopped at a pizza parlor and ate inside. Finishing his meal, he returned to the car and sat awhile before leaving. What he was doing remained unknown.

When the car finally moved, the couple trailed it to the hotel where the driver was staying. He entered the lobby, and Diane followed. Hank left his car to inspect the Chevy. Finished, he waited for Diane to return; and together, they sat in the car talking. Hank then dialed Jerry on his cell phone and reconfirmed the dinner meeting, asking Jerry to contact Shomazzi and Stacey as to the location.

"Diane and I may be fifteen or twenty minutes late. I have an idea, and if I'm right, the two of us will have a few things to do. By the way, be certain to drive Stacey to the restaurant in your car. Leave hers at her home."

When Diane and Hank arrived, the others were discussing strategies. In Hank's hands was a large box, which he placed on an empty table.

"Drinks?" Shoe asked. "Tonight's on me. I like the idea of being on the offense rather than the defense. So order whatever makes you happy."

After he was served, Hank apologized for being late but continued, saying that Diane and he had been "nosing around" and discovered something interesting.

"Stacey, when you left for your luncheon meeting today, something happened. A car, a black Chevrolet, was in the parking lot across from your building. And when you left, it began to follow. Did you notice it?"

"No. Guess I had my mind elsewhere, a conversation at the luncheon meeting probably."

"This time, it may have been just as well. But in the future, be alert to whom and what is near you. You don't want to be taken by surprise.

"Today, because of the traffic, changing lights and road repairs, you were able to put distance between the Chevy and you. In fact, your pursuer lost sight of you. Yet when Giant, Windy, Diane, and I arrived at the restaurant, the pursuer was already there. And then when you went to your second meeting, he followed, waited, and left when you later went home."

"My god," she whispered, behind a mouth-covering hand.

"After leaving you, he went to his hotel, and we followed. There, we examined his car and then drove to your house and inspected yours. As I surmised, he has a GPS vehicle tracking system, and he's bugged your car."

"Damn it," muttered Giant. "No wonder he got to her second meeting so easily."

Stacey sagged in the chair, her face ashen.

"You removed it, didn't you?" demanded Shoe.

"No, I left it there."

"Left it there! Why would you do a damn fool thing like that?"

"Several reasons! First, I don't want him to know anyone is on to him. But more importantly, I want to use it to our best advantage."

"White, you're not going to turn my goddaughter into a decoy. I won't allow it."

"I have no intention of doing that. If you'll remain calm for a few minutes, you'll hear the plan. Then say whatever you think! Diane, take over!"

Rising, Diane walked to the table where Tom had placed the box.

"Stacey, what size are you?"

"A six."

"Good. You and I are the same size. At home, have you a pair of black slacks, black shoes, and a button-down-the-front white silk blouse?"

"Doesn't everybody?"

"Plain black slacks or designer?"

"Both!"

"Good."

From the box, Diane removed a three-quarter-length red jacket, sunglasses, and red cap.

"Tomorrow, drive to *Mama's Kitchen* for breakfast, wearing your plain black slacks, white blouse, and this red jacket. Also wear these sunglasses and red cap. Arrive at seven thirty as you normally do but not a minute earlier. Try on the jacket and cap see how they fit."

"Perfect. And nice-looking too."

"Good. When you arrive, Hank and I will be in the restaurant. Ignore us completely. No eye contact, no waving, no conversation. Order what you normally do, and once you're finished eating, request another cup of hot coffee. Stand, place a newspaper next to the coffee along with the breakfast check if you've already received it. Go to the ladies' room. Tell the clerk where you're going and have her leave everything, including the coffee at your spot, along with a breakfast check if you haven't received it. Hank and I will have a booth near the restroom. I'll make certain no one goes in. When you stand up, I'll go in the john. Then you come in. You'll give me the jacket, your pocketbook, cap, sunglasses, and car keys. I'll give you a full-length black coat, a hat, another pair of sunglasses, a pocketbook, and a hat. You'll put on the garments, leave the restroom, and join Hank in his booth. Shortly thereafter, I'll exit the ladies' room, go to your table, drink the coffee, pick up the breakfast check and paper, and go to the cashier and pay for your breakfast.

"Once I leave the restaurant, I'll get in your car and drive to the Scenic View on Rocky Mountain Pass. At that early hour, no one is likely to be there, and with a good performance by each of us, your stalker should be drawn to the location."

Hank interrupted. "Timing is critical. When Diane leaves the restaurant, she'll get in Stacey's car and fiddle around. That'll give me time to pay my bill and leave with Stacey for the parking lot just as Diane is pulling away.

"During all this time, Giant and you, Windy, will be waiting away from *Mama's Kitchen* but in view of it. When you see the stalker leave to follow Diane, the two of you will trail along. Stacey and I will be the third car in this parade. Between the three of us and Diane, we should be able to grab the killer at Scenic View. And I can't wait until that moment."

"What if he doesn't come to the restaurant?" asked Stacey.

"Oh, he will."

"Hank, that's a damn good plan," said Jerry. "But what about me? I don't like being left out of this caper. I think my interest in Stacey's well-being is equal to everyone here."

"And that's the reason you're out of it. If he sees you, he'll become suspicious. We need him to have his guard down, and we can't risk failing because he's alerted. I hope you understand."

Together, over dinner, they reviewed the plans, making certain everyone understood his or her role and how it should be played.

CHAPTER 68

SURPRISE! SURPRISE!

The following morning, Diane drove away from *Mama's Kitchen* as planned, and a black Chevrolet followed. When the two cars were out of sight, Hank and Stacey headed for *Scenic View,* following Giant and Windy.

When their cars arrived, only the convertible was there.

Exiting his car, Hank walked to Diane. "Did the Chevy show up?"

"No, just the four of you. Did you see the Chevy leave the lot?" asked Diane.

"Yes, but I never saw the car between here and there. I wonder what he's doing. You wait here. The four of us will go up the Pass a quarter of a mile or so, park, and wait for ten or fifteen minutes. If he arrives and begins giving you trouble, lay on the horn."

Going to Shoe's men, Hank told them of the change then headed to his car. As he was getting in, the Chevy appeared and drove next to the convertible. The three men dashed to the vehicle, and Hank pulled open the driver's door. Seated behind the wheel was a teenager.

"Who the hell are you?" demanded Hank.

The boy stammered. "I'm-I'm-I'm a messenger! I have-have this note for the lady," he said and handed it to Hank.

Opening it, he read:

Lady, you nearly fooled me. You're a tad taller than McDonald. She arrived in three or four-inch high heels. But you're in flats. Maybe I'll have the pleasure of meeting you some other time, but not today.

Grabbing the teenager by his coat, Hank dragged him out of the car.

"The guy who gave this note to you, where is he now?"

The lad, fear showing all over his face, said, "Honest, mister, I don't know. He nearly ran me off the road . . . up the hill. Handed me fifty bucks and told me to . . . to take his car down here and give that note to a lady in a convertible."

"The Chevy? What are you supposed to do with it once you give the woman the note?"

"I'm-I'm-I'm to take it back to where we met. And leave it."

"With the keys in the ignition?"

"No, on the floor . . . under the seat! I'm to lock-lock the car and go away. Honest, mister, honest! That's all he told me! I don't mean no harm. I'm just trying to do what he called 'a good deed.' I don't want-don't want any trouble, mister. Here-here, take the fifty bucks! Just let me go. Please."

Hank shook his head. "Keep the money! You earned it. Now get going!"

Windy said, "You going to just let him go? Like nothing happened?"

"Windy, follow him and try not to be seen. Giant, get in the Cadillac with Stacey. Drive her home. Stay there until I arrive. Diane and I will follow Windy.

"Damn that guy. Now, I have another reason for getting my hands on him. How I hate being outmaneuvered. The scumbag made fools out of us."

As they drove up the hill, Diane said, "He's certainly good. Can you believe it? A woman's shoes. Heels, no less. No wonder he's hard to catch. He's alert and notices the smallest things. Takes nothing for granted."

"Maybe so. But he's no different than any other hood. He's ahead of the game right now, but wait. He'll make a mistake, and it'll cost him . . . cost him plenty."

Diane said nothing. Sitting motionlessly, she stared silently into space.

Nearly one half mile later, the female investigator shouted, "Stop the car! The dirt road we just passed! There was dust rising from it. Bet the cars went that way."

Hank backed up and made a hard right, moved rapidly to a clearing. Trees aligned each side of the road. After another hard right, he slammed on the brakes and skidded to a stop. Less than a foot away was the Chevrolet, parked and empty.

Hank backed up and drove around the Chevy and continued several hundred yards further. Unexpectedly, the teenager came out of the trees, riding a bicycle. Diane and he followed at a distance, and Hank watched the lad turn off the road. Coming to where he had turned, they saw the walking trail the boy had entered. "There's no way we can follow him. He's gone. We'll go back to the Chevy and wait. I wonder how far Windy went before he realized the kid got away."

Fifteen minutes turned into a half an hour! Then another thirty minutes dragged by.

"Well, there's no sense sitting here any longer. If the stalker's around, he knows we're here, and he won't be showing up. I hate to leave because he's bound to come back for the car, but he'll do it at his convenience. Damn it all! Now, I've got to admit to Jerry and Shoe that this guy played us for fools."

CHAPTER 69

THE MAKING OF A BELIEVER

The front door opened, and the big man nodded his head! "Good morning, Ms. Whittingham!"

"Hello, Giant! Is the lady in?"

"She will be for you, ma'am. She's in that room across the hall."

Walking to the den, Diane saw Stacey sitting at a table sipping a cup of coffee.

"Hi, Diane! This is an unexpected visit. Would you like a cup of coffee? It's fresh and piping hot."

"No, thanks! I was up early and already have had three. My stomach's starting to growl."

"How about some coffee cake then?"

"No, I'm good. I just thought I'd drop by and see how you're holding up."

"Today, pretty well. Last night . . . a different story. Yesterday, I expected things to go well, really well. In fact, I thought all my problems were finally behind me. Then, when things didn't go right, I was drained."

"Thought that might happen. So why the change today?"

"Yesterday, my annoyance led to self-pity. So I poured a glass of wine, sat down, and chided myself 'Quit feeling sorry for yourself.

What are you going to do? Give up? Spend the rest of your life looking over your shoulder? Being constantly frightened and unhappy?'

"Then after the second glass of wine, I began to think about what happened and what my godfather said, 'I like being on the offense rather than the defense.' And the more I thought about that, the more convinced I was that it was time to take the play to the enemies. To do that, I needed a plan. So for the past few hours, I've been thinking, strategizing so to speak."

"And what have you decided?"

"Well, it's rough, really rough. And not thoroughly thought out. That's why I'm so glad to see you. Your arrival couldn't be more timely."

"Timely? How so?"

"Because my plan needs you. Hear me out! As mentioned, to be proactive, I need to be in charge. Not subservient to the enemy. And to do that, I need someone with experience. Someone who's creative. Someone who can guide me. And I know of no one better qualified than you.

"All my life, I've been making decisions—deciding what needed to be done to achieve whatever objective I set out to accomplish. This has evolved in habits and characteristics that have enabled me to take on the challenges confronted. Challenges not too different from others faced. But now I'm in a different arena, an alien setting, one for which I have no experience. And I need expert guidance, guidance that will draw out, fine-tune, and complement the skills and abilities I need to apply to overcome the barriers I face. That type of guidance you possess. You can provide the direction required because you have the experience needed."

"I thank you for your confidence in me. And those words are very consoling. Very encouraging. But they are generalities. I have no idea what you are planning and am, therefore, uncertain that I'm qualified in being of any help."

"Hold on! Don't formulate any conclusions until you hear what I have in mind. Ever since this whole nightmare began, I've been on the receiving end with one or two . . . I not only don't know the number, but I don't even know how to label them . . . Animals—for sake of a word—calling all the shots. My plan will put the man who impregnated the mother I never knew in an uncomfortable, defensive position. A plan that hints at something happening to this animal but without specifically telling him what, when, or where. Here's my plan."

* * * * *

Upon learning what Stacey intended to do, Diane said, "That's pretty good. But consider this, also." And the women, together, finalized the strategy.

"Something else, Stacey. I can't side with you without first apprising Hank and Jeff of your intentions."

"I assumed that. In fact, Diane, I won't let you do anything to jeopardize your employment or relationship with either of them. I'm only asking you to withhold telling them for a short time."

"A short time? What's a short time, and why is that important?"

"Because I want to begin this game without any stumbling blocks. High heels and flats! You know what I mean, Diane?"

"Oh, I understand." She laughed. "But how long is a short time?"

"No longer than those first two steps we'll be taking. Then the fish should be nibbling at the hook."

"I'll go along with that. As long as it's no longer. But understand this, Stacey. If any danger is about to pop up, I'm bringing in the cavalry."

"That's fine!"

CHAPTER 70

LETTERS AND A PHONE CALL

Friday morning at precisely 11:42 a. m., a messenger moving a two-wheel wire-basket cart entered the building lobby. Walking to the bank of elevators, he pushed the button that carried him to the upper management floor. He headed down the hallway, stopped at the door to the president's office, knocked, and waited for the invitation to enter.

"May I help you?" Anna asked.

"I have a letter for Mr. Jensen."

"Sorry, but he's away for the day. Give it to me, and I'll see that he gets it tomorrow."

"Are you his secretary?"

"Yes."

"His regular one or a substitute?"

She frowned but replied, "His regular one."

"Okay. Please sign here."

On the delivery slip, preceding the line with Jensen's name were six other signatures, indicating deliveries to people at other locations. Following his name were another seven people who had not yet been seen. She signed the slip, accepted the letter, and the messenger left the office.

Outside the building, he walked two blocks to a restaurant and headed to a booth in the back. There, he removed his gray jacket and cap and threw them on top of the remaining undelivered letters in the cart. From a bench, he picked up a red high school varsity basketball jacket and put it on. Then he handed the signed delivery slip to a woman sitting across from the bench where his jacket laid.

"How did it go?" the woman asked.

"Fine. No problems at all."

"Good. Care for a hot chocolate, Danish, or something else?"

"No, thanks. I have to be going."

Reaching into her purse, she handed him twenty-five dollars.

"I really appreciate the help!" And the boy departed, never expecting to see Diane again.

The following day, Walter Jensen arrived at his office.

"Good morning, sir!" greeted Anna. "How was the trip?"

"At times, argumentative then demanding. But we made the sale and can keep the factories open for another year."

"That's wonderful. The last few months have been pretty lean."

"Tell me about it."

As he walked to his office, she handed him a number of pink telephone message slips.

"You've been missed."

"I wish." He laughed.

Scanning the slips, he entered, walked to the closet, and hung his coat. Still absorbed with the call slips, he did not immediately notice the lone letter on his desk. Finally, seeing the envelope, he dropped the slips next to it and reached for a letter opener.

> Dear WJ,
>
> Our contact suffers from serious lapses in time: first at the tennis courts in Bermuda over a month ago and now this belated remembrance letter. But I promise not to be so out of touch in the future.
>
> I have a party planned, and I know you'll want to attend. Otherwise, it will be so incomplete and less vocal without you, the guest of honor. We have so much to share with others. Don't you agree?
>
> AM

Rereading the message one more time, he rose and walked to Anna's desk. "This letter!" he demanded. "How and when did it arrive?"

"Yesterday, by an outside delivery boy." He returned to his desk without closing the door and stared at the bare mahogany surface.

A week passed with neither Stacey nor Diane receiving or sensing any response from the letter. On the following Friday, again precisely at 11:53 a.m., Diane entered the building lobby. Sitting on a bench, she watched the elevators. Minutes passed before Jensen exited with a cadre of lower level executives at his side. They moved through the revolving door and headed for a downtown luncheon meeting.

Diane got off the bench and went to the elevators. When she reached the seventh floor, she walked into the cafeteria looking for Anna and nearly backed into the secretary at the cashier's station. "Sorry, clumsy of me! I wasn't looking!"

"No spill, no harm." said the executive secretary.

Returning to the elevator, Diane went to the president's floor. Outside his office, she tested the doorknob. It was locked. She removed a set of picks from her purse and let herself in. She approached Jensen's door. It too was locked. Again, she dropped the tumblers and gained access to his office. At his desk, she repositioned some papers and file folders, giving her an open space where she placed a second letter.

As she left both offices, she locked each door and exited the building. She then searched for a public phone booth where she telephoned Stacey.

To a voice recording, she merely said, "The letter's been delivered. What's our next step?"

Jensen, entering the executive office suite, gave Anna a perfunctory nod. He continued into his office and immediately noticed the rearrangement of papers on his desk. An annoying scowl was replaced by astonishment when he saw the envelope with its familiar script. He grabbed the letter opener and ripped open the flap.

> Dear WJ,
>
> Soon it will be party time, and tomorrow is ideal for you and me to become reacquainted. Say at your house. You'll be able to review, in a comfortable setting, the list of people who will be invited and the plans made for the upcoming party. There are so many who need to know what

we mean to each other. Don't you agree? I'm so excited and hope you are too.

I'll let you know when I'll be arriving. Don't go to any trouble over refreshments. All I want is your presence.

Your long lost,
AM

Jensen shouted, "Anna, get in here now."

Running into his office, she asked softly, "What's wrong, Mr. Jensen?

"This letter! When did it arrive? Who delivered it? And don't tell me it's another outside messenger carrier."

Looking at the envelope in his trembling hand, she said, "I don't know. I've never seen it before. Where did you find it?"

"On my desk! Did you leave the office doors unlocked?"

"No, sir! I unlocked them when I returned from lunch."

"Well, someone has access to these rooms, and I want security to find out who it is. Now close my door and make the call."

He immediately grabbed the phone. Dialing numbers known only to him and to the person being called, he listened to three rings and then heard "Hello there! It's been a while."

"Too damn long, in fact! And don't be so damn cheery. I want to see you tomorrow, at my house by noon!"

"Hold on a second! Do you know where I am?"

"I don't give a shit if you're in Beijing, Melbourne, or Moscow. We have problems, and I want your ass here now. Today, if I thought possible."

"What's the problem, Walt?"

"Don't Walt me, you bastard! If you'd done the job you were hired to do, I wouldn't be in this fix. The McDonald bitch is making threats. And from the vibes I'm receiving, she seems to know that I knocked up the one you drowned years ago. And unless you do something to close her mouth permanently . . . tomorrow . . . she'll have both of our asses in a sling. Do I make myself clear?"

"Oh, I hear you, and so will everyone in your company, if you don't lower your voice."

"Don't you lecture me! You're nothing more than a clown. A failure! Over twenty-four years, and she's still around. If you were half as good as you think you—"

"Shut up!"

"What did you say?"

"I said shut up. We've had this conversation before . . . down in Miami, at your condo. I'm sure you remember, but if not, let me remind you. You threatened me, calling me names and promising to destroy me by spreading a story about my failing this assignment. And when you said that, I promised I'd make your life miserable. As I recall, I said I'd gouge out your eyeballs, break your bones, and crush your balls. And I still remember the fear on your face, that sickly white wimpy, cowardly face. Well, it's not too late. I can still provoke the pain."

"Don't try intimidating me. The fear I once had for you was caused more by the dread I had in the McDonald woman learning I was her father. Now she may know. I've come too far in my life to have the world know that I, Walter Jensen, president of Jensen International, have an illegitimate daughter. And I'll do whatever is necessary to protect my name and reputation.

"Now, you're going to do what I want, what I'm paying you to do. You be at my house tomorrow. Come through the tunnel by the tennis courts. No one will see you. And when you arrive, I'll tell you how you'll fulfill my contract. I'm tired of your fuck-ups. Be there tomorrow, damn it, or expect to become the laughingstock among your circle of friends and followers."

With that, he slammed down the receiver.

The man of many names stared at the receiver in his hand. *Oh, I'll be there all right, you bastard. And I'll take care of the bitch you sired. But after that, you'll find out what it's like to be my enemy. Tomorrow's going to be the happiest day of my life.*

CHAPTER 71

TAKING EYES OFF THE BALL

The man of many names retrieved his overnight bag from the airport carousel. Planning on staying no more than one night, the bag was small enough to have been stowed in an overhead luggage compartment in the main cabin. But inside the bag were keepsakes that never would have cleared security.

At the car rental, he removed a blackjack, forceps, and Freddie's knife from the bag before tossing the carrier in the vehicle's trunk. Pressing the button several times, the blade sprang into action. Satisfied, he slid the knife and forceps into his jacket pocket and attached the club to his belt. Then he walked to a public phone and called Jensen at his home. "It'll be two hours before I arrive. My plane had mechanical problems," he lied. While Jensen was not happy, he said he would stay occupied.

Following an often-traveled route, he arrived near the woods behind the Jensen estate in the customary forty-five minutes. He entered a seldom-traveled dirt road, weaved in and out of the trees, and parked, leaving his bag in the locked car. From there, he hiked to a gazebo where tennis players often sat before and after matches to watch others compete on Jensen's two courts.

Behind the main house was a crown of trees fronting on a brook with a crossover bridge leading to the free-standing structure. Entering the main door of the gazebo, he went down a flight of steps and through a tunnel. At the end of the tunnel were two locker rooms, one for women and the other for men. There players showered and changed before entering the main house for refreshments and dinner.

Separating the locker rooms from stairs leading into the house was a large room where tennis rackets, balls, and other paraphernalia lay on tables for unequipped guests to use when invited to play several sets.

Mounted on two opposing walls and held in place with brackets were two mannequins, one in a serving stance and the other in a receiving crouch. Trophies, ribbons, and photographs identified tournaments—nationally and internationally—wherein the host had both competed and won. People visiting the room not only realized how avid a devotee Jensen was to the game but how immodestly he considered his abilities and accomplishments.

The intruder ascended steps into the living quarters and examined rooms on the main floor. He saw no one. The house appeared empty until he finally found the man seated in front of a television in his library, concentrating on a tennis match.

With his back to the door, the stalker mocked, "Hope you're enjoying that game because—"

Wheeling around to face the newcomer, Jensen interrupted, saying, "Damn, you! Why didn't you—"

Before completing the question, the blackjack landed violently on Jensen's head, with the attacker finishing what he had intended to say.

"Because it's going to be the last one you ever watch."

Across town, Stacey dialed Diane. In response to a recorded message, the caller said, "Hi, it's Stacey. Wish you were home. I wanted to share my thoughts on the next move. With no response to our letters, I've decided to be pushier. So I'm going to Jensen's house to confront him face to face. I want to hear his sorry-ass excuses and hopefully see him squirm. I'll be in touch after I leave."

Having never been to the house, she took several wrong turns before arriving at the long driveway leading to the front door. *Talk about mansions! This guy must be loaded.*

The door was open, and deciding a surprise visit might put him on the defensive, she entered quietly. Moving from one room to another, she discovered nothing other than a tennis match appearing on a TV screen in an empty room. Near the kitchen, she heard voices, indistinct and rather distant. Continuing toward the sounds, she came to an open door leading to the basement.

From below, she heard, "Why in hell do you have me tied to the wall like this? Are you out of your fucking mind? You've had your fun. Now let's get serious and talk. Cut me loose!"

But there was no response.

"My god, no! You can't! Not me! We've been . . . partners . . . too long!"

Finally, the other broke his silence. "Oh . . . partners! Is that what we've been?" A long, loud, macabre laugh followed.

Drawn to the sounds, Stacey quietly descended the circular stairs. Near the bottom but remaining hidden in the shadows of a bend, she saw Jensen shackled to the wall where the tennis-serving mannequin had been. And moving toward the captive was the invader of her apartment at *The Quad*. Passing from one hand to the other and back again in uninterrupted exchanges was a switchblade.

"I can't, says you. Well, you'll see what I can and cannot do. Upstairs, you watched the last tennis match you'll ever see. In fact, it will be the last thing you ever see because now you're about to enter the world of total darkness. I'm going to remove those eyeballs of yours, and then I'm going to leave you hanging, there on that wall, bleeding to your well-deserving death, one that's painful, agonizing, and slow. No one speaks to me the way you have. Calling me a fuck-up . . . a clown . . . a failure! No one says that to me and lives."

Suddenly, Jensen's near-hysteric "no, no, no!" was joined by a loud, overriding voice. Turning, the killer saw Stacey standing at the bottom of the stairs.

"You're right! Jensen's no good, but he doesn't deserve to die the way you're suggesting. Leave him to wallow in his own misery—his memories and the disgrace he's caused others. But let him live!"

"Well, well, well! Little Miss Do Good! Would you feel that same way knowing he hired me to find you, ravish you, and scatter your remains for no one else to find? Along with that, would you feel differently if you knew he had me kill the woman who gave you birth, and he ordered me to dispose of your adopted parents, and he had me come to Bermuda so I could drown you? Knowing all of that, do you still feel the same way about this old fool's life? Over twenty-five years, I've been searching for you. And now you come to me of your own free will."

Inching toward her slowly, tentatively, he continued, "Think about this! Once I kill this bastard, I'm going to rape your naked body, and then I'm going to touch you in ways you'll never forget. For you see, my dear, I need a reward for all the troubles you've caused me, the time I've spent chasing after you, and the money I'm about to lose with Jensen's death."

From eighteen feet away, he took two rapid three-foot steps toward her. But Stacey was already holding two tennis balls and a racket in her hands. Bouncing one ball, she drove it twelve feet into his face. He staggered back, clutching a swelling eye with one hand. Quickly, she dropped the second ball and propelled it into his groin. As he fell to the floor, Stacey raced around him to the steps and ascended them two at a time.

Jensen pleaded, "Cut me down, Daughter, cut me down. I am your Father. Save me, save me!"

At the main door, a terrifying outcry caused her to stop momentarily.

"No, no, no," followed an agonizing scream that echoed throughout the house.

Outside the front entrance, Jerry, Tom, Diane, and four policemen were leaving their cars. A terrified look on Stacey's face evoked from Jerry. "Darling, are you all right?"

One floor below, blood was everywhere. Two empty eye sockets in a downward tilted head stared openly at two eyeballs lying below the victim's feet. Jensen's neck was slashed from side to side. In front of the man stood the violent smiling killer, an assassin of victims long forgotten. Slowly, meticulously, he wiped Freddie's switchblade on the dead man's shirt.

The sound of steps overhead prompted the killer to exit through the door leading to the locker rooms. He shut the door and wedged a chair under the knob against the floor. From a table, he grabbed several towels and a sweatshirt, dashed down the tunnel to the gazebo and through the woods to his car. As he drove to the highway, he began to casually hum from *Oklahoma, Oh, What a Beautiful Morning* . . . .

Back at the house, Stacey led Tom, Diane, and the four policemen to the basement where they followed bloody prints to the locked door. Unable to open it, they broke through the upper wood panel before reaching down to remove the door-blocking chair. By the time they arrived at the gazebo, the killer's trail was nowhere to be found.

CHAPTER 72

MISMATCHED

It was dark and windy with little traffic on the roads. The killer came to a service station that was closed for the night. Parking by the outside restroom door, he picked the lock, entered, and removed his bloody shirt. He washed his face, chest, and arms then dried them with the towels taken from Jensen's locker room. Carefully, he scrubbed away streaks of blood that had sprayed on his trousers. Relatively clean, he put on the Jensen sweatshirt, combed his hair, and drove to a restaurant. The evening activities had made him hungry.

After a three-course meal, he returned to his car and drove to Rocky Mountain Pass. In Stacey's driveway was Jerry Forrest's car.

Ah, two instead of one! Immobile, he'll be able to watch me fondle and fuck his girlfriend, again and again. Then after I slowly kill her, I'll torture him to a prolonged, unpleasant death. Oh, this will be a rewarding night.

He once again parked beneath the limbs of the willow tree on Destiny Lane and stepped from his car. Outside, trees were swaying in the breeze, leaves fluttering, and occasional sounds of hooting owls and barking dogs could be heard.

Good, keep up the noise, Mother Nature. All the better for what I have planned.

Running across Rocky Mountain Pass and through the trees, he arrived at the back door of Stacey's house. He tried the doorknob and found it locked. Crouching, he began to pick the lock. Suddenly, his body lurched forward. Two strong hands pushed down on his shoulders, and another hand slammed his head repeatedly against the door. The uninvited guest was unconscious, and Mother Nature's sounds muffled all noise of the attack.

The following morning, after Stacey and Jerry awakened, made love, and showered, they headed to the kitchen for breakfast. After eating, Jerry left for the office, and Stacey organized the breakfast dishes for a later washing. She was anxious to arrive at *TH&E* early in order to seek guidance on issues involving client agreements.

Hurrying to the garage, she discovered an envelope on the front seat of her car.

> *My Dear Stacey,*
>
> *After a busy day and a good night's sleep, one should awaken to good news. And I am pleased to be the bearer of tidings you have waited your entire life to hear.*
>
> *The uninvited one, the trouble maker, the assassin has disappeared forever. He will never be seen or heard from again, by anyone. His whereabouts will remain forever a secret.*
>
> *Live the remaining years of your life with the happiness you richly deserve.*
>
> *From the one you can always count on.*

A smile appeared on Stacey's face. *Oh, Windy. My lifelong protector, my guardian! Always helpful, ever considerate! Thank you, thank you, thank you, Dear One.*

Your letter will remain our little secret. Even my lawyer-lover will never learn of it. He's too honest and too law-abiding, and it's best not to awaken his curiosity over this missing, evil person. Yet, someway, somehow, I must show my appreciation to you. You're too much of a friend to go unrewarded.

CHAPTER 73

ANOTHER TIME, ANOTHER PLACE

A little girl, struggling with a bucket of water, spills some as she half carries, half pulls it to her brother. He smiles. Scooping sand out of a hole, he piles it into a mound then dips his hands into the water and fashions another turret to his castle.

Off to the side, an older woman, sitting in her beach chair, looks proudly at her grandchildren. Turning and about to say something, she remains silent. Her husband snores softly with a newspaper resting on his chest and stomach.

A teenager, running in shallow water, glances over her shoulder and laughs, daring the boy who is chasing her to toss her into the water as he threatens. And in the deeper, clear blue water, swimmers enjoy the calm, warm, rippling waves of the Atlantic Ocean.

As far as one can see, people—young and old, together and alone—lie on beach towels, reading books, doing crossword puzzles, and capturing the remaining moments of the afternoon sun. Enjoyment and pleasure are everywhere.

And off in the distance walks a couple, heading to their private Bermuda beachfront cottage; she holds one hand of his in hers, carrying a can of tennis balls in the other; he holds two rackets resting on a shoulder. As they speak, as they look into each other's eyes, observers know they are in love. They are newlyweds, three days into their honeymoon. Anastasia and Jerry Forrest are destined for happiness, professional success, prosperity, and the new beginning that awaits them.

How can one be certain? Because it is written in the cards. The Arcana speak. *The Sun,* the *Ace of Cups,* and the *Six of Wands* stand upright.

ACKNOWLEDGMENTS AND CONFESSIONS FROM THE WRITER

THE UNKNOWN

One not known . . . something requiring discovery . . . the unexplained.

These words define *unknown* and foster the intrigue, violence, and unexpected that surfaces throughout the mystery in this novel.

- *Those Not Known:*
  - ./ The Heroine: a woman who, at the age of twenty-five, learned her infant body had been discarded in a dumpster, left to die, and to be trucked away.
  - ./ The Evil Ones: killers who continue their search for the heroine with the intention of completing what they failed to do when she was born.
- *Something Requiring Discovery:*
  - ./ The Heroine's identity: abandoned as an infant but found and raised by a couple living off the streets, she has no heritage and is, in a sense, an *unknown* to herself and to others.
  - ./ The Evil Ones: Unseen, *unknown,* but ever present; they have to become known to be avoided and curtailed from their menacing intentions.
- *The Unexplained:*
  - ./ What unknown secret does the heroine possess that requires the Evil Ones to devote twenty-five years to dispose of both her and the secrecy?
  - ./ How do an unopened letter, swimming, horse racing, a devious friend, a newly acquainted woman, and Tarot cards contribute unsuspecting consequences to the mystery, its secrets, and the central characters?

The Unknown is fiction. While there are actual cities identified, true historic events cited, and words of published songs quoted, the cast of characters, *The Quad,* the *Bermudian,* the Royal Tournament of Tennis, along with street names and actions taking place are fabrications of this writer's imagination. Any association the central characters in the plot have to living people is unintentional.

Furthermore, I am not a Tarot card counselor and use this medium of divination merely to focus on the plot. To illustrate, when one prepares an entrée for family or guests, the cook wants to preserve the basic taste; however, a particular herb may be added for seasoning. In *The Unknown,* the characters and their actions are the "entrée." The Tarot cards are merely the "seasoning." Other elements cited in the paragraph immediately above are more critical to the plot and its conclusion.

Many an hour, both day and night, have been devoted to this fiction. It has been a commitment producing considerable satisfaction. Hopefully, the story captures your interest as much as it has mine.

In concluding, I want to thank the people at the self-publishing company Xlibris, whose editing assistance and ever-dependable presence was always available: Kay Benavides, Taylor Gil, Charles Ortiz, and Maria Rosario Legarde.

A second novel, *Vengeance,* is now being written. It too is fiction but not a mystery. Instead, it is an intense action-moving tale revolving around an important event in history. Hopefully, on release, it will appeal to you.